W9-BSZ-417

# As the Night Ends

*Also by Audrey Howard*

The Skylark's Song
The Morning Tide
Ambitions
The Juniper Bush
Between Friends
The Mallow Years
Shining Threads
A Day Will Come
All the Dear Faces
There Is No Parting
The Woman from Browhead
Echo of Another Time
The Silence of Strangers
A World of Difference
Promises Lost
The Shadowed Hills
Strand of Dreams
Tomorrow's Memories
Not a Bird Will Sing
When Morning Comes
Beyond the Shining Water
Angel Meadow
Rivers of the Heart
The Seasons Will Pass
A Place Called Hope
Annie's Girl
Whispers on the Water
A Flower in Season
Painted Highway
Reflections from the Past
Distant Images

AUDREY HOWARD

# As the Night Ends

Hodder & Stoughton

Copyright © 2005 by Audrey Howard

First published in Great Britain in 2005 by Hodder and Stoughton
A division of Hodder Headline

The right of Audrey Howard to be identified as the Author
of the Work has been asserted by her in accordance
with the Copyright, Designs and Patents Act 1988.

1 3 5 7 9 10 8 6 4 2

All rights reserved. No part of this publication may be reproduced,
stored in a retrieval system, or transmitted, in any form or by any means
without the prior written permission of the publisher, nor be otherwise
circulated in any form of binding or cover other than that in which it is
published and without a similar condition being imposed on the
subsequent purchaser.

All characters in this publication are fictitious
and any resemblance to real persons, living or dead,
is purely coincidental.

A CIP catalogue record for this title
is available from the British Library

Hardback ISBN 0 340 82407 7

Typeset in Plantin by Hewer Text Ltd, Edinburgh

Printed and bound by
Mackays of Chatham Ltd, Chatham, Kent

Hodder Headline's policy is to use papers that are natural, renewable
and recyclable products and made from wood grown in sustainable
forests. The logging and manufacturing processes are expected
to conform to the environmental regulations of the country of origin.

Hodder and Stoughton Ltd
A division of Hodder Headline
338 Euston Road
London NW1 3BH

I have taken some liberties with dates and names
during the Women's Movement of 1860 to 1918
but each event described actually took place.

# I

He first saw her in what the police would describe as a 'scuffle' but it proved to be more than a scuffle and it was the noise of it, the screaming, the shouting, the yelling, floating over the water, that drew him to it.

It was the beginning of June. He had intended crossing Westminster Bridge and strolling along Bridge Street, down Millbank, turning at Dean Stanley Street and into Smith Square where he had rooms. After the distressing surgery he had performed that morning he felt an even greater need than usual to clear his head of the sights and sounds and smells of the accident ward and the operating theatre where he had been working since seven.

When he had left St Thomas's, nodding to the porter at the main entrance, stepping out into the pleasant June sunshine, there were comparatively few people about though it was almost noon. He had been looking forward to this, his afternoon off, glad to be away from the despair of the mother whose child, a boy of seven, had lost his leg. He himself had amputated it after he and Dick Morris had done their desperate best to put together the smashed limb, crushed beneath the wheel of a horse-drawn cab under which the child had fallen. It had been hopeless and they had had no choice but to take it off just above the knee, condemning the lad to the life of a cripple. A prosthetic limb would be fitted, of course, but the boy, who was a keen footballer, his broken-hearted mother kept repeating, would be maimed for ever.

St Thomas's was by far the largest 'pavilion-plan' general hospital, with beds for over 600 patients, one of the most modern and hygienic in London and the boy had been fortunate – if such a word could be used in the dreadful circumstances – to have been brought into its care. The wards were large and airy, replacing the small rooms that had once been usual, for then they had believed that large wards produced disease because of the sheer numbers of sick gathered in one place. Now the long wards contained beds placed in two rows with the heads against the wall. When the hospital had been built six adjacent ward pavilions had been provided with plenty of space between each one. There were bathrooms and lavatories, sculleries and closets on each ward with a ventilated lobby separating the wards from the sanitary facilities to prevent smells from entering the ward. There was ample space around each bed to allow for the presence of students and the requirements of clinical teaching. It was here that he himself had been first a student, where he had qualified and now after many years' training was, despite his comparative youth, a surgeon, and it was in one of the immaculate beds that the boy lay, still unconscious, his distraught mother beside him, for he had given instructions to the tight-lipped sister on duty that she was to be with her son when he awoke.

He walked the length of the Albert Embankment towards Westminster Bridge, trying to identify the noises he heard, which appeared to come from somewhere in the vicinity of Westminster Yard, at the same time breathing in the scent and the sight of the deep pink begonias which provided bold splashes of colour among the white of the allysum and the blue lobelia in the hospital gardens that lined the Thames. The contrast between them and what he had seen and done this morning could not have been stronger and he wondered if he would ever become immune to the suffering of the humanity he served. Perhaps that sounded pompous, he brooded, or even priggish, as though he were the only surgeon to care for those who were brought to him to be mended, but he sometimes wished he could develop the dispassion of others in his profession.

The old man who cared for the gardens leaned on his hoe for a moment, lifting his cap and wiping his forehead with the back of his hand.

'Mornin', Doctor,' he said in his nasal Cockney. 'Nice day fer it.'

'It is indeed, Jack.'

'Dunno what's goin' on over there,' nodding in the direction of the Houses of Parliament. 'P'raps them 'oo works there is hengaged in fisticuffs. Wouldn't put it past them.'

'You could be right.'

With a smile he continued towards the bridge. When he reached the end of the walkway an old derelict sprawled by the public urinals held out a grimy hand and whined for 'tuppence fer a cuppa, yer Lordship,' and putting his hand in his pocket he withdrew some coppers and threw them into the old chap's cap.

'Thanks, guvner.'

It was then he noticed that the previously quiet bridge was becoming crowded with people who were in distinct danger of being run down by horse-drawn vehicles and the occasional motor car which puttered along the road. They were mostly men, hurrying across the river towards the Houses of Parliament, and they appeared to be excited about something. Although he had intended a pleasant stroll in the sunshine towards his rooms overlooking the lovely old church of St John, he found himself swept along in the sudden surge of yelling, fist-waving men.

Coming off the bridge and moving with the crowd along Bridge Street, since he had no option but to go with it, he turned the corner into Parliament Square as they did and was appalled, for the area of Westminster Yard was boiling like the scene of a revolution. Mounted police were laying about them with stout batons, striking anyone who got in their way. Foot policemen were doing their best to seal the area in front of the statue and several prison vans were drawn up with the doors open and uniformed constables on the steps. Hordes of women swept in from the far side of the square and he was forced back against the railings to which he clung for dear life lest he be dragged underfoot.

'It's them bloody suffragettes,' the man who was crammed against him shouted in his ear. 'Bloody whores, the lot of 'em. Should be whipped . . .' The man's voice was carried away as he fought to get to the heart of the riot where scores of women, mostly well-dressed ladies, were grappling with as many police and plainclothes men. Fists were flailing, hats and umbrellas and dainty parasols were flying, police helmets rolling on the ground beneath the hooves of the horses, along with women who had fallen, or been shoved in a flurry of white petticoats. Women were being propelled up the steps of the Black Maria, punched and even kicked by a man in a straw boater, his nose streaming with blood, his face a mask of fury. The van was already full but the man, whoever he was, seemed determined to push in more dishevelled women like pickles in a barrel, women with torn clothing, women with blood on their faces, their hats lost, their hair straggling down their backs. Other females were dragged from the crowd, thrown from one demented man to another, each laid into by their fists, some seized by the coat collar and pushed helplessly into a side street where severe beatings were taking place. 'I'll teach you a lesson,' one incensed man was shrieking as he struck again and again, his fists bloody. It was not his own blood! 'I'll teach you a lesson you'll never forget so that you'll not come back again.' A young chap in a cap and no collar was bashing an elderly woman against a lamppost, hitting the post with the point of her jaw, beating, punching with such demented fury one wondered what was in his mind except an intention to terrorise and intimidate. Or perhaps just like some men in the crowd he had never had the chance to brutalise a woman without retribution and here was the perfect opportunity.

He had become trapped against the railings, pinioned by the mass of struggling humanity, aghast at the brutishness of the scene and it was then, as a gap suddenly appeared in the crowd, that he saw her. Two uniformed policemen had her, one to each arm, while a third walking behind passed his arms about her body as they frog-marched her towards the steps of the van, her booted toes scraping the cobbles. Her skirt had been lifted almost to her waist, showing her pretty lace-trimmed drawers but more horrific was the grinning policeman's hand which had torn down her blouse and underwear to reveal one perfect white breast and a pink nipple as sweet and ripe as a cherry. His hand fondled it as her mouth opened on a silent scream: of terror, the watching man thought, then he realised that it was not terror but defiance that creased her lovely face into a snarl. Her hair was a tumbled mass of dark and glossy curls and her eyes which glared out at the world were the most incredible blue, bluer than the bluebells in the woods of Old Swan where he had played as a lad, bluer than the summer sky, and yet with a clear brilliance. Quite extraordinary, he remembered thinking, not just their colour but his own strangeness in noticing them at a moment such as this. Her head turned frantically and she seemed to stare directly into his face, her own still contorted, whatever she was shouting unheard in the baying of the crowd. The top of her head barely reached the shoulders of the three tall constables who hustled her towards the van. Her feet left the ground completely at that point and she was thrown like a sack of potatoes into the second van, gathered up by those already packed into it. Trampled underfoot were torn banners on which were written, 'Votes for Women'.

It took an hour to clear the square, not just of screaming women who had come to demand their rights but of infuriated men who had come to see them refused. A couple of policemen stood where the vans had been, looking so ordinary, so amiable, so completely the British 'bobby' it was hard to believe that an hour ago he had seen them abusing women in the most indecent manner imaginable.

'Where will they take them?' he asked one abruptly, for though he did not approve of the women's militancy neither could he approve of the way they had been manhandled.

'Sir?' the policeman queried politely.

'Those women.'

'Bow Street Magistrates' Court, sir. They'll be busy there tomorrow.'

'Oh, yes?'

'Aye, over a hundred of 'em at my reckoning an' some gents an' all. Can yer believe it? Holloway's gonner be a bit packed fer some time ter come. P'raps they'll keep their gobs shut from now on.'

He recognised her at once as she was hustled in to the dock alongside a dozen other women. She still wore no hat but some time during the night she had managed to sew up the rent in her blouse and her hair had been bundled into a tangled knot on the top of her head. It was far from tidy, curls falling in wayward knots about her ears, across her forehead and from her hairline at the back of her neck. In repose she was lovely, serene even and he found it hard to associate this composed figure with the virago she had been the day before. She sat with several of her companions on the bench awaiting her turn, not leaning forward with her arms on the rail that surrounded the dock as the others were, their chins in their hands as they listened to Christabel Pankhurst address the court, but settling back calmly as though this had really nothing to do with her.

But he knew, just as if her thoughts had taken wing and roosted in his own mind, that she was inwardly seething and that the moment she was called she would turn back into the violent creature who had defied authority the day before. Christabel Pankhurst was a brilliant orator and for several minutes, though they did their best to stop her, she ranted on in the manner he and the rest of the male population had heard or read of in the newspapers and he barely listened. His whole attention was riveted on the young woman waiting her turn. The court dealt with Christabel and two other women who refused to pay their fines and were sentenced to various prison terms depending on their previous records, and then it was her turn.

She began at once. 'For ten years, no, that is not correct, for more than *fifty* years we women have fought to have equality with men. At first we campaigned peacefully, lobbying for support from MPs but forty years of this approach has not persuaded . . .'

'Oh, put a bloody sock in it,' a male voice from the body of the court shouted, 'we've heard enough from the other one . . .' but she continued as if he had not spoken.

'. . . to take the demand seriously. We have been treated with ridicule whenever it was raised in Parliament. Women of this land . . .'

'Madam, we are not here to listen to you lecturing us, so be quiet.' This from the judge himself. 'We have heard enough from the other one.'

Again she went on regardless. '. . . indeed the world over must secure for themselves a parliamentary vote, as it is granted to men. Mr Asquith dismisses us as a small problem but believe me he is making a mistake. So I refuse to recognise the proceedings of this court . . .'

She did her best to make herself heard above the catcalls and jeering but a well-dressed elderly gentleman several rows in front of him stood up and, interrupting her, begged permission to address the bench. The bench looked astonished but then what else could you expect from these women and their followers.

'No, Father, no,' the woman began to shriek. 'You must not interfere. I know what you're going to do and I won't have it. I shall serve my sentence with the others as I am entitled to do and I won't allow you to . . .'

The hubbub that erupted drowned what she was trying to express, for it seemed every man in the court had something to say on the matter. Most in loud, angry voices but the elderly gentleman ignored her, and them, continuing to speak to the judge with great courtesy.

She would have leaped over the rail had not two policemen grabbed her by the arms, holding her in much the same manner as those of yesterday. He himself had stood up with the rest of those in the court and with a total disregard for the men hooting and hissing about him began to elbow his way towards the dock. The judge banged his gavel and at last the elderly gentleman made himself heard.

'Your Honour, this is my daughter you see before you and I am here to claim a father's rights to pay the fine, whatever it may be, and take her home.'

'No, you have no right, Father, none at all.'

'Darling, you have suffered enough for this . . . this cause, and your mother and I cannot stand it a moment longer.' Those in the court listened with fascination, no less than did the man who was at last standing so close to the prisoner he had time to notice that her eyes, which yesterday he had decided were blue, were indeed a soft shade of lavender as she looked with love, despair and anger at her father.

'Let me go, Father, please, you have done enough . . .'

'I cannot, Alex. You are ruining your health and if I go home without you your mother will never forgive me as I will never forgive myself. You are not strong . . .'

'Father, I am as strong as I need to be. I shall serve whatever sentence I am given.' She swayed slightly and the two police-men tightened their grip but the matter was settled as far as her father and the judge were concerned when she slid to the floor, disappearing behind the rail of the dock.

The doctor sprang forward and with an athlete's grace vaulted over the rail and knelt beside the fallen woman. Her father, too old to leap as he had done, peered anxiously over the rail, then spoke harshly. 'Take your hands off my daughter, or . . .'

'I'm a doctor, sir, and she has merely fainted. Now if you will pay her fine we will get her out of here before she comes to, away from the prying eyes hoping for some sort of show.'

The fine was paid and they had her in a cab, her eyelids beginning to flutter, a sigh emerging from her soft mouth. Her father gave the cab driver an address and both the men watched her anxiously as she began to recover consciousness. She was leaning heavily on the doctor's shoulder but the moment she came to she began her tirade, heaving away from him, glaring at her father.

'You had no right, Father, none at all. How dare you interfere with my life. I am over twenty-one and can do as I please. We must take our tactics to the streets to be noticed and identified . . .'

'Alex, you have spent the last two years stone-throwing, breaking windows, setting fire to buildings, even attacking the Prime Minister in his motor car. How many times have you been in prison?'

'That is not important, Father.'

'It is to your mother and me. You are precious to us and we want you to come home for a rest.'

'I advise you to listen to your father, Miss . . .' Patrick

O'Leary began, but he was no match for Miss Alexandra Goodwin.

'And who the devil are you?' she hissed, snatching her hands away from his as he did his best to take her pulse. 'And who gave you permission to lay your hands on me? Dear God, you're all the same. You always know what's best for the little woman, don't you? And what I'd like to know is how you knew I'd be there, Father? I thought you and Mother would understand, particularly Mother for she has been part of it since she was a child. Yesterday was an important day for us, for me, and well you know it.' She stopped to draw a breath and her father spoke mildly before she could continue.

'I have some little influence, darling, and I was well aware of what was to happen probably before you were. I came up yesterday, for your mother swore she could not bear to see you locked up in the Third Division, which you would have been with your record. Three months' hard labour, and dearest, you wouldn't have survived it. How many times are you to suffer it? How many more times is she to . . .'

'Father, oh Father, you know I can't stop now.' Her voice was soft, patient, loving and the pair of them seemed to have forgotten him. 'They will none of them pay the fine. Emmeline and Christabel and the rest, and I shall be the only one not to be with them. Ever since 'Black Friday' we have been waiting for the Conciliation Bill but there is still no progress. It was then we began our militancy and I know the public are shocked but we must draw attention—'

'Alex, darling, I know, but will you not just have a rest, come home with me for a week or two. The WSPU can manage without you.'

'We have been beaten up by gangs of men and boys . . .'

Her father winced and Alex put out her hand to him. 'Darling Pa, I know how this distresses you but we simply can't let them grind us down. Not now. So won't you take me to Clement's Inn where I can at least help in the office? We are putting together a reply to that fool Sir Albert Wright whose letter was printed in *The Times* stating that 'the failure to recognise that man is the master, and why he is the master, lies at the root of the suffrage movement'. Did you ever hear of anything—'

'Miss Goodwin, is it? Miss Goodwin, I would strongly advise you to return to your home and go straight to bed. Your father is right. I saw what happened to you, and the others, yesterday and as a doctor I believe you would benefit from a rest. I don't suppose you slept much last night and may I ask what you have eaten? I believe—'

She turned on him in astonishment and the doctor saw her father sigh and shake his head as though in exasperation.

'Dear God, don't tell me we have another one who believes that women are fragile little creatures who need protecting by the superiority of man.'

'Alex, please, Mr O'Leary is only trying to help. As a medical man he knows—'

'He knows nothing, Father. There are thousands upon thousands of men out there who think as he does and anyway, what the devil is he doing with you and me? Are you acquainted with him?'

'Miss Goodwin.' Patrick O'Leary could feel the annoyance run through him, annoyance that would change to real anger if this voluble young woman did not be quiet. 'Perhaps you do not recall – in which case you would definitely be better in bed – but you fainted in the courtroom. As a doctor I advised your father to pay your fine, which was pretty hefty, and bring you home. This he did and we are on our way there now. You will not go to Clement's Inn, which is, I believe, the headquarters of the WSPU, but home with your father where I shall make sure you are put to bed. I shall give him instruction to keep you there for at least a few days where you should be fed a light but nourishing diet.'

He remembered the feel of her in his arms. The rather voluminous blouse she wore, decorated with rows of ruffles down the front, the puff sleeves, the full gathered skirt, again with ruffles round the hem which reached the top of her black boots, had camouflaged the true fineness of her. She had looked fairly well fed as you would expect a woman of her class to be. Slender with small breasts certainly, but not emaciated. And yet in his arms she had been no more substantial than a sparrow he had once held in his hand as a boy. Stick thin her wrists were and her neck looked barely strong enough to support her head. She had lost all colour when she fainted but now it was back in a hectic flush on her cheekbones and he suspected she was feverish *and very angry*!

'How dare you dictate to me what I should or shouldn't do. Sweet heaven, isn't this the very thing we are fighting for, the right not only to vote but to control our own lives?'

'Oh, for God's sake, woman, get down off your soapbox. Go where you like, for what is it to me?'

'Exactly!'

'Alex, will you listen to Mr O'Leary? Let's get you home and Nan can put you to bed.'

'Father, I'm not a child.'

'Then stop acting like one, Miss Goodwin. Unless you want to damage your health permanently as many of your . . . your comrades are doing, then do as your father asks, even if it is only for a few days. You will be better use to your cause if you are fit and healthy.'

'There, Alex, will you not listen to Mr O'Leary?' her father pleaded.

Alex Goodwin looked properly into the face of the man who was doing his best to hold her hand while he endeavoured to take her pulse with long, strong fingers. It was certainly not a handsome face, neither was it young. There was even a touch of grey above his ears. He had removed his brown bowler hat or she had removed it for him with an unconscious movement of her hand as he placed her in the cab and it lay on the floor at his feet. He wore spectacles. His hair was dark, dark as treacle and was straight and heavy, even now falling over his forehead. But as he had been intrigued with *her* eyes she found it difficult to look away from his. They were steady, surrounded by a heavy fringe of black lashes which made him look somewhat foreign but it was the colour that claimed her attention. They were a smoky brown with points of gold radiating out from the pupil to the edge of the iris, and wrinkles fanned out from each one. His lips were firm but at each corner they were inclined to curl as though at any moment, given the right circumstances, he might break into a broad smile. A cleft slashed each cheek from nose to mouth and there was another in the centre of his chin.

The cabbie clucked at the horse and they came to a stop.

'Bedford Square, guv,' he announced, and at the sound of his voice Patrick O'Leary and Alex Goodwin came from the strange reverie that had embraced them for a fraction of a second and looked away from each other, but not before something had been kindled which they both refused to recognise!

'Open the door, Mr Goodwin, and I will bring your daughter.' Without further ado Patrick O'Leary swept Alex Goodwin into his arms and carried her to the front door of the house at the edge of Bedford Square. To his surprise she did not struggle.

# 2

Patrick O'Leary was the only child of a small but successful grocer in Liverpool and though his parents, good Catholics both of them, had regretted that they had been blessed with only this one boy they had comforted each other with the thought that it had at least enabled them to give him the best education a child of their class could ever hope to have. Had they given life to the ten or twelve children that were usually bestowed on an Irish Catholic family none would have had but the most cursory education offered to children of the day: to read and write, add up a few sums and learn the catechism which would befit them for casual work in a factory or the warehouses of Liverpool, the work of labourers, dockyard workers, maidservants and other menial positions that were the lot of their class.

Patrick O'Leary was the shining beacon held up by the Irish community – for it was their custom to live and die among their own – to illustrate what could be achieved by their offspring if they worked as diligently as Fergus and Mary O'Leary's lad, as with the cheerful insouciance of their race they did not stop to think that it was the size of their families that prevented each child having what Patrick had been given.

His parents, Fergus and Mary, were the children of Irish immigrants who had left the devastation of Ireland and the failed potato crop in the 1840s. Fergus's father had not, like many of his race, relied on the charity of the Church or the casual labour that was on offer to the Irish immigrant, but had somehow built a handcart from bits and pieces of wood and a couple of wheels which he pulled himself and began to sell anything in the way of provisions he could buy cheaply from the sailing boats moored in the docks. Stuff the crews had pilfered from cargoes: tea, sugar, vegetables, potatoes, fish, bacon, mutton, food that was on its way to being rotten by the time he got it and on which the poor lived. He sold cheaply, just about making a profit and the wherewithal to support himself, his wife and their two remaining children, the other six having died in the famine. In two years he had saved enough to rent a small shop in Scotland Road where the Irish congregated and again, working from five in the morning until midnight, he was moderately successful. In 1851 a boy whom they named Fergus was born and it was he who, with a flair denied his father, turned the small business into a thriving concern. When his father died Fergus married Mary Connelly, left Scotland Road and rented a bigger shop in Newington Street just off Bold Street where a better class of customer gave him their business. Their only child, Patrick, was born above the shop in 1881.

He had first attended, as many of the Irish community did, the Roman Catholic school in Limekiln Lane at the back of the church where they went each day to hear Mass and once a week to confession. But when, at the age of thirteen, his playmates left school to take up work as their fathers had, at the docks, in the factories or as maidservants, Patrick had 'gone on' to the Mechanics Institute in Mount Street where he had been instructed in English grammar, literature, writing, arithmetic – which did not mean the simple sums he had been taught at St Albans – philosophy, chemistry and biology, among other subjects. It was there he had decided upon medicine as his career. He did not even know why but had felt drawn to it. His parents had been delighted, bewildered, afraid, overwhelmed by this clever lad of theirs who still spoke, as they did, with the lilt of the Irish in his voice, but when they saw him off to Edinburgh and the university to study medicine, they knew quite conclusively that their son was lost to them for ever.

He had been at St Thomas's for ten years when he met Alex Goodwin. As he carried her protesting figure up the shallow steps to the front door of the house just off Bedford Square, following her father into the narrow hallway he was greeted by a plump dumpling of a woman who screeched her horror in the broadest Lancashire accent he had ever heard.

'What's ter do wi't lass, Mr Goodwin? Eeh, I'm afeart every time I open't door there'll be a bobby standin' there ter tell me she's bin took badly or she's locked up in that there gaol. What ails thee, lass, that tha' can't leave it alone, this daft notion that women are't same as chaps? I knew last night when tha' didn't come 'ome tha'd bin took again an' where it's all ter lead us, only' t good God knows. Eeh, Mr Goodwin, can thi' not put a stop to 'er gallop . . .?'

'It seems I can't, Nan, but this gentleman at least prevented them from putting her in gaol this time. He's a doctor and he's told her she's to go to bed and stay there for a few days. She fainted, you see, which allowed me to pay her fine and bring her home.'

'Thank the good Lord fer that—' the person called Nan pronounced but was wildly interrupted by Alex Goodwin.

'If this gentleman would put me down I shall decide what I am to do and where I am to do it. I cannot spare the time to be lying in bed when there is so much to be done at Clement's Inn. Put me down, sir, put me down at once,' struggling so madly Patrick had no choice but to obey. At once she made her unsteady way up the passage towards what he decided must be the kitchen area and he noticed with a medical man's interest that she walked with a slight limp as though one leg were shorter than the other. The left one, he thought. The maid, if that was what she was, followed her along the hallway, still berating her though no notice was taken of her. It seemed she must be an old family servant who felt she could speak her mind on whatever subject she chose and the one she chose now was the young woman's madness in getting mixed up with 'them daft beggars 'oo should be at 'ome mindin' their business' which was, in her opinion, being wife and mother. Mind, she pronounced sharply and to no obvious effect, she blamed Miss Alex's mother and grandmother who had stuffed her head with this nonsense ever since she could walk, and she, Nan Meredith, didn't hold with it and if she had her way the lass would go home with her pa and stop there. Patrick was left to wonder where 'home' was.

Her voice died away as she entered the kitchen on the heels of her young mistress, shutting the door to behind her and the two men exchanged ironic glances.

'Will your daughter take my advice, Mr Goodwin?'

'The answer to your question is "no", Alex will not. As Nan says, she has been fed the rights of women and their fight for equality with her first milk. She took it in in the nursery and wherever my wife went, parades, political protests, rallies, speeches, lectures, gatherings to raise funds for the cause, Alex went with her. But won't you come into the drawing-room and have some refreshments? Unless you have urgent business elsewhere.'

Patrick had arranged for Dick Morris to keep an eye on his patients for an hour or two while, for some reason he couldn't fathom, he had felt compelled to go to Bow Street to find out what had happened to the girl with the lavender-blue eyes, though he hadn't told Dick this, and had promised to be back at the hospital by lunchtime. He was not the only surgeon in a hospital the size of St Thomas's and if any emergency arose there was always one on call. Dick, who was training to be a surgeon, was a good doctor, sensible, practical, compassionate and did not stand in awe of the ward sister as many doctors did and Patrick trusted him above all others. He had promised to keep in touch with him by telephone and as he had noticed one in the hallway he asked Mr Goodwin if he might use it.

'I must keep in touch with the hospital, you see, but I would also like to make sure that Miss Goodwin follows my advice and with the help of the . . . er . . . maidservant might be persuaded to stay in bed for a day or two.'

Archie Goodwin turned in the doorway of the drawing-room, smiling ruefully. 'Mr O'Leary, no one will ever persuade my daughter to take advice if she feels like ignoring it. She is twenty-five years old and has lived in London ever since she came of age. She wanted to be where the Pankhursts were, you see, for though there are branches of the WSPU in Liverpool and Manchester where she might just as well have gone, she felt she could do more good here. I rented this house so that she would have somewhere decent to stay instead of the rooms the WSPU advertise to their members. For a while she worked at a desk at Clement's Inn, putting together the facts, collected by others, about the underpayment of women in sweated industries, the filthy, overcrowded conditions in which they were forced to labour. But that was not enough for her, for apparently there are a great many elderly and infirm members who could undertake such work. The movement was badly in need of young, able-bodied women like herself who would work in the field. Her words, not mine. So she became a . . . a . . . what I suppose you would call a "soldier" fighting injustice where she saw it. For the past four years she has been as violently militant as Emmeline, Christabel, Annie Kenney, the Pethick-Lawrences, Lady Constance Lytton and all the others who are involved. She carries a hammer in her handbag, did you know, and at every opportunity smashes the windows of shops like Selfridge's, and Marshall and Snelgrove.' He bowed his head sadly and his shoulders, which were broad and looked strong, sank wearily. 'We can do nothing to stop her, and, I'm afraid, neither can you. Short of locking her in her bedroom, from which she would undoubtedly find some means of escape, there is no more we can do but pray she will come to no serious harm. But enough of this, make your telephone call and then take a cup of coffee with me while, hopefully, Nan gets Alex to bed. I don't believe there is anything seriously wrong with her except overwork and the weakness compounded by her stays in prison and being force-fed a dozen times. But if you could persuade her to come home with me for a week or two I would be eternally grateful.'

'I will do my best, sir, but she sounds a very strong-willed young lady. Perhaps, if I may call tomorrow I might give her a sleeping draught that will keep her drowsy for a day or two.'

'Well, you can try, but your chances of success are slim.'

Patrick made his call and was relieved when Dick informed him that there were no pressing reasons for him to return at once to the hospital. 'The lad's doing well. No sign of fever and though he's been told his leg is gone he seems cheerful enough. Having his mother on hand has made a big difference, Patrick, though Sister Mills is not best pleased. You realise that you have totally disturbed her routine and defied her rules, and if you do it for this one does that mean all patients are to have their families gathered about their beds? And the abdomen case is doing well though the woman whose breast you removed is feverish and I suspect an infection. I'm keeping an eye on her if Sister Mills will allow it. Jesus, Patrick, you'd think the bloody hospital belonged to her personally.'

'I'll deal with Sister Mills this afternoon, Dick. I'm held up at the moment but I'll get away as soon as possible. I'll be in within the hour, I'm sure.' He hesitated and he could tell Dick was intrigued. 'There's just . . . well . . . someone I must speak to and then I'll be back.'

Dick was astonished, Patrick knew, for Patrick's life outside the hospital was virtually nil. So what was his friend up to that he had to take the morning off? Dick would be thinking. He began to wonder himself.

The drawing-room at the front of the house, which he entered hesitantly, was quite splendid. He had expected Victorian opulence, a sombre hush, rich drapes and hangings, plush furnishings, knick-knacks on every surface, the walls hidden behind dozens of framed pictures. Instead it was light and airy with a high ceiling, elegant, the feminine touch very much in evidence. There were a few pieces of good furniture, comfortable sofas scattered with cushions, two deep arm-chairs, in one of which Mr Goodwin sat, pale sand-coloured walls and a plain carpet of the same shade. The curtains were duck-egg blue silk and under the large window, which was open, stood a ladies' writing desk. Sounds of laughter came from outside where well-starched nannies were walking children in the railed garden. Vases of fresh flowers were arranged next to pretty electric lamps with delicate glass shades, while in the grate of the white surround of the fireplace a large copper urn held more flowers. On the mantel was a row of silver-framed photographs, a man and a woman, handsome and laughing, three children at play, a small boy on a pony and an elderly couple, the man in the photograph sitting opposite him. A large gilt clock under a dome of glass sat in the centre.

'What a charming room, Mr Goodwin. Your daughter has impeccable taste, if I may say so.' He looked about him admiringly, thinking of his mother's parlour which had been furnished, *overfurnished* in the style of the old Queen with hardly enough room to walk about, which was probably why she and his father had lived in the cosy kitchen on the first floor at the back of the shop.

Archie Goodwin laughed. 'This is not Alex's doing, Mr O'Leary. My daughter has no time for what she calls the "frivolities" of women. My wife furnished the house when we took it and I must say it is useful when we come to London.

Now do sit down, but will you ring the bell first and we'll have coffee.'

'But won't the maidservant be busy with your daughter?' In his opinion Alex Goodwin, unless supervised, would be off to Clement's Inn and the woman called Nan gave the impression she was the one who might prevent her.

'Oh, Nan has a handmaiden by the name of Nelly,' Mr Goodwin answered and sure enough a slip of a girl in an immaculate uniform sidled into the room and bobbed a curtsey.

'Coffee for me, I think, Nelly, and you, sir. . .?' casting an enquiring glance at Patrick.

'The same, if you please, and then I must have word with Miss Goodwin, if I may.'

'Miss Alex be in 'er bed, sir,' the maid piped up.

'Well, thank goodness for that,' her father sighed, leaning his head back on the headrest of the chair. 'Nan has managed to make her see sense.'

'Miss Meredith's ter wake 'er in an 'our, she ses,' the little maid added. 'She's far too busy ter loll about all day, she ses.' She spoke with authoritative importance of one who basks in the glory of another.

'Well, we'll see about that,' Archie Goodwin told her, 'but fetch a pot of coffee for the doctor and myself and then we'll tackle Miss Alex Goodwin.'

Alex Goodwin, though she had argued forcibly with Nan, had been glad of a hot bath in the modern bathroom her father had installed in the house, and then, despite her intention of going at once to the WSPU headquarters, could not resist sinking with great relief into the bed in the front bedroom over the drawing-room. She had slept not at all the night before in the cell in which she and the others had been crammed. Neither had she eaten, but she promised Nan that the moment she

woke she would take a bowl of 'pobs', which was Nan's name
for bread and hot milk with a spoonful of sugar to sweeten it. It
would put a lining on her stomach, Nan told her and was easily
digested, and yes, Nan promised she would wake her in an
hour.

She could hear the murmur of male voices in the room
below and guessed that her father was doing his best to
convince the doctor – what was his name? . . . Oh, yes,
Patrick O'Leary – that the best place for her was bed. Father
would be aware, of course, that she would take no notice of
any man, not even himself whom she loved with all her heart.
She smiled as she relaxed in the depth of the comfortable bed.
For several moments she found herself picturing the man who
had, against her will, which was something that did not
happen often, picked her up in his arms and carried her, first
from the court into the cab and then from the cab into the
hallway. She could still see against the lids of her closed eyes
the smoothness of his freshly shaved face, the high cheekbones, the flat planes of his cheeks, the deeply scored clefts to
the side of his unsmiling mouth, the firmness of his jaw which
said he would stand no nonsense and then the incredible
softness of his golden-brown eyes which belied it all. His chest
had been hard, his arms strong and muscled and yet he was
not powerfully built. She had, incredibly, felt a great longing
to nestle . . . *her, nestle!* . . . against his shoulder, she who had
nestled against no man except her father when she was a child.
She had had no time for that kind of thing and she was amazed
at herself for pondering on it now. He had smelled nice, too.
Some sort of lemon soap, or was it cologne, clean and,
considering his profession, without a hint of disinfectant.
She derided herself for her silliness and snuggled deeper
under the covers.

Nan, who was maid, housekeeper, friend and sometimes
even nurse when she, Alex, had crawled from Holloway more

dead than alive, was drawing the curtains against the lovely golden sunshine that crept across the carpet.

'Don't forget, no more than an hour,' Alex murmured drowsily. Nan did not answer and if she had Alex would not have heard her, for she fell at once into a deep sleep where she remained for twenty-four hours, unaware that the most terrible tragedy in the history of suffragism had taken place.

Patrick read the news in a copy of the *Daily Mirror* dated 5 June 1913. It reported the serious injuries of the militant suffragette Emily Wilding Davison, who, on Derby Day, knowing that the King's presence at the most prestigious event of the racing calendar would guarantee plenty of press interest and therefore maximum publicity for the WSPU's campaign, had stepped in front of the King's horse.

*Anmer struck her with his chest and she was knocked over, screaming. Blood rushed from her nose and mouth. The King's horse turned a complete somersault, and the jockey, Herbert Jones, was knocked off and seriously injured. An immense crowd at once invaded the course. The woman was picked up and placed in a motor car and then taken in an ambulance to Epsom Cottage Hospital where she still remains.*

The headlines had caught his eye that morning as he moved on his rounds with a group of students. A male patient with a badly infected foot which might or might not have to be amputated, since Patrick was pretty sure it was gangrenous, was propped up on his pillows reading about it and as Patrick, a group of students and the ward sister approached his bed he placed the newspaper on the immaculately folded sheet across his chest. At once sister hissed her disapproval, for the man had been arranged neatly for the doctor's inspection and the print from the newspaper would be bound to leave a mark on the sheet.

The patient saw her face and at once mumbled an apology, moving the newspaper to his locker. To the consternation of the students, the sister and the patient himself, Mr O'Leary, who surely never looked at any newspaper bar *The Times*, picked up the *Daily Mirror* and began to read the front page.

For several moments there was total silence then sister cleared her throat, because if Mr O'Leary had time to stand about reading the news, she hadn't. The students exchanged glances, for who were they to interrupt this great man?

Patrick felt a wave of something he could only describe as despair wash over him, then wondered at the feeling. Dear sweet Mother, he whispered softly, his Catholic upbringing almost persuading him to cross himself, as he knew what this would mean, not only to the women of the WSPU but to her. *To her!* And yet why the devil should he be concerned with a woman he had seen for the first time only days ago? He had not gone back to the house as he had said he would, because when he had left, shaking hands with her father, the maid Nan had told them that Miss Alex was sleeping so soundly it was her opinion she would not wake again that day.

'Leave 'er be, sir. I'll see to 'er,' she had announced firmly, and looking into the small, bright and loving eyes of the maid Patrick was convinced that she would. Now the whole lot of them would be up in arms, meaning the suffragettes, including her, meaning Miss Alex Goodwin, and there would be chaos on the streets of London and all the big cities of the nation. If the damn woman died God only knew what might happen.

'Sir!' He was confused for a moment as he pictured the frail loveliness of Alex Goodwin embroiled in another affray and dismayed by his own reaction to it. What the hell did it mean to him? He had nothing to do with women except in the most casual way to satisfy his male needs, and those he treated on the wards. He was far too immersed in his work to think of women in the social sense and went nowhere to meet them. Yet he could see those incredible eyes, luminous, enormous in her thin face and he knew he could not simply walk away and pretend he had never met her. Her savagery in Westminster Yard in the hands of the policemen had appalled him. She had been like a captured tigress, snarling and snapping to escape the clutches of her captors. She had revealed a fiery exultation that had driven her into battle. This was *right*, what she was doing, her maddened attitude was telling those who tried to prevent it. He remembered now that as she screamed her defiance the words 'Votes for women' had been on her lips and though, like most men, he did not agree with what she demanded he began to wonder why. Why should women not have the vote?

The very sister who ran this ward with the efficiency of a sergeant major was surely more capable of deciding who should run this country than some of the ineffectual and indifferent men who already had the vote. She was sensible, intelligent, quick-witted but, along with lady mayors, other nurses, mothers, lady doctors and teachers, she was denied the vote, while convicts, lunatics, drunkards and other unworthy male counterparts had the right to decide who they wanted in the government. He supposed, if he was honest, though he had seen these women, very well-dressed women, ladies even, at the end of Downing Street, several carrying placards decorated with the convict's arrow which meant that they had served a term in prison for their involvement in the campaign, it had not touched him. They were just a bloody nuisance blocking the road, some of them hiring tradesmen's carts to make a platform from which they addressed hooting, jeering men. Elegantly dressed ladies strolling along Regent Street or Knightsbridge wearing French hats and then suddenly opening their handbags, taking out their hammers, as he supposed she did, and demolishing the plate glass windows of Harrods.

In the corner of his mind that would not be silent, he had admitted to himself that he had admired their bravery but at the same time he had thought them foolhardy and she was as rash as the rest. What would she do when she heard of the drama at the racecourse? Did he need to ask? He was not involved, he told himself, but now because of a pair of lavender-blue eyes which turned icy in her rage, striking daggers at him, and a voice that told him stridently to mind his own business and let her get on with hers, he was.

# 3

He next saw her, as he knew he would, on the day of the funeral of Emily Wilding Davison who had died from her injuries four days after the terrible event at the racecourse. He stood among the dense crowds, so packed and restless that policemen had been called out to control them, and he noticed that though some men in the crowds removed their hats in a gesture of respect as the cortège went past, the policemen didn't. There were even men and women seated in comfortable chairs on the railed balcony over the shop window of Boyle and Co, Tailors, as if they had reserved seats to watch a procession of some grand, or even royal personages go by. Shop workers hung out of windows and even stood on the first-floor ledges of the Vienna Café, which proclaimed itself to be the first of its kind in London. It had been reported that all through the night a suffragist bodyguard of honour had kept watch over their fallen comrade and he was pretty sure that Alex Goodwin would have been among their number.

To the roll of the drums and the muffled chords of Chopin's funeral march the great procession slowly moved forward, headed by a young cross bearer, her fair hair uncovered. Immediately behind her came twelve white-clad girls with laurel wreaths and a banner inscribed, 'Fight On and God Will Give the Victory'. The banner was in purple worked with silver. Following came more girls and young women in white and she was in the front row wearing a black armband as they all did. Her face was like paper it was so pale under her wide-brimmed hat and her huge eyes were set in deep shadows. He could see that Alex Goodwin, though he barely knew her, was grieving and the icy flash of her eyes, which he had seen at the affray at Westminster, was softened by sadness, which he saw in the other women's eyes. These women loved one another as sisters and were mourning the death of one of their own.

Then came a dense throng of women in black carrying bunches of purple iris. These were succeeded by others in purple, carrying red peonies, and these in turn by a long stream of members in white with madonna lilies. The coffin was placed on a low, open bier and was covered with a purple, silver-edged pall showing silver arrows and three laurel wreaths inscribed, 'She Died for Women'.

The procession was headed towards St George's Church, Bloomsbury and though the crowd began to disperse as soon as the bier had passed, since the spectacle was over, he walked slowly beside it, wondering at himself as he did so and when the service began he edged into a packed pew where he could just see the bowed head of Alex Goodwin. He knew she was weeping though just how he knew escaped him for he could not see her face. Inside he could feel her pain and he supposed it was then that he knew he loved her, which was bloody ridiculous since he had spoken to her, and she had ranted at him, only once on the day he and her father had brought her from Bow Street.

The coffin was to go to the railway station on its journey to Morpeth where the dead woman was to be interred.

He was waiting for her as she came out of the church and though she was with a group of her comrades, after a start of surprise she walked across to him. Again he noticed that she limped, not a very noticeable limp but she favoured her left leg, which made her bob slightly to one side as she walked.

She shook her head as she smiled sadly at him. 'Mr O'Leary, I don't know why you're here but I'm glad that you are. Thank you.' She held out her hand and he took it, holding it between both his own and though she seemed somewhat bewildered when he held on to it she left it there. Could this soft and gentle creature be the termagant he had first seen in Westminster Yard?

'I knew you would be here, and I saw you in the procession. The last time we met you hurled abuse at me but there was something in you that fascinated me. In all of you. I would like to know more about your movement, to try to understand, and if you have a moment one day I would be glad to . . . to take you somewhere . . . perhaps to tea where you could explain to me what you and your friends . . . what your thoughts are. What you mean to do in the future and why—'

'Why we carry on as we do? I would have thought that pretty obvious to any man with intelligence. We have said it over and over and over to the government but it won't take us seriously. All we want is to secure for women the parliamentary vote as it is, or may be, granted to men; to use the power thus obtained to establish the quality of rights and opportunities between the sexes; to promote the social and industrial wellbeing of the community. There, I have learned it off by heart and though I repeat it parrot-fashion, it is the truth. But I must go with my friends now. Perhaps you might like to telephone me and I can tell you more about these brave women.' Then she was gone, limping even more as though she were tired, and with a doctor's detachment he knew she was bone weary, almost at the end of her strength and with his man's heart he knew he must do something about it, for having found her he did not want to lose her.

Since he had qualified he had taken no more than a day off here and there, since there was nowhere he wanted to be, or to travel to. His whole life from being a youth until he became a man had been concerned only with medicine. He could not imagine any other way to be, to live, to work and it was not merely a philanthropic notion that guided him. He wanted to heal, true, but he also wanted to advance the course of medicine and with that in mind he had little time for anything else, particularly what was known as a 'holiday'!

Dick Morris was amazed but delighted for him, he said, his pleasant face splitting into a wide grin when Patrick told him he was to take two weeks off. Dick was his only friend, if that was how to describe their relationship. He respected the younger man and his dedication to the sick, unaware that it was this very attribute that made himself such a fine surgeon. They had now and again had a night out at a theatre, and it was Dick who had introduced him to the discreet house where might be found attractive and clean women who were well paid for their services.

'Of course we can manage without you, you daft beggar, though I must admit the thought of dealing with Sister Mills by myself terrifies me. But where do you plan to go? They say Switzerland is grand, or perhaps Italy. Now don't tell me you are going alone . . . Yes, I can see it in your face, you *are* going alone.' Dick was a gregarious young man who had friends all over London and could not imagine doing anything by himself. He loved company and pretty girls but his nature was kind and he was fond of old Patrick. The idea that 'old Patrick' was to spend a fortnight wandering about by himself was one he could not understand 'Surely you have a pal who could . . .?'

Patrick laughed and as a few had been before him, Dick was bowled over by the change in his appearance. The clefts in his cheeks deepened. His face creased into a wide grin and lit his brown eyes like candle lamps in the dark. His good white teeth gleamed as his lips curled at the corners in merriment. He looked five years younger when he laughed and very attractive. The shape of his face altered and seemed to be lit up from within, and Dick was astonished that some woman had not snapped him up years ago. Even the way he spoke was attractive, with the lilting brogue of his Irish forebears on his tongue.

'Never you mind, you spalpeen, I know what I want to do and I shall try my very best to achieve it. And no, it's not Switzerland or Italy but I promise when I come back I shall tell you all about it.'

Dick sighed, then his grin became even broader than Patrick's. 'It *is* a woman, isn't it, you dog.'

'Away with you, man. Now get on your rounds or Sister Mills will smack your bottom and put you to bed without your tea.'

She heard the telephone shrill in the hall but barely had the strength to turn her head on the pillow as two or three minutes later Nan entered the room. She had reached the end of her staying power, at least temporarily, she told herself, and had been sent home to rest after a night in which she and several others had set fire to a racecourse stand and because of her weakness the others had been forced almost to carry her away into the dark. She had endangered herself, and them, because she would not admit to the strain that hollowed her out, parched her, scorched her brain so that she could no longer think clearly and she knew she must do as she was told.

'I know you are determined to see this through to the end, my dear,' Mrs Pethick-Lawrence, who was editor with her husband of *Votes For Women*, told her, 'but you are no good to us, to the cause, if you are severely debilitated which you are after your last hunger strike and force-feeding . . . when was it? March? It's very obvious you are seriously weakened. That last stretch in prison nearly killed you and what would have happened last time if your father had not been there to pay the fine at the beginning of the month is unthinkable. You would have been sentenced to, and probably would have died in, the Third Division. That is what it will be next time,

Alexandra, for with your record they would show no mercy. Now go home and I mean to your parents' home up north, rest, eat well and come back to us renewed. We have many plans for the future and you shall be part of them but only if you are strong enough.'

Nan had thrown open the bedroom door with a flourish, her round rosy face wreathed in smiles. Nan had begun her working life as a scullery-maid, moving up the servants' ladder until she was head parlour-maid at Lantern Hill, which had been Alex's grandparents' home until they went to live in Lytham where Grandfather Goodwin had bought a house on the sea front. He and Grandmother Goodwin were getting on and all the Goodwin businesses, of which there were many, were now run entirely by Alex's father, Archie. Lantern Hill had been sold and the servants dispersed to decent jobs except for Nan who had chosen to accompany Miss Alex.

'Guess 'oo that were,' she said with a toss of her head, for Nan did like a good drama.

Alex turned to look disinterestedly out of the window at the gently moving leaves of the trees beyond, listening to the sound of the children's voices in the square's garden. She didn't know, nor care who had rung because her whole mind was concentrated on the enforced expulsion from what had been her life ever since she came to London. Before that she had shared with her mother the political rallies, the bazaars to raise money for the cause, the garden parties, the parades, travelling about the north to listen to Emmeline, to Christabel, to Mary Eleanor Gawthorpe, who was a northern lass like herself, to Ada Flatman, to Grace Roe and many others, and even to speak herself. But it was to London that her zeal called her and eventually her mother and father had let her go. This was the first time in four years that she had been ordered to rest and she didn't know how she was to get through the next few weeks.

'I can't imagine, Nan,' she answered listlessly, then with a show of weak enthusiasm she tried to sit up, 'unless it's one of the members come to visit.'

'No, it weren't. It wcrc that doctor chappie wantin' ter call on yer. I told 'im ter come right over.' Nan sniffed triumphantly, for it was her dearest wish to see Miss Alex set up with a decent chap in her own home with children at her knee and what could be more suitable than a doctor?

At Nan's words Alex felt the smile begin to form about her lips and a pleasurable flutter moved through her. She had felt so nauseous, her stomach rebelling at every tasty morsel Nan placed before her but she knew that if she didn't eat she would never recover enough to get back to her rightful place in the world. After so many spells in prison, hunger strikes, the horror of being forcibly fed through a tube in her nostrils or forced down her throat, she wondered if she would ever be able to eat, to smell, to touch or taste anything with enjoyment again, but strangcly the image of Patrick O'Leary calling on her put a touch of gladness in her, a gladness she had forgotten existed. But she must not let Nan see it, or anybody, and evcn as the thought passed through her mind she didn't pause to wonder why.

'How dare you take it upon yourself to invite all and sundry into my home, Nan Meredith. You know I am to remain in my bed until I am fit to work again . . .'

'Oh, give over, Miss Alex. Don't talk so daft. The man's a doctor. 'E was 'ere t'other week when tha' was poorly so why shouldn't the lad come an' see 'ow tha' gettin' on. Now see, put this mornin' gown on' – Nan still lived in the days of Victoria when women wore such things to breakfast – 'no, not that 'un. Summat pretty. Tha' want ter look nice, don't tha'? 'Appen me an' Nelly'll give thi' a 'and downstairs. Tha' could lie on't sofa and put a rug over tha' . . .'

'I'm going nowhere, Nan,' Alex stated resolutely. 'You can just tell the good doctor that I'm not at home.'

'But I just said tha' was.'

'Well, you will have to turn him away.'

Nan became very quiet but in her eyes was a knowing look. For some reason Miss Alex didn't want to see this fine gentleman, or so she pretended. In fact she looked nervous but Nan had known Miss Alex since the day she was born and could read her like an open book.

With a firm step she crossed the room, threw back the covers and put out a hand to help her young mistress to her feet. 'See, put this on,' holding out the pretty, but very discreet, gown of lavender-blue velvet which exactly matched her eyes. There were satin ribbons at the throat and wrists and she thought Miss Alex, if she could just get a bit of colour in her cheeks, would look a treat. She guided her to the chair in front of the mirror, ringing for Nelly on the way, and with a gentle hand sat her down and began to brush her hair. She was glad that her young mistress had been persuaded not to cut her hair as she had threatened, for it hung down her back almost to her buttocks in a rippling banner of waves ending in curls. She tied it back with blue satin ribbons and when Nelly came bobbing and smiling into the bedroom, summoned her to help her get Miss Alex downstairs.

'I can manage perfectly well on my own,' Alex said impatiently, throwing off the helping hands of the two maids, but she found she was very weak as she reached the top of the stairs, looking down to the hallway which seemed a long way off.

They had just got her down and settled on the sofa when the doorbell rang and as she sent Nelly scurrying off to answer it, Nan smiled again in triumph, and secretly, for she was pleased by the quick flood of colour that came to her mistress's cheek.

He strode into the room almost angrily as though he were quite put out at being here but Nan was having nothing to do with this custom of a fifteen-minute call where the visitor kept his hat and stick beside him to signify he was to obey the rule, and before a word was said, she had deprived the good doctor of both, bearing them away to the hallstand.

'Good morning, Miss Goodwin,' he said formally, looking round him in confusion and was glad when she invited him to sit down. 'I said I would telephone at our last meeting and you seemed not to mind so I took the opportunity today since I am about to start a fortnight's holiday.' He stopped abruptly, for the sight of her in her pretty gown with her hair hanging in a shining mass quite silenced him. He wished she would say something. He was not accustomed to the niceties of polite conversation, the customs of what was called 'polite society' and he found himself to be as tongue-tied as a boy. 'You did say . . .' he began, but was stopped by her smile which lifted the corners of her rosy mouth, her bottom lip, he noticed, full and pouting.

'Please, Mr O'Leary, you don't have to explain. And I'm glad to see you. You were kind enough to come to Emily's funeral which many men would have thought out of the question and I appreciated it. You were, I admit, rather high-handed in your treatment of me that day at Bow Street but I forgive you.'

'Dear lady, you fainted. I had no choice but to be "high-handed" as you call it. As a doctor I felt it—'

'I did not call for your help, sir, and I thought you took too much upon yourself.' She began to pale, the soft flush at her cheekbone fading away and the flashing angry blue of her eyes dispersing the colour of lavender in a way he was beginning to recognise.

'Miss Goodwin . . . Alex, don't upset yourself. You are too fragile at the moment to make a fight of it which I know you long to do. Just forget what is gone and let us chat amiably, if that is something you are capable of.' Again he knew he had made a mistake, for she immediately took up the challenge.

'I can be as amiable as—'

'I'm sure you can but shall we both agree to be gentle with one another? If I ring the bell will your maid bring us some coffee? Then I will tell you of my plans for a holiday and ask your opinion as to where I should go. I hear the Lake District is very lovely at this time of the year.'

'My father has a house near Grasmere.'

He wasn't sure how she meant him to respond to the remark. It sounded as though she were inviting him to make use of her family's home but then that was hardly likely on such a short acquaintance. He rose to ring the bell to hide his deepening confusion, cursing himself for becoming entangled with this woman, but how could he be any different for she was the first, and he suspected the last, woman who would ever interest him. No, that was not true, he felt more than an 'interest' in her as though she were some subject matter he had come across in a medical journal. His feelings for her were strong and though he had experienced nothing to which he might compare them he knew them to be enduring. He also knew himself to be what young Dick would call a 'dry old stick' but this woman had awakened something in him so here he was, probably making a complete fool of himself and, what's more, not caring!

'I am thinking of going there for a rest,' she said casually. 'I intend to travel tomorrow up to St Helens where my parents live. There is a train to Manchester with a change there to St Helens. Nan and Nelly will accompany me.'

'Miss Goodwin, as I am going that way myself why don't I give you a lift?' he heard himself saying, wondering what the hell was the matter with him. He didn't even own a motor car and certainly had no idea how to drive one so what had happened to his usually incisive brain? Miss Goodwin must have had the same thought, or perhaps was also no longer in control of her senses.

'A lift?'

'Yes,' he answered airily. 'A fellow doctor has a motor car

which I'm sure he would let me borrow. There is room for yourself and your maids and we could take it in stages, staying perhaps . . . well, I would have to make enquiries but I'm sure . . .' He began to falter but Alex scarcely noticed. Her father was talking about buying one of the new and exciting means of travel but as yet she had never ridden in one of the wonderful contraptions. The very thought of doing so, of bowling up to Edge Bottom House in one brought colour to her cheeks and a flash to her expressive eyes. Patrick saw it and was elated.

'I think that would be . . . would be grand, Mr O'Leary. I could telephone Father . . . No . . . no,' she interrupted herself sharply, 'he would not agree so best just to turn up and give them a surprise.'

At that moment Nan entered the room, balancing a tray on which stood a silver coffee pot, a silver sugar bowl and milk jug accompanied by the 'best' porcelain teacups and saucers, the ones Nan trotted out when anyone of importance came to call. Which wasn't often!

'Nan, put the tray down and then scoot upstairs and start packing, for we are off home tomorrow. Mr O'Leary has kindly offered us a lift in his friend's motor car. Isn't that so?' turning an excited face to Patrick.

'*A motor car*,' gasped Nan, teetering with the tray in the centre of the room. She was in imminent danger of dropping it she was so confounded and it was not until Patrick stood up and took it from her that she could find her breath, for like her mistress she had never been in one of those infernal machines, as they were popularly called by all those who did not own one. 'Nay, tha' pa'll never let thi'—'

'That's why we're not telling him, Nan, but I think it's a splendid idea. Oh, do pour the coffee, Mr O'Leary. I would do it myself but I know that if I emerged from beneath this rug, Nan would have a fit. The niceties of convention have already been severely tested, thanks to Nan.' She smiled impudently at her maid because she knew full well that Nan had brought about this meeting in the hope that she, Alex Goodwin, would fall for the doctor and give up all this nonsense she had indulged in for so many years. Was the doctor to go with them to Grasmere? she would be asking herself.

What would Mr Goodwin make of it all, not to mention the lass's mother when they roared up the drive at Edge Bottom, thought Nan. . . . Oh dear God, she wished she'd left the whole damn thing alone, for where were they all to end up? She without a job, probably, and Miss Alex locked up in her bedroom. It wasn't proper, was it, travelling alone except for servants in a stranger's motor car. She was speechless with apprehension!

Patrick O'Leary was in much the same predicament but for a different reason. He not only had to persuade Dick Morris to lend him his Darracq which was his pride and joy, but he had, overnight, to learn how to drive the thing!

He poured the coffee and it was only his training in the field of surgery where a steady hand was absolutely necessary that allowed him to do it and hand the cup and saucer to Alex, smiling like the bloody idiot he was!

# 4

Patrick O'Leary had believed that any fool could drive a motor car. Surely all one needed to do was get in, switch on and steer the bloody thing, but for three hours, while Dick Morris cursed obscenely, not only at Patrick, but himself for agreeing to it, he struggled to learn the complexities of getting the woman he couldn't erase from his mind from London to St Helens in one piece.

'*NO! NO! NO!*' Dick shrieked, for by the end of an hour he was convinced that Patrick was either an imbecile or one of those men who had no empathy with machinery and would never learn in a month of Sundays! 'Put the bloody clutch in before you step on the accelerator and *then* take the handbrake off. You've stalled it again and now you'll have to get out and crank the bloody thing once more. Patrick, I'm having serious doubts about letting you take my motor all the way up to the Lake District. They have *mountains* up there, man, and nothing but muddy tracks for roads.'

'Dick, I promise if I wreck your motor I'll buy you another one. Holy Mother, if I had time I'd purchase my own but I haven't. I promised the . . . the . . . my friend . . . my friends . . . that I'd convey them to Lancashire. I know I must have been out of my head when I made the promise but it was the only way I could . . .'

'Impress your girl, that's it, isn't it?' Dick grinned impudently and at once Patrick reared up in outrage, causing the bloody thing, as he called the automobile, to stall again.

'It's no concern of yours, Dick, what I am to do, where I am to go. I am going on a holiday for the first time for years and I have a fancy to see the lakes. Some . . . some acquaintances are travelling to Lancashire and I told them I would take them there.'

'In *my* motor car. And what if I'd said no?'

'Well, I suppose . . .'

'You could have gone to a motor showroom and bought one and they would have taught you to drive it in an hour. What about that?'

'I didn't think . . .'

'Paddy' – sometimes Dick called him Paddy which he knew Patrick hated – 'Paddy, my lad, why don't you tell the truth? There is a woman involved in this and there's no use trying to hide it. No man goes to all this trouble for some *acquaintances*!'

'Mind your own bloody business,' Patrick snarled savagely and then, suddenly, he relented. Dick was the only friend he had, or ever had had, and why couldn't he confess that he . . . well, he wouldn't admit to having fallen in love, but at least he had met a young lady he liked and there was nothing wrong in trying to further their friendship by obliging her with a lift up north, was there? If he had thought of it in time he would have bought himself a motor car, for he had money saved but it had not worked out that way and Dick's rather smart automobile was his only chance. He had been going up north himself anyway though he had intended travelling by train, but this way he not only arrived there but in style which was what Dick had deduced. He was trying to impress Alex Goodwin in a way that was contrary to his very nature . . . Oh, sweet Jesus, he was babbling inside his own damned head but he was, he knew, a private, even a shy person, one who did not reveal his feelings easily and to admit to Dick, of whom he was fond, that he had fallen head over heels for a woman in the space of a few weeks was something he just could not do.

Luckily Dick, who had a kind heart, did not press him further and with quiet patience continued with the lesson and by the time dusk had begun to fall he admitted that Patrick had mastered the rudiments of driving and allowed him to drive back to his apartment in Smith Square among the horse-drawn carriages, the broughams, the cabs, the omnibuses, the wagons and the occasional automobile that clogged the road.

'Well, old chap, I can't do any more with you. Just remember in what order you do things, ignition, gears, clutch, accelerator, clutch out . . .'

'Yes, Dick, and thanks. You'll never know what this means to me . . .'

'It is a woman, isn't it?'

'Yes.'

Dick was bowled over by the expression that crossed Patrick's face, for it transformed him. It revealed a gentleness, a gladness, a delight that the emotions he had often wondered about but never experienced had entered his heart. He was thirty-two years old and had never known or been given the love of a woman but this one, this special one that all men secretly dream of, had come at last into his life.

'Good luck, old man.' Dick turned away, his own face working, as this was the first time he had seen Patrick O'Leary, his friend, with any softer expression than pity for a patient. Although men of medicine must possess serious dedication combined with an impersonal approach to people, Patrick had the former but was hard put to combine it with the latter. If Patrick had fallen for this woman it would be no light thing and he hoped to God she would not hurt him.

He was at the door of the house at Bedford Square at nine sharp, having battled and sweated and cursed his way through the early morning traffic from Smith Square by way of Charing Cross Road, which had been a nightmare, and the square. He rat-tatted sharply on the brightly polished brass door knocker, turning to look back at the gleaming splendour of the Darracq, finding that he had an impetuous longing to jump down the two steps that led up to the front door and give the motor car another rub-over with the chamois leather that Dick had provided. He was amazed at himself but it really was a splendid machine and he promised himself he would have one the day he got back from his holiday. Gleaming black paintwork, red leather seats, a brass horn polished as magnificently as the knocker on the door of the house, gleaming brass lamps, four of them, and a spare tyre fastened to the side of the automobile where the driver, *himself*, sat. As he gloated at the thought of what the next two weeks would bring, the door was thrown open by an obviously terrified Nan.

'All ready, Nan?' he asked cheerfully, looking over her shoulder into the hallway. There were boxes and a trunk and it was then his heart quailed, for where was all this luggage to go? There was a rack behind the two back seats but was it strong enough to bear the weight of his own suitcase and what the ladies obviously thought necessary for a fortnight's holiday?

'Oh, sir,' Nan moaned, overcome and almost ready to weep. In her mind it was possible for a man to dash about in one of these dreadful things. Men understood such intricate contrivances but surely the good Lord did not mean for women to do the same?

'Is she ready, Nan?' he demanded heartily, for it would not do to let this woman, any of the women, know that he too was filled with apprehension, and not only that but his own madness in thinking in a cocksure way that he could drive them, on the basis of one lesson, the 196-odd miles from London to St Helens.

He had put up the hood of the Darracq, for though the sun shone from a cloudless blue sky, a June sky in the height of the summer, if it should turn cold, or begin to rain he didn't want the ladies to suffer. Even so there was no protection from the weather to the side of the motor car so he had brought several rugs which the ladies must sit on, he explained, but were there just in case.

'Just in case of what, sir?' Nan mumbled anxiously from the back. She and Nelly were wrapped up in so much clothing it was difficult to recognise them but Miss Alexandra Goodwin, who had been settled first in the front seat next to himself, was positively beaming, full of sparkle and zest, and he knew with his doctor's instinct that already this trip was doing her the world of good. She looked a different woman to the one he had left languishing on the sofa the day before. She was warmly dressed, obviously ordered by Nan, and had a rug over her legs. After some struggle with the luggage, firmly tied on with rope that Nelly had to go back into the house to fetch, they were off.

They did not need goggles since the automobile had a windscreen. At first, until they were out of the mainstream of traffic in London, he kept to less than ten miles an hour but even this terrified the two women in the back. They clutched at each other and moaned pitifully, recoiling from every wagon or omnibus that came close to them, afraid that a horse might put its head through the window, and indeed anything that came within two feet of them, but at last they were in the quieter streets of Hampstead moving sedately along what was known as Watling Street in the direction of Elstree. They had almost 200 miles to travel and he told them it would take three days, so they were to spend the first night at Fenny Stratford where he had telephoned ahead to an old inn Dick had recommended and booked three rooms. Thank God for Dick, he had said to himself, and his experience of the more sophisticated way of life, the intricacies of which he had passed on to Patrick!

The day continued fair, with a blue and white loveliness that seemed to soothe the two maidservants. They passed along roads and lanes bordered with hedges laden down with white blossom and in the ditches grew dusky cranesbill, of pink and blue, comfrey of a brighter blue and purple, silverweed the colour of the sun, hairy willowherb in a glowing pink and all in harmonious flower. The fields were a rich summer green sown with masses of scarlet poppies and golden buttercups in which cows grazed knee-deep, inclined to shy away from the clattering sound of the motor as they passed.

They stopped for a while at lunchtime and Alex picked a bunch of wild guelder roses from the hedgerows and stood to watch the dance of tiny blue butterflies, and his professional opinion was that she looked better with every hour that passed, already with a touch of carnation at each cheek. Nan, elated, had told him privately that Miss Alex had eaten a boiled egg and some toast for breakfast which was the first real food she had eaten in days. Nan had made up a basket of food for a picnic, she whispered to him, which she held on her knee. They sat in the sunshine beside a flowering hedge and ate cold chicken legs, dainty cucumber sandwiches, Nan's home-made biscuits of almond and nuts, and slices of fruit cake washed down with elderberry wine, which she admitted she had brewed herself from a recipe given her when she was parlour-maid at Lantern Hill. She and Patrick watched Alex as she lay back, her face to the sky and, as though she were unaware of what she did, ate a chicken leg, two cucumber sandwiches and a biscuit. Not realising that they did so they exchanged triumphant glances. She fussed about Alex, who seemed not to mind in her relaxed state and Patrick watched her, and in turn, as he did so, was watched by Nan. He was dressed casually in grey flannel trousers, a white open-necked shirt with the sleeves rolled up and a pullover, the day being warm so that even the ladies threw off much of their outer garments. Nan knew what was in his mind, for it was in his eyes and in his expression every time he turned to look at her young mistress. It was lovely but she did wish he wouldn't do it so often because when his eyes were on Miss Alex they weren't on the road. Mind, there was not much traffic about so they seemed quite safe in his hands.

They travelled over sixty miles that day, taking just over six hours, and by the end of it Patrick considered he was an experienced driver. One or two farmers striding along beside wagons of hay or milk churns jumped hastily into a hedge then turned to stare in open-mouthed wonder as they clattered past. They capered in the dust the automobile threw up and shook their fists, for it was believed, as had been believed when railway trains took to the open countryside, that the sound and sight of them would cause their cows' milk to dry up.

The inn at Fenny Stratford was welcoming, comfortable and clean and Patrick blessed Dick for his advice. He ate alone as Nan had insisted Miss Alex must eat before the cosy fire in her bedroom and then retire for the night since she was tired. It was true and he did not argue with her. Alex had spoken little on the journey but he had felt her relax, sink down in what seemed to be great relief and enjoyment as they had driven through quiet villages, along country lanes filled with the smell of grass, of wild flowers and the country sounds of lowing cows and plaintive sheep.

The next day was a repeat of the first, though they made better time since the ladies in the back, feeling they were seasoned travellers by now, were more at ease, pointing things out to one another and engaging in conversation so that he was able to drive a little faster in the hope they would not notice. When they reached Ashbourne they alighted from the by now dusty motor car with all the aplomb of ladies who were quite accustomed to this way of travelling, ushering their young mistress up the stairs to the bedrooms he had booked and again he was forced to eat alone.

They reached the outskirts of St Helens and from there to Edge Bottom House just as Beth and Archie Goodwin, Alex's parents, were about to sit down to dinner. The commotion a couple of dogs made at the back of the old house brought them to the front door, for no motor car had ever driven up the lane at the side of the house in its lifetime. Maidservants crowded at their back and from the yard came a host of stable lads and grooms and gardeners to stare in wonder at the contraption which came to a perfect stop beside the garden gate. Patrick was by now cock-a-hoop with himself, for not many gentlemen who owned one of these machines had driven 200 miles in three days as he had and he clambered over the array of gearsticks and brakes, hurrying round the front of the automobile to hand out Alex. She swayed a little, leaning against him for a delicious moment as she regained her balance.

'Alex,' he whispered beneath the brim of her ridiculous hat, his lips close to her cheek where her dark hair curled, 'are you all right?'

'Yes, Patrick, and thanks to you I will be in full health in a couple of weeks. Now, come and meet my parents.'

Patrick thought Archie Goodwin was about to embrace him when he had done with his tired daughter. She had been put in her mother's arms and it seemed certain that they would all be weeping soon for the sheer joy of it.

'Mr O'Leary, how can we ever thank you enough?' he blurted out, wringing Patrick's hand between his own. 'I knew she was very fragile when we brought her from Bow Street but how in heaven's name did you persuade her to come home?'

'Sir, I can take no credit for it. I believe it was the WSPU who told her she was not well enough to . . . to carry on—'

But Archie interrupted him, holding out his hand to his wife who still held Alex in a grip that said she would never allow her out of her sight again. 'Beth . . . Beth, come and meet Mr O'Leary. He it was who saved Alex at the Magistrates' Court and now he has brought her home to us. Where are Will and Tom, for God's sake? They should be here to greet their sister.'

'They are still at the works, darling,' she answered. 'You told me there was a big order and—'

'Of course, but come and shake hands with . . .' He had no time to finish his sentence, for his wife, whose face was wet with tears of gladness, did more than shake his hand. She put her arms about him and kissed his cheek, leaving her tears there. Patrick was astonished, because his own mother, who was the only woman he had known well and who he knew loved him and would have died for him, had never embraced him in his life. A dry kiss on the cheek as a greeting or farewell but nothing more.

Alex's mother was nothing like her in colouring, or indeed in anything else. She had hair that had once been a lively copper but which had faded to cinnamon and her eyes were a shining silvery grey. Her husband was grey-haired mixed with a silvery blond, with faded blue eyes, nothing like the lavender blue of his daughter. They ushered him into the hallway of the weathered stone house which sat four-square before a long garden bursting with summer flowers of every colour under the sun: purple-blue of delphinium, bright golden orange of marigold mixed with the vivid blue cornflowers. They crowded the borders to the edge of the smoothly mown lawn, and all over the walls and an arched gate to the right-hand side were climbing roses, the scent quite heady as the evening dusk fell. There was an ancient oak tree, a wrought-iron garden seat with a table to match where he supposed the family took afternoon tea in fine weather. It breathed peace and dignity and wellbeing and it crossed his mind that he would like a house like this one day, with Alex Goodwin in it!

He was pressed to sit down to dinner with them, though he argued that he did not wish to impose on their hospitality. He thought Mr Goodwin was about to take offence at that, for after all, he said, he had brought their girl back and were they to turn him out as though she were no more than a straying cat? In fact if he did not agree to stay a night or two he, Archie Goodwin, would be inordinately wounded, and so would his wife, turning to her and holding out his hand which she took.

Patrick looked to Alex who had been prevailed upon to sit herself in a comfortable leather chair by the empty fireside in the wide hallway. The servants were bustling about, smiling and chattering quietly to one another, carrying the suitcases and the trunk indoors, then awaiting their mistress's orders as to where Mr O'Leary was to be put. And before he knew it he was ushered into a large, beautifully furnished bedroom at the front of the house with orders to come down as soon as he had washed. He must not bother to change, for they were very informal at Edge Bottom House. There was plenty of food, Mr Goodwin told him, holding his arm as though afraid he might dart away, turning for confirmation to Mrs Adams, the cook, for the boys would be in soon and there was always more than was needed since they ate like two wild horses.

They were all there waiting for him when he came down the stairs, smiling hugely, every last one of them, even Alex who had been spruced up by the efforts of Nan and was drinking a glass of sherry, which Mr Goodwin hoped Mr O'Leary would not object to his patient taking. Patrick, not aware that he was now considered Alex Goodwin's physician, could only nod his head and take the glass of brandy put in his hand by his host.

There were two tall and handsome young men lounging against the fireplace and it was evident at once that they were the sons of Mrs Goodwin though there was nothing of their father in them. They had coppery curls falling untidily about their head and silvery grey eyes just like hers. They were lean, confident and smiling their good nature, eager to be about something, since they were young and in excellent health and were only staying to pay their respects to their parents' guest as he was evidently nearer their father's age than their own, or so they seemed to tell him with their respectful manner and the way in which they called him 'sir'.

'These are my sons, Tom and Will, Mr O'Leary, just come from the works: the glass works we own, and as you may have noticed they are keen to get away to whatever it is young men do these days.' Even Mr Goodwin seemed to consider him to be too old for his sons' social pastimes.

The only thing that interested the 'lads', Will being the elder at twenty-three and Tom twenty, was the Darracq which stood in the lane beside the house. It had been surrounded by a crowd of bemused men, servants of the Goodwins and men from the neighbourhood, for the news soon spread of its marvel. They had all seen one of these 'infernal machines', those who ventured into town, but none had actually *touched* one and Alfie, one of the grooms, had begged to be allowed to clean it. He had high hopes that Mr Goodwin would one day purchase one and that he might be called on to drive it. Horses were a thing of the past, or soon would be, he was overheard to say, and it seemed Tom and Will agreed with him.

'Mr Goodwin, sir,' Patrick interrupted courteously over the splendid dinner – fried whiting, followed by pork cutlets with tomato sauce, then meringues *à la crème* – 'the motor car does not actually belong to me. A colleague very kindly lent it to me so that I might travel up to the Lake District where I am hoping to spend a couple of weeks. Probably walking and—'

'Where are you to stay, Mr O'Leary?' Archie Goodwin cut in sharply.

'Pardon?' Patrick raised his eyebrows enquiringly.

'Where are you to stay? Please do not think me inquisitive but if you have not booked a hotel, may I offer you our house at Grasmere. It is set on the hill overlooking the lake. It is the least we can do, is it not, darling,' turning to his wife who sat serenely at the head of the table, smiling in great joy at her family, all together under her roof.

'Of course, Mr O'Leary, after what you have done for Alex we won't hear of anything else.' Here she frowned a little. 'Unless you have . . . perhaps you are to stay with friends?'

*Friends!* Patrick was ready to smile at Mrs Goodwin, for he had had no friends since he had started school in Liverpool at the age of five. Even then he had been what his classmates called a 'swot' who would rather have his nose in a book than play their high-spirited games in the playground because he had been eager to learn from an early age.

From the corner of his eyes he saw Alex lower her head and heard what he thought was a chuckle. She had mentioned her parents' country house knowing full well that they, being the generous, kind-hearted folk they were, would offer to put him up while he was travelling about the lakes. And, since she was an unconventional, independent young woman, made so by the life she led, she fully intended to go with him, but he was not aware of this as he looked about him from one face to the other.

'Mrs Goodwin, Mr Goodwin, I couldn't possibly do that. You scarcely know me and it would be unfair of me to take advantage—'

'Scarcely know you! After what you did for Alex.'

'I did nothing, Mr Goodwin, really. Any doctor would—'

'Mr O'Leary, I absolutely will have my way on this.'

'Father, while you and Mr O'Leary argue about who should do what, to whom, and where, may Tom and I be excused? It's not often we get a chance to study an automobile at close quarters. And perhaps when you have settled this between you, whatever it is, you will come outside and have a look at the . . . it's a Darracq, isn't it, sir?'

Will pushed his chair back and stood for a moment, ready to take flight, while Patrick nodded distractedly, hoping to God these two boys, for that was what they seemed to him, just boys, would not fiddle with anything attached to Dick's motor.

'Perhaps you could come yourself, sir, and . . . well . . . would it be too much of an imposition to take us for a spin?'

'Will, Mr O'Leary is—'

'Patrick, please.'

'I'm sorry?'

'Won't you call me Patrick?' for this family seemed to him to be so delightfully unorthodox. The females were allowed to be members of the suffrage movement, the upheaval of women where anything might be said or done, even their unmarried daughter, when most of her class were kept at home until they were married, passing from a father's protection to that of a husband. He wasn't absolutely sure he approved!

'Patrick, of course, and let me warn you that if these lads of mine have their way they will be driving your friend's motor before it's dark. But first let's make it quite clear that my wife and I will be offended if you don't take up my offer for Grasmere.'

'Mr Goodwin—'

'And I shall come with you, Mr O'Leary. A couple of weeks at Fellgate House will do me the world of good.'

Every head turned to stare in wonder at Alex Goodwin as she calmly spoke of sharing, not just the motor car but the house at Grasmere with a man who was not related to her. Though he couldn't think of anything he would like more, Patrick frowned, ready to give her the length of his tongue as his mother would have said, but her mother smilingly defused the moment. Beth Goodwin and her family might be unconventional, their rules more relaxed than many of their friends liked, but she knew when to draw the line and to keep on the correct side of it.

'What a wonderful idea, and your father and I will come too. It's about time we had a holiday.'

# 5

She couldn't remember when she had last felt so happy. And so free! She and Patrick walked for hours, laughed and argued, particularly the latter, but amicably, for hours, listened to music on the gramophone, a contraption with an enormous horn that had to be cranked up by hand for each record. The thunder of Wagner, the phrasing of Mozart and Mendelssohn, waltzes by Johann Strauss, which were her mother's favourites, echoed through the old house and though Patrick knew none of them he found intense enjoyment in listening to the music with the Goodwin family around him, the old man beating time on the arm of his chair.

But for the first few days Alex found she really did need to rest, which she did, sleeping the clock round, and when she woke eating the good Lakeland fare that Mrs Stone put in front of her. The clap bread made from oatmeal, hasty pudding eaten with butter, milk and treacle, bread hot from the oven, fresh milk, quantities of cheese from the farm and crowdy, a form of delicious and nutritious soup, herb puddings consisting of the leaves of Alpine bistort eaten with veal. Mrs Stone, who was a splendid cook, made pies from minced mutton seasoned with salt and pepper. She cooked fresh fish caught the day before and brought overnight from Whitehaven, as well as the more sophisticated dishes that the Goodwin family were used to. Patrick told Alex he could literally see her putting on weight!

Fellgate House was perched on the lower slopes of Rydal

Fell, set in a grove of trees which had been cleared to the front of the house allowing for superb views over Grasmere and the small island that appeared to float in the centre. The house was situated on a plateau cut into a steep slope, solid, built of local stone with a wide terrace which led in a series of stone steps down to tiers of lawns with a cobbled path to a wrought-iron gate let into the garden wall, the lane beyond leading to the village of Grasmere. Each lawn was bordered by a bed of flowers, at this time of the year ablaze with colour. Jake Stone, husband to the cook, and Curley Mounsey, a local man from the village, were in charge of the outside, keeping the woods at the back and side of the house from becoming overgrown, especially the wild garlic which was a 'bugger' to keep down, according to Jake who, with his wife Ethel, were permanent caretakers at Fellgate House. Three local girls were employed when the family was in residence: Jane Bibby in the scullery, Annie Garnett to help Mrs Stone in the kitchen, and Betty Mounsey, Curley's daughter, as parlour-maid. The three village girls went home at night, as did Curley, but Jake and Ethel Stone had their own quarters at the top of the house which Archie Goodwin had converted into a private apartment for them, all very comfortable. There were seven bedrooms on the first floor, one of which was Mr and Mrs Goodwin's with a small sitting-room and its own bathroom attached. Patrick O'Leary's bedroom also had its own bathroom, as did two of the others. He was overwhelmed at the luxury of it all, particularly as the Goodwins only used the place for part of the year, deciding as he unpacked his rather battered suitcase, looking around him and out of the windows at the lovely gardens, that Archie Goodwin must be a very rich man indeed.

Alex had her own room and bathroom at the further corner of the house, also overlooking the front but with a window at the side from which she could see the summerhouse and the peacock which fanned its tail for her pleasure. Nobody knew where it had come from but it was now a permanent feature at Fellgate House. Everywhere were deep-piled carpets in pale colours, mostly a dove grey, with deep and comfortable armchairs in peach and pale green. The silk curtains matched the carpets which the Goodwins strode carelessly across with no thought to the mud or grass they trekked in and which the sunny-natured Betty cheerfully cleared up.

The Goodwins were the most unique family Patrick had ever known, agreeable, unconventional and independent, seeming to care not at all for the principles of the era, which was why their daughter had been allowed, he surmised, to live in London and become a member of the most militant suffragette party in the country. It seemed that Mrs Goodwin, and before her her mother, had been part of the movement for the enfranchisement of women for nearly fifty years so was it any wonder that this passion for women's equality had rubbed off on the men in their lives, making them more tolerant, or, as he would himself put it, somewhat careless of their womenfolk. Perhaps he was Victorian in his outlook, he brooded, but any woman of his – daring to allow his thoughts to wander to Alex Goodwin – would be too busy with her home and the children he would give her to concern herself with the degradation, the humiliation and danger that were the fate of the members of the WSPU.

The journey from St Helens to Grasmere had been managed in just one full day. Mr and Mrs Goodwin, Nan travelling with them, had done the trip by train, arriving at Windermere and taking a coach from there to Grasmere, getting to Fellgate House at almost the same time as Patrick and Alex in the Darracq. Patrick, without the little shrieks of anxiety from the back seat from Nan and Nelly, had got up to a heady thirty miles an hour on the open road, since Alex seemed to be as delighted as he was himself with a turn of speed, begging to be allowed to drive herself, which he refused saying the motor was not his but as soon as he had one of his own he would teach her. She seemed to find nothing unusual in his assumption that when the holiday was finished and they were back in London their friendship would continue. He even left the top down which pleased her more and a fine colour tinted her cheeks. They stopped for lunch at an inn on the outskirts of Lancaster, then continued on through Kendal, following the winding road until they saw the shining silver water of Lake Windermere. Again they stopped for tea before climbing back into the motor and roaring along the road that ran beside the beautiful lake. They had not talked much because the going was so noisy and Patrick found he needed all his concentration to guide the automobile through the narrow lanes, which had not been created for such a machine. At every turn he encountered thunderstruck farm labourers plodding along on a horse and cart, wagons of hay, even flocks of sheep and, once, a herd of inquisitive cows. Alex fell asleep as they drove through Windermere and as they entered Ambleside he was forced to waken her for directions.

Mr Goodwin, with Jake and Curley, were waiting anxiously at the gate in the lane, ready to help with the luggage, and with an exhausted Alex, leaving a perplexed Patrick wondering where to put Dick's machine. Then a scrap of a lad said something unintelligible in what Patrick took to be the dialect of the district and pointed emphatically at a field gate further up the lane set in a hedge of brambles. It was invisible to the traveller but the lad obligingly opened it and Patrick found he could drive up a rutted path to the stables at the back of the house. Alex had been put straight to bed before he had even entered the house and he, who had driven perhaps the same distance in one day as he had in three, soon asked to be excused, sinking into the comfortable bed with scarcely a thought, even for Alex.

After several days just sitting on the terrace with her face to the sun she had recovered enough to accept his invitation to walk down to Grasmere for her first excursion, but being Alex she told him she wanted nothing to do with people and buildings but needed to get the fresh, reviving air of Cumberland in her nostrils. No, they would climb up to Rydal Fell, she said, and yes, she would stop when she had had enough, she promised. Her mother and Nan protested loudly but she shook her head, her hair moving in a ripple of curls and straying tendrils about her ears and neck and he was so enchanted he did not add his protests to those of her mother. It was an indication of the freedom Alex enjoyed that her family did not try to oppose her, treating her as a mature and practical woman who knew her own mind and would stand for no objections. As she grew stronger he could see in her the woman who had screamed her defiance at those who tried to restrain her in Westminster Yard on the day he met her.

It was as they climbed the rock-strewn slopes that Alex realised how joyful she felt, an emotion she had not known for a long time. She was dressed in sensible boots and a walking dress of light cotton cut just long enough to clear her footwear. It fitted her figure neatly yet was loose enough to allow for free movement. It was in a soft shade of azure and again her eyes changed colour, taking on the very same shade, Patrick noticed bemusedly, whether the result of the clear air of Lakeland, or a reflection of the colour of her dress he couldn't tell.

The weather had continued warm and in her hand she carried a stout walking-stick which she had taken from the stand in the big hallway at the house. As they moved up towards Helm Crag which Patrick had decreed was high enough for her first day, having studied the map, they did not talk until they reached their destination. There Patrick laid out the groundsheet he had brought, made her sit on it with her back to a grey, moss-pitted stone and produced the sandwiches Mrs Stone had made up for them and, as a treat, he said smilingly, a bottle of white wine that he had tucked into his rucksack.

'When we've eaten we'll rest here for a while and drink that wine slowly, macushla, or I'll be forced to carry you down the trod . . . is that the right word, a sheep trod?'

'It is and if you don't mind I'm not accustomed to taking orders from a man,' but she was smiling.

'Sure and don't I realise that but it seems I've been employed as your doctor and everyone knows that a doctor's orders are law.'

'Is that so, and what is all this lapsing into an Irish brogue? You'll be saying things like "begorra" next.'

'My forebears were Irish. My grandparents came over to Liverpool during the famine of the forties and we Irish have this dreadful habit of hanging together, so for the first years of my life I lived among my countrymen even though we were settled in Liverpool.'

They were gazing out over the Vale of Grasmere with the lake shimmering in the midday heat haze and in the distance they could see Rydal Water and the top end of Windermere. The fields were covered with a moving pattern of white on green where the sheep grazed, hemmed in by the criss-cross network of dry-stone walls. Higher up was the umber of bracken and the purple of heather but round the lakes trees grew thickly. Across the lake rose the magnificent beauty of High Raise, Silver How and Loughrigg Fell, all of which she had climbed as a girl. Peace entered her and she leaned back against the rock with a sigh of content.

'What does macushla signify?' she asked lazily, closing her eyes and resting her head against the rock.

'It's Irish,' he said abruptly.

'I thought as much but what does it mean?'

'It's a term of . . . endearment.'

She opened her eyes lazily and was startled to see his face close to hers as he leaned up on one elbow but he turned away hastily, grinning. 'It's what mothers call their naughty children.'

'Am I a naughty child?'

'Sometimes. You were being very naughty when I first saw you and if I had had my way I would have turned you over my knee and tanned your bottom. That's what many of your women need. A good spanking.' He was about to go on but she sat up slowly and her face hardened and he knew that he must not spoil the day by going head first with his own views on suffragism so instead he smiled and took her hand. 'So that is why I called you macushla. Now then, tell me if there is a boat we can hire to get across to that island in the middle of the lake, and while you do let's finish the wine.'

They drank the wine and once again relaxed against the rock and when he turned to her she had fallen asleep. Her face was flushed with wine and the sun, and her eyelashes touched her cheekbone. Her hair was tangled about her head, a long tendril curling across her parted, rosy lips and very delicately he slipped a finger under it and tucked it back. Unable to stop himself, not even thinking of it, if he was honest, or what the consequences might be, he laid his own mouth, soft as a butterfly, against hers. She did not wake and he was glad, for he knew if he moved too fast she would escape him. She was stubborn, with a desire to tackle the problems of the women she championed head-on but at the same time she had an unexpected sparkle of humour. She was intelligent, with intuition and sensitivity, but there was that recklessness in her, that passion for her cause that made her unpredictable. He loved her, he knew that. For the first time in his life he was in love and at his age it was not a light thing nor would it go away when she did. He must move slowly, gain her friendship before anything else. He lay back and closed his eyes and, like her, fell into a deep sleep from which he woke to find her studying his face with an intensity that amazed him.

'Have I not shaved to your satisfaction?' he asked her, grinning, though his heart was thumping madly.

She reared back then grinned with him. She stood up and held out her hand which he took and got to his feet and the moment was defused, but they both knew something important had happened to them both here though neither was aware that the other knew.

They walked each day after that and even hired a boat which he rowed erratically with much hysterical laughter across to the island, nearly tossing them both into the lake. They motored to Bowness, taking the steamer the length of the lake, dreaming, both of them, in the summer heat which continued day after day. Alex discovered that far from being the rather serious, dedicated man she had first thought, he had an ironic, whimsical, rather ribald sense of humour which made her laugh with delight. All the men she had known, who were mostly the sons of her father's business associates, had treated her as an innocent girl who must be protected from anything that might upset her delicate sensibilities. And she certainly must not be talked to about indelicate subjects such as the ones Patrick spoke of connected with his work. They knew of her association with the suffrage movement, of course, which was probably why none had made a bid for her hand, and her father's fortune, but Patrick talked of many things, the hospital, his patients, the surgery he performed with the help of Dick Morris, who had made this holiday the success it undoubtedly was, taking it for granted, since she was an adult, that she would understand.

'We must repay him in some way when we get back, Patrick,' she said as though it were the most natural thing in the world that when they returned from this magical life to their own they would continue to see each other. 'We'll treat him to a good night out. Does he have a lady friend?'

'Many,' Patrick told her ruefully.

'Well, he must bring his favourite and we will dine out at the Ritz and then see a show. I'll find out what's on and . . .' She stopped speaking abruptly and he knew she was suddenly thinking of her responsibilities to the WSPU.

'Dick would enjoy that,' he said softly and did not add, as he was tempted to do, 'and so would I'.

It was on their last night as they were dining on the terrace that the question of war came up and to Patrick's amazement it was Archie Goodwin who spoke of it. The table had been carried out through the conservatory and placed in the soft evening warmth, candles burning without a flicker in the windless night, the gleam of silver and brilliantly white napery, even a great bowl of roses in the centre of the table, their scent mixing with the smell of newly mown grass, of rich, sun-soaked soil, of the very earth that lay placidly about them so that it seemed almost an obscenity to speak of something as dreadful as war. They had not dressed for dinner as was the custom but the men wore ties and the ladies a pretty gown. It was also the custom for the ladies to leave the gentlemen to their brandy and cigars but the Goodwins had no truck with that sort of thing.

'What d'you think of the Kaiser, Patrick?' Archie asked diffidently.

'The Kaiser?' Patrick asked, surprised.

'Mmm. Do you not think there is danger in the rivalry between Germany, France, Russia and Great Britain?'

'I'm afraid, for my sins, I take little interest in politics, Mr Goodwin,' he said mildly.

'Like the majority of the men in this country, I fear, Patrick.'

'If women had the vote they would be taking an interest, Father,' Alex said hotly, but her father held up his hand.

'Let us not have the WSPU for tonight, my darling,' and Alex subsided resentfully. 'The Germans, rightly or wrongly, fear encirclement, Patrick.' Archie drew on his cigar, watching the smoke from it curl up into the evening air. 'They see Russia as barbarians and France as an irresponsible nationalist mob though I believe they would like to come to some sort of an agreement with Great Britain.'

'Are you saying you believe they would go to war, sir?'

'Well . . .'

'Surely not even a crass idiot like the Kaiser would challenge the British Empire? Men like Asquith and the pacifist group in the cabinet would resign in a body if—'

'Oh, take no notice of me, lad. Everyone I know thinks I am a scaremonger but I have this feeling that . . . something is about to happen. Perhaps not immediately, or even this year but one day.'

A strange silence fell around the table then Beth Goodwin stood up suddenly, for the thought of war was not one she cared to contemplate. She had two sons and if that wasn't enough to frighten any mother, she had a daughter who would not simply sit at home and roll bandages.

'Enough, let's go inside and have coffee.'

They had gone to bed, leaving Patrick and Alex alone. The windows were wide open and the scent of roses was over-powering from a vast climber that tangled up the front of the house and was smothered in cream blooms. Alex was conscious of a tension between them as though something might be said that would alter their lives but which neither of them felt they could speak of. Neither of them wanted to break the silence. It was heavy with promise, a promise of what? she wondered. Then, going back over the past two perfect weeks when she and Patrick had walked, laughed, talked endlessly, boated, even swum in the icy waters of the lake, she knew that she could barely contemplate their coming parting. He was lounging in an armchair, his long legs stretched out before him, crossed at the ankles. He was smoking a cigarette, the smoke in a cloud about his head, his eyes on the moths that had entered the room and were circling the lamps. His face, which had become so familiar to her over the past fortnight, was in shadow but she knew his eyes were now on her and as suddenly as lightning strikes she knew why. There was electricity in the air, moving between them, but she, who had no experience of men, had not the slightest idea what to do about it. She knew at that moment that she did not want this . . . this . . . what was she to call it? She didn't know, she only knew she could not bear it to end. She could say so, of course, but in her world it was the man who made the first declaration and indeed, who was to say he would make one?

Her voice was harsh when she broke the silence. 'What would you do if there is a war as Father seems to think?'

'Fight, I suppose.'

'But you're a doctor, not a soldier.'

'Alex, I can't believe there will be a war. What concerns me more is . . .'

'Yes?'

'The thought of you in *your* war.'

'Patrick . . .'

'I know, you can't give it up. Don't you think I don't know that? It is tearing me apart that as soon as you get back to London you will resume the activities that, if you keep them up, will eventually kill you. They will put you in prison again, probably for months. You will go on hunger strike. They will force-feed you and they will kill you. Alex, say you will stop.'

'Don't be a fool, Patrick. How can I? My family have been fighting this government and other governments for nearly fifty years. My grandmother, who is in her sixties, my mother, who is forty-six, and now me. Can I let them down?'

'There are others who can continue.' He sat up abruptly and the light from the lamps fell on his harrowed face. She had never seen such pain and for a moment she felt it melt the very bones of her. She loved him, she knew that now. He was everything that she had dreamed of in a man, if you could say she had dreamed at all. He was strong and gentle, compassionate and funny, he was considerate of others, mannerly and yet not pompous. But he wanted from her what she could not give and it would drive them apart. He had tried to hide it but she knew he hated what she did and hated the women who had made her what she was. He was telling her that she could just step down and let the others fight on. Let them go to prison, be humiliated, be hurt and weakened. She knew now because she could see it in his expression that he loved her, that he was consumed with the need to protect her, from herself, she supposed wearily, but it was impossible and as he sank back she knew he had seen it in her face.

'No, I suppose not,' he said bleakly, though she had not spoken. He stood up and with a savage gesture lifted her from her chair and pulled her into his arms. She sagged against him in her need and when he put his mouth against hers, her lips parted, opened willingly, hungrily. His kiss was hard, then soft and warm and he breathed her name into her open mouth.

'Alex, leave it.' His mouth slipped to her cheek, to her jaw, to her throat and she began to moan with longing but at his words she stiffened for she knew what he meant. He continued to kiss her, attempting to return her to the submissive state his long, lean body had brought about but she was beginning to struggle, to push at him and at once he let go of her so that she almost fell.

'I do beg your pardon. It seems I am offensive to you. I'll let you get to your bed. We have a long day tomorrow so I will bid you goodnight.'

She wept in the night, wetting her pillow with her tears, but finally she slept, still weeping in her dreams for what she had thrown away and when she went downstairs in the morning, her face ashen, her eyes like huge waterlogged lakes, he was gone, leaving only a note of profuse thanks for her parents, wishing them well and making no mention of her.

# 6

At first she was put to work in the Woman's Press shop in Charing Cross Road which had been opened in 1910. The rapid growth in the sales of suffragette literature and merchandise necessitated the move to this central London location and it was here that women who had been badly weakened in Holloway by long sleep strikes, hunger strikes that led to forced feeding were employed until they were deemed fit to return to more arduous duties.

It was a smart little shop, its window a blaze of the movement's colours in purple, white and green displaying beautiful motoring scarves in shades of purple, white muslin blouses, bags, belts, the bags named 'The Emmeline' or 'The Christabel', and 'The Pethick' tobacco pouch. The WSPU were very keen for their members to wear the uniform of the Union if possible when leading a procession or at a meeting, which was a purple or green skirt, a white-jersey golf coat which could be purchased in the press shop for seven shillings and sixpence, and a golf hat which sold for two shillings. Regalia should be worn over the right shoulder and fastened under the left arm. Not all the members could afford to buy the uniform, particularly women from the working classes, but it had been found that their membership was gradually falling away since they did not agree with the increasing violence advocated by the Pankhursts. The movement was, therefore, mostly made up of women from the middles classes, ladies who did not depend on a husband's wage to support them.

Hung in the window of the shop were placards advertising forthcoming meetings, others declaring, 'Votes for Women', and on shelves were teapots, mugs, teacups and saucers, all with the symbol known as 'Sylvia's Angel' decorating them. Sylvia Pankhurst, who had designed them, had received an artistic training before she became involved with the women's movement. There were books, pamphlets and leaflets, stationery, games, blotters, playing cards and indeed almost everything that could be produced in purple, white or green or a combination of all three. There was even a suffragette cookery book with a recipe for cooking and preserving a good suffrage speaker! Alex bought one for her mother, knowing it would appeal to her sense of humour.

*First: Butter the speaker when asking her to come and speak by sending her a stamped addressed envelope with which to reply.*
*Second: Grease the dish by paying all the speaker's expenses.*
*Third: Put her to warm, or cool as the case may be in a room by herself before the meeting so that she may be fresh and in a good condition for speaking.*
*Fourth: Beat her to a froth with an optimistic spoon, making light of all disappointments. Carefully avoid too strong a flavour of apologies.*
*Fifth: Do not let her cool too rapidly after the meeting but place her considerately by a nice bedroom fire with a light supper.*

Alex quite enjoyed her stay at the Woman's Press shop, for it gave her great satisfaction to talk to the rather diffident women, a few of them from the working classes, who were not sure about joining the movement since their Fred or their Albert wouldn't care for it, but nevertheless they longed to talk of it and promised to come to the next meeting at the Queen's Hall in Langham Place if the old man could be persuaded to mind the kids. Many of them showed an acute interest in – spoken in a hushed whisper – birth control since they already had six or eight or even twelve! But those interested dropped off considerably as the violence, particularly the death of Emily Wilding Davison, continued to escalate.

When she had been back three weeks Miss Kerr, the General Office Manager at Clement's Inn, asked her to call in at the WSPU office in the Strand and when she was shown into her office, surprised her by asking if she could drive a gig.

'A gig?' Alex was bewildered and disappointed since she had been expecting, hoping, she supposed, that Miss Kerr was about to tell her that it had been decided she could return to her normal duties, which sounded a foolish description of the militant activities she had been concerned with. She was longing to be of more use than what she thought of as merely a 'shop girl', which was something the older or more infirm ladies could manage and the mention of the gig puzzled her.

'Yes, dear, a gig, or what we like to call the "press cart". Among other members you will be in charge of the distribution of our pamphlet *Votes for Women* in central London. You must make sure that all our pitches are supplied with copies. Helen Craggs who drives the gig has been arrested for trying to set fire to a house in Oxford, which is where she comes from, and Rose Kellett, who usually accompanies her, has never driven a gig, indeed knows nothing about horses. I heard that you used to ride when you were younger and I wondered if your family owned a gig. In which case I presumed you drove it.'

Miss Kerr was a woman in her fifties, a spinster who had, from an early age, devoted her life to the 'cause'. She had grey hair, almost white, fastened back into a neat coil, wore a white shirt-like blouse with a stiff collar and a mannish tie. She had once owned a secretarial business but had given it up to work full time for the WSPU and though she was fair, even kindly, she was a woman who stood for no nonsense. She raised her eyebrows as Alex hesitated, leaning back in her chair waiting.

'I had hoped to get out canvassing, Miss Kerr. I heard there was to be a deputation to—'

'Soon, my dear, but I think you may find the job of distributing copies of *Votes for Women* can be quite hazardous. Lady Constance Lytton and the Honourable Mrs Haverfield were almost dragged from their seats by a crowd of bullies who accosted them. They were pelted with rotten fruit but they fought back, as we all have to do.'

'It's because of my leg, isn't it?' Alex's voice was indignant.

'No, it is not. You have been in the thick of it for four years now, Miss Goodwin, and your disability never stopped you from doing anything the others did. You have been arrested many times and have suffered great hardship.'

'I'm not the only one, Miss Kerr.'

'I appreciate that, Miss Goodwin and we are proud to have you work for the movement but we must place our members where they can do most good and at the moment we have no one to drive the gig. Not at such short notice. Now we shall send you out soon. There is to be a march from King's Cross to Tower Hill to show our support for two suffragettes who are on hunger strike in Mountjoy Gaol in Dublin. They are close to death and will no doubt be released very soon but we thought a protest might have some results for other prisoners. The high-sounding Prisoners' Temporary Discharge for Ill-Health Act which the government rushed through in April, what you and I call the 'cat and mouse', will see to that, for it would do the government no good to have women die on them, would it? We have suffered many injustices, Miss Goodwin. You know the Lincoln's Inn House headquarters was raided by the police, don't you. I was myself arrested and now the public are attacking our shops and offices. We are beginning to annoy them, you see, with our bomb hoaxes and so many of our women are being arrested that until I can find a replacement for Miss Craggs I must ask you to deputise for her. Believe me, it is not an easy job. I know you are longing to *fight*, to be used in more . . . more war-like activities, so perhaps you can go along with your colleagues to the church service on Sunday where they are to chant in protest at the treatment of their colleagues in prison. Will you do that? I can't guarantee you will not be arrested again but it will be a start. Are you well enough, d'you think?'

'Of course.'

Miss Kerr smiled at her enthusiasm. 'But in the meanwhile will you drive the press cart? Let me warn you that women undertaking such "unwomanly" and "unsexing" activities have made a strong and unfavourable impression on passers-by. You will be dressed in and carrying accessories of purple, white and green to maximise your impact.'

It was nearly four weeks since she had returned to London and in that time as she walked from home to the offices in Charing Cross Road she had looked out for Patrick, castigating herself for doing so. Every man above average height was scrutinised and she had even run after one tall gentleman who was, unusually, bareheaded, dark-haired, startling him considerably when she touched his arm. He had smiled agreeably, for what man can resist a pretty woman, ready to respond to her approach, but with a mumbled apology she had hurried on, almost running in an attempt to escape the awful hole that had opened in her life with the loss of Patrick O'Leary. She had hoped he would forgive her for what must have seemed to him to be a total rebuff at Grasmere. The love he had revealed to her and which she returned could not be accepted if it meant he would do his utmost to make her give up her life's work. That was what he wanted. What *all* men wanted, which was what Gladstone had called years and years ago *the angel of the hearth*, a woman who would be there at all times, in the management of his home, his children and be what he wanted in his bed at night. He would be a good husband but she could not be a good wife, not until the fight she fought was won. She wore her brooch proudly, the brooch of a tiny portcullis and broad arrow in purple, green and white which had become the medal awarded to those who had seen service in Holloway. And they surely were beginning to win. By imprisoning so many literate, articulate women the government had unleashed upon itself rather more than it had bargained for and it was her duty, being one of those women, to explain to the electorate the vile conditions its elected representatives condoned. She had given herself to the suffrage cause as she could not give herself to a man, no matter her feelings for him, which were strong, she admitted to herself, until the cause was won.

The next day the press cart stood outside the press office with the copies of *Votes for Women* stacked in the back. At each side of the gig was fastened a poster with 'Votes for Women' printed on it in large letters and beneath it in smaller letters an advertisement for a forthcoming meeting at Caxton Hall, Westminster. Already perched on the seat was a young woman who was surely the loveliest Alex had ever seen. She had a perfect oval face beneath her pretty flowered hat, glossy black hair and a great deal of it, fastened loosely in a huge coil at the back of her head beneath the hat's brim. She had long-lashed violet eyes that shone with enthusiasm. She was smiling in what seemed to be huge delight, a warm, friendly smile as she held out her daintily gloved hand.

'You must be Alex Goodwin. I'm Rose Kellett but all my friends call me Rosie. I haven't been doing this for long because it took an age, in fact until I was twenty-one and able to please myself, to get my father's grudging permission to come to London. He gives me just enough money to pay for a tiny room in Cheyne Walk . . . oh, please forgive me. I'm inclined to babble on, or so my father says, but I'm here at last and that's all that matters.'

Alex couldn't help but respond to this delightful child, for that was what she seemed to her. She had only just begun the long road she herself had travelled and how could she dampen her high spirits, which reminded her of a little girl going to her first party.

They had dropped off all the copies at the various pitches where their women sold the magazine for one penny and were on their way back to Charing Cross Road to pick up another batch, travelling at a smart lick along Millbank towards the Houses of Parliament, with Victoria Tower Gardens on their right and beyond the gardens the river. The traffic was not unduly heavy but a hansom cab was forced to swerve when the group of young men, who must have been warned they were coming, erupted from Great College Street. They were rough men, caps slung on the backs of their heads, no collar or tie and threadbare jackets, obviously men out of work and looking for a scapegoat on which to vent their frustration. Suffragettes were fair game and might be attacked without too much interference from the law.

'Hang on, Rosie,' Alex said through gritted teeth, snapping the reins and doing her utmost to urge on the elderly horse. It did its best to break into a canter but one of the rowdies grabbed at the bit, hauling at the horse's head. The animal panicked, rearing so that the gig tipped backwards and both women were thrown off into the road.

'Gerron, yer daft bitches,' one of the roughs called out, aiming a kick at Rosie, who had fallen awkwardly, one leg bent up and caught beneath her body and though she was not heavy she had obviously damaged it, but for good measure, as she lay dazed in the road, he aimed a booted foot into the side of her head. He was taking an inordinate amount of interest in her frilled white drawers which were revealed as her skirt fell back

about her waist. The man, his eyes gleaming with lascivious-
ness, was reaching out to the elastic at her waist, ready, it
seemed, to pull down her drawers, here in broad daylight in a
road along which people walked and vehicles drove but none
was prepared to intervene. She screamed but not more loudly
than Alex who struggled to her feet and tore into them all, and
there were five of them, with the wrath of one of the furies,
hitting and kicking and even biting the hand of one of the men
who, incensed, drove his fist into the point of her jaw. She was
brought down now beside Rosie and a reluctant crowd had
begun to gather and as they did so the men slipped away,
regretfully muttering among themselves that they wished they
had had time to drag the women into an alley, for some fun
might have been had. Real fun!

They hesitated, those in the group gathered about the two
beaten women, because they were against what these women
did but they were, after all, human and could not see two
defenceless women kicked and beaten almost to death without
doing something.

Alex was only semi-conscious, her hat gone, her hair trailing
about her head in the mucky road and as she slipped in and out
of consciousness she could hear a woman's voice and then a
man's and though they seemed to be arguing the woman was
determined to have her way.

'. . . it's only sensible. After all, hospital's only across
river . . .'

'. . . they ask fer all they get . . .'

'. . . man, we can't just leave 'em. That 'un's unconscious.
Such a pretty thing . . .'

'. . . pretty or not she should . . .'

'See, fetch the ambulance somebody . . .'

'. . . an' what about poor bloody 'orse . . .?

She came to lying on a high, spotlessly clean but narrow bed
in what she presumed was an examining room in a hospital.

Everything was white from the tiled floor, the curtains that separated the beds, the sheets on the bed, the starched apron of a nurse and the equally starched coat of a man who was bending over the figure in the next bed beyond the half-drawn curtain. She was not sure if she was seeing double, which she supposed was possible when you had been kicked in the head but there seemed to be two white-coated men bending over the other bed.

'. . . leg's broken and she's concussed, I'd say, wouldn't you, Dick? Best get her ready for . . .' Then she slipped away again and when she came to she was tightly fastened beneath a sheet that came up to her chin and her head and jaw were swathed in what she presumed was a bandage. It reached down to her eyebrows and met the sheet beneath her chin and she wondered what had happened to her hat, which she distinctly remembered putting on this morning. Her jaw ached unbearably and she carefully ran her tongue round the inside of her mouth feeling for broken teeth. There seemed to be none. She was lying next to a window and when, slowly and painfully, she turned her head on the starched pillow she could see the river and the dozens of boats, big and small, that glided along it. She made a great effort and turned her bandaged head the other way and looked into the still, white face of Rosie Kellett. Rosie's eyes were closed and there was an enormous bruise across one cheek with a deep cut slashing her eyebrow. It had been stitched and from it sprang bits of bloody twine, or whatever it was they had used to close the cut. Poor Rosie, she would have the mark of the attack for the rest of her days! She had not yet received the badge, the medal of honour that was given to women who had been imprisoned but she would wear the badge of the battle she had just survived.

She tried to move, to sit up, to escape the binding of the sheet and was amazed when Patrick spoke to her, gently pushing her back on to the pillow. She was amazed and filled with joy, for he bent over the bed in which she lay and smiled into her face. She thought, and hoped that he was about to kiss her as his hand lovingly cupped her cheek then a woman's voice, sharp and resolute, interrupted her lovely dream.

The nurse, presumably the sister in charge of the ward and fourteen stone of starched uniform, voiced her disapproval of such conduct from a doctor.

'She's only just come to, Mr O'Leary, but the other one is still unconscious. I don't know what these women think they can achieve with their violent behaviour. I for one think they deserve all they get in the way of insults.'

She was obviously accustomed to deference from timid nurses with downcast eyes, to patronising doctors and bullying all those beneath her, including patients.

'These women were not treated insultingly, Sister,' Patrick told her sharply, 'they were beaten up by a gang of roughs.'

'They ask for it, sir, in the way they go round.'

'Please, Sister, let it be. I must continue my rounds but I am to be called at once if there is any change in either of them.'

'Why you should feel the need to place them side by side is beyond me, if you don't mind my saying so.' It was evident she did not care if he did. Sister Mills had been taught her nursing at this very hospital in the nursing school founded by Florence Nightingale herself and the sister had been privileged to meet the famous lady and even shake her hand. No doctor was going to get the better of her, even if he was a surgeon! 'To move Mrs Brown further down the ward so that—'

'Mrs Brown didn't seem to mind, Sister, and since these two were obviously attacked together I thought it might be of help to them both to wake up and find themselves still together. I don't agree with them. Their ways are anathema to me, Sister, but I'm inclined to think they are very brave. Now, I will look at . . .'

His voice faded away as he moved down the ward and she felt the loss of him again pierce her in the middle of her chest where she supposed her heart lay. He had seen that she was conscious, since she had opened her eyes and he had smiled and that had been a caress he had given her but he had chosen not to speak to her. She supposed the nurse would have been filled with prurient curiosity if she had discovered that the great Mr O'Leary was acquainted with one of the hysterical women who called themselves suffragettes. At the moment nobody knew who she and Rosie were since there would be no identification on them except in the bags – hers was an Emmeline – that had probably been snatched away by the attackers. Patrick knew her, of course, and he would be forced to admit, at least to her, that they were acquainted, but in the meanwhile she found she could not keep her eyes open, unaware that she had been given a recent injection to make her sleep.

She was awakened by the soft touch of a woman's hand on her cheek and when she opened her eyes there was Miss Kerr, a warm expression on her face and a smile about her rather thin lips. It was July and the summer continued warm so she wore no coat over her mannish blouse but on her head was pinned a straw boater with a broad ribbon in the women's colours round the crown. She wore her badge – for Miss Kerr had done her time in prison – pinned to the ribbon.

'Well, my dear, you have been in the wars, haven't you, and Miss Kellett. The other ladies who have been employed in the same task have had rotten fruit and vegetables thrown at them but you two are the first to be seriously injured.'

'I'm not badly hurt, Miss Kerr,' she tried to say but it came out as a slurred mumble. Her face ached abominably and her mouth felt as though it were twice its normal size, swollen and cut. She ran her tongue round it then cast her eyes to the locker beside her bed where a glass jug stood covered with a net from which coloured beads hung. Miss Kerr understood. She poured a glass of water and with the aid of a glass straw curved at one end helped Alex to drink.

Alex reached for her hand as she returned the glass to the locker and managed to mumble something that sounded a bit like, ' 'Osie'.

'Miss Kellett, you mean. She's broken her leg, the doctor told me, but it has been splinted and will, the Irish doctor told me, be as good as new. You must not worry, my dear. Her face is as bruised as yours and she has had a stitch or two and must remain in hospital for the time being. We have been in touch with her parents, and yours, but we will look after you. I told your mother so and though she wanted to come I told her not to.' Miss Kerr was not in favour of the women being constantly interfered with by parents who still wanted to treat them as children. 'I believe you have a servant at home who can look after you until you feel well enough to come back to us. My dear, you have been unlucky, haven't you?' And Alex got the impression Miss Kerr thought her a poor sort of a creature who was forever weakened by her experiences.

She did her best to speak slowly and carefully. 'I . . . I shall be home . . . shoon and back a' work . . .'

Miss Kerr patted her hand briskly and seemed prepared to leave. 'I'm sure you will . . .'

'And Roshie'll come t' me. Nan'll look after ush.'

When Miss Kerr had left she and Rosie smiled at one another but were both too bashed about to hold a conversation. Rosie tried. 'Come t' oo . . .?'

'Yeth . . . shoon . . .'

As she smiled at Rosie her heart missed a beat then began to quicken as she saw a white-coated figure approaching. It was not Patrick but another doctor she did not remember having seen before. At the same time as Rosie turned to see what Alex was looking at, her smile deepened, though she winced as her face creased.

'Itsh Mr Morrish . . .'

The doctor was all smiles as he came to the end of the bed in which Rosie lay. 'Miss Kellet,' he began, then seemed unable to go on and Alex saw it all there in his face as he looked at the battered one on the pillow. What the devil will he look like when he sees her after she has recovered, Alex asked herself, if he looks as foolish as he does now when she is stitched and bruised and not at all her beautiful self?

'And Miss Goodwin.' He dragged his gaze reluctantly away from Rosie and his cheerful, boyish face beamed at her. 'How are you both feeling?' He did not wait for an answer and indeed expected none from these two pretty women who, Patrick had told him, were suffragettes who had been in the wars.

'Ah, here's sister. It's examination time, I think.' And at once he became professional with the help of Sister Mills who would have no truck with romance, and certainly not on her ward. She had been surprised when Mr Morris had come on his own, for Mr O'Leary usually accompanied him on his rounds, or rather Mr Morris accompanied Mr O'Leary who was the senior man. He had made the excuse that he wanted to study some notes in his office and Mr Morris was perfectly capable of doing the rounds alone.

She did not connect his absence with the dark-haired patient in the end bed who was to be discharged tomorrow.

# 7

'Rosie, what is the advantage in you living in that poky room in Cheyne Walk when I have this enormous house all to myself? There are five bedrooms, for God's sake and two women in the kitchen who absolutely adore you and long to do anything for your comfort. Nan was almost in tears when I told her you were going back to Cheyne Walk and begged me to persuade you to stay here. Oh, I know you are almost recovered and your leg is healing nicely but . . .'

'Alex, dearest, I cannot impose on you another day, honestly. I have been here for four weeks and have been waited on hand and foot and I have never been so spoiled in my life but I cannot . . .'

'Why, for God's sake? If it will make you feel better you can pay me rent, whatever it is you pay for your room. I really enjoy the company, what with Dick Morris spending every spare moment he has with you, though sometimes I think he wishes I would beggar off and leave him alone with you. He is quite besotted.'

Rosie blushed, not the horrid red contusion that afflicts most young girls, but a pretty flush that stained her cheeks a soft, rose pink. She did everything beautifully, with a laugh that sounded like the chuckle of a baby, a sneeze that sounded like a kitten and when she wept, which she had done when she was first injured and pain had attacked her, it was without the sniffles, snuffles, red nose and eyes of other women but a lovely silvery spilling of silent tears which could break the heart of any man. And yet she was totally without guile and Alex, Nan and Nelly could not help but love her. And Dick, of course, who had already begged her to marry him! Even the scar on her eyebrow had healed with barely a trace!

'You are returning to work at headquarters in the treasury department where you will be able to sit down all day and as soon as you are completely better, and that means when Dick says you are better – though I suspect he will lie in his teeth about that one – you can start campaigning again. So please, won't you come and live with me? I would be dreadfully lonely without you.'

The two young women were sitting one on either side of the bright drawing-room fire in the tall, semi-detached house at Bedford Square for which Archie Goodwin paid a rent of £50 a year. The houses had been built for the prosperous middle classes and had five bedrooms, a dressing-room and a bathroom, besides the drawing-room, dining-room, kitchen, scullery and WC off it downstairs. Alex slept at the front of the house on the first floor and when Rosie came out of hospital she had put her in the back bedroom overlooking the long, narrow back garden. On the second floor Nan and Nelly shared the bedroom directly above Rosie's, the front side bedrooms above Alex's kept for guests, and her parents who liked to come up to London now and again to see a show and for her mother to do a bit of shopping in the smart shops such as Liberty's, Derry and Tom's, and Peter Robinson's. The bathroom was on the first floor directly behind the bedroom Rosie had occupied.

They could hear Nelly's voice raised in song from the scullery behind the kitchen. There was a great clattering of pots and pans and Nan shouted to her to be quiet or she would disturb the ladies, but it was said half-heartedly for no one liked a song better than Nan, and Nelly had quite a decent voice.

'Goodbye, Dolly, I must leave you, Though it breaks my heart to go . . .' and so on until 'Goodbye Dolly Grey', a great favourite during the Boer War in which Nelly's father had served.

It was September and the days were drawing in so that already at seven o'clock it was almost dark. They had eaten what Nan had decided was a nourishing meal for ladies who were convalescing, though Alex had been back in what Nan called 'the thick of it' for three weeks now. A fresh and tasty piece of hake done in Nan's own sauce, pork chops with sautéed potatoes and fresh minted peas followed by apple pie and cream, Nan's own baking, naturally, all the ingredients purchased at Covent Garden market where Nan did most of her shopping. They were both doing well on Nan's meals, putting on weight even, which gratified Nan who thought they were both too skinny for their own good. Not until they were the same roly-poly shape as herself would she be totally satisfied. And it pleased her to feed that long stick of a doctor who was Miss Rose's gentleman caller, for the lad lived in 'rooms' whatever they were and didn't eat a decent meal from one week's end to the other, except when he dined with them.

Alex sighed dramatically to let Rosie see how frustrated she was with this argument Rosie would insist on giving her. Only yesterday Alex and others had been involved in burning down St Catherine's Church in Hatcham, which had been destroyed in just over an hour. Four of her comrades had been caught and arrested and this morning had been up before the magistrates at Bow Street where they had all been sentenced to nine months in prison with hard labour since this was not their first offence. Alex, with several others, had managed to slip away round the back of the church and through a belt of trees where a motor car, a large Vauxhall belonging to one of their wealthy members, was waiting and into which they had crammed themselves and escaped. She had been part of several arson attacks in the past three weeks, one of them a country residence belonging to Lady White, another the house of Mr Arthur du Cross. Both buildings had been carefully reconnoitred to make sure that no humans or pets were killed in these attacks.

Tomorrow she was to stroll with a dozen other comrades about the West End and, when the moment was right, open her handbag, take out a hammer and break as many windows as she could! They were to split into groups to target the Strand, Cockspur Street, Kensington High Street, Downing Street, Whitehall, Piccadilly, Bond Street and Oxford Street and smash as many windows as possible. There would be such a crash of shattered glass and angry exclamations from the shopkeepers that the fracas would be heard as far away as Buckingham Palace where it was hoped the King would flinch from it. Some of them would be arrested and one of them might be her and it comforted her to know that if she were sentenced Rosie, of whom she had become very fond, as fond as if she were a sister, would be well looked after by Nan and Nelly. Rosie was as delicate-looking as a piece of rare porcelain and was not really suited to the rough and tumble she herself had known for years. Dick, who was absolutely besotted with her, would do his best to keep her from the kind of activity in which she herself was to take part tomorrow.

'Say you will, Rosie, please. I would feel better if I knew you were looking after the house for me should I—'

'Get arrested tomorrow?' Rosie's face was ready to crumple in tears, those lovely tears that were so enchanting, then she steadied herself for it did not do to weep for a comrade, a 'sister' in the war they fought. She was just waiting for the chance to show her own mettle, wondering at the same time if she would be as brave as Alex. Could she stand up in a hall packed with angry men at a political meeting and ask the speaker if he was prepared to give votes to women? 'Deeds not Words' was their motto and her heart quailed at the thought. She had stood with other women at street corners with banners and copies of their newspapers to sell. She was good at that, for the men were quite delighted to be solicited by such a pretty woman and bought her newspapers enthusiastically, glowing in her smile, for Rose Kellett was not daft and knew the power of her own loveliness. But as yet she had not been arrested nor stood in front of the magistrate at Bow Street and been sentenced to a term in prison. But if it would help her new friend to know that the house at Bedford Square was occupied should she be sent to prison, could she, Rosie, deny her that?

'Very well, I'll go over to Cheyne Walk and get the rest of my things.'

'Dick'll take you in his motor car.' Alex laughed, then sobered as she thought of that magical fortnight she had spent with Patrick and the Darracq in June. It was a memory she took out each night as she lay sleepless in her bed, going over every sweet moment, touching with her fingertips her lips which he had kissed with such passion, with such tenderness and her own response to him. She had revelled in it for several heart-beats, then she had wrenched herself away from him, offending him, for she had known that deep down he would try to make her give up her life's work, the fight he disapproved of. She had not seen him since, apart from that brief and tender moment in the hospital when he had caressed her cheek then strode away without a word. His name was forever on the lips of Dick Morris who called regularly to see, and woo, sweet Rosie, as he called her. It was Patrick who had sewn up Rosie's face so skilfully and had helped with setting her fractured leg, so Dick told them reverently and it was plain he considered Patrick the most clever and compassionate surgeon he had ever met and only a little less omnipresent than God Himself! He wanted to be just like him, he told them and was honoured to work with and learn from him. Alex listened to him, hanging on his every word, though it was anguish to do so. Dick, of course, knew that Patrick had spent a fortnight in the Lake District but it seemed Patrick had told him nothing of where he stayed, or with whom. He had borrowed Dick's Darracq and gone off on holiday after obliging a lady with a lift to her home in St Helens and it seemed, as far as Dick was concerned and apparently Patrick had confided nothing more, that was that!

He was in Kensington High Street and about to go into Lyons Corner House for a cup of tea when he saw her and for several moments he was paralysed with shock. There were three of them, three well-dressed, even elegant ladies with pretty flowered hats and dainty, high-heeled boots strolling side by side among the crowds, laughing, talking, perhaps intent upon a bit of shopping. The traffic was particularly congested with house-drawn carriages, horse-drawn cabs, brewers' drays, horse-drawn traffic mingling with the low-pitched roar of the ever growing popularity of automobiles; omnibuses packed with would-be shoppers and sightseers and people crossing the busy road as though unaware of the traffic that swirled about them. There was the smell of fresh manure filling his nostrils blending with that of petrol. He had left his own small motor car, of which he was inordinately proud, in a side street and walked in the September sunshine to which the chill of autumn was beginning to cling.

He stopped dead when he saw her, much to the annoyance of a lady with a parasol who walked into the back of him, but so pole-axed was he at the sight of Alex he scarcely noticed. Suddenly, as though one had given a signal, they opened their bags and produced a hammer apiece, and to the danger of those about them lifted the hammers to shoulder height and drove them with great force into the windows of Pontings Department Store. The noise was appalling, the crash of the hammers, the shower of falling glass that scattered across the pavement but worse, far worse, was the shrieks of the women, for with each blow they gave out their war cry: 'Votes for Women! Deeds not Words!' Men were shouting in outrage and women passing by, some with children, were screaming. From further down the street there came the shrill sound of policemen's whistles and as he stood there, his heart racing, dithering, he admitted, for he wanted to do no more than run to her, grasp her arm and hustle her to safety, three enormous police constables pushed through the crowd and did their best to put their brawny arms about the struggling, screaming suffragettes. One of them managed to slip away and a constable gave chase, but it wasn't her, for she was clasped with her back to the chest of a policeman, her feet off the pavement and kicking wildly in the air.

The policeman held her wherever he could get a grip which seemed to be in the region of her breasts. He was actually laughing and Patrick began to realise what these women were up against. The policemen, at least this one, was thoroughly enjoying handling a pretty woman who was showing off her lace-trimmed drawers to the jeering crowd of men. All those who watched were men, for the passing women on the pavement hurried by with averted eyes, shocked and bewildered and embarrassed by the antics of members of their own sex. A horse-drawn Black Maria came galloping up the street and drew up, the door opening at the back to allow the crowd to see the packed interior, all women in a state of disarray, some of them bruised in the face, and without undue haste she and the other one were dragged, literally dragged for they refused to walk, across the pavement and stuffed unceremoniously into the van.

A man who crowded at the entrance actually spat at them and the spittle landed on Alex's face and as it did so she saw him in the crowd. 'Votes for Women!' she shrieked as the van door shut and he knew she was telling him, not the others who watched, but *him* that she would never give it up. He wanted to weep for her. He wanted to bang on the back of the van and ask to be admitted so that he could hold her in his arms and let her

know the depth of his feelings for her brave self, her courageous, defiant self, but he knew she was lost to him. She had
been arrested before. She had been sentenced to a month, three
months in the past. She had gone on sleep strikes, thirst strikes,
hunger strikes and been fed forcibly through a tube in her
nostrils and, when they were damaged, through a tube thrust
down her throat to her stomach. It was no more than three
months ago that he and her father had saved her from again
being sentenced by paying her fine, but this time there would
be no such chance. It would be nine months' hard labour and
when she went on strike, as he knew she would, until she was
seriously ill, they would send her home to recover and then
when she was well enough would arrest her again to suffer the
same horrors. Cat and mouse, the women called it and he really
did not think he could stand the thought of it. If he could just
*talk* to her, make her see reason, let him care for her, love her,
soothe her pain and weary mind, *marry her* for God's sake, but
he just stood there and watched the van drive away with his love
and unless he could somehow do what he had done in June, he
must allow it.

He leaned against the door frame of Lyons Corner House so
that those who wished to enter were forced to push past him,
tutting some of them, as he blocked their way, but he seemed
unable to move his feet. He was devastated by the strength of his
feelings for her, his anger, his sorrow, his pain for what she
herself would suffer. He turned and to the consternation of those
trying to pass him banged his forehead against the door frame,
breaking and bruising the skin until a young waitress came out to
ask him if he was all right. He was so obviously of the middle or
even upper class, those inside didn't know what to make of him.

He came to himself and turned a stiff smile on the young
woman, doing his best to pull himself together, anguishing that
a woman could do this to him. He who had been immune to all
females, their wiles, their pretty ways, their sexuality, for there

had been those who had done their best to interest him but until now not one had touched the inner core of his heart where love hid. Love that he longed to give to a woman who did not care a jot for him. And yet . . . and yet he had felt there was something in her that moved towards what was in him, only to be diverted by this bloody women's cause. This curse, these militant women who had something that appealed to her as he did not.

He went to Bow Street the next day and watched as she was dragged in on her knees, refusing to walk, held up by a constable. He had her by both arms but she wrenched herself free and tried to climb over the dock rail and at that moment a bag of flour was thrown, scattering its contents over the court like fine snow on a winter's day. The dozen women, all shouting defiance, refused to give their names and Alex was designated Number 11. It was like a bloody circus, he thought, belittling the women who were being treated as though they were clowns, and silently he spoke to her, begging her to be still for he could not bear the way she was treated. He sent the message of his love over the heads of the shrieking crowds, holding his gaze on her, keeping his eyes from the fiasco that boiled about him and suddenly, as though by some mystical telepathy, she turned her head and saw him. Her face, which had been ugly with anger, became still, almost serene and to the astonishment of all those about her she seemed to smile.

'I love you,' he mouthed silently and he saw her body relax and her eyes fill with a lovely light. She kept her eyes on him, as though for courage, as the judge sentenced her to nine months' hard labour. No fine could release her and as he watched she became again the virago who had been dragged in as she was dragged out again.

He was the last to leave the court, the image of her as she had been for an interval of perhaps five minutes scalded in his heart.

★    ★    ★

She was sentenced in September and in November they released her under the Prisoners' Temporary Discharge for Ill-Health Act, which meant that as soon as she was recovered enough she would be rearrested. Long before eight o'clock, the hour of her release, as was the custom, a number of Alex's friends and members of the WSPU gathered wearing the colours of the Union, ready to welcome her and bear her away in celebration, but they were astonished when a well-dressed but officious gentleman who stood beside a smart two-seater motor car struggled through the small crowd. They were prominent members of the Union but they were so surprised by the gentleman, and by Alex herself, who, as soon as the small gate opened and she staggered through, allowed him to pick her up bodily, place her in the passenger seat of the motor and drive away with a great tooting of the horn. Fortunately there were several other women released that day so the band, the flowers, the carriage that would be drawn through the streets to the delight of the crowds were not wasted. There was a great deal of speculation among the women as to who the gentleman might be. One of her brothers perhaps, but as none of the women knew her family they decided they would carry on with today's celebration and one of them would call round to Miss Goodwin's house and enquire. It was a shame, for the young woman who lodged with her, Miss Kellett, had been imprisoned only the day before or more information might have been gleaned from her about the mysterious man.

Nan and Nelly wept as they took her clothes from her limp body and placed her in the hot bath Mr O'Leary had recommended. She was so thin they could see every last bone of her sticking through the wafer-fine flesh, and she was covered with bruises, old and new, for she had not submitted to force-feeding with good grace. It had taken four strong wardresses to hold her down three times a day while the doctor inserted the ghastly tube, either up one of her nostrils until they became badly damaged, or then down her throat through her mouth which was held wide open by a metal gag. She was near to death's door, Nan sobbed to the doctor, who paced frantically up and down the hallway until they had her in her bed. He was strung up with such anger Nan felt constrained to stand a decent distance from him, from the fists he clenched at his side and it was in her mind to bar his way to Miss Alex's bedroom but even as she stood to one side, holding the bedroom door open, she saw his face change to one of such love she wanted to cry all over again. He loved her young mistress, she could see that and perhaps, to the great joy of her and the Goodwin family, he would persuade Miss Alex to marry him and give up this madness that was killing her. She stood on the other side of the bed as he examined the withered, semi-conscious figure stretched out on it, exposing her tiny breasts, her stomach, the skin of which surely touched her spine, her spindly legs and arms, and held her sitting upright, her poor head lolling while he sounded her chest, frowning at the wheezing, rattling sound that came from within. Though Nan knew he loved her mistress she did not think twice about allowing him to examine her in such an intimate way. For who but a doctor, who loved her as he did, could bring her back to full health? If it was the last damn thing she did, she'd kill herself before she'd let Miss Alex put herself through this again, and now the other one had gone and got herself arrested and thrown in gaol, and her as delicate as a bit of gossamer.

Nelly was left sitting beside Alex's bed, Alex's hand in hers and as she continued to sniffle, the irony of Alex trying to comfort *Nelly* was lost on both of them, while downstairs Nan and Patrick conferred on how they were to restore to full health the woman they both loved. And not only that but how to keep her out of the authorities' hands when she was!

'Don't cry, Nelly,' Alex whispered to the little maid. 'We are doing this . . . for you . . . for all women. You shall . . . have the vote . . .'

'I don't want bloody vote, Miss Alex, not if tha've ter do this ter get it. Oh, miss, please . . . give it up. Tha' ma an' pa'd have a fit if they could see yer an' now there's Miss Rose goin' same way . . .'

'Where is Miss Rose?' Alex faltered, but as Nan and the doctor had ordered her Nelly told the lie that Miss Rose was out.

'What's . . . she . . . doing . . .?'

'Nay, I don't know, Miss Alex. Tha're all mad if tha' ask me.'

She had been home two days before they told her Rosie was in Holloway. She had slept most of the time, only waking to use the 'po', as Nan called it, under her bed, or to be spoon-fed whatever Nan thought fit to give her. Mostly milk with eggs beaten in it, bread and milk, nourishing custards, eggnogs to which sherry had been added, food that her stomach could digest. Patrick came each evening and lay beside her on the bed, holding her gently to him, her head on his shoulder, saying very little, but loving her in the very way he looked at her, kissed her tenderly whether she liked it or not, held her, stroked her hair which had not been washed for two months and she made no objection.

'What am I to do with my hair, Nan?' she begged.

'When tha' take yer next bath, me an' Nelly'll wash it but not before.'

'Pass me the scissors then, if you please.' For by now she was beginning to recover some of her fighting spirit.

'What for?' Nan asked suspiciously.

'I'm going to cut it off.'

'Over my dead body.'

'Then I'll ask Rosie to do it. It was my hair that disgusted me the most when I was in prison. It was so long and filthy with . . . *things* in it. Next time, if it's short all over I shall just be able to push my hand through it so let's get it cut off. Please, Nan, if you won't do it, then send Rosie in. Where is she by the way? I can't just remember how long it is since I came home but I'm surprised she hasn't been in to see me.'

They told her about Rosie then and though she had suffered so much on her own and the Union's behalf somehow the thought of Rosie, who was such a little bit of a thing and would never be able to manage a stretch in Holloway as she herself had done, devastated her.

When Patrick came that evening she wept in his arms as she had never done before and it was in his mind that perhaps this, the thought of young Rosie enduring what she herself had endured might turn her away from what he saw as insanity.

'Why didn't someone pay her fine? A first offence . . .'

'Believe me, Dick tried, but she screamed in the dock that she didn't know this man and it was not to be allowed. Poor Dick, I fear he may have a breakdown. He knows what you went through. He has been up to see you and was speechless with horror at the sight of . . . well . . . You were asleep, and the sight of your sleeping face on the pillow and that hacked-off hair which he thought had been done to you in prison just about finished him.'

'I'll never forgive myself if she does not survive.'

'My darling girl, she is as strong as you, and she will survive.'

He stroked the short cap of curls which Nan had at last been persuaded to cut and wash for her, resting his cheek against its fragrant softness and swore, as Nan did, that he would not let this happen to her again.

# 8

Her first task when she came to London had been at the WSPU headquarters helping with the publication of *Votes for Women* newspaper, cutting and pasting at the 'making-up table' which she had found exactly to her taste. She was a warm-hearted, sociable young woman and got on well with her fellow workers. She enjoyed the freedom away from her family, dearly as she loved them, and was enchanted with the bustle and excitement of the capital city.

She had been there for several months when she had been asked to sell the newspaper she helped to create at one of the WSPU's pitches and then, later, to sit beside Miss Craggs on the press cart and distribute the newspapers to the pitches. Again she enjoyed what she was doing and it was not until she had been introduced to Alex Goodwin on the day Miss Craggs had been absent, she herself being unable to drive the press cart, that she realised that she could not ignore the fact that she was young and healthy and was quite capable of doing what Miss Goodwin usually did. But they had been attacked, a first for her but not, it seemed, for Miss Goodwin, and with her leg broken and her face cut and bruised she had been forced to postpone her entry into what the militant suffragettes were participating in until she was recovered.

She had been shocked and devastated by Alex's imprisonment. She had known that Alex had resumed her militant activities, for each night over dinner – since by then she had moved in with Alex – she had listened to Alex's accounts of what she had been up to. Arson attacks, smashing windows, attending political rallies where she had shouted her defiance and been thrown out into the street, addressing a crowd at Hyde Park or wherever one could be gathered. In the past Alex had been arrested more than once, doing 'time' in Holloway but never for longer than a month. Until now. Nine months' hard labour she had been given and here was Rosie Kellett doing nothing more challenging than any woman twice her age could do.

Her leg still ached when she stood on it for long and Dick was like a bull run mad when she told him what she proposed to do.

'You are not fit enough to get up to the tricks those . . . those women carry out. You must rest, sweet Rosie,' he protested, shaking her as though a bit of brute force might do the trick. The argument became fierce when she told him that not only was she was well enough but old enough to make her own decisions.

'I am perfectly well, Dick Morris' – raising her small, stubborn chin – 'and I will not listen to you babble on about my welfare. Oh, I know you are concerned—'

'*Concerned!* Christ, I love you, have I not told you that a thousand times.'

'Not quite a thousand, Dick.' She smiled, doing her best to defuse the situation but Dick was having none of that.

'I cannot bear to think of you being . . . manhandled by those bobbies.' For he had come upon several scuffles between the police and the suffragettes and like the decent man he was, though no believer in what the women were doing, he had been appalled. 'Look at you, no bigger than twopennorth of copper . . .'

'Stop it, Dick, I must do as my conscience dictates. With Alex locked up for nine months I must take her place in the war.'

It went on and on with Nan and Nelly listening in the

kitchen, both ready to weep, for with Miss Alex in Holloway how could they stand it if Miss Rose was to have the same happen to her? Every one of the 'soldiers', as they called themselves, in the battle for equality were, sooner or later, arrested and put in prison, but Miss Rose, sweet Rosie, listened to none of them and the next day she presented herself at Union headquarters as a 'soldier', one who was prepared to fight physically as Alex had done.

The day after that she was told by Miss Kerr, one of the co-ordinators of the everyday activities of the campaign, to go with two others to a political rally on behalf of the Liberal government at which it was rumoured Prime Minister Asquith might be present. He was not, but a Liberal cabinet minister was, and with a nudge from Madge Atkinson, who sat next to her, she jumped to her feet and forced through her dry throat the classic suffragette demand: 'Will this Liberal government grant votes to women?' She was immediately set upon as she had expected, both arms pinned behind her back, hustled between rows of jeering faces and thrown out into the street where she landed in a heap of horse manure.

She had done it. She had climbed that first hurdle and though she stank to high heaven and felt repelled by her own state, she had crossed that threshold of experience, the one Alex had crossed a dozen times and so surely from now on it would be easier? She would take Alex's place until Alex was released or she herself was arrested. Every call to arms would be answered and though Nan and Nelly were appalled at the state of her when she returned home, declaring that Doctor Dick would soon put a stop to it, which, of course, he tried to do again, so much so that she told him not to call any more and having no right nor responsibility towards her he was forced to back down, or lose her completely.

One night at the beginning of November she was told to accompany Madge Atkinson to a meeting at which a Liberal minister was to speak. This time it was Madge who jumped to her feet and began to yell the familiar words, Madge who was ejected from the meeting hall and began to hold a meeting of her own on the pavement outside. The Liberal minister was furious and demanded that the police should be called to move her on. Rosie, who had followed Madge outside, objected strenuously, and the noise made by Madge, by Rose and by the crowd, who were vastly entertained by it, further incensed the honourable gentleman who was still on the platform doing his best to hold the attention of the audience. The police were ordered to take action and in the ensuing scuffle Madge was knocked to the ground where she hung on to a constable's leg. To no avail for she and Rose, who warbled 'Votes for Women' into the face of anyone who would listen, were hauled away. The next morning at Bow Street Magistrates' Court she was told to pay twenty shillings in a fine or serve three weeks in the Third Division.

'I will not pay the fine,' Rose whispered, doing her best to 'speak up' as the magistrate told her, and though Dick tried to catch the attention of the gentleman, prepared to pay her fine for her, nobody took any notice of him since Rosie was screaming by now that she did not know him and he watched in despair as she was half carried away to the Third Division.

She had listened to Alex speak of the First Division where prisoners were allowed to wear their own clothes, even have their food sent in and might receive and write letters. Prisoners in the Second Division were obliged to wear prison uniform and manage on a diet that included meat twice a week and could write one letter and receive one letter a month.

But those sentenced to the Third Division were simply incarcerated and were never seen nor heard of again until their sentence was up. In this division were confined prostitutes, vagrants, drunkards and suffragettes. Madge, who had a bruise the size of her hand across her cheek and eye where the constable, in an effort to dislodge her from his leg, had kicked her, was to serve three months. She did her best to support Rosie through the coming ordeal though she herself was in a worse state.

'Keep your chin up, duckie. You'll find nothing worse than a few head lice and fleas. Grit your teeth and try to remember what we're fighting for.'

They were taken from the court to Holloway in the Black Maria that had brought them the day before, along with assorted sweating seamen, swearing prostitutes and thin, defiant girls who it turned out were shop-lifters. Though it made her flesh crawl, the flesh that all her life had been clean and pampered, she would bear it, she told herself. Alex had borne it, *was* bearing it at this precise moment, and so could she. But when, having been shut in a cubby-hole for what seemed hours, she was dragged out and told to undress in a room full of other women, one of them Madge, and to get into a bath filled with tepid water in which all the women before her had bathed, she knew then, quite categorically, that she could not do it. But she did. When she was examined roughly and told to put on a soiled uniform and white cap she knew she couldn't do it. But she did. She was given a number, 14, and, losing sight of Madge, was hustled into a tiny cell with a plank bed, a slop pail, a tin mug and a wooden spoon.

Twice a day she was permitted to go to the lavatory in the corridor, a lavatory that was filthy with the . . . well, she had no idea how to describe what was on it never having seen it before in her well-ordered, servant-administered life. Twice a week she was allowed to exercise in the yard and three times a day she was served with one pint of oatmeal and water and a slice of brown, dry bread. Sometimes there was a small bowl of unsweetened suet pudding and now and again a spoonful of potatoes. She was not surprised when the day came for her release to find her own clothing no longer fitted her but hung on her frame as though on a coat-hanger.

But far worse than this was her own shame at her inability to face the ordeal of being forcibly fed. She had eaten what was given her and though she had been bitterly cold all the time and her head itched as did her flesh as if something crawled over her, she had slept each night. In other words she had complied with the enemy. She would do better next time.

It was the end of November when the two young women met again. Alex, though by no means recovered from her own incarceration, wearing a hat swathed with a veil to hide her face, was there with a deputation of suffragettes at the gates where Rosie was presented with a bouquet of flowers, taken out for a celebration breakfast and presented with the traditional brooch.

Dick had brought the Darracq in the hope that he might take the two women back to the house where he could take care of his love in the comfort of her own home, but he was brushed aside, not only by Alex but by the women, for this was their triumph, this slip of a girl who had withstood the trials brought upon her by her bravery. Patrick was on duty or he would never have consented to Alex leaving the house, though he and Dick were becoming increasingly aware that they had no authority over the women they loved. Alex took a risk in going to meet Rose, for if she was recognised and the magistrates decided she was recovered enough, she could be whipped back into gaol to finish her sentence, or until she became ill again.

The four of them dined at Bedford Square several evenings later, the gentlemen exchanging glances at the half-hearted 'picking' at their food the two young women showed. The meal was splendid, for, even more than she had ever done in the past, Nan prepared and cooked what she hoped might tempt her two young ladies to eat. Miss Alex was painfully thin and so was Miss Rose though she had not lost the weight Miss Alex had, and it was evident that even now, when Miss Alex had been out of gaol for several weeks, it was still an effort to eat. There was soup, a good hearty soup, the stock made from four pounds of shin of beef, a knuckle of veal, three onions, three turnips, celery, mushrooms, a tomato and herbs. It was cooked slowly for five hours, then strained through a sieve. Into the stock went one large sliced cucumber, butter, two eggs and a gill of cream and if that didn't put the pair of them to rights she didn't know what would, she grumbled to Nelly.

Next came a herb soufflé, light and fluffy, which had risen to exactly the right height and must be eaten immediately, she ordered them, then they could have a break before she brought in the main course which was a pie made with the best cut of beef, sprouts and cauliflower, now in season, fresh from the market, roast potatoes and gravy. If the four plates weren't cleared by the time the apricot cream, into which she had put sixteen ripe apricots, sugar, milk and the yolk of eight eggs, was served she would know the reason why!

'She's worse than my nanny,' Dick grumbled as he attacked with great gusto what was put before him.

'You had a nanny?' Patrick was clearly flabbergasted.

'I'm afraid so, old chap, and was she a tartar. She used to burn my bottom with an old slipper and my poor sisters were . . .' Suddenly aware that the others were staring at him with knives and forks poised to eat, he looked from one to the other in bewilderment.

'What? What's wrong with having a nanny?'

Alex, Rose and Patrick exchanged glances then burst out laughing. Both Alex and Rose had had what might be called a privileged upbringing with servants to wait on them, and still did, but Patrick, thinking of his working-class mother and father who had slaved in the shop his grandfather had begun, was shaking his head and sighing.

'I can see I had a deprived childhood, for my mother scrubbed floors and did a wash every Monday, ironed on a

Tuesday with an old flat iron, holystoned the front steps and even scoured the pavement in front of our door. She black-leaded the oven and cleaned the brass and washed the windows with vinegar and old newspaper and certainly gave no thought to employing a servant. I went to the local council school and won a scholarship to go on to 'the grammar' and it was due to them that I got to university and medical school. Bloody hell – I beg your pardon, ladies – but a nanny . . .'

He began to laugh and though they were none of them sure what was so humorous about the tale of Patrick's rise to be a surgeon at the prestigious St Thomas's hospital, they began to laugh too and as Nan said delightedly to Nelly, it was grand to hear Miss Alex and Miss Rose in high spirits after what they had been through.

It appeared that both Rose and Alex had been taught at home by a governess and their education had been somewhat sketchy, but Dick had gone to boarding school at eight and to be truthful, he told them, he scarcely knew his parents.

'I don't know mine at all,' Alex declared quietly and when the three of them turned to her in astonishment, for they had all seen the affection with which Mr and Mrs Goodwin treated her, she smiled.

'Oh, don't think I suffered from the loss of them. My father, my *real* father, though he was not real to me, is dead, and my mother lives in America with her second husband. I was adopted at birth by Beth and Archie, and have lived with them as their daughter ever since.'

'Holy Mother,' Patrick breathed, then stood up and moved round the table to stand behind her, putting his hands on her shoulders. He caught Dick's eye and with a nod of his head indicated to him to take Rose somewhere, anywhere, perhaps the drawing-room, while he talked to Alex.

At once Dick rose to his feet and, taking the bewildered Rose by the hand, led her from the dining-room. 'What the dickens . . .' she began then bit off the words abruptly as she saw Alex's hand move up to take one of Patrick's. Nan, who was just leaving the kitchen to enquire if they would have coffee in the drawing-room, watched with consternation as Doctor Dick and Miss Rose crept from the dining-room and along the hallway to the drawing-room, holding their fingers to their lips and smiling at her. At once, in high glee, she went back to the kitchen and through to the scullery where Nelly was up to her elbows in sudsy water, clattering pans and singing under her breath.

'I think this is it,' Nan chortled, unable to settle.

'What, Nan?'

'I think he's proposin'.'

'Proposin'? 'Oo to?'

'Why, Miss Alex, yer daft 'apporth.'

'Doctor Patrick?'

' 'Oo else an' there's no need ter leave them there pots. We'll know soon enough. Now I'd best tekk coffee inter't drawin'-room.'

There was an old sofa in the big dining-room; no one knew why it had been kept or why it should be there but, lifting Alex to her feet, Patrick led her there and sat her down. He sat close beside her but did not attempt to put his arm about her, or hold her hand. The intimacy they had known when she was so ill after coming out of prison had stopped the moment she came downstairs. At first they had been doctor and patient, dearly as they loved one another, but now the circumstances were different and though the love was still there, they were more circumspect with one another. He was courting her, they both knew that and even without Nan to oversee the proprieties they were aware that they were no longer as they had been when he brought her home.

'When I brought you home from Holloway, as your doctor I examined you. Nan was there, naturally, but I saw parts of your body I might never have seen unless we were husband and wife. Your foot, for instance, which I know causes you to limp. I have never asked but I'm asking now for a reason. I have seen . . . infirmities in babies, bone damage, infections, blindness, even brain damage, caused by . . . well, men who consort with unclean women can contract sexual diseases and then pass them on to their innocent, sometimes pregnant wives—'

'That is what we are trying to do, you see, Patrick. We *must* make men more responsible,' she interrupted eagerly, but he took her hands in his and held them for a moment to his lips.

'Listen to me, Alex. Did your biological father pass this disease on to your mother, causing you to have a deformed foot? There are no toes on your left foot and though I saw that you have had surgery toes cannot be replaced. No. *No!* my darling, don't hang your head as though you were at fault. It makes no difference to me and if it is your slight limp that has prevented other men from speaking for you I can only thank the Blessed Mother for it. You know how I feel about you. I love you and I want you to marry me but . . .'

'Don't, Patrick . . . don't . . .'

'Don't what, my love?' he asked in surprise.

'Don't put conditions on our relationship.'

'My dearest love, yes, that is what you are to me, my dearest love, and I'm not making conditions. I want to marry you. I have from almost the first moment I saw you shouting your defiance at those constables who were dragging you to the Black Maria. If the crowd hadn't been so dense I do believe I would have leaped to your rescue like a knight saving a damsel in distress. I can't bear you to be humiliated, to be hurt and . . .'

'I don't like it much myself, Patrick, but if one of the conditions of our marrying is to give it all up then I'm afraid I must refuse. It's my life . . .'

'Make *me* your life, sweetheart,' he begged her fiercely. 'A doctor's wife can be of enormous help to other women. We could open a clinic for the very women you are trying to help. Please, oh please, my love, say you will . . . say you will.'

He wanted to gather her in his arms and kiss her into submission but she stood up and began to stride about the room while he watched her helplessly, for it all seemed so simple to him. If women were to get the vote, then so be it. If they were to have equality with the male population, then so be it, but it would make no difference one way or the other if Alex Goodwin was fighting with them or not. He had passed the end of Downing Street the other day and three of them, bloody suffragettes, he privately called them, had chained themselves to the railings. The police were trying to cut them out of their padlocks and chains while all about them men were swearing, jeering, making menacing gestures while the women stood stoically in their chains, submitting to the rough handling of the police. He had walked on, thanking the Blessed Mother that Alex was still too weakened to be with them.

Suddenly she stopped her pacing and sat down quietly by his side. She slipped his arm about her shoulder and rested her head on his chest, then she lifted her face and offered her mouth for his kiss. He laid his lips gently on hers then, as they opened beneath his the kiss became more urgent.

'Sweet Jesus,' he groaned, 'I love you so much being without you is an agony I can't bear.' His hands slipped into the short curls on her head, tilting it back as he looked deep into her eyes which had become soft and unfocused. His hand slipped down to caress her cheek and chin, the soft curve of her throat then dropped to cup the swell of her breast. Through the fine silk of her gown he could feel the peaking of her nipple and his whole being surged in triumph for he could see she was his, to do with as he pleased. Now, in this room in this house which contained four other people who might, especially Nan, come in at any moment.

He smiled and kissed her again, smoothing her hair, cupping

her cheeks while she swayed towards him, wanting this as much as he did.

'No, my love, not yet, not here. We shall be married soon, as soon as possible and then I will take you to bed and do things to you that will amaze you. I love you so . . . I love you . . .'

To his amazement the lovely soft womanliness of her became stiff with some anger he could not understand. She wrenched herself out of his arms and her voice shook as she spoke.

'I see, you will make me your wife, allow me to give help and advice to other women, if I give up my work. If I go into headquarters and say that I am to be married and therefore I can no longer be of help to them, to the women of this land who long to be enfranchised, to be equal in all *things* to men. To betray the women who have suffered for so long. Fought and suffered and *died* for this just cause. For fifty years they have—'

'For God's sake, get off your bloody soapbox and be a real woman for once. You speak to me as though I had offered you an insult of the worst kind.' He stood up and she took a step backwards. Her stomach clenched at what she saw in his face. 'Goddammit, woman, I swear I could spiflicate you,' using an expression he had heard his mother say a hundred times. It clawed her heart to rags and yet at the same time she wanted to laugh hysterically, for she had heard it too in the northern county from which she came.

If they had laughed then, or even smiled at the comic side to it, all might have come right but they were both paralysed with their own beliefs. Her heart began to sink, heavily, coldly in her breast. She had noticed before that he had a trick of wiping all expression from his face when he wished and he did so now. His brown eyes, such a soft velvet brown minutes before, had turned a flat peat colour and he gave her a cool appraising stare.

'I'll take my leave of you, then, Miss Goodwin. Thank Nan for a splendid meal and may I wish you whatever you wish yourself in your fight for equality. I don't agree with it, of course, since I think it proper that women should be at—'

'I know,' she spat at him, 'at home with the children husbands foist on their wives every nine months. I dare say you would be the same and I would not care for it.'

'No wonder you are still a spinster, Miss Goodwin. You should have been born a man then—'

'Leave this house before I hit you, you insufferable sod.' She was shaking with rage and something else which might have been terror at the thought that he would be in the world but she would never see him again. It was unbearable and she could not stand it but she would, as she had stood everything she had suffered for her cause.

When the front door slammed, Nan crept from the kitchen for their words had been heard as far away as the scullery, and Rose peeped from the drawing-room, Dick behind her. They were just in time to catch Alex as she fell to her knees in a storm of anguished weeping.

# 9

She resumed her duties far earlier than she should have, or so Nan, Rosie and Dick told her vehemently, for she had barely regained any weight and was forever in trouble with Nan for not eating enough.

'Pick! Pick! Pick! That's all yer ever do. An' how you expect ter get ter end o't road, never mind ter that place where them women are up ter all sorts o' tricks is beyond me. An empty sack won't stand, yer know that, fer 'aven't I told yer so a dozen times a day. There isn't a pick on yer. See, lamb, eat this porridge,' Nan would wheedle, 'just a spoonful and then drink this milk, or would yer rather 'ave pobs? It'll put a linin' on yer stomach.'

'Please, Alex, just have another day by the fireside. It's too cold to go out today. Sit with your feet up and read that new book by D.H. Lawrence I brought from the library,' Rosie coaxed her. '*Sons and Lovers*, it's called and I guarantee you'll love it.'

'You're storing up trouble if you go on at this pace, Alex. Your body can't stand it. Some of the suffragettes, so I've been told, have ruined their health with the prolonged force-feeding which is why the government have brought in this new Act. Patrick says—'

'I don't give a damn what Patrick says, Dick, and you'll oblige me by not discussing me with him. I can't just sit at home and do nothing, Nan . . . Rosie . . . Dick' – whoever happened to be berating her – 'I'll go mad staring at the four walls of the drawing-room.'

'Then why don't you go home and have a few weeks with your family?' This from Rosie. 'A bit of country air will put the roses back in your cheeks.'

'For God's sake, Rosie, don't you start talking to me as though I were an invalid. Put the roses in my cheeks, indeed. You sound like Nan.'

'Nan cares about you, as we all do. Dick said he was speaking to Patrick about you the other—'

'I've told Dick before not to discuss me with that . . . that . . .'

'Alex,' Rose said patiently, 'you must not continue with this feud. Patrick loves you and wants to marry you and what is wrong with that? He—'

'Nothing, except he is like most men in that he will not countenance my work with the WSPU and wants his wife to sit at home and have babies.'

'Don't you want children, Alex?'

'Yes, I do, one day, but not at the expense of the work I do. When women are enfranchised, when we can vote for who we want to represent us in government, as men do, then I will marry and have children, a family . . .' Her voice trailed away wistfully.

'It might be too late by then, dearest.' Rosie, so sweet-natured, so patient, so concerned for her friend who was, after all, nearly twenty-six and long past the age of making a good match, would not give up. She herself was four years younger than Alex and was considered in this day and age to be on the shelf, even at her age, but she at least had the prospect of a good marriage. She had promised Dick she would marry him in the summer and had got his promise that he would respect her views on female enfranchisement, but she was not awfully sure if he meant she could go on *thinking* as she liked, or she could go on *working* as she liked. She would meet that problem when it arose, she told herself, but should she become pregnant after they married she would no longer be a soldier but would work in the offices at headquarters or the press office. Anywhere she could help the cause.

She did not tell Dick that, as a suffragette with access to suffragette literature, she had read many letters and pamphlets from women who advocated birth control and meant herself to resort to it until she was ready to give birth to their family. One letter had been sent anonymously from a woman whose grandmother had given birth to twenty children, eight of whom had lived to the age of fourteen and only two to a good old age. Another was from a woman whose sister had borne seven children in seven years. The first five died at birth, the sixth lived and the seventh had died taking its mother with it. Though not all the feminists in the suffrage movement agreed with it there were several forms of contraceptives to be had and indeed it was rumoured that a third to a half of all married couples were already practising some method of birth control.

But she said nothing of this to Dick even though Dick was less intransigent than Patrick. Patrick had, in the last weeks of the old year, been nowhere near Bedford Square and had refused all her and Dick's efforts to arrange a meeting with Alex. They were both stubborn, self-willed people, their own beliefs set in stone in their minds and neither would consent to speak to the other.

By the time 1914 was a couple of months old, Rose and Dick had given up.

'It's no good, my love,' she told him. 'When I mention Patrick's name she simply gets up and walks out of the room. Did you know she offered to take Mary Richardson's place at the National Gallery? It's as though she is determined to put herself in as much danger as she can.'

'Who is Mary Richardson?' Dick was somewhat weary of this constant talk of WSPU matters and he had finally accepted that 'old Patrick' had cast Alex from his life. To tell the truth he was also weary of Alex herself, who had begun to look her age,

or even older in the scrapes she got into, although as yet she had
not been recaptured to continue her prison sentence. She was
rarely at table when he dined at Bedford Square, for which he
was thankful since it gave him precious time to be alone with his
love. They were to be married in August and already he was on
the lookout for a suitable house to rent for himself and his
bride-to-be.

'They call her "Slasher" Mary Richardson.'

'*Slasher!* She hasn't cut some poor chap's throat, has she?'

'No, she attacked the *Rokeby Venus* by Velasquez at the
National Gallery last Tuesday. It was damaged they think
beyond repair and it's no wonder, for she smashed it with an
axe. The National Gallery, the National Portrait Gallery and
the Wallace Collection are closed to the public and it's said that
when women are allowed to enter again they must have no
muffs, wrist bags or sticks. Even then women can only enter
when accompanied by a man who will accept responsibility for
them. Of course, women who are not suffragettes are up in
arms.'

'Well, can you blame them, sweetheart. Your women are
giving all women a bad name.'

'But it's for them we are doing it, Dick.' Rose was outraged
and slamming her soup spoon down she stood up and made
her way towards the dining-room door which Nan had left ajar.
But Dick caught her wrist and dragged her on to his lap,
beginning to kiss her with all the passion *she* put into her work
for the WSPU. At first she resisted, flailing at him with her
slender hands but gradually she calmed down and even kissed
him back so that when Nan entered to clear their soup plates
she was filled with embarrassment, for Doctor Dick had his
hands . . . well, where they shouldn't be, she told Nelly, her
face crimson. That young woman had better get married soon,
by the look of things, then, remembering her Alex who wandered in and out of their lives like a pale ghost, she wished to

God Doctor Patrick had been as bold as Doctor Dick. If he had got Miss Alex in the family way, though it would have been scandalous, at least they would have married quickly and the bloody women of the bloody WSPU could find someone else to do their dirty work. This from Nan who detested bad language! She couldn't for the life of her understand why women wanted the damn vote, anyway. They had husbands, fathers, brothers who could vote for the family and even if she herself was given this enfranchisement that Miss Alex babbled on about, what would she do with it, for she knew absolutely *nowt* about politics and didn't want to, neither!

It was a week later when Rose asked Alex if she would care to dine with her and Dick at the Ritz. It was Dick's birthday on 1 April . . . yes, an April Fool's baby, and he would be delighted if she would come.

'There's no need to buy him a present, dearest. His family are motoring in from Sevenoaks and are staying a few days; it seems they are rather rich, Alex,' she pronounced, not gleefully, which another woman might have done, but with innocent astonishment. Alex knew she would marry Dick, rich or poor, wondering how the Morrises would take to this daughter of a country parson from Yorkshire. They were probably hoping for one of this year's debutantes at least!

'Will his sisters be coming?'

'I suppose so . . . oh dear, I feel really nervous.'

'Anybody else?' Alex's voice was suspicious.

'I really don't know. Dick only mentioned family.'

'I see, but Rosie, my love, you must not be nervous or shy. Just be yourself. We all love you and how could any mother not be overjoyed to have you as a daughter-in-law?'

It was a lovely spring morning and Rose and Alex had walked the length of Tottenham Court Road, turning left into Seaton Street and on into Regent's Park. The world and his wife – and their children – were in the park which was a delight to the eye. Carefully groomed grass, neatly brushed walkways, and beds filled with every spring flower imaginable. It was a riot of colour, the blue of periwinkle mingling with the bright yellow of nodding daffodils, white narcissi, a brilliant bed of wall-flower, bronze, orange, yellow, and the shy, virginal beauty of lily of the valley half hidden by the trumpeting arrogance of tulips in every shade from yellow to scarlet. They strolled across the grass to the Zoological Gardens where they peered at monkeys, lions, antelope and were in total agreement that they should miss the reptile house. They finished in the refreshment room where they drank hot chocolate and Rosie said she wished Nan was here to see Alex eat *three* scones! There was a bandstand where the uniformed musicians played stirring martial music with great enthusiasm. Children ran and jumped and skipped and screamed, those not superintended by stiffly starched nannies. The anticipation of the summer to come was in the air so that even dogs on leads barked and wagged their tails and the cheerful atmosphere put a smile on Alex's face and a touch of peach in her thin face.

'Well, that's better,' said Nan, as they discarded their hats and coats in the hallway, peering closely into Alex's face. 'Yer'll have ter tekk her out more often, Miss Rosie, if yer fetches her back like this. Anyroad, yer've a visitor an' no need ter tell yer who it is.'

Knowing it would be Dick, Alex excused herself, saying she would go and have a lie down for half an hour. 'Don't go on my account,' a cheerful voice said from the direction of the drawing-room. Dick lounged into the doorway, his hands in his pockets, doing his best to appear casual but his eyes went at once to his Rosie. He moved towards her, dragging his hands from his pockets and reaching for hers and it seemed it was all he could do not to pull her into his arms in front of Nan and Alex. 'I can't stop long as I've to help . . . er . . . a colleague in a rather ticklish bit of surgery this afternoon,' and they were all in no doubt who that colleague would be. 'I wanted to know if Rosie' – squeezing her to him in a paroxysm of love – 'had mentioned Saturday.'

'Your birthday, you mean,' Alex began.

'Yes, and I warn you I won't take no for an answer. My sisters . . . well, Mother doesn't agree, but they are keen to be suffragettes and they are longing to question the pair of you and besides, I have to know the numbers to book the table.' He grinned engagingly, his eyes warm and kind, and Alex was aware that Rosie would have a husband who would give her a life glowing with loving kindness.

'Well, you see . . .' she began.

'I told you she would argue,' Rosie told him.

'I won't let her argue. If she says she won't come I shall hail a cab and fetch her. Alex, sweetheart,' he appealed, 'you would be doing me *and* Rosie a big favour. You would help to smooth an awkward moment when Rosie meets my family. Not that they are ogres but with you there it would be easier for Rose.' He looked down into Rosie's rapt face and Nan and Alex were made aware that he would jump through flames to make things easier for his sweet Rosie.

How could she refuse? 'Very well, but this is for Rosie, remember that, not for you, fond of you as I am. Now go and perform your operation while Rose and I talk about what we shall wear to impress your mother.'

Mr Morris, that is Mr Edward Morris, Dick's father, sent his chauffered Rolls-Royce to pick up his son's guests, causing such excitement at Bedford Square it affected the two young women as they were handed deferentially into the back seat in a state of flushed excitement themselves. Nan and Nelly, standing on the steps to see them go, were ready to curtsey to the uniformed chauffeur, the colour of his uniform an exact match to the motor car, a shade somewhere between burgundy and port. The automobile was brand-new, the chauffeur told them, evidently as proud of it as if it belonged to him, and was called the 'Silver Ghost' and was ornamented with glowing, polished brass. It seemed that Mr and Mrs Morris with their two daughters, both younger than Master Dick and named Miss Catherine and Miss Christine, were staying at the Ritz and would be waiting there for Miss Goodwin and Miss Kellett in the cocktail lounge.

Both Rose and Alex had splashed out on a new evening gown and looked such a lovely picture as they hesitated in the doorway of the cocktail lounge that there was a momentary hush among the guests downing their cocktails before dining in the restaurant that César Ritz had made famous. Rose had chosen a pale, rose-pink chiffon studded at the neckline with tiny crystal beads, the neckline itself cut just low enough to show a hint of the valley between her small breasts. It had an ivory satin underdress caught at the feet with the narrow crystal insertions and the dress was straight and tubular but not clinging. Her satin slippers were the exact shade of the dress and in the heavy coil of her dark hair she wore a pink rose. Alex's dress was in a shade of azure that brought out the incredible blue of her eyes and though the style was similar to Rose's it was plain with no ornamentation bar a single long string of pearls caught on a strand of gold. The pearls had belonged to her grandmother, a gift from her doting husband but had been given to Alex on her twenty-first birthday. In her short riot of curls which fell over her forehead and ears she had placed a beautiful azure butterfly whose wings were studded with gold. Although trains were fashionable neither girl wore one.

The Morris family were grouped round a low table, an elderly couple who were evidently Dick's father and mother and two young ladies who might have been nineteen or twenty but were in dresses far too young for their age in white gauze with blue sashes and silver knots of ribbon. Mrs Morris was resplendent in purple brocade and was bristling with diamonds at her throat, ears and fingers. It seemed to Alex in the few moments she had to appraise the sisters that their parents, or probably Mrs Morris, were intent on keeping their girls in the style and upbringing reminiscent of the Victorian age, which boded ill for poor Rosie!

Besides Mr Morris there were two other gentlemen: one was Dick, the other was Patrick!

Rose gripped Alex's hand fiercely, afraid, Alex was inclined to think, that she might turn tail and run away, smiling inwardly, for didn't Rose know her better than that. Her heart might be leaping in such a way she thought it might break free from her breast but she was a woman who had faced many challenges and never shirked them. Though she might be boiling with rage she would not let anyone see it, especially Dick who must have devised all this, for it was plain that Patrick was as aghast as she was.

The three gentlemen stood up as she and Rose approached and she saw Mrs Morris's eyes dart between herself and Rose, wondering, she supposed, which was the woman her son intended to marry. They were both beauties and dressed with elegance and taste but Alex knew instinctively that neither of them would do for Mrs Morris.

She almost laughed out loud at the expression on Dick's face. It shone like a beacon with his love, and his hands, as they had done earlier in the week, were itching to take Rosie's but he restrained himself, making the introductions, though when he said, 'Mother, Father, this is Rosie, Miss Rose Kellett,' the declaration of his love was in his face, in his demeanour as his body swayed towards her, his hands, which should have known better, reaching out in a most improper manner, or so Mrs Morris believed, and taking both of hers. She was stiff with outrage and his father, wanting to side with his wife but failing completely, was simply bowled over by Rosie's shy and in-nocent smile, by her lovely serene face which turned to his son with the love not many men receive or experience.

'And this is her friend, and mine, Miss Alex Goodwin. Rose and Alex live together in Alex's father's house.' The introductions continued: 'My sisters, Christine and Catherine, and of course you both know Patrick O'Leary . . .' mumbling somewhat, for it was very evident that Alex and Patrick, though they would be polite for his sake, were not showing any sign of relenting their feud as he had hoped when he had invited them both without telling either of them that the other would be there.

'Won't you sit down, Miss Kellett,' Mother Morris said, indicating the seat next to her, her manner determined that Dickon, as she called her son, should not sit with this pretty but totally unsuitable girl. She immediately began to press her about her family, her background, her father's profession, what she herself was doing in London living with Miss Goodwin, while the others were left to sit wherever they liked. They drank lemonade, all the ladies, for Mrs Morris did not believe in drink, frowning at her husband and son when they ordered a brandy each. Mr O'Leary was totally beyond the pale, being of Irish extraction and coming from Liverpool where his father had owned a shop, he had told her. It was perhaps this, as Mrs Morris manipulated them all in the seating around the table in the dining-room, that made Alex relent and speak coolly but politely to Patrick who was placed next to her. Mrs Morris's daughters were placed one on either side of their brother with Alex next to Catherine, Patrick next to Mr Morris and Rose captured between Mr and Mrs Morris.

'And how are you, Mr O'Leary?' she asked him. 'It's a while since we saw you.'

'I'm well, thank you, Miss Goodwin. And yourself?' He sounded very Irish, for when Patrick O'Leary was being someone other than himself, he lapsed into the brogue of his childhood. And he was not himself tonight. He wanted nothing more than to get Dick Morris on his own somewhere and knock the living daylights out of him. He had engineered this, inviting Alex and himself in the hope they would make up their quarrel, if you could call it that. Inside he was hurting with the beauty of her, her cool poise, her smile, which never quite reached her eyes, and by the flutter of her thin hands as she broke a bread roll in two. For Dick's sake she was being courteous, her upbringing demanding good manners as she turned to Catherine Morris who began at once to question her on her suffragette activities.

'That will do, Catherine,' Mrs Morris, who seemed able to listen to everyone at the same time, said. 'We want none of that here, if you please. Remember you are a lady.' She could not have uttered a more deliberate insult to Rose and Alex. Dick got to his feet, his face a flaming, fiery red and was ready to grab Rosie's hand and leave, but his father shook his head.

'Sit down, Dick, your mother meant nothing. She does not happen to agree with the—'

'I know that, Pa, but—'

'Let's drink a toast to Dick on his birthday,' Patrick interrupted smoothly, 'and I think a bottle of champagne would be in order, don't you, Mr Morris?' Before the startled gentleman could answer or his wife could show her outrage, Patrick lifted a hand to summon the waiter, asking for a bottle of his best champagne, and later tried not to wince at the price. There was a flurry of activity as champagne glasses were brought to the table and although Mrs Morris firmly refused a glass for herself her husband said that a sip would not hurt her daughters.

The rest of the meal passed off in comparative peace with desultory conversation and it was evident from poor Dick's usually cheerful face that he knew the evening had not been a success. His sisters sat in silence, speaking only when spoken to, by their mother! Dick was not able to talk to Rose who was overwhelmed by Mrs Morris and her searching questions, and with Alex and Patrick barely speaking to one another . . . He had had such high hopes for the evening. His parents would adore his sweet Rosie, as he did. His sisters would be able to question Alex about suffragism, hopefully being put off by her tales of the ordeals she herself had endured and, last but not least, Alex and Patrick would be friends again, if not lovers! He knew what Patrick was suffering. The Irishman was not a man to bare his feelings to a living soul but he had been devastated by his parting with Alex, which showed in the monosyllabic answers to Dick's bright chatter and cheerful attempts to 'bring him out of himself'. He was reserved at the best of times but now he hadn't a word for the bloody cat except in matters to do with his work.

The tables were set round a small dance floor where, during the meal, couples waltzed or tried a sedate foxtrot. When Patrick rose to his feet and asked Christine if she would care to dance, they all looked astonished, and then turned their gaze to Mrs Morris as though to hear what she would have to say to that! Though she hissed at Christine to behave, just as if the girl were about to perform a striptease, Christine stood up defiantly and was led on to the floor by Patrick. The silence was appalling and became worse when, emboldened by Patrick's rebellion, Dick stood up and held out his hand to Rose.

'Well!' said Mrs Morris, clearly mortified, and Alex, who vowed, if she could manage it, never to be in Mrs Morris's company again, watched as Patrick floated by with Christine, who appeared to be a good dancer. She was chatting brightly to him and he was smiling and for the first time in her life Alex felt jealousy sink its poisoned fangs into her heart. She had loved this man for a long time, and he had loved her but they had been separated by their individual beliefs. Was it worth it? He was hers and she was his and what did anything else matter?

The sight of him laughing and dancing with another woman, a pretty, and, now she was away from her mother, a vivacious woman pierced her as nothing else could. Dear God, what was wrong with her? Patrick was not the kind of man who passed from woman to woman like some men. When he gave his love, it was given for life and he had offered it to her. She had thrown it back in his face so what the devil did it matter who he danced with, who he flirted with, as he was so evidently doing now? He was nothing to her. He could not be part of her life since he did not believe in it. Did not approve of it. They were like oil and water and could never mix as Rose and Dick did. Dick was a more tolerant, even indulgent man and Rose was the sort of woman who, though she had been brave in her fight for women's freedom, would always choose love of a man above love of her fellow women. She might deny it but it was true. She was truly a woman . . . Oh dear Lord, the pain inside was terrible, so terrible she turned frantically for a way to escape it and there was dear Mr Morris – how on earth had he got into the clutches of the woman who was his wife? – standing at her side.

'I promise to try not to step on your toes, Miss Goodwin, but may I take you on the floor?'

If looks could kill both she and Mr Morris would now be lying dead on the floor but thankfully Mrs Morris had no powers there and with a grateful smile Alex stood up and put her hand in that of Mr Morris.

It was later that the gentlemen, given permission by Mrs Morris, lit their cigars and drank another brandy. The talk between Patrick and Mr Morris turned to the Irish problem and the problems Mr Asquith had to deal with; the manner in which Germany was building up its navy which Mr Morris seemed to consider something of a threat and Patrick appeared to agree, not once glancing in Alex's direction. Dick was daydreaming across the table at his love, since Mrs Morris, with her daughters dutifully in tow, had sailed off to the ladies' room.

It was after two when Alex and Rose were dropped off at home in the Rolls-Royce. Patrick had his small Austin Seven, he said, so would take himself back to his lodging. Neither Alex nor Rose was given much chance to bid Dick farewell as Rose would have liked, for Mrs Morris clung possessively to his arm.

The two girls said goodnight to one another in such a sober mood it was difficult to believe they had drunk champagne at a birthday party and it was not until Alex was in her own room and had emptied the small evening bag in which she kept her handkerchief and tiny flask of French perfume, that she came across the note. It was short and incisive.

*Meet me in the Royal Botanic Gardens at eleven o'clock.*

So sure was he that she would know who had written it and slipped it into her bag, probably while she danced with Dick, he had not even signed it, nor did he seem to think she might ignore it which, of course, she would!

# 10

He was there, standing just inside the gateway of the Chester Road entrance to Regent's Park. He was casually dressed in grey flannels and a tweed sports jacket in shades of beige and brown with a round-necked beige jersey beneath it. His brogues were brown and well polished and he wore no hat. In the bright sunshine his hair, which looked newly washed, was a shining brown but with bands of copper in it and his eyes glowed a deep chestnut, the gold flecks in them very noticeable.

Due to the splendour of the weather there were many ladies and gentlemen enjoying the soft spring air, some of the ladies dressed as she was in a moderately full skirt just touching the instep, a high-necked blouse banded with lace, a broad leather belt, and a flat straw hat known as a boater, and high laced boots. Others wore a walking costume, the lapels and hem of the skirt faced with contrasting material with a high-necked, side-buttoning jacket, gloves, and a large brimmed hat decorated with feathers, birds, flowers or artificial fruit. The gentlemen were more formally dressed than Patrick, in lounge jackets with waistcoats and trousers to match, bowler hats or what was known as a Homburg.

It was evident that Patrick was indifferent to current fashion. He was leaning against the dappled trunk of a stately cedar of Lebanon tree, one of the many clustered in a grove to the left of the gateway. As she approached, ready to give him the rounds of the kitchen, as Nan would say, for daring to presume that she would come when he called, he stood away from the tree and without warning gripped her arm, and before she could protest dragged her into the deep, densely packed grove. He said nothing but at once put his arms fiercely around her, pinioning hers to her sides and placing his mouth on hers. His lips were warm, firm, demanding, cruel even, then they became soft, caressing, tender and to her astonishment she found herself responding, unable to resist him. Her body was held close to his, or, rather, was sagging against his and her legs were inclined to tremble, barely able to hold her up. He had kissed her before, and before that first kiss, had had time to disarm her when she would have repudiated him. But not this time and she had a fleeting moment to reflect that he could not have chosen a more successful way to weaken her resolve. Perhaps he had planned it but his action and her response to it told them both the truth of their feelings. Had he tried with words, explanations, even apologies, she would have responded with words of her own and they would have become entangled in such a web of verbiage they would never escape it. She was articulate. She had stood on a makeshift platform at the gates to a factory and talked to men, working-class men and with her wit and a joke or two, mainly against herself, she had held them to her, listening to her good-naturedly as she explained her mission. And he was Irish. He had the gift of the gab, inherited from his paternal grandfather, though he rarely used it unless, like her, he was addressing a crowd, in his case a crowd of would-be medical doctors. Had he given her a chance they would have tied each other up in recriminations but without stopping to think of the consequences he had taken her in his arms and it was their bodies, female to male, male to female, that spoke.

He sensed her surrender, moving his lips across her cheek, to her chin and the soft flesh beneath, brushing her throat with the tip of his tongue and heard the soft whimper that told him she was his. If he could have laid her down on the earth beneath the trees, thrown her skirt over her face and taken her before she came to her senses, he would have done so, so great was his need, but, of course, he couldn't and besides, he wanted their first time to be special, private, unseen and unheard by a living soul. There were dogs and children capering about the park and there was a chance that one or the other might invade the grove of trees.

'My love . . . my dear love,' he murmured against her mouth, 'I love you. God, how I love you . . . last night . . . you were so beautiful . . . my beauty . . . my heart . . . my very soul. I can't go on without you, not the way it has been.' Capturing her lips again he could feel the pressure of her body surge against his and he knew he must strike while the iron was hot, so to speak. Take advantage of her willingness at this moment and hope to God she didn't change her mind, as women did, and slap him in the face for his impudence. He wanted to be sure of her and he knew, once she had given him her body, taken his inside her, she would never look elsewhere. He had loved her since that first moment in Westminster Yard and though no words had been spoken he knew she loved him.

'What . . . what . . . where are we to . . .' She was dazed, her eyes unfocused and such a dark blue, a blue he was to come to know well in passionate moments such as this.

'I want to make love to you, so I do, and I want it now, bejasus,' reverting, as he always did when deeply moved, to his Irish lilt. 'And so do you, say you do.'

'I don't know . . . last night when you danced with that . . . that gobbin' – which was another of Nan's sayings – 'I . . . felt . . .'

'You were jealous,' he said, delighted. 'You were jealous of my dancing with whatever her name was, which means you *do* love me . . . say you do.' But she wouldn't. Even now the femininist core of her, which despised men who tried to subjugate women, stopped her mouth, as he did, with his lips. His tongue searched for hers, then he took the full softness of her lower lip between his teeth and bit it, bit it hard and she was sure he had drawn blood.

'I want to make love to you, dammit,' he almost snarled, 'in my bed . . . d'you hear . . .'

'Yes . . .' she sighed, her breath sweet as a child's, as submissive as a child, her eyes great pools of blue darkness. He felt an amazing happiness, piercing and sweet, and without wasting another moment he took her hand firmly in his.

Without another word he dragged her out of the trees, bursting on a small family, husband, wife and two young children who were walking along the path. The mother and father looked outraged, drawing their children close to them as though the decently dressed couple, who must have been larking in the bushes, might contaminate them. They ran like giddy children across the park where they were stared at by passers-by, and by people idling in the sunshine as they dashed headlong to where he had parked his motor. Into it he roughly placed her, driving like a racing motorist dodging in and out of traffic along Charing Cross Road to Smith Square. They were in great danger of colliding with another vehicle but Patrick was afraid that if Alex was given time to think she might change her mind and it seemed to him that this was the instant in which he must act. It sounded premeditated, which in a way it was, but he must grab at this chance if he was to get her, keep her, love her to the end of their days. Today was the starting point. If she was to belong to him it must be today. This was the moment. Everything in some strange way led to it. It was Sunday and Mrs Dawson, who came in each day to clean, to do his laundry and, if he was there, to cook him a meal, was not there. The house would be empty. Dear God, he hated himself for being so . . . so devious – was that the word? – but surely his deep and endless love for this woman excused him.

The house in Smith Square where Patrick had an apartment was very similar to the one Alex lived in, tall, narrow, semi-

detached with area steps leading down to the cellar. He un-
locked the front door and stepped back to allow her to walk into
the hallway and already he could see she was hesitant. Her
passion, the passion he had aroused, was slipping away as
reality took over. He reached out for her in the gloom and took
her in his arms, very, very gently. He removed her boater and
dropped it to the floor, then placed his cheek on the soft curling
darkness of her short hair. They stood for two or three minutes,
their bodies again speaking for them, but gently, and he felt her
relax against him. Her arms rose and her hands clasped one
another at his back.

'We don't have to do this, my darling,' he murmured, 'not
now. I have rushed you over here and you came but if you want
to wait . . . another time perhaps, I will understand. If you are
not ready, or want marriage, I'm your man but it is up to
you . . .'

'Patrick, stop babbling and . . . well, I suppose what I'm
saying is take me to bed.'

His bedroom was the second one along the narrow hallway
with the drawing-room at the front, the kitchen and scullery to
the back of the house. He led her into the bedroom which was
as neat and clean as though one of her mother's parlour-maids
had 'bottomed' it. There was a big double bed with snowy linen
and a patchwork quilt of many colours, a wardrobe and a
dressing-table, his hairbrush on it, a ticking clock, a few books
and what looked like medical literature, all tidily placed. She
supposed in his profession he would have to be tidy, she had
time to think, then he swept her into his arms, no hesitation this
time, no talk of leaving it, of waiting for another day. She could
feel the enormous bulge in his trousers and was startled to
realise that she had a great desire to put her hand down there
and cup it. His hands went to the buttons down the back of her
blouse, flinging the garment from her, then her skirt and in a
moment she was naked and so was he. He laid her none too

gently on the bed, his face grim, serious and set into an expression she had never seen before. It was the face of a man who is fully roused and is determined to satisfy his need, and then he sighed and rested on his elbows, his face relaxing into a smile of such love she wanted to cry. He was an honourable man who wanted to marry her but he was also a male with a female in his arms and nature must run its course.

'I'm sorry, my love. I'm going too fast for you.'

'No . . . no . . . please . . .'

'Let me look at you.' And his eyes, his hands, his tongue, his mouth moved up and down her body, exploring every part of her from her mouth, her ears, her breasts, taking particular interest in her nipples which peaked into his mouth, her flat stomach, the inside of her silken thighs to her feet. He examined her deformed foot, not with a doctor's interest but as a lover who finds his beloved's imperfections perfect then kissed the stump where the toes should have been.

She was beginning to squirm, to moan, to claw at his back, to drag at his thick hair and, knowing she was ready, he plunged himself into her, hurting her, and when she winced he hesitated but she arched her back, urging him on. He had taken her maidenhead, as the quaint saying went, and without sparing her he went deeper and deeper, deeper and stronger and when it was too much for either of them they both cried out and rode the wave again and again until it flung them on to the shores of ecstasy, of rapture. He was groaning but she would not let him go, holding his buttocks to keep him inside her and was surprised when he began to laugh gaspingly.

'My darling, I can do no more. It will take a while for me . . . see . . .' He pulled away from her and rested on an elbow, directing her gaze to his penis which was innocently resting among the thatch of his pubic hair.

'But . . .' She was bewildered, for she remembered the great organ that had been so much in evidence earlier.

'You don't imagine I go round with an erection at all times, do you? I wouldn't be able to walk. My dearest love, you have a lot to learn and so have I, since I have no great knowledge of women. It will come again,' and under her fascinated gaze it began to swell. 'Hell's teeth, can you not see what you are doing to me . . . you are . . .' He groaned as though in pain and again he plunged himself into her, rolling over until she was on top of him. She smiled and lifted her arms, flaunting her breasts, loving it, loving him, moving with him until they both shouted with the joy of it as she fell on to his chest.

They lay then, satiated, drowsing, murmuring love words to one another, stroking but this time with a tenderness, a gentleness a mother might use on a child.

'I suppose I must go or I'll have Nan giving me the length of her tongue. She was bad enough when I left this morning without telling her where I was off to. She is probably imagining me in the thick of one of the daft activities the daft sufragettes get up to.'

'Mmm, I don't think I can manage to get out of bed after my exertions. I need someone here to see to my needs.'

'Well, it's not me, Patrick O'Leary.'

'Put the kettle on, there's my wee macushla, for to be sure wouldn't I love a cup of tea?'

'You what!' She rested her chin on his chest then sat up and explored him from his head to his toes, taking her time, sitting astride him, exclaiming over the marvel of his body. Her innocent face was full of wonder, since she had never seen a naked man before. She laid her mouth on his throat and he purred like a cat, then told him to lie still as she hadn't finished with him yet and their laughter was simple and uncomplicated. He had told her she was beautiful but she discovered that so was he. He was tall, lean and wiry but well proportioned with graceful bones and muscles that flowed smoothly from the curves of his chest and shoulder to the slight concavities of his belly and thigh. He had a spring of curls on his chest and tight nipples. His hands were large, blunt-fingered but slender and they rose to touch her face, her eyebrow, to cup her face and bring it down to kiss her lips and she thought she would die of love for him. This was her man. She was his woman and the simplicity of it amazed her.

They dressed reluctantly, still inclined to stop and sigh over the lift of her breast, the curve of his buttocks, to kiss and touch until he warned her that he would never let her out of this room if she didn't behave.

He drove her up to the corner of Bedford Square but said he wouldn't come in.

'Why not? Nan would be thrilled to see you.'

'My love, if you hadn't noticed Nan surely will.'

'Notice what?'

'You've a glow about you, a sleekness, a brilliance in your eyes that a blind man on a galloping horse couldn't miss. It says you have just been in some man's bed. You have been thoroughly made love to. There's even a smile in your voice which Nan cannot fail to miss and bejasus, I take full credit for it. Besides, I have to go up to the hospital. I have a very sick child who—'

'Oh, my darling, why didn't you tell me?' She was full of contrition, and compassion too, for him and for the sick child to whom he was to give his skill. He glanced round him then kissed her gently. 'May I telephone you later?'

'Please, Patrick . . . and . . .' She took his hand, looking down at it shyly.

'What is it, my darling?'

'Thank you.' Then she ran to the door, not looking back.

He was smiling, fatuously, he knew, as he hurried back to his apartment.

⋆ ⋆ ⋆

Nan was made up, as she constantly told Nelly, that Doctor Patrick was back on the scene. 'Thank the dear Lord,' she kept saying, for it was evident that he was doing her young mistress the world of good. She was forever smiling and humming and glowing like the sun in the sky and now and again Nan felt a pang of misgiving, for was the girl *too* gloriously happy and if so, why? Oh, she loved the man, there was no doubt of that and he loved her. You only had to see them together to realise that. His eyes lit up when Alex entered the room and hers followed him as he rose to help himself to a brandy. They were forever touching each other, a hand caressing an arm or cheek and she knew damn well that the minute she left the room they were kissing each other. She had caught them at it once and the good doctor's hand was down the front of Miss Alex's low-cut gown and Miss Alex was certainly not objecting. The familiarity of it disturbed her, for it spoke of a couple who knew each *very well* which brought her round to the fact that every Sunday Miss Alex disappeared, saying vaguely that she was going for a walk or she had some suffragette business to attend to. Nan approved of Mr O'Leary. He was just the man she would have chosen for her lamb if it had been up to her. He was no young sprig who might break Miss Alex's heart. He was well set up in a splendid profession and would make Miss Alex a wonderful husband, but as March moved into April and though Doctor Patrick was a regular visitor at Bedford Square, they didn't seem to *move on*. Of course he had met her parents and it had been clear that both Mr and Mrs Goodwin thought the world of him. So why was no engagement announced? Tell her that and tell her no more, she said fretfully to Nelly. Nelly was only a young girl but she had been with the Goodwins since she left school at thirteen. She had willingly come to London five years ago now to be part of Miss Alex's household and she had a wise head on her shoulders. Nan often unburdened her worries on Nelly but the girl was half in love with Mr O'Leary herself and was captivated by the budding romance between him and Miss Alex.

'They should be announcing their engagement bi' now, Nelly,' Nan said to her. 'I've a good mind ter speak to 'er messen. Miss Rosie an' Doctor Dick are deep in their plans fer their weddin' an' Miss Rosie were tellin' me they're goin' ter look at a house terday, not far from 'ere, she said, so why aren't Miss Alex an' Doctor Patrick doin't same?'

She sighed and Nelly sighed with her. It was the end of April, a Sunday and as usual Miss Alex had gone off with a vague tale of a meeting somewhere or other but she had that flushed, even feverish look about her that Nan didn't like at all. Surely she couldn't be . . . well, Nan didn't even dare to think about what Miss Alex and the doctor got up to but with no wedding in the offing it worried her to death, for if they were . . . well, up to something, what would she do if Miss Alex should . . . no, not Miss Alex who had been brought up proper and the doctor such a gentleman. Mind, them suffragettes went on about women being as free as men and where would that lead, she brooded, while in Patrick's bed her Miss Alex was moaning like a wounded tigress, which Patrick said she was sometimes, her head flung back in the pillows, her body arched to receive Patrick's as it had done every Sunday for weeks now.

It was later when they were lying entwined on the bed, Patrick's cheek on one breast, his hand caressing the other that she told him she was to go to Liverpool the next day.

At once his head shot up and his hand left its delightful place on her breast and that familiar expression she had come to dread crossed his face.

'Why?' That was all.

'I have some business there. Several of us are to go to a meeting that is to take place—'

'I suppose you mean that at that meeting you are to stand up and insult the speaker.'

'No, it is a suffragette meeting. One of our members is to speak to the women of Liverpool about the Conciliation Bill which Asquith is—'

He flung up his hand to stop her, his face harsh, his mouth, which so recently had been warm and tender in many intimate parts of her body, grim, his lips thinned in his outrage. 'Don't tell me any more, for the Lord's sake, or I swear I'll . . .' He dared not say what he would do, for he had no power over her should she decide to have her own way. He had been patient as he waited for her to tell him she would marry him, which he longed for with all his heart. He knew how much she loved him but whenever he became serious she would back away from him and to keep her he knew he must not tie her too tightly, but for some reason she had on this day mentioned the suffragettes, which she never did, and he could not hold his tongue.

'I'm sick to death of that bloody woman who I suppose will be there, for wherever there's trouble she's in the thick of it, taking you and other decent young women with her. She's an outrage to respectable women.'

'I suppose you are referring to Emmeline.' Her voice was icy.

'Emmeline, is it?' he sneered. 'Well, bugger Emmeline and all the trouble she has caused among the women of this land.'

'You mean the trouble she has caused the men, don't you? The trouble she has caused men in her fight, and *my* fight as well, don't forget, and the men can't forgive her.' She had leaped from the bed and as though she could no longer bear to be in the same room as him, never mind the same bed, she was flinging on her clothes, hurriedly trying to do up buttons he had undone so tenderly hours ago.

'Can I ever forget it? The state of you when you last came out of Holloway and the way you are forced to act, hiding and nipping round corners in case you should be hauled back in again. I won't have it, d'you understand? It's more than a man can stand, watching the woman he loves putting herself in danger. Oh, sweet Jesus, Alex . . . my love . . .' He hung his head, his chin on his chest, naked and beautiful in the pale rays of the sun that crept through the window and fell across the bed. 'Don't go . . . please, give it up, marry me and be safe. I promised I wouldn't bring it up,' he mumbled, 'but you are so dear to me, you are my very life and to think . . .'

She flew on to the bed and wrapped her arms about him, weakened by his pain, by his love for her, but at the same time somewhat uneasy, for there was nothing in the world, even this man she loved with all her heart, would compel her to give up the fight which her mother had begun before she was born. Even her grandmother, Abby Goodwin, had made a stand against men who wanted to keep women subjugated. Three generations of them, though Abby and her daughter Beth had been moderates and had not fought the militant fight, as women were doing now. Tomorrow she would go to the meeting in Liverpool which hundreds of women from different parts of the country were to attend. There would be banners – 'Deeds not Words,' they would say – and a procession in which they would all take part. A brass band to lead them and in the procession Emmeline Pankhurst, Christabel Pankhurst and many others who were up in arms because it was rumoured that the prison authorities were drugging their members to reduce their resistance to force-feeding. The WSPU attacks were becoming more and more severe and a deputation of their members were planning to see King George V at Buckingham Palace. She was to be among them but she dared not tell Patrick though in her heart she wanted to. She hated the deception, for it went against all that she was fighting for.

'Don't, darling, don't,' she began.

'Don't what?' he answered savagely. 'You expect me to pat you on the head and tell you to go and fight for your cause as though it were nothing to me. Your bloody cause. I hate it, *I hate it,* d'you hear. I want to keep you safe. Alex, please, don't go . . .'

She fell back from him, from his anguish, from the despair on his face. She stood up and continued to dress while he slumped on the bed, his chin on his chest, defeated. There was nothing she could do or say to make him see what this meant to her. The women's movement had been her life for so long and then she had met him and inside her were feelings that hurt, both physically and mentally. But she must go on, despite what it did to this man she loved with every fibre of her being, with every beat of her heart, with everything that was in her: she could not stop now.

'Patrick . . .' she murmured as she stood at the door, her composure almost broken on the pain of his distress. She felt lost and frightened and at the same time astonished that any man could make her feel as she did. She nearly broke and if he had looked up he would have seen it in her, but he didn't.

'For Christ's sake, go,' he said harshly and, with tears raining down her cheeks, she went.

# 11

'Have . . . have you and Patrick quarrelled?' Rose asked hesitantly.

'You might say that.'

'May I ask why?'

'Oh, the usual thing. He does not like my work for the movement and when I refused to give it up he told me . . . to go. He inferred that he didn't want to see me again, and he hasn't.' Alex's voice was brisk and artificially cheerful.

'Oh, Alex, and you love one another so much. Anyone can see that. Dick said only the other day that he had never known Patrick so genial and now he hasn't a good word for anyone. He works all hours God sends and will make himself ill, Dick says . . .'

'I don't want to hear another word about what Dick says, if it is to be about Mr O'Leary, Rose, and now if you will excuse me I must get ready for the march. Thank goodness it is fine.'

Rose looked at Alex with a troubled expression on her face, then sighed sadly, saying no more, for she knew it would do no good. The picture that Dick had painted of Patrick's retreat into that private world of his, letting no one in, like Alex herself, she suspected, seared her loving heart, as she and Dick were so . . . so – what was the word? – so compatible. Dick was good-natured, cheerful, and never remonstrated with her about her work for the WSPU even though she knew he didn't care for it. He was tolerant, if not exactly encouraging, but it seemed Patrick and Alex shared none of these feelings.

Alex rose from her chair in the breakfast-room where she had picked at a piece of toast and drunk a cup of coffee, smoothing down the practical grey serge skirt she wore. She had on a plain white blouse with no lace or frills, a wide leather belt and sturdy boots, her straw boater ready on the hallstand.

'Yer not goin' out on that!' Nan wailed, eyeing the crumbled toast on Alex's plate as she entered the room with a bowl of porridge with which she hoped to tempt her young mistress. 'A bit o' toast an' a cup o' coffee. I've told yer time an' time again, an empty—'

'I know, Nan, an empty sack won't stand, but I promise you I'll try and eat something before we set off.'

'Set off where?' Nan demanded to know.

'To see the King.'

'*Ter see the King!* Well, I never did! When were you an' your lot pally with 'Is Majesty, that's what I'd like ter know.'

'We're going to petition the King. We've abandoned all hope of any parliamentary progress on women's suffrage so we're off to Buckingham Palace.' Alex's voice was cold as she answered Nan, just as though it were nothing to do with her what the suffragettes did.

Nan was appalled. She had had such high hopes when Doctor Patrick had returned to Alex, high hopes that included marriage, of course, and an end to this madness both of her young ladies were involved with. And Miss Alex had been so happy, filled with some joyous emotion, it had affected them all. Nan had never been in love, being a plain, homely sort of a body, but she had seen it in Alex and she had seen the light that had been lit in her fade away and go out when Doctor Patrick stopped coming to the house.

She turned now to Rose, her face red with outrage. 'An' I suppose you're goin' an' all.'

'I am, Nan. Many women are coming from all parts of the country to—'

Nan threw her apron over her head and began to cry in despair. 'An' yer never said a word, neither of yer. That'll mean two of yer ter nurse, I suppose, or 'appen pair o' yer will end up in gaol. Does Doctor Dick know about it?' She wept, her voice muffled, then she whipped her apron from her wet face and turned to Alex. 'An' what about your lad? What about Doctor Patrick? Us've had neither sight nor sound of 'im fer weeks now and onceover 'e were never off bloomin' doorstep.'

'This is nothing to do with either Patrick or Dick, or you for that matter, Nan. Rose and I are prepared to stand up for our beliefs—'

'Don't you sauce me, young lady! An' I suppose yer said that ter Doctor Patrick and that's why 'e's done a flit. Eeh, lass, it's muck or nettles wi' you an' it's high time yer came ter yer senses. A likelier lad yer'd never wish ter meet an' there's you with not a pick on yer . . .'

'That's enough, Nan. What I choose to do, or not do, is none of your business. Now, Rose, are we ready? I think we'll get the tram. Save ourselves for the . . . for whatever lies ahead.' For they both knew that they might not see this comfortable house, this weeping, pleading woman who loved them both, for a long time.

There were hundreds of them marching shoulder to shoulder along the Mall carrying their banners, wearing their colours of purple, white and green, cheered, booed, and even spat at by men and women in the crowds who lined the route, for it was not only men who abhorred the suffrage movement. It was said later that 20,000 to 30,000 persons formed up in Constitution Hill, the Mall and on the forecourt in front of the railings of Buckinghan Palace. It was 21 May, another lovely spring, almost into summer day and those who seemed to be in the know prophesied a long, hot summer. The trees along the Mall were almost in full leaf, throwing dappled shadows across the women who marched steadfastly towards their goal, ignoring the crowds who had come to make fun of them, or do worse than that in some cases. Many of them were ladies, smart and elegant with their lovely, flower-laden hats, dainty gowns of muslin and lace, even pretty parasols, for there were women from every station in life marching to see the King. There were women in clogs and shawls come from the machines they 'minded' in Lancashire, from Wales with frilled caps under their tall stovepipe hats, their aprons as white as snow.

He saw her at the head of the procession behind Mrs Pankhurst, her head held high, her banner even higher. She looked so stern, so absolutely resolute on her mission he felt his heart contract with love for her, though he hated every other woman in the procession and, worst of all, Mrs Pankhurst who had started these militant activities when she left Manchester to come to London over ten years ago. Rose was there among the women, her sweet face pale with emotion. She was frightened, he could see that and perhaps because of it was the bravest of them all. It was not easy to go ahead with an action that terrified you.

'Do they imagine the King will see them?' one woman in the crowd standing near him said to her neighbour. 'Daft beggars. A deputation to demand votes for women, that's what they're calling it. I don't want the damn vote, do you, Cissie? Well, never mind, the police'll see 'em off. Lord, I've never seen such a crowd. Now stick hold of my arm, Cis, or we might get separated.'

He kept pace with the leaders which included Alex and it was almost four o'clock before the great gate at the top of Constitution Hill was closed, but by that time Mrs Pankhurst and the women with her had passed through the police cordons at the bottom of the hill. No attempt was made to arrest Mrs Pankhurst but as she, and the rest, Alex among them, reached the palace she was recognised and was at once surrounded by the incensed police. The petition that Mrs Pankhurst hoped to present to the King was in her bag but a huge inspector of police, his face purple with rage, seized her bodily and carried her, her feet off the ground, to a waiting motor car. She was lifted in and two detectives leaped in after her and the car drove off. Just before it moved, seeing Mrs Pankhurst's distress, two St John's Ambulance men ran forward and offered their help but it was coldly refused. As she was carried past a group of reporters Mrs Pankhurst called out, 'Arrested at the gates of the palace. Tell the King,' then she was gone.

He was caught in the crowd, a crowd of excited spectators come to see the fun, for it was often a good show when a demonstration of this sort got under way. They were not disappointed. Some of the women not yet captured by the police rushed for the gates of the palace, and the railings to the side and he heard Alex's voice over the tumult, yelling for them to climb over.

'Get on to the crossbars,' she was shouting, herself hanging like a monkey from the top spike, scrabbling with her feet to try to get purchase, her hat gone, her shirt torn at the sleeve. She was hanging on despite the attentions of an enormous plain-clothes policeman and her voice was carried across the seething crowds.

'We protest at the torture of our women,' she was shrieking. 'We are here to demand votes for women and claim equal treatment for militant Ulstermen and militant suffragettes. Let us . . .' And then she vanished into the crowd at the foot of the railings, torn down by cruel and vicious hands. The other women, those who had not been able to reach the railings, were attacking the police and trying to force them out of the way. Many of the police were in plain clothes and they waded in as though at a free-for-all in a public bar where rough working men were ready to lock horns. There was no quarter given, no recognition that these were women and weaker than themselves. Even some of the women in the crowd who watched began to mutter among themselves at the brutality of it. The police, both in and out of uniform, were pummelling the suffragettes unmercifully, their fists aimed at their breasts, which they had learned were the most vulnerable part of their body, dragging them from the railings and throwing them savagely to the ground.

'Nay,' said one woman next to him. 'There's no need to treat them like that, poor souls. See, he's got that woman's skirt in his hands and it'll be her drawers next, I shouldn't wonder.' She had her hand to her mouth but she was a single voice in the crowd of baying men.

He watched in horror, searching in the group of struggling, screaming women for Alex, but though he caught sight of Rose being dragged by two rough types who he presumed were plainclothes policemen, and forced into a Black Maria, there was no sign of Alex. He pushed and shoved and earned a few curses and black looks to get to the front of the crowd but when he did they had all been taken away. On the ground beside the railings were torn banners, umbrellas, hats, shoes and even, God forbid, a pair of lace drawers. Policemen on horseback stood guard but the 'fun' was over.

'Move along there, sir,' one constable told him politely, his face, which Patrick could see would be kind in different circumstances, unsmiling. He was minus his helmet and was none too pleased about it, but his manner said that this was a gentleman to whom he must show respect. Patrick wondered at the irony of it. One minute they were knocking seven bells out of women but as soon as order was resumed and the women dragged off to where they belonged, the constable was politeness itself to one of his own sex.

The crowd began to disperse, drifting along the Mall towards Admiralty Arch and he went with them, his feet dragging as though he had just run a marathon, which he felt he had. He was about to turn for home at Nelson's Monument when he felt a touch on his arm and when he turned there was Dick, his face like putty, his eyes burning, his face, usually shining with good nature and laughter, now pale and filled with horror.

'What the hell are we to do, Patrick? What are we to do with them? I don't think I can stand any more of this. God in heaven, I try to understand, to keep my bloody mouth shut but when you see the woman you love being manhandled as though she were some whore soliciting in the street I want to kill someone. Where will they have been taken, d'you think?'

Patrick knew his own face would be exactly the same as Dick's but he said nothing, for what was there to say that had not been said a hundred times before. It was almost twelve months since he had first seen Alex in the same situation as the one he had just witnessed and, like Dick, he knew he could take no more. He would have to get away, get away from London, away from Alex, from all these women who were fighting and at the same time taking away his one chance of happiness, or if not happiness then peace of mind.

Sixty-six women were arrested that day, among them Alex and Rose who were sentenced respectively to six and three months in the Third Division. He did not go to Bow Street as Dick had done, for he felt if he was to make the break he must do it now and it was Dick who told him the news. He would never see her again, he would make certain of that, though poor old Dick, who was not as clever at hiding his feelings, was in a terrible state.

'We were to have been married in August and if she stays in that place for her full term how can we be married as soon as she comes out? She'll go on hunger strike this time, I know she will, so perhaps they'll set her free under the cat and mouse.' Dick was almost in tears and Patrick felt story for him, but he was in too much pain himself to do more than comfort him with stupid words that meant nothing to either of them. It was as though the women they loved were soldiers who were off to war, leaving them behind to worry, as women did when their men marched away. But he was too numb, too frozen, too paralysed with grief at his loss to comfort Dick.

'I'm leaving,' he said abruptly, cutting through Dick's agonising and was almost ready to laugh, and might have done if there had been any laughter left in him, at the blankness of his friend's expression.

'Leaving? Leaving where?'

'The hospital. London.'

'But where to?'

Dick had just come from the Magistrates' Court and they were sitting in the cocktail bar of the Ritz where last they had been on Dick's birthday. They had drunk several brandies apiece and were about to have lunch but somehow neither of them seemed capable of doing more than summoning the waiter for two more drinks. The place was crowded and Patrick hoped to God that none of Dick's cheerful pals would suddenly appear. He didn't even want to be here at all and had only come because Dick had turned up at his apartment after the hearing at Bow Street in such a dreadful state.

'Do you not read the newspapers, Dick?' he asked mildly, so mildly Dick wondered if Patrick O'Leary had ever had real feelings for Alex Goodwin, like his for his sweet Rose. He was so bloody calm. It was as though Alex Goodwin were merely a passing fancy who had just happened by, but then why was he going away? It was a terrible dilemma for Dick to understand, at least in his present state.

'The newspapers?'

'Yes, surely you can see what is coming.' Patrick drew deeply on his cigarette, gazing sightlessly at the smart crowd that shrieked with laughter about him.

'No, I don't understand. What—'

'There's going to be a war, lad.'

'A war, for God's sake what are you talking about?' Dick's jaw gaped and he stared at Patrick as though he had gone mad.

'Oh, it doesn't exactly say so but I've been watching, as have those in the government, I suspect, Germany building up its navy and its gold reserve and it seems, to me at any rate, that they are determined on war. The Kaiser has been entertaining all the leading personalities and he doesn't want peace, or so it has been reported, and neither do his cohorts.'

'His cohorts?' Dick said, bewildered.

'They are just waiting for something to give them an excuse and when it comes we'll be in the thick of it.'

'Jesus, Patrick, you can't mean it. We're not warmongers.'

'No, lad, we're not but it's inevitable, so I'm joining the army as a surgeon.' Patrick snapped his fingers at the waiter and ordered another two brandies, wondering why it was that though he and Dick must have drunk at least half a dozen each, both of them were stone-cold sober.

'But . . . but what about Alex?' Dick lit a cigarette. They both dragged the smoke deeply into their lungs.

'What about her?'

'Are you just to march off to war? Bloody hell, Paddy, you can't mean it.'

'Alex is none of my business any more, Dick. You must know that. She goes her own way to damnation and lets me go mine so that's where I'm headed. As to the prospect of war, there'll be something to set the Germans at it, you'll see.'

He was right. On 28 June, when Alex and Rose had been in gaol for five weeks, the Archduke Franz Ferdinand, heir-apparent to the crowns of Austria and Hungary, was murdered by Serb nationalists in the Bosnian capital, Sarajevo, and the fuse was lit to the bomb that would soon blow the world as the population of many countries knew it to smithereens.

★   ★   ★

They tottered from gaol at the end of July. While they had been imprisoned it had been decided by their comrades that despite demonstrations and mass meetings, legalised torture in His Majesty's prisons had not been enough to sway public opinion and so window-breaking became even more prevalent, letter-boxes were set alight or the mail was destroyed by pouring acid and tar through the slots, and telegraph wires were cut in a last desperate attempt to gain equality for women.

And on Tuesday, 4 August, a hot, still, listless dog-day when war with Germany was declared, taking most people by surprise, they neither of them could understand why, its political and economic origins a mystery to them both. Nor, if they told the truth, could they expend part of the tiny amount of energy left to them to care, for it had all been drained out of them during the past weeks of imprisonment.

Dick looked after them, and Nan and Nelly were his hand-maidens, for had they not been through it all before with Miss Alex. They were fed on milk and eggs, which should be easy to get down and were nourishing, but sometimes Alex, and she supposed Rose too, for she also had been force-fed, remembered the mixture of milk and raw eggs that had been poured down the tube to her stomach and which she had immediately vomited back. But there would be no more of that, no more feeling the unremitting cold of her cell, the sense of unreality that had possessed her as she lay alone in light-headed doze with the pale phantom of Patrick hovering near. No more reaching into her numb brain for something, anything to take her from her suffering, a poem, 'Come live with me and be my love,' she had whispered and he came to her then, seeing her through the agony of a torn mouth, the panic of being held down, a beloved ghost who soothed her red-hot flame of agony and humiliation. Patrick . . . Patrick . . . where are you, where?

Alex's mother came to stay and Beth cried when she saw her daughter's wafer-thin body, the hollows and angles of her brittle bones, the bruises on her almost non-existent breasts, green and black patches on the inside of her arms.

'My darling, what have they done to you? I can only thank God your father can't see this. I blame myself, really I do, for it was my belief in the enfranchisement of women that persuaded you to take it up.'

'Mother, stop it. I have a mind of my own and you were wise enough in allowing me to make my own choices, which is what we women wanted. Choices! And it was my choice that took me to Holloway. Yes, Mother, I have been beaten and it takes four great wardresses to hold down a woman who is to be forcibly fed, but, darling Mother, you were not to blame and' – holding out a thin hand to her mother – 'it will be the last time. We have been told that the WSPU has completely abandoned its campaign for the franchise and we are to devote ourselves entirely to the war effort. Emmeline is a patriot and also has a lot of common sense. Someone must run the essential services while the men are at war, she says and if we prove ourselves efficient and show we are capable of shouldering these tasks then the government of the day might find it awkward to refuse us the same legal and political rights as men when the war is over. Just think, by this time next year we may all have the vote, men and women alike. They say it will be over by Christmas but I have a feeling Father does not think so. And what of the boys? I suppose they are wildly excited at the thought of going to do their bit?'

Her mother sighed, holding Alex's hand, looking down at it as she clasped it between hers. 'Oh, you know what young men are like. Will is fascinated by anything mechanical and has already bought himself a motor car but he wants to fly, can you credit it. Archie is beside himself, for not only is Will to be off but Tom has already enlisted and has gone to an officers' training camp up north. The world is turned upside down and I don't know who to worry about most, you or the boys. So what are you to do now, darling? You and Rose. Will you take up some kind of war work?'

'I don't know, Mother. We must both get our health back before deciding on anything.'

'Why don't you come home for a while before you make any decision, you and Rose? Neither of you is strong enough even to think of . . . well, I don't know. What will young women do until the war is over?' Or until they get married, she might have added. Even Rose was unofficially engaged to Dick Morris and would be officially if he could escape the tentacles of his mother's domination. Mrs Morris did not care for Rose, or so Beth Goodwin had been told in private by Alex. A domineering mother she was and no wonder Dick had fled to London to begin his career as a doctor. What she wanted for her son was a mystery, for could you meet a sweeter, more good-natured girl than Rose? And pretty too, coming from a good but impoverished family, but then Beth had a feeling that the world was going to be a very different place from now on, or so Archie told her sadly.

'You and Rosie could even go up to Fellgate House for a couple of weeks, take Nan and Nelly and rest while you get your strength back. It will be cooler up there and with some of Nan's good cooking inside you you'll soon be yourselves. Don't think about anything else, Alex. Concentrate on getting strong.'

Alex knew her mother was scheming in some way to keep her, Alex, at home in Edge Bottom House where she could be fussed over and where Beth would not have the constant worry of what Alex was up to now that the WSPU was disbanded. She would be picturing herself and Alex doing their bit for the war, rolling bandages and knitting socks, perhaps doing a little light nursing in a local hospital where only wounded officers were in residence. Alex did not enlighten her!

Great Britain was traditionally a leading sea power with

neither a large standing army nor conscription. The British Expeditionary Force comprising 160,000 men, a 'contemptible little army' in the Kaiser's opinion, were, between 9 and 22 August, ferried across the Channel under the watchful guardianship of the navy. They fought their first battle at Mons on 23 August.

Among them was Patrick O'Leary.

# 12

She mended slowly; the body blow delivered by Dick when he told her gently that not only was Patrick in the Royal Army Medical Corps but had gone over to France with the British Expeditionary Force, or the BEF as it was to be called, affected her deeply. It seemed bizarre that now her fight was ended his was just about to begin and although Rose picked up quickly, no doubt due to the good food that Nan stuffed into her and the loving kindness the Goodwin family showed her, Alex could not seem to care much for anything. Her purpose in life had been taken away from her and the man she loved had marched off to war without a backward glance or even a word of goodbye. She continued to look pale and strained. Despite the glorious August weather, the long, hot days, the sunshine that blazed down from a cloudless blue sky, she was still cold. She could not get rid of the feeling that her body was parched, hollowed out, drawn out in strain. Her head ached and itched and though she slept in a clean bed, obediently ate everything Nan put in front of her and sat all day under the oak tree in the garden of Edge Bottom House where her father had taken herself and Rose, she was continually tired. Her mother and Nan worried over her for why could she not recover as Rose was doing, but then Rose had young Dick Morris fussing over her whenever he could get away from St Thomas's, loving her, holding her hand, and it was plain to the two women that their lamb, their lovely Alex was grieving badly for Patrick O'Leary and with nothing to take her mind from it, which her work with the WSPU had successfully done, she was not recovering as they had hoped.

Will had joined the Royal Flying Corps and was a second lieutenant with one pip of which he was inordinately proud and was training to be a pilot. He would be involved in air reconnaissance over the battlefields in France, which was the only activity the powers that be thought suitable for these strange machines, these aircraft, most of which had been designed for sport, aerobatic displays, contests and such like. But they would be useful for scouting and artillery spotting, they admitted, which was what Will was training for.

Tom was at an officers' training camp in Northumberland. Lord Kitchener had become Secretary for War and though the BEF was the best trained, the most competent army in the world, they were sadly lacking in supplies, particularly for trench and siege warfare, though naturally the people knew none of this. A sort of war fever erupted in London and all the big cities as men marched off to this great adventure. They were cheered on by crowds, Union Jacks waving, by the great surge of patriotic enthusiasm, the men rushing madly to enlist, for the damn thing would be over by Christmas and they were terrified they might miss the fun. The rumours were horrific: German atrocities such as violated nuns, and babies with their hands cut off and the outraged Englishman, gentry or working class, could not allow the horror to go on. Poor, gallant, little Belgium was a phrase on everybody's lips and every man was determined that he must get out there and defend these innocents from the deranged depravities of the German army. The recruiting centres were overrun with men who were desperate to get to France, where the fighting was, and Archie said privately to his wife that Dick Morris would be the next to go. And so it proved.

The next weekend at Edge Bottom House Dick, of whom they had all grown so fond, told them that he was off to France.

He had enlisted, as Patrick had done, in the RAMC, for already in September losses in the BEF, who were fighting so courageously at Mons, were mounting and the seriously wounded were being brought back to hospitals in the south of England, while those who might be returned up the line were in field hospitals where Dick would serve and where presumably Patrick was already. By the end of 1914, of the 160,000 of the BEF who had gone over in August, 95,654 of them were casualties and the new army, 'Kitchener's Army', hundreds of thousands of volunteers, all of whom required training, were to cross the Channel to France.

Dick was still begging Rose to marry him before he went but she stood firm and only Alex knew the reason why.

'Why don't you marry the poor fellow and put him out of his misery? He absolutely adores you and I suppose he wants to leave a bit of himself in England. Probably wants to get you pregnant and tied up in domestic trivia while he's off doing his bit.'

'Which is precisely why I don't want to marry until the war is over. A married woman has no will of her own, Alex, no choice when it comes to what she wants to do, we both know that more than anybody. I love Dick and I hope to marry him one day when this is all over but I don't want to sit at home and twiddle my thumbs until he comes back. Married women will be barred from doing anything useful to help win this war. Oh, I suppose there will be ladies' groups knitting and sewing and doing useless little things for the troops but the *real* war work, for women, I mean, will only be allowed to single women. There is so much that can be done, nursing, driving ambulances, driving staff cars . . . I don't know, but I mean to find out. There is voluntary work in hospitals but I must have something that pays me a wage, for, unlike you, who has an allowance, my father has no more money to support me.'

They were sitting in the shade of the enormous oak tree in the garden at the front of the house, Alex drinking one of Nan's concoctions, eggnog with milk and sherry. Almost hourly, or so it seemed, Nan sallied forth with forceful directions to 'get this down yer an' no arguing' thrusting the glass into Alex's hand. Rose was looking her old self again, but then Rose had been in prison just the once and had not had five years of being in and out of the cells, of starvation, manhandling, force-feeding, and had not lost the weight that Alex had. A scarecrow, Nan called her and at every opportunity forced some nourishing drink on her. Mind, she did look better than when Mr Goodwin brought them both home, despite the fact that Patrick O'Leary had dropped out of her life for reasons unknown to Nan.

'D'you feel able to go for a walk?' Rose asked Alex solicitously. 'Just as far as the paddock to—'

'I do wish you'd stop treating me like a damned invalid, Rose Kellett,' Alex snapped irritably. 'What with you and Mother and Nan forever at me I feel about ninety-five.' The trouble was that for years Alex had had a purpose in life, had known that what she did was worth while. Her days had been filled with marches, rallies, mass meetings, demonstrations, protests, always some goal to achieve, some challenge to be overcome and now, apart from the deterioration in her health, she had lost the only man who had meant anything to her and she despaired, since she knew there would never be another. Her life was empty and at the same time she knew if she was to get back on her feet and do something worth while in the war effort, she must put up with the constant 'nagging' as she privately called it from Nan, Rose and her mother. Even her father, when he returned from the works, hung about her asking if she was feeling any better. She had for over five years been her own mistress, and this need to 'mollycoddle' her was driving her to despair. She put up with it for one reason only and that was she knew she could not hang about at Edge Bottom with no purpose in her life. She wanted, like Rose, to do something and, again like Rose, she wasn't sure what but if she was to be well enough to be accepted in some useful capacity she must be patient.

She put a hand on Rose's arm and when Rose turned to her she smiled. 'I'm sorry, Rosie, I'm an absolute bear but this inertia is driving me crazy. I must get well . . . I must and so I must put up with you all fussing over me like mother hens. And yes, I do feel I can totter as far as the paddock but you must promise to give me your arm if I should feel faint.'

'Of course I will, dearest, you are . . . oh, you.' She laughed when she realised that Alex was teasing her. 'And I won't even offer to help you from your chair.'

They strolled across the paddocks at the back of the house where what was left of the horses were peacefully grazing. Most of them had been commandeered by the army, for there were still generals of previous wars who believed the conflict would be won with brave cavalry charges, but the mowing pony was still there and the slow, elderly mare, too old for duties at the front. They both lifted their heads as the girls sauntered by, their ears swivelling at the sound of human voices. There was little to be done now in the stables, even the carriage horses gone and in their place was a rather splendid, silver-grey Vauxhall which her father had bought and learned to drive. Harry Preston was the only man, apart from the old gardener, left about the place, the rest having headed for the recruiting office in St Helens. Harry, along with his master, had had lessons and learned to drive the motor car, and he had his head under the bonnet as the girls passed through the yard. Harry's mother, who had once worked for the old people at Lantern Hill, was pensioned off in a cottage on the estate and Harry, no longer young himself, lived with her.

'Nice day, ladies.' He smiled, touching his finger to his cap in the old way.

'It certainly is, Harry. And how is your mother?'

'Nicely, thanks, Miss Alex,' watching his master's daughter limp across the cobbles, remembering the days when her real mother had abandoned her and left her to the care of Mrs Beth and Mr Archie. She'd made a lovely looking woman, though he'd heard she'd been mixed up with them madwomen up in London burning other folk's property and such. Well, perhaps she'd settle down now and find herself a nice chap. A couple of kids would do her the world of good, though she was getting on a bit. T'other one was a pretty little thing an' all and was said to be engaged to that chap who drove up in his Darracq now and again. Harry felt himself to be quite knowledgeable about motor cars though he did miss them horses!

Alex and Rose idled their way across the big meadow at the back of the house, the hems of their skirts brushing against the wild flowers that grew there and releasing their fragrance into the warm air. The scent of poppies, ragweed, meadowsweet, harebells and from the hedges where honeysuckle abounded, the drenching perfume rose about them. Butterflies were everywhere, a red admiral and scores of small tortoiseshell, and against the hedge, tall and stately, were the deep pink of foxgloves. The air was filled with country sounds, the buzzing of bumble bees frantically going about their business from flower to flower, the lowing of cows standing wherever they could get a bit of shade, and from somewhere far off the frantic barking of a dog.

They sat down, the two young women, each chewing on a blade of grass and Rose remarked idly, 'You look a lot better, Alex. More your old self. Mind, how could anyone not put on weight with Nan forever urging you to eat up? I love her, you know, and Nelly, and all of you. Especially you, dear Alex. My mother died when I was twelve and my father cares for nothing but books. I was an only child and as long as I wasn't "mithering" him – as Nan would say – he didn't really mind my coming to London when I was twenty-one. I don't think he knew what the dickens was going on. That's why I . . . I'm so fond of you all and why it will grieve me to leave you.'

Alex smiled and shook her head but continued to nibble on the stalk of grass. 'Now why am I not surprised, sweet Rosie, as your loving admirer calls you? When is Dick to go to France?'

'Next week.'

'And so you are off to see what you can find to do in his absence?'

'I can't loll about here for the rest of the war, Alex, and neither can you. We are not like . . . well, we have been fighting, working, doing things no well-bred lady should do. We know hardship and heartache. We have proved we are both strong-minded if our bodies are weaker than a man's so we must do something, not waste our strength. Let women who have known no hardship roll bandages and . . . and knit balaclavas and send packages to the troops. We can—'

'Nurse, perhaps?'

'Yes. They are advertising for recruitments to the Voluntary Aid Detachments in London or in France. Are you game?'

Alex laughed out loud and Rose was 'made up' as they said in Lancashire with the improvement in her dear friend's looks. Her face had taken on a rosy hue, for she had caught the sun and her hair, which she kept cut short, stood up in attractive curls on her head. It bounced when she walked and since there was a bounce in her step these days she was almost herself again. If she wept for Patrick O'Leary she did it in private and none of them, least of all her, mentioned his name. He was in France, no one knew where, and Dick, who as Rose had said was to go next week, made a promise at least to Rose that he would find him and send them news. Rose would not give up on the hope that one day Alex and Patrick would reach for one another again, especially now that the WSPU no longer stood between them.

It was a sad moment for them all at Edge Bottom House,

even the servants, as Rosie Kellett bade them all a mournful farewell. Not that Rose wanted it to be mournful but Mary and Ruth in the kitchen, Dottie, the parlour-maid, Mrs Adams, Nan and Nelly standing at the front door to wave her off, sniffing sadly, handkerchiefs to their eyes, all seemed to believe she was off to the trenches and would never more be seen, at least by them. Harry, Mr Goodwin's chauffeur, was to drive her to the station in St Helens and old Solly, the gardener, surprised them all by bringing her an enormous bunch of Mrs Goodwin's roses, all white which to him symbolised the purity of Miss Kellett's actions. The servants were sadly depleted in this month of September, for most of them had gone charging off to the nearest recruiting station to join up like the rest of the wildly excited young men. Sidney, the butler, Billy and Nathan Williams, both gardening lads, and Alfie and Robbie who had worked in Mr Goodwin's stables and who had all reacted to that pointing finger of Kitchener's. Whatever position you took up, Billy told Harry Preston, the finger was always pointing at you and how could you turn your back on it? He and his brother Nathan couldn't, although their mam gave them the rounds of the kitchen when they told her!

The world as they knew it was coming to an end, though they weren't aware of it. The weather was so beautiful and up and down the country garden parties, tennis parties and village fêtes were all taking place, not that those concerned the servants in the big houses, and especially at Edge Bottom House where the two young ladies were recovering from their fight, which had taken place with that daft lot up in London. They marched away, the young men, many of them under the age of nineteen, which was the legal age for joining up, whistling 'It's a Long Way to Tipperary' which was to be *the* song of the war. It had become a hit in 1913 and its appeal had by no means worn out a year later when the first great cavalcade of British soldiers marched to war.

So they all cried when Rose left to whatever she was to do, for she was such a lovely lady, but perhaps that sweetheart of hers, whom she was to meet in London before he went to France, would persuade her to marry him and then she would be safe at home, which was where all young ladies like her and their own Miss Alex should be.

Alex did not weep. Soon it would be her turn and as yet she had made no definite decision as to what she would do. She could drive a motor car since Patrick had taught her one weekend when they had motored up from London to visit her parents – aeons ago it seemed to be now – but her subconscious mind urged her to be where she might see Patrick. He was in France, she had been told, and though they needed ambulance drivers to carry the wounded from the front to the hospitals, she held back for a week or two, marking time, first to get back her strength fully, and second to make some enquiries about the possibility of becoming a member of the Voluntary Aid Detachment, a VAD. Here her parents' old friend, Doctor John Bennett, old in years as well as experience, was able to pull a few strings and secretly, for she did not want her parents to be worried, found her the information she needed. She was not awfully sure whether nursing appealed to her, particularly after a chat with Doctor Bennett. She must join one of the Voluntary Aid Detachments, he told her, of which there were at least 2,000 spread across the country, comprising 74,000 enthusiastic members, but if she was serious he could probably again pull some strings and get her into one of the teaching hospitals. She would learn to put on splints and bandages and although she would be attached to a nursing unit she would probably never touch a wounded man. She would scrub floors in the hospitals, clean sluices, push the sister's trolley round, accompanying her from bed to bed and be a general dogsbody.

'Will I get to France, d'you think, Doctor?' she asked him,

and felt the old man's eye on her. His gaze held suspicion. He had known Alex since the moment she was born, for it was he who had delivered her and he knew of her activities during the last five or so years. His wife had been her grandmother's dearest friend and the lives of the Goodwins were inextricably linked to those of himself and his wife. He knew of this young woman's strength of character, her determination to do or be whatever she chose. So what was she up to now, apart from asking him about the VADs? All the young women of the upper middle classes who had, from birth, led lives of privilege but not the freedom Alex Goodwin had known, wanted to do their bit. They 'came out' when they were eighteen, lived very comfortably with lots of servants and did no physical work at all but this young woman knew what it was to suffer and was therefore more likely to understand the sufferings of others. He had heard she had what was euphemistically called a 'young man' but nothing, it seemed, had come of it so he supposed she now wanted to fill the gap that the end of suffragism had left.

'Why do you want to go to France, Alex?' he questioned her. 'There are many hospitals in Britain would take you as a VAD. An old friend of mine runs a VAD convalescent hospital down south and if I asked her she would probably take you on at once. But as for France who can say what is to happen there?' He smiled ironically. 'It might all be over by Christmas and then . . .'

'You don't believe that, do you, Doctor Bennett?'

'No, I don't, Alex. Already there are heavy casualties. Sixteen thousand in the retreat from Mons, so I've been told, and don't ask me how I know – let me just say I have friends in the military. An old man of my age picks up many acquaintances during his life's span. There's heavy fighting and during the Battle of the Aisne many wounded and dead had to be left behind. And, my dear, we have hardly begun. It will get a lot worse before it gets better. Now how is that cough of your mother's? I hardly get out these days and Laura's the same. That new young Doctor Jameson is a good man but he tells me nothing. I think he believes I am senile and will not understand. How is she?'

Beth Goodwin who was, after all, only forty-seven, had developed a little cough, nothing to disturb her family who got used to the small dry spasms that shook her, and Nan, eagle-eyed where her family were concerned, dosed her with a mixture of honey, lemon and glycerine and kept her niggling little worries to herself. She knew Mr Goodwin would fall apart if his beloved wife so much as sneezed and Miss Alex was herself not totally recovered, but still Nan didn't care for the persistent little cough.

'Oh, she still has that bit of a cough but Doctor Jameson seems to think nothing of it.' Alex stood up and reached for her hat, prepared to leave, but Doctor Bennett put his hand on her arm to detain her.

'D'you think you could get her in to see me?' he asked casually.

Alex looked at him sharply, then sat down again, for she was not sure she liked the tone of Doctor Bennett's words.

'Why?'

'Oh, just humour an old man, my dear. I've been looking after the Goodwin family's health for a long time now and although I know Doctor Jameson will consider me an interfering old fool, I can't help it. Ask her to pop in some time, or perhaps you could bring her to see me yourself before you go gallivanting off back to London.'

'Doctor . . .'

Doctor Bennett got stiffly to his feet and put a reassuring hand on her arm. 'Now then, Alex, I only want to have a visit from an old friend and I'm sure Laura would be pleased to see her. She misses your grandparents since they moved to Lytham and although Abby writes regularly and begs us to go and stay with her we are getting on and the journey is a bit much at our age.'

'Doctor Bennett, why don't you let me drive you there in Father's motor car? I know he wouldn't mind and at the same time I could bring my mother to visit you. I'm not planning to return to London yet awhile, not until I've made up my mind where I can be of most use and I'd be glad of the change. I'm treated like an invalid at home, you know what Nan's like, although Mother doesn't fuss me as much. Now, what d'you say? Shall we all go to Lytham at the weekend and then the following weekend, or later if you want, I'll come and pick you up and bring you home. Please, go and consult Laura. I'll wait here and then—'

'Alex, my dear, shall we wait until I've had a look at your mother? You always were a lass who dashed into things without—'

'Thinking about the consequences?' She smiled and her face lit up, her eyes turning to that incredible lavender blue that never failed to astonish. 'I've been told that before now and . . . and . . . well . . .' Her eyes dimmed, for the last person to say it to her had been Patrick.

'Shall we say tomorrow then and if that doesn't suit tell Beth to telephone me and we'll make further arrangements.'

Harry had driven her over, as he was still inclined to consider her an invalid and he knew his master would not be best pleased if his precious daughter overdid it. He was in the kitchen with Doctor and Mrs Bennett's old servant, Biddy, who had come to them as a kitchen-maid. They were drinking tea and discussing the sadness of the war and all the young men, many from St Helens, who were marching off with a song on their lips and excitement in their hearts. They had both been employed for years in the same households and considered themselves to be part of the family and the thought of young Will, who was to fly one of them 'airyplanes', and young Tom, who was off to

France soon, was one neither of them cared to contemplate. Doctor and Mrs Bennett had no children or grandchildren but just the same it was a dreadful thing to see the trains going from St Helens to God alone knew where filled with the youth of the town.

Alex held her mother's hand as Doctor Bennett examined her, watching his face carefully, trying to decide what it was that, though he did his best to hide it, had warranted his unusual request. He smiled throughout the examination and chatted light-heartedly, smiling, though the smile did not reach his eyes. Alex prided herself that during her five years as a militant suffragette she had learned to read a man or woman's face and what was going on behind it. Sometimes it had been the difference between capture and escape if a constable or a plainclothes policeman let his intentions be known by his expression or the shift of a shadow in his eyes and she did not like what she saw in Doctor Bennett's eyes.

He sent her mother off to the sitting-room where Laura was waiting with tea, then when they were alone, he turned to Alex.

'I want your mother to have an X-ray. A chest X-ray.' His voice was serious. 'They have a new machine at the infirmary and—'

'Why?' She found she could say no more.

'She has . . . I can hear . . . but there is no good speculating. I don't care for this cough and from the sounds in her chest . . . well, my dear, you are a grown woman and an intelligent one. She has . . . it's her lungs that trouble me and so . . .'

'Please, is she seriously ill?'

'Not yet but it is better to be safe. What a silly old man I am . . . your father . . .'

'My father will not be able to cope, Doctor Bennett. There is no question of me leaving, not until she is recovered.'

# 13

By November the expectation that the war would be over by Christmas was accepted as false by the soldiers who fought in it and by the people at home. Antwerp had fallen and the first Battle of Ypres had begun, and in every town and city up and down the land young men besieged recruiting offices in answer to Lord Kitchener's call to arms.

Alex received a letter from Rose to say she had applied to the Red Cross to become a VAD and had been accepted. She had decided against being an ambulance driver, since no matter how hard she applied herself she just could not grasp the intricacies of the ambulance engine and a driver who could not maintain her ambulance was of no use at all. She had been made to realise that she was not mechanically minded and Dick had declared when she had practised in the Darracq that her talents lay elsewhere. The Darracq, by the way, was to be stored in a garage Dick had rented so that when he was on leave they would be able to get about. It had been rather sad to think of the lovely times they had had in her. Dick said she must call her 'her'! Anyway, she was to start work the next day at Number 3 General Hospital on Wandsworth Common and had already been issued with her uniform: a long grey dress, an apron that totally swamped her with a red cross on the bib and an enormous handkerchief headdress under which it was impossible to ascertain whether she was bald or not! She had visited her father and he had promised her a small allowance so that she could join immediately. Not much but enough to live on since she could eat at the hospital and would take up Mr Goodwin's kind offer to live at Bedford Square which would save her paying rent. She had seen Dick and they had spent a few days together before his unit was shipped across the Channel. But if he could see her in her VAD uniform she was sure he would break off their engagement immediately. Yes, she had agreed to compromise on the subject of marriage and Dick had given her an engagement ring before he sailed and she was now what was officially known as a 'fiancée'. Not that she could wear the ring on duty but it had made Dick happy, or at least *happier*. When was Alex to start on whatever it was that she was to do? she asked. She rather hoped she would join her, Rose, for she really felt as though she were doing her bit at last. She hoped all the family was well and to give them all her love. Again she must say that she was so grateful to Mr Goodwin for allowing her to use the house at Bedford Square, though she only used the one room, the kitchen and bathroom. Write soon, she told Alex, and if Alex was agonisingly disappointed that there had been no mention of Patrick in the letter she let none of them see it.

Her mother had had her X-ray and though Doctor Bennett smiled and told them not to worry, Doctor Jameson, being a younger and more 'modern' man, did not believe in obscuring the truth and drawing Alex to one side, recognising that she was the one with the strength to cope with it – he had heard she had been a suffragette and therefore must have what he called 'guts' which his patient's husband had not – told her that a shadow had shown on the X-ray which would need more investigation.

'In the meantime I want her to rest as much as possible. Get her to stay in bed until lunchtime and then perhaps an hour or so downstairs in the afternoon on the sofa. Make her drink plenty of milk, eggs, broth – she is not strong – get that cook of yours to feed her nourishing dishes: egg custards, that sort of thing and I'll look in a couple of times a week to check up on her.'

'But what is it, Doctor? Are you saying she has the consumption . . . or perhaps her heart . . .?'

And it was here that Doctor Jameson became a little vague and was disinclined to meet her eye. 'We must wait and see, Miss Goodwin. Doctor Bennett—'

'Why didn't you advise my mother to have an X-ray earlier?' she cried accusingly. 'Doctor Bennett—'

'Is an old man, Miss Goodwin, but he seems to have—'

'He is an experienced old man, Doctor.'

'Then you must consult him if you are dissatisfied with my treatment, Miss Goodwin.' It was plain that Doctor Jameson was highly offended and later that month when he left to go to Flanders as so many medical men were doing now that the casualty lists were growing longer and longer, Alex was relieved.

She made it her business either to drive over to Claughton Street where Doctor and Mrs Bennett had lived for nearly fifty years, ever since he and Laura had married, or to send Harry to fetch the old man. He often brought Laura Bennett as well which her mother enjoyed immensely though at the end of the visits she would be breathless and flushed. Alex began to notice that her mother appeared to have shrunk of late, as some people do with age but then Beth Goodwin was only forty-seven. When she came down in an afternoon she would seat herself carefully, arranging her skirt with slow, thin hands, her face sad and drawn, and Alex knew she fretted for her sons who were now both in France.

'You mustn't worry, Mother,' she would say cheerfully. 'You know how those two scamps avoid trouble. How many trees have you seen them climb and fall out of with nothing more than a scratch?'

'I know, darling, but everything is changing and I find it hard to get used to it.'

'Don't say that.' Alex moved to kneel in front of her. 'You know we all love you and . . .'

'I know you are eager to be off and that I am holding you back.'

'No, no, Mother, you mustn't say that,' even though it was true.

'Don't shout, darling, it gives me a headache.'

'Mother, I'm sorry.'

'I think I'll go back to bed now, dear.'

'Of course, let me . . .'

'Ask Nan to come, will you, darling.'

'I can help you, Mother. Let me . . .'

But Beth smiled faintly and shook her head. This girl of hers whom she loved dearly was too strong, too overpowering for her at the moment and when Nan came at a run, for that's how they all were in the despair of Beth's illness, Beth turned to her, relieved.

Half an hour later Nan came downstairs, her face haunted. Alex stood up and when Nan put her arms about her she began to cry. Nan didn't cry, for nothing could alter the fact that Beth Goodwin was leaving them.

Christmas came and went and the house moved carefully and slowly round the needs of the dying woman and the man who was her husband and who would die too when his wife did, they all thought. There was little left of Beth now, both in body and spirit. The wax of her beauty had all but melted away as the precious flame wavered and guttered but it was still there in a serene and delicate way. Archie had sent for Will and Tom and they had both been given compassionate leave. They came, Tom still with the mud and blood of France dried on his uniform, his young face, which had been as engaging and impish as a boy's, drawn and strangely old as so many of the young soldiers were these days. They did not talk, either of them, about their experiences. In his BE2 Will was engaged in reconnaissance and his young man's heart had been overwhelmed by the devastation he was forced to watch from the skies over the battlefields.

They smiled at their mother, what was left of her, and held her tiny, bird-like hand but had nothing to say and neither did she, for these silent, harrowed young men were not the handsome, laughing boys she had waved to as they marched off to war, excited, thrilled at the thought that soon they would be in it.

They had arrived just in time, for Beth Goodwin died the following day. It was March and across the lawn to the front of the house daffodils stood thickly, bright and lovely, and beneath the hedgerows in the lane that led to the church celandine threw out its cheerful yellow glory with primrose and wood anemone. Thrushes, blackbirds, robins, skylarks and chaffinches sang their hearts out as though in farewell to the woman who had loved the meadows, the fields, the house and garden where she lived all her life. The funeral was attended by so many folk who had known and loved Beth Goodwin since she was no more than a toddling child; a great crowd was forced to stand outside the church in the pale spring sunshine. Abby and Noah Goodwin, Beth's parents, had come over from Lytham, too devastated to speak, for it did not seem right that a child should die before her parents. They left soon after the interment, hurrying back to the place where they could be alone together in their sorrow.

Nan, Nelly, Mary, more friend than servant, Dottie and Ruth, who had been so brave and constant, never letting their mistress see their grief, wept openly now but Beth Goodwin's family stood straight, tearless, even her husband who, some said, would not be far behind her. His devotion to and reliance upon Mrs Goodwin had been well known and it was a good job that feckless daughter of hers, for so they thought of any woman who had any truck with suffragettes, was there to see him through. Her sons, stiff-faced and silent in their uniforms, stayed close to their father and it was noticed he was inclined to lean on one arm or another.

There was a funeral tea, small sandwiches passed round to Doctor and Mrs Bennett and others who had been close to Beth in her own suffragist's day, for she had been an ardent member of the women's movement which was where Alex Goodwin got it, they presumed. At the last moment, before they had gathered their hats and coats to leave the grieving family alone, a motor car driven by a chauffeur drew up at the side gate. The company stared, even the family, for all who had been invited were present. Out of the motor car a handsome woman stepped, helped out by an equally handsome man and a younger man, who was so like the two of them in a mixture of ways he could be no other than their son.

'Archie,' the woman said hesitantly, gently, and those present were stunned when Archie Goodwin stepped into the woman's embrace. They murmured a while, so overcome with emotion they could not seem to part, then the older man stepped forward and smiled, holding out his hand to Will.

'We are come from New York,' he said in an accent none of them had heard before, since they had never met an American. 'I am Todd Woodruff and the lady clasped in Archie's arms is my wife, your aunt Milly, your mother's twin sister. This is our son Noah. We left the rest at home. Noah is determined to enlist so . . . oh dear, I do beg your pardon. I am rattling on and I'm sure Milly is longing to put her arms round . . . is it Alex? It *is* Alex, isn't it?'

It took several long minutes before the mourners were sent on their way, for they longed to stand and gape at this man and woman who had had them all by the ears almost a quarter of a century ago. What a scandal it had been and yet would you look at them now, as respectable-looking as any of them.

But at last they had gone all except Doctor and Mrs Bennett who were such old friends and had been so irrevocably linked with the Goodwin family since before Beth and her sister Milly were born that they were persuaded to stay. It couldn't have happened at a more opportune moment, for though Archie had just buried his beloved wife and was sunk in despair, the arrival of Milly, her husband Todd who had shared the schoolroom with them as children and their son Noah, took his mind off the sadness of the day. There was great excitement in the kitchen where Cook, Nan, Nelly and the rest of the kitchen staff rushed about preparing a meal for the latecomers.

Milly was dressed in the latest fashion, expensive, elegant. She wore a day dress with a high-collared, jacket-like bodice and an open tunic overskirt in a rich tawny shade which was the same colour as her hair. Alex decided that it owed none of its hue to nature! She wore a perky hat almost like a beret on which was curled a long feather, and on her feet patent leather laced 'Russian' boots. She carried a long, furled parasol. Her husband, evidently influenced by transatlantic styles, was casually dressed in what had become known as a lounge-suit with broad shoulders, an easy, deep cut to the armholes and peg-top trousers tapering to the ankle. Their son, who was tall, lean and amiably grinning at them all, wore a knitted jersey with a number nine printed on the back, full, casual flannel trousers, no hat and what he explained later were a pair of American shoes with a blunt, round toe. He had his mother's deep brown eyes but the rest of him was his father: dark untidy hair, powerfully broad shoulders, lean-waisted and was obviously the apple of his mother's eye.

Milly explained, through her tears for her sister, that though they had received Archie's telegram they had been unable to get passage on a ship in time to see Beth before her . . . her death. Todd had a lot of influence in New York where he was a successful businessman but what with the war and one thing and another this was the best they could do. She would go at once to visit her sister's grave and place flowers there if Archie felt up to accompanying her, and Alex could see that this bright, intelligent and sensible woman was the best thing that could have happened. The first visit to Beth's grave, even if the interment had only happened that very morning, would be got through with her help. She was not the sort of woman to stand for any undue sentimentalism. She had loved her sister and been fond of Archie in their younger days and would, if she could be persuaded to stay a while, allow Alex to leave. She felt a pang of remorse and guilt that this thought should occur to her on the day of her mother's funeral but it was March, the war seven months old and she needed to do her bit, as they were all saying.

Her aunt Milly . . . Dear God, *her aunt Milly was in reality her very own mother* and Noah was her half-brother but some-how she could not get to grips with this phenomenon of her birth. Her mother lay buried in the graveyard to where her father – her adopted father – was preparing to take Milly, Todd and Noah Woodruff to pay their respects.

It was while they were gone, tooting off in the splendid, chauffeur-driven motor car, that Tom drew her to one side and asked her to sit with him and Will in the drawing-room, the room that still seemed to be gently filled by their mother. Will appeared to be sunk in some world of his own, fiddling with cigarettes and a box of matches, and though he was listening he did not seem to be unduly interested in what Tom had to say.

'What is it, Tom?' Alex asked him softly. It was strange the way her brothers hung together, treating everyone else almost as though they were strangers in whose home they had been billeted. There was a relationship between them that had nothing to do with being brothers and she knew they were not at ease. They seemed to want more than anything to get back to France, about which they never spoke. As though that were the real world, and this where they had been born and where they had grown up was no more than a dream from which they would soon awaken.

'I saw Patrick a few weeks ago,' Tom said shortly, drawing deeply on his cigarette. Alex drew in her own breath with a gasp and her chest felt as though a fist had been thumped against it. She could feel the blood draining from her head and was thankful she was sitting down otherwise she might have fallen. It was twelve months since they had quarrelled so bitterly and she had not seen him since. Rose and Dick must have talked to each other about him and about her but Rose never mentioned him so it seemed pretty apparent that Patrick had confided to Dick that he never wanted to see Alex again. Her heart was breaking as it had done for months now, a dull ache that constantly nagged at her and she wondered dreamily how long it took for a heart and a soul, for Patrick had that too, to mend.

'Oh . . .' was all she could find to say.

'He's in a field hospital behind the lines at Neuve Chapelle. There are many casualties, Alex. The whole of the front, some 350 miles of it, is bogged down but the high-ups in their wisdom continue to throw men at the defensive barbed wire and machine-guns and there are heavy losses. Jesus, I'm sorry, I shouldn't have told you that but you must understand. Will and I should get back as soon as possible.' He smiled a bright and artificial smile. 'Now you mustn't worry. Will and I are—'

'Don't talk such bloody rot, Tom,' she answered harshly. 'I'm not your usual well-bred young woman who cannot be told the true picture of what's going on. Anyway' – she had had time to recover some of her composure – 'how was Patrick?' She could think of nothing else to say, or ask.

'Well, I was down from the line on an errand for my captain and there he was, sitting outside a café drinking coffee. I was surprised to see him there when the casualties were so . . . but he said that he couldn't stand another . . . well . . .' He coughed to cover his confusion, for the haggard, expressionless face of the man who had once been in love with his sister had shocked him. He had himself seen enough sights to drive any man over the edge of sanity but Patrick looked as though he had come from an abbatoir instead of a field hospital, even to the dried blood on his hand and under his fingernails, and he supposed that must be how it was. He hoped to God he himself would never see the inside of one!

'He asked after you and I said you were nursing Mother. "I wondered why I hadn't seen her over here with the others," he said. "She did love a good fight." That's all he said then he stood up and walked away.'

He and Will left the next morning, as eager to be away as though they were off to a school reunion. They looked better than when they had arrived, for Nan, being Nan, had almost force-fed them with every good thing she could lay her hands on. Their uniforms had been stripped off them and the women in the kitchen had cleaned and pressed them, polished their boots, wiping off the tears that fell on them, and saw them off with cheerfully smiling faces which, the moment the Vauxhall was out of sight, became wet with tears. Archie stood for five minutes looking at the curve in the lane where they had disappeared and would have drifted into a brooding state of grief had not Milly and Todd whisked him off on some pretext or other in the splendid Rolls-Royce Todd Woodruff had hired for the duration of their stay in England.

Alex was polite to the woman she called Aunt Milly but she could not forget that this woman who was her blood mother had abandoned her at birth. Doctor Bennett had told her when he thought she was old enough to understand that her father, her blood father, had given her mother some dreadful disease that had been passed on to her in the womb which was why she had a deformed foot. No, she owed her life and everything she had done in it, which included her fight for the enfranchisement of women, to the woman they had just buried and to the man to whom she had been married. They had given her all that a child needed to grow strong, to become a complete adult, a responsible, fully developed grown-up, allowing her to think and to decide on her own future. She knew she was different from many young women of her age who had been protected from life and had passed, like a child, from father to husband with no thought in their heads but what their protector, whether it be father or husband, had put there. So perhaps that was why Patrick had decided that she was not the woman for him. She was too independent and men did not like independence in the women they chose to partner them through life.

She lay in her bed at night, or sat at the open window smelling the night scents of the fields and woods about her, sleepless, restless, filled with a longing she could not crush, swamped with despair which she knew would be with her for ever if she did not leave here and reach out for some worthwhile labour, some job of work that would challenge her. She had led an active life, done a job of work for the women of the country ever since she had been old enough to join the WSPU. She admitted to herself that she could not have left her father to cope with her dying mother. She had done her duty as a loving daughter but now she must leave. She must get to London, join *something* that would help to win this war which was wiping out young men in their thousands. She could not stop here weeping for a love that was lost, for that was not her nature but it would be hard to leave her father in his sorrow.

The next day her problem was solved for her by Noah Woodruff who she had of course realised was her half-brother. At luncheon, as they were eating one of Cook's superb soufflés with salad, Noah put his knife and fork on his empty plate and with a rather guilty smile directed at his mother declared that he was to be off the following day.

'Off where, son?' his father asked, though he knew damn well why Noah had come with them to England. Like a lot of young Americans who were aware that America must enter the war at some time, he was eager to get to France and fight alongside the 'Tommies'. He especially, since both his mother and father, although they were now American citizens, were of English blood, felt the need to get in on it.

'To London, Pa. You knew that was what I had in mind when I came over here. I intend to join up and help—'

'Now, Noah, darling, there is plenty of time for—'

'No, Ma, there isn't. You've seen the casualty lists in the newspapers.' Which was perhaps an unfortunate remark for a son to make to his mother. But Milly Woodruff was made of stern stuff and though Alex could see she was upset she was not the sort of woman who shed tears in order to get her own way.

'Now, Noah—' his mother began again but he interrupted her gently.

'Now, Ma, you know we agreed.'

'I know that, darling—' but this time it was Alex who interrupted.

'I intend going to London myself as soon as . . .' She stopped, for she had been about to say, '. . . as soon as Father can be left.'

But Archie Goodwin stood up and came round the table to where she sat. He put his arms about her and rested his cheek on her springing hair. 'My darling, you are to go whenever you are ready. You and I have . . . have looked after your mother. You have been my support and I love you for it but your work is somewhere else and I can't . . . won't stop you. Go with Noah with my blessings on both of you . . . but . . .'

'Father . . .?'

'Take care of yourself. You are very dear to me, daughter.'

*     *     *

She and Noah caught the through train from St Helens to London, a journey of 202 miles, slightly ill at ease with one another, both aware that they were half-brother and -sister. She had invited him to stay with her and Rose at Bedford Square until he enlisted and went to France and he had been volubly grateful. He was of English heritage, had been born in St Helens so there should be no difficulty in him getting into the army, he said optimistically and she found she was beginning to like him, for, after all, his mother's, *her mother's* transgressions were not his fault. He was so cheerful, so full of the joys of spring, longing to be in on it, to have a big adventure. He was not after a commission, he told her. He wanted to be an ordinary Tommy fighting beside other ordinary Tommies from all over the country and then he would go home, as he called America, and settle down, with no thought in his cheerful heart that he might go the way of thousands of ordinary Tommies who were being flung indiscriminately against the German lines.

They took a cab from the station to the house since between them she and Noah had a considerable amount of luggage. She looked about her as they travelled the length of Gower Street towards Bedford Square and she was amazed at the number of men in uniform. As they were about to turn into the square a police constable stepped out into the road and held up his hand to stop the traffic. It was as though a funeral were about to pass, so hushed did the usual hubbub become, but along the road came a procession of ambulances, about a dozen of them with a huge red cross painted on the side. It was halted for a moment and from one of the vehicles drifted a sound that she could not identify. A sort of sighing, choking, moaning sound, a rustling of wounded men who were on their way to the Middlesex Hospital, the cab driver told them.

They did not speak, either of them, until they reached the

house and there was Rose smiling on the doorstep, dressed in her uniform and as she held out her arms and smiled at Alex her eyes were on Noah and his on her and as brown eyes met violet the expression in them was not hard to fathom.

# 14

Rose had been awarded her First-Aid Certificate which entitled her to dress cuts and grazes and bandage broken limbs. She was allowed to smooth pillows, make beds, sweep floors, empty ashtrays, scrub lockers and concoct a very tasty beef tea, but was not to think of taking a temperature, she told Alex and Todd over dinner that evening. She was nothing but a glorified housemaid, she laughed, but with the retreat of the BEF at the end of last year the wounded were beginning to flood the hospitals and they had been so busy sister had actually directed her to hold the stump of an amputated leg while it was irrigated. A solution of eusol and peroxide is poured over the stump and . . . well, she shouldn't talk about it when they were just about to eat but . . . pus flooded over her hands . . . oh, dear God . . . it was horrific! Yes, she sighed, she had nearly fainted, but she had done it and against all the rules she had held the soldier's hand afterwards, for he had suffered a great deal of pain and could she in all conscience have walked away and left him to bear it alone? Sister had given her what for afterwards but it had been worth it to see the soldier relax into his pillows. No matter how hardened she was supposed to become she would never achieve it. The soldiers came first, didn't Alex agree?

Both Alex and Noah listened in reverent awe and great admiration to Rose's tale. Alex had put her arms about her and whispered how proud she was to be her friend and Noah was ready, given the slightest encouragement, to kneel and worship at the feet of this young woman who, an hour ago, he had not known existed. He had loved her at once, of course, and could you blame him, for not only was she brave and kind, she was the loveliest girl he had ever met. She was nursing what was left of the BEF which had suffered ninety per cent casualties in their retreat from Mons and Noah Woodruff was longing to join the men of the Territorial Force that was flooding to France to reinforce them.

It was a makeshift meal, for neither girl had learned the art of cooking having always had someone like Nan, or, in Alex's case, Cook at Edge Bottom House, to see to their needs, so they were both surprised and delighted when Noah told them he made a 'swell' omelette and with salad he promised them it would be delicious, that's if they were agreeable. It seemed he had gone to summer camp, as he called it, as a boy and it was there he had been taught to knock up a meal. Since it was only the three of them there was no need to open the dining-room, where the furniture was covered in dust sheets. Surely they could eat in the kitchen, he asked with raised eyebrows, its huge scrubbed pine table adequate not only for preparing the salad but for them to eat off. No, they didn't need a tablecloth, this was a picnic and perhaps if a bottle of wine could be found, what more did they want? Cheese, grapes, a bit of fruit and they had a feast.

The kitchen was enormous, probably the biggest room in the house, with a dresser of scrubbed pine to match the table. The dresser held scores of plates of different sizes, meat plates, dinner plates, gravy boats, cups, saucers, oval fish plates, jugs, sugar bowls, all in the same pretty blue pattern of willow trees on a background of white. There were copper pans, again of every shape and size, hanging on the walls about the room, a poss tub, a poss dolly and a mangle with wooden rollers with which Nan and Nelly had dealt with the household laundry. Filling one wall was a blackleaded cooking range with a fire at its centre on which a kettle could be boiled or a pan be placed to fry bacon or indeed the omelette which Noah had whisked up with a dozen eggs. On either side of the fire was a roasting oven and above it a shelf for warming plates and above that another shelf where stone storage containers stood in a neat line. Before it lay a rag rug stitched together by Nan and on the rug was a tuffet on which she rested her feet. There was a rocking-chair on one side of the fire and a plain upright Windsor chair on the other where Nelly had been allowed to rest of an evening when her chores were done. Everything shone and winked and on the wall a clock ticked cheerfully.

Alex and Rose found Noah to be good company, easy-going with a sense of fun that delighted them, Alex particularly, since there had been little laughter at Edge Bottom in the last few weeks. She had been glad to get away, for the sight of Milly Woodruff – there was no way she could call the woman Aunt and certainly not *Mother* – giving orders to her mother's servants was unbearable. She had buried her beloved mother in the churchyard at St Cuthbert's Church where she and Father had been married and where the Goodwin family plot was situated. She could not bear to see Noah's mother sitting in what had been *her* mother's favourite chair nor listen to the reminiscences of the childhood she had shared with Beth and Archie Goodwin. But she was quite charmed by Noah, and so was Rose. Alex loved her brothers who had left for France and worried about them, for they were both so changed from the cheeky-faced lads they once had been; but this one, her half-brother who had not yet suffered the trauma of war, quite delighted her with his confidence, which was in no way over-bearing, his unhurried movements about the kitchen, his sunny good looks, and it was evident that Rose thought so too. Rose looked like some angel of mercy, at least that was how she would seem to Noah in her nurse's uniform, which she wore since she was to go on duty at midnight. She had not yet put on her headdress and her dark, glossy hair, which she still wore in a huge coil at the back of her head, her small, slender, graceful figure, the perfect oval of her face and the impact of her incredible violet eyes were very evidently much to Noah's liking. He was not aware, of course, that Rose was engaged, for she did not wear the ring Dick had given her.

While Alex was setting the table and Noah was at the stove with the frying pan, Rose hovering at his back in her role as kitchen-maid, there was a good deal of laughter between them and it was as though they had known one another for years.

When she had put out the plates and cutlery and found three wine glasses, searched in the cellar for a bottle of white wine and filled the glasses, Alex sat down at the table with the small ginger kitten, which Rose said had wandered in and which she had adopted, purring in ecstasy on her lap. She watched them and some inner sensibility, a female instinct, though instinct was not the exact word, told her that something was happening between them. *Sparking* between them which she had never seen between Rose and Dick. Whether they knew it or not, she couldn't tell, for they were both teasing one another in a most natural way, laughing, talking ten to the dozen, almost like children, and yet there was a tension in Noah that had not been there before. She chided herself for being silly, for Rose loved Dick and anyway, how was she to know what her half-brother's nature was. Perhaps he was just one of those men who will flirt with any woman passably pretty and since he could hardly flirt with his own sister Rose was the obvious choice. Alex had never met an American before but it was generally believed that they were far less formal than the English, even his casual manner of dress told her that. He seemed to wear nothing but knitted jerseys, a cap with a large button on the top, a tweed jacket with his flannels and his happy-go-lucky, come-day-go-day attitude was like nothing she had known before. Her own brothers were inclined to be undisciplined in the confines of their own home and its environs but they would not go about without a tie, or travel the world with nothing more formal than a knitted jersey! She found she liked Noah but she was not too certain that she approved of the way he was looking at Rose, nor Rose's somewhat startled return of that look.

'Where did this thing come from?' she asked, referring to the kitten purring on her lap, forgetting that Rose had already explained, doing her best to divert Rose from her attentions to Noah.

Rose turned and in a lovely gesture, which Noah watched with dazed eyes, she scooped the kitten from Alex's lap and held her up with two hands, her shining eyes gazing up at the delightful little creature, the lovely pure line of her throat causing Noah to pause in his task with the frying pan. 'Isn't she a sweetie? I call her Ginger, obviously, but I found her mewing piteously on the doorstep a couple of days ago. I couldn't turn her out, could I?'

'Of course not,' Noah said quite fatuously, the spatula with which he had been just about to lift out the omelette limp in his hand.

The omelettes were delicious eaten with the salad stuff which was the only food Rose had in the pantry since, she explained, she mainly ate at the hospital.

'But you will come home tomorrow when you are off duty, promise me . . . promise us,' Noah begged, looking as piteous as the kitten which had fallen asleep on Rose's lap. 'I'm off to the recruiting office.'

'Are you to enlist?' Rose sounded anxious and Alex could not help but think of poor Dick who was off God knew where in France fighting, not in the battles, but to save life. He had loved Rose for a long time but for some reason, a reason that she had explained to Alex and which had seemed quite logical at the time, she had put off marrying him. Now here they were, the pair of them, Rose and Noah, gazing speechlessly into one another's eyes, then dragging themselves so obviously back to this world, to Alex with such exaggerated politeness she was ready to laugh at them and tell them they were fooling no one.

'Oh yeah, the Yanks will be here soon, you mark my words. They won't be able to keep out of it, or so Pa says, and I want to be in it from the first. Already there are medical units in France and men from the United States longing to fight side by side with the limeys.'

'Limeys?' Alex and Rose said in unison.

'Yeah, it's what we Yanks call you, but never mind me. There's just one thing that bothers me, of course, but Pa says it will make no difference in the end. Any American who fights in a foreign army is likely to lose his American citizenship. Now, since I was born in England and Ma and Pa were too, I might get away with it but what the hell . . . oh, I do beg your pardon, ladies. Now that's enough about me. Tell me what you're up to, Rose. Are you nursing the wounded at . . . where is it?'

She had been reassigned to the Middlesex Hospital on the corner of Cleveland Street and Goodge Street, she told them, which was very handy for Bedford Square, but she was hoping for a post at Number 6 London General Hospital at Wandsworth where she might be allowed to do some real nursing. After all she had been a VAD for over five months now. It had once been an orphanage but the orphans had been despatched elsewhere and the building was now at the hub of a vast, sprawling encampment of hutted wards which received the never-ending stream of wounded men from France. 'I've heard that they are so overrun with casualties in France they are asking for volunteers to go there who have had three months' hospital training at home and who are twenty-three.'

'But you're not twenty-three, Rosie.'

'I'm twenty-two, Alex, and I mean to go. Even if I have to lie about my age.'

Noah looked horrified and Alex was convinced he was about to pick up Rose's hand and kiss it, to hold it firmly in his to prevent her pursuing this mad and dangerous scheme, but he refrained as common sense told him he had only met this lovely girl an hour or two ago and must behave accordingly. He knew how *he* felt and was pretty certain she felt the same but nevertheless, he must be patient, he told himself, especially with his newly found sister looking on.

Leaving Alex to clear up he insisted on escorting Rose to the Middlesex even though she protested that she had been doing it every night for weeks.

'It doesn't matter, Rose, while I am here you will allow me to walk with you to the hospital. After all, it is nearly midnight and then tomorrow, after I have enlisted we' – turning hastily to include Alex – 'will take in a show and a meal. Don't you think that would be swell? We must see as much as possible of each other until I get overseas,' looking at Rose but doing his best to include Alex.

When Rose and Noah left, the ginger kitten who had been placed on a cushion on the chair launched herself at Alex in a fit of fright and for half an hour she sat with her purring on her knee before the fire. As usual her thoughts turned achingly to Patrick and she pondered on the possibility of becoming an ambulance driver because if she did the first thing she would do would be to put in for a transfer to France. She was slowly coming to the realisation that no matter what she did, or in whose company she found herself, she could not get on with her life until she had seen him again. He might recoil from her. He might have another life, another love but she must know, she must be absolutely certain that there was to be nothing more of Patrick O'Leary in her life. He was presumably in the thick of it in France with very little time to consider the woman he had once loved but she had had weeks, months to brood on it. She had no idea what would, *could* be said between them but she needed it and if he should spurn her – *dear God, she could not bear the thought* – then she must find something to fill her empty days. Universal enfranchisement would surely be granted when this war was over so how was she . . .

The sound of the front door opening cut off her sad thoughts. The kitten awoke and stretched as Noah came into the kitchen, ready, she could see, to eulogise about Rose but with a forced smile she rose to her feet and after showing him, reluctantly on his part, to his room, she went to hers, the kitten still in her arms, and without even a wash flung on her night-gown and crept into bed.

The BEF had suffered enormous losses and the call for volunteers vastly exceeded the ability of the tiny pre-war army, which had been so decimated, to cope with the need to train and equip those who were sent over. A fortnight's training was all that could be managed and most of that was in drilling, which was of no use whatsoever at the front. The army was overwhelmed with the problem of equipping 100,000 newly enlisted civilians and turning them into soldiers. Join up, join up, they exhorted them and when they did the War Office was engulfed. Noah Goodwin, now Private Noah Goodwin, some-where on the South Downs, he didn't know where, he wrote to Rose, was marched about, taught how to fall out and have a smoke, played football and did physical jerks and when, eventually, he crossed the Channel with his new rifle he had never even fired it!

Alex had been to the Red Cross headquarters in the Mall and was accepted as an ambulance driver since she could not only drive, but repair her vehicle, which many of the girls could not. She had received her uniform and taken part in a short course on the most rudimentary aspects of first-aid delivered in the form of lectures. She was introduced to ambulance driving by taking turns in the three ancient Siddeley-Deasy models kept by the Red Cross for this purpose, and since she had rooms of her own in London was allowed to return home each night.

The others, who had come from many parts of the country, were billeted in a dormitory close by the ambulance station in what had once been a convent school.

Up to the end of March 180,000 casualties had passed through the hospitals in France. It was towards the end of April that the really heavy casualties began to arrive in England, the war suddenly knocking on the doors of the military hospitals from the Battle of Ypres. On 22 April the Germans made the first effective use of gas poison to attack a French and British position at Ypres and many of the soldiers caught in it were sent home, since the casualty stations in France were overrun with the wounded and could not cope with them. The casualty lists were quite horrendous, day after day, column after column in the newspapers, filling whole pages. Since the day in August when the army had first crossed the Channel, the BEF had practically been wiped out, and Alex agonised on the fate of Patrick who had gone with them, frantically sharpening her skills, not only as a driver but with first-aid, desperate to be ready when the call for an ambulance brigade came through. Noah wrote that the Yanks were spilling into the front lines with breathtaking speed, for thousands of young men like himself had poured across the border into British Canada and enlisted there. They too had not been deterred by the United States law that said any man who enlisted in a foreign army would automatically relinquish his US citizenship.

Both Rose and Alex were wakened nearly every night by the shrilling of the telephone with orders to report at once to their respective posts.

'Charing Cross, Goodwin,' the sister in charge shouted at her, 'and take a VAD with you, one with some experience.' And so it was that Rose and Alex who had shared so many frightful, frightening experiences as suffragettes were to share their first horror of gas warfare which no one in the medical profession had yet encountered.

They drew up at Charing Cross Station, Alex expertly parking her ambulance in the line of others waiting for the casualty train to draw up to the platform, long grey trains with red crosses on the side. Alex was given a number and when she heard her number called she was to bring her vehicle as near as possible to the platform. There were detachments of stretcher-bearers with their own commandants and they waited, nurses, ambulance drivers and stretcher-bearers standing together.

'I have a dreadful horror of one night looking down at a stretcher and seeing the face of someone I know,' Rose whispered and for some reason her hand, which had stroked so many pitiful, dirty, bloody faces of unknown men in her compassion, slipped into Alex's and they clung together as though at some premonition.

'I know,' Alex replied in a low voice, then said, 'Rose, when Tom was home for Mother's funeral he told me he had seen Patrick. I didn't say anything but if Dick mentions him to you in a letter would you let me know. I . . . I want to know where he is.'

'You still love him?'

'Yes.'

'You never mention him so I didn't either. I didn't want to open a . . . well, you know what I mean. In Dick's last letter he said that Patrick was . . . was close to the line in a field dressing station.'

'Yes, he would be.' Alex's voice was sharp with bitter agony.

'But the need for surgeons called him back to a casualty clearing station beyond the range of the enemy guns.'

'Thank God.'

'Is that why you want to go to the front?'

'Yes. One of the reasons.' They could hear in the distance the rumble of the approaching train and every man and woman on the platform tensed.

'Oh, darling . . .'

'Please, Rosie, don't say any more.'

'No, of course not.'

It was eerily quiet at the station as the train slowed and drew to a stop. Most of the ambulance drivers had, of course, met trains packed with wounded before and with the help of the stretcher-bearers, who actually lifted the wounded from the train, had really done nothing but back their vehicles to the required position, waited until the ambulance was filled four into each and, at the signal and their destination, driven away to the designated hospital. They had listened pityingly to the moans and rustling whispers, the occasional scream of a wounded man as a stretcher was jolted, but their job was to get the soldiers from the station to the hospital as quickly as possible where, again, stretcher-bearers lifted the soldiers from the back of the ambulance and carried them into the hospital.

But this was the first time any of them had had anything to do with gas cases. The men on the stretchers were struggling for breath, a terrible rasping sound in their throats and chest as they tried to get air into their damaged lungs. Their faces were blue and livid but worst of all was the terror in their eyes as the fluid rose higher and higher in their lungs, threatening to drown them. Those whose eyes had been affected by the gas were blinded and trapped in their suffocating bodies and others had, beside the agony of the gas, wounds caused by shrapnel.

'Oh, dear sweet Jesus,' Rose moaned, for a moment hesitating in what she knew was her job. It was her nature to comfort, to soothe and she had been in trouble many times with sister since it was beyond her to be dispassionate as she was told to be. 'You must harden yourself, Nurse, for without detachment you are no good to these boys. We are too busy for you to sit by a wounded man's bedside and hold his hand. Do you understand?'

'Yes, Sister,' her face calm and steadfast, and sister had sighed, for she had known Nurse Rose Kellett would continue to 'pet', as sister called it, any man whom she was nursing.

Now, in the face of so much agony she was momentarily overwhelmed. She spent a great deal of her time polishing floors that had been stained with Condy's fluid and scrubbing acres of skirting board with a small brush, all in the interest of hygiene, washing windows, sluicing stone floors, but recently since there were so many wounded and so few nurses she had been allowed to take temperatures, give injections and even dress wounds that were healing.

'Come on, sweet Rosie,' Alex said harshly, 'it's no good weeping over them,' unaware that her own face as well as Rosie's was wet with compassionate tears. The inhumanity of man against man, the beastliness of this scene from hell had rendered them all speechless and paralysed, and not until a commanding voice brought them out of their trance of horror did they leap into action. Alex's number was called and she backed her ambulance to the side of the train. Four whimpering, sighing, murmuring men, still with the mud and blood of the trenches on their uniforms, in their hair, and plastered across the bandages some of them wore, were placed as gently as though they were crates of eggs into the back of her ambulance. Rose was in the back with the soldiers and Alex could hear her soft, low voice murmuring to them and knew Rose would be holding each hand in turn, dripping her tears on each face. She heard one hoarse male voice, barely able to speak, thanking Rose and telling her she was not to upset herself. Many of these soldiers were from rough and ready homes and had never spoken to a lady, a real lady in their lives and they were pathetically grateful for the attention the ladies gave them. And to have one of them cry for them helped them to bear their suffering more calmly. It was like having their own mam beside them. The gas had seeped into their uniforms as they had stumbled to the aid post and since then they had been on fire, with festering sores where the gas had eaten into their bodies. Their eyes had been scorched by a flame and were gummed together with sticky pus. They were all four of them panting and choking as the gas destroyed their lungs and yet they were distressed because they had made her cry! It was almost more than she could bear.

Rose was never to weep again, at least where she could be seen, over the men she cared for, since she knew, though she had comforted the gassed men, the blinded, choking soldiers, she had not really done her job. She was loveable, sweet-tempered and steadfast, wanting with the greatness of her gentle heart to take each wounded man in her arms and hold him, but from that day on she steeled herself to be as sister told her. If she was to be any good for the soldiers she nursed she must stiffen her resolution and her heart.

She was surprised when one of the men, an officer she thought, for his uniform was different to the others, spoke her name. Just a harsh rattling in his throat which at first she did not recognise. She smiled in the blurred darkness of the ambulance and moved to bend over him and again he said something which at last she recognised as her own name.

Her heart thrust wildly against her ribcage, for his uniform could belong to any of the men she knew who had gone to the front. Patrick, Dick, Noah or even Alex's brother whom she had met last year at Edge Bottom House. They were all in khaki but in the darkness and covered in filth it was difficult to identify anyone, or even their uniform.

'What is it?' she asked fearfully, for if it was Noah Goodwin lying choking on the stretcher she would be destroyed, wondering as the thought exploded in her mind why she had not admitted it to herself before this.

'Rose . . .?'

'Yes . . . who . . .?'

'Alex's . . .'

Writhing on the stretcher with his face swathed in bandages was Tom Goodwin.

# 15

They marvelled at the fates that had decreed that they should stay together. For nearly two years, ever since they had set out eagerly to deliver the WSPU newspaper in the gig which Rose could not drive since she had never had anything to do with horses, they had been inseparable. Like sisters they had been, as fond and close as sisters, suffering the torment of Holloway together, the manhandling that had led to it, the force-feeding and the draining of their health which they had recovered together at Edge Bottom House.

Since then they had dodged through the busy streets of London in the ambulance carrying their precious, damaged cargo of casualties and though Rose was a VAD and Alex an ambulance driver, chance seemed to throw them together as it did when they were both told they were to go to France. That year of 1915 was to be remembered as one of stalemate, with the allies making little advance on the position they had held since August the year before.

As Archie Goodwin, lonely and growing considerably older-looking without his dear wife and the departure of his three children into the theatre of war, said to Alex when he came up to London to visit his wounded son, 'There's too many bloody men in command, Alex. There's Lord Kitchener who believes he is the commanding voice, General Joffre and the Grand Duke Nicholas in Russia, all with different ideas on how this war is to be won. The Germans, with their usual Teutonic thoroughness, are producing ammunitions and enlisting soldiers as fast as they can and in the meanwhile poor lads like Tom are getting crucified. We cannot stand any more losses like those at Neuve Chapelle and Ypres and I can tell you . . . oh, darling, I'm sorry but Tom's wounds have made me . . . what will be next? First your dear mother and now this with Tom.'

Tom Goodwin was threatened with blindness. At the age of twenty-two he had lost his sight in the gas attack at Ypres but the surgeon in charge told Alex privately, since he didn't want to raise the hopes of Tom's father, that in his opinion when the last of the treacherous gas, which was being treated with eye drops, had been cleared he might have some vision left. Each day his eyes were bathed, the gummy substance that glued his lids together soaked away, and each day he stared out at nothing and wished to God he was dead. And he hadn't even been fighting which made it all the more bitter. As he said to his father, he was standing in the bottom of the trench cooking his bit of breakfast of fried bacon and cheese. Though he was an officer he did enjoy the homely, domestic task of cooking. Sergeant Albert, who took a fatherly interest in his young officer, had made tea in his dixie and they were about to sit down in the comradely way that had sprung up in the trenches between officers and the ranks when one of the lookouts had shouted that lyddite shells were bursting along Jerry's trenches. Out of curiosity they had all jumped up to watch the yellow smoke, but about five seconds later the same lookout had shouted that it was not lyddite but gas. 'I at once ordered the chaps to open with rapid fire, but by this time the gas had reached us and then . . . well, our throats were blistered and men began to scream. We had nothing but a roll of bandage in our first-aid kit so we bandaged each other's eyes and when a soldier saw us just sitting there waiting for someone to take pity on us he led us back, each with his hand on the shoulder of the man in front. We got to the first-aid station and lay down in a field and then . . .'

Here Tom became silent. They couldn't even hold his hand, she and Rose and her father, for his flesh was still blistered, but he was a strong, well-nourished young man, come from a family who had never known want, and slowly he was recovering. Many others who had enlisted from the slums of London and the industrial cities of Britain and should not have been accepted into the army had died like flies, since they had not the stamina of men like Tom. Out of the 250 men who had been gassed only thirty-eight had survived and most of them were blind.

In a strange, sad way, though he would have gladly given his life for his son, Tom's blindness had put fresh impetus into Archie Goodwin's days, for he now had someone who needed him, someone to protect and care for, as he had protected and cared for Tom's mother. And now his daughter was going to that hell that had just spewed out his son. But he would look after Tom and he meant to get the best eye man he could to look at Tom's eyes.

On the day before she and Rose were to sail for France she went alone to say goodbye to Tom. The ward was jammed with beds, all holding a wounded officer, gentlemen who, though they had fought side by side with their men, had been wounded with them, had even been rescued by them, were segregated from the other ranks. There was scarcely room between the beds, only enough to allow the movement of a nurse or a doctor. The men in here were not allowed to smoke, since the smoke would irritate the lungs of the men who had inhaled the gas. This was the Fulham Eye Hospital and most of them had eye as well as lung injuries. Tom was in the end bed, sitting up, his eyes and hands bandaged and his head was turned towards the window as though he were gazing out on to the broad expanse of the common where children played with kites and dogs chased balls.

She spoke his name as she approached the bed and at once

he turned hopefully and it seemed to her he had been wishing for someone else. She thanked the nurse who had insisted on escorting her to Tom's bed as though she suspected her of being a danger to her patients, and then moved away to speak to a man who was bandaged from head to toe, or so it seemed, despite his pyjamas.

Alex kissed the bit of cheek that was visible under Tom's bandages. She heard herself ask the usual ludicrous question on the state of his health and was not surprised when he answered sarcastically, 'How the hell d'you think I am, for God's sake?' Then he bowed his head to his chest. 'I'm sorry, Alex, it's just the utter boredom.' He did not speak of the pain. 'I can't even read a bloody newspaper but then why should I want to? It's not going well over there, and . . .' He took a deep breath which made him cough and the nurse came hurrying over.

'You must not make your brother cough, Miss Goodwin,' and Alex was rewarded with a smile from Tom. For several minutes it seemed that neither of them knew what to say, then Tom, as though he could not keep it in any longer, whispered, his throat raw after coughing, 'I have had several visits from Rose, did you know?' Beneath his bandages he looked shy.

'Rose? She didn't say.'

'She was usually on her way to somewhere or other and just dropped in, she said. She's a lovely girl. Not that I can see her but I remember what a beauty she was when she came to Edge Bottom and her kindness . . . I look forward to her visits.'

Dear God, how many other men were going to fall in love with Rose, Alex thought wildly, wondering how her friend was going to manage this abundance of admirers, that's if you could call Dick, her fiancé, an admirer, and that's if they all survived the holocaust of the Western Front. Rose received letters from both Dick and Noah almost every day but their contents were not revealed to Alex. As Tom said, she was the kindest, most sweet-tempered girl, with a heart that did its best to enfold every soldier in her care so was that what she felt for Tom? Well, whatever she felt for any of them, someone's heart was to be broken.

'She said I had to tell you . . . well, I told *her* that when we, my men and I, were taken to the casualty clearing station . . . she said you ought to know because you were . . . asking after him . . .'

Alex felt the air about her press against her flesh and Tom's face seemed to blur and even tip as though someone had shoved against his bed. Her heart missed a beat then thumped erratically and her hands started to shake.

'What? Who?' she quavered and even though he was bandaged like a mummy and could not see her Tom put out a comforting hand, then withdrew it.

'Alex?'

'Yes, tell me.' She wanted to grab his poor damaged hand and shake it out of him, whatever it was he was going to tell her. Please, dear God . . . oh, sweet God . . . let him not be injured . . . dead, but then surely Rose would have found some other, more compassionate way to tell her.

'He treated me—'

'Where is he, tell me?'

'Well, I will if you'll shut up.' Tom was peevish as though he wished his sister would go, for the effort of talking to her was too much for him. When Rose came she didn't talk much, just touched his cheek or some part of his arm or hand that didn't hurt and often when she did this he fell into a healing sleep. But his sister was tense, tight with some emotion that played on Tom's already stretched nerves though he wouldn't have told her so for the world.

'It was a casualty clearing station at Bailleul. We were there for two days, the wards were full of men gasping for every breath but the word was to try and get in the care of "Mad Paddy".'

'Mad Paddy?'

'Yes, it seems he was the best of the lot. Caring and taking endless trouble even though he was run off his feet. He shouted a lot at the staff in an Irish accent, though it was said he came from Liverpool. It turned out to be Paddy O'Leary, the best doctor in the hospital, they said, and so when I asked for him and told them to say it was Lieutenant Tom Goodwin, he came. Alex, he looked after me like a baby and the other men began to think there was something . . . well, funny between us. D'you know what I mean? Have you heard of . . .'

He was frightfully embarrassed to be talking to his sister about the 'forbidden love', which was what it was called, but he was trying to explain what had happened.

'He even did what the nurses usually do, bathing my eyes and coming in during the night, or when he was off duty to look at me. The bandages I had on in the ambulance were the ones he put on. They had no time to clean our uniform, of course, so we arrived in Blighty pretty much in the same state we had been in when we left the battle.'

'Did he ask after me . . . mention my name?'

'No,' Tom admitted sadly.

'Bailleul?' Her heart was still racing, her pulse beating crazily and she found when she came to stand up, for really she must get out of here, that her legs refused to support her.

'Are you all right, Ally?' Tom asked her anxiously, using the name they had called her as a child. 'You were a bit gone on him for a while, weren't you?'

She managed to stand up and, leaning over him, gently kissed his cheek. 'Yes, I was a bit gone on him, lad. Now I must go. I'll ask Rose to come and see you before we sail tomorrow.'

'Yes.' His voice was glum and his bandaged hands plucked at the sheet. She touched them and they stilled and she began to realise the true effect Rose Kellett had on the men she nursed. Any gentle female physical contact, just that of a hand on theirs gave them the courage to go on. 'Goodbye, Tom, let's hope we'll all be home safe and sound before long.'

'Yes,' sighed Tom, though the very nature of the sigh told her he didn't believe it, no matter how much they hoped.

They were the only females on the troopship, Alex and Rose and several other girls who were VADs. They had said goodbye to her father and to Nan who had come up to London with him to 'see to him and Master Tom' as she put it at Bedford Square. And that rascal would need feeding up when he came out of hospital, she said and who better to do it than Nan Meredith who had known him since he was a cheeky little lad.

The boat was bursting at the seams with raw recruits come to Lord Kitchener's call, most painfully young and filled with the joys of spring in their optimism. They had never been away from home before and the Channel, which was ruffled by a disconcerting wind, made them sick and half of them hung over the sides for the whole voyage but they were off on the big adventure and that was all that mattered.

They were met at Boulogne by a command leader under skies that had turned grey, clouds scudding across the sky, while behind them the harbour was turbulent and the temperature noticeably lower.

'Detachment of ambulance drivers for Camiers,' someone shouted, and the girls, whose names they had not yet found out, stood up, Alex among them. There was Garvey, Kellett, Fenwick, Thorpe and Goodwin, all to go to Camiers and the VADs, all but one, were to go on by train to Etaples. The miracle was that Kellett, since one of their VADs had been sent home seriously ill, had been picked to report to Number 4 General Hospital at Camiers to replace her and was to go with the ambulance drivers. They couldn't believe it, Rose and Alex told one another in whispers, that even now they were not to be separated and how much easier it would be to get through whatever lay ahead if they could be together.

Along the whole of the battlefront, which had been hastily dug and fortified, the British Tommy lived in trenches and died in the blood, mud, slime and shell-holes of what was to be called no-man's-land. Barbed wire and entrenched machine-guns necessitated a prolonged artillery barrage before an attack which in turn removed the crucial element of surprise. So, on the Western Front a monstrous war of attrition developed in which hundreds of thousands of soldiers were thrown in repeated and hopeless assaults against the enemy. The allies dug in opposite the German army which had been halted at the Marne.

Throughout that summer the wounded poured into the hospitals at Camiers, at Etaples, Rouen, Bailleul and others, and Rose was thrown into it from the start. She had time only to change into a dress of mauve check cotton with a high starched collar fastened with a collar stud. There was a voluminous apron that covered her from neck to ankles, thick black stockings and flat-heeled black shoes. She wore a headdress made of a three-cornered handkerchief hiding her hair and dropping down to her eyebrows. The shining coil of her dark hair was totally invisible. She had gone beyond the confusion of sights, sounds and smells, which had initially horrified her, even terrified her, since she had been a VAD for seven months and though her heart still ached with the pain of the young soldiers she had learned to hide it, except from the men themselves. She had learned to cope with bedpans, thermo-meters, bed making, changing dressings and giving enemas; to steel herself against vacant, staring eyes and senseless inco-herent mutterings as delirious men rambled on about Mother, Bessie, the apple orchard, football, the four-ale bar, pints of beer and all the precious things that had been an accepted part of their lives before this one. She held mutilated stumps while sister irrigated the wound and changed the dressing, she shaved men and fed them, cleaned them up when they became incontinent, but worst of all, had learned how to make decent the broken bodies of the dead whose relatives, too late to see them alive, wept at the side of their loved ones.

There were two men in France of whom she thought a great deal and every day as fresh casualties were brought to her ward, from Neuve Chapelle, from the second Battle of Ypres where the first gas had been used and from the horror of Hooge where liquid fire had reduced the soldiers to living flame, she hesitated before looking down at the face of the wounded soldier on the stretcher in case it should be Noah. Dick was in a casualty clearing station about ten miles behind the line and in his letters he told her that as soon as he could he would borrow a bicycle and get over to see her, a visit she dreaded, for how was she to meet him and tell him of her feelings for another man? She had loved Dick and still did in a way, but her feelings for him were not to be compared to what she felt for Noah Goodwin. He also wrote to her, agonising on the danger she was in serving at a clearing station in France, but so far she had been granted no leave, not even an afternoon off.

The first time Alex was called out was a mere two days after she had arrived in France. The Battle of Neuve Chapelle was her first introduction to the task she had elected when she had joined the Ambulance Brigade. She and the others had spent their first full day checking the engines of the ambulances they were to drive but it was during the second night at about ten thirty that the whistle they had been told to expect shrilled out. Andrews, who was their section leader, put her head into their hut and began to screech, 'Convoy up the line! Convoy! Everybody out,' and now that they were fully awake they could hear the distant thunder of the guns.

'Oh God, oh God,' Garvey was muttering as she struggled

into her uniform, and even in the dim light Alex could see the paleness of her face.

'Bear up, Garvey,' she said, wondering if she would ever get used to calling a woman by her surname and having them speak to her the same way. The others were clattering down the steps at the end of the outside corridor and she could hear the cough and rattle of engines being started up.

She raced along the line of vehicles and cursing with impatience attached the handle. The engine sparked and spluttered at the fifth attempt and, trying to stay calm, she joined the queue of vehicles turning out of the grounds and on to the road. It was a clear night, not cold, for it was still August. The ambulance was a Buick with a canvas top and the forward movement of the vehicle flapped the canvas top like the wings of a large bird. She was next to last in the line but she could see the others in front of her with just a faint pinprick of light as the third and sixth ambulances were the only ones permitted to show lights.

They drove into the railway station before the hospital train had arrived and for several minutes Alex felt curiously helpless. The tension with which she had begun her journey, ready for the worst, she supposed, had fizzled out to nothing. They all parked their ambulances in the road, backs towards the platform as they had been told, Garvey, Thorpe, Fenwick and herself, gravitating towards one another as they waited anxiously.

'It's like an exam,' Garvey murmured. 'The anticipation is worse than the actual examination.'

'Oh, I do hope so,' Thorpe whispered. Thorpe was a dainty little thing, all big eyes and rosy mouth who would prove to be as strong and as tough as an old boot, as she laughingly described herself. A firm favourite with the wounded for her prettiness, her rosy, innocent face was like an angel in a dream to the tortured men.

'I do hope it's not too awful,' Fenwick remarked and the others laughed in a wobbling sort of way, for how could it be any other. She offered them all a cigarette and they each took one though none of them had ever smoked. Somehow it helped, though there was a lot of coughing and choked laughter which Alex realised was no more than a release from something that might become hysteria.

They were on the platform when the train pulled in and as the doors were opened it was the smell that nearly had them over. It streamed out like sewage as the harassed orderlies jumped down from a coach marked 'Wounded 1'. It was a smell with which she was familiar, soiled clothing, which by the time the wounded reached Charing Cross was a great deal worse than this. The air seemed to move with moans and coughs and retching and laboured breathing, a whole orchestra of small rustling, creaking, gurgling sounds as the suffering humanity on board the train tried to ease its own pain.

But there was little time for reflection. The train was full and the ambulance drivers had to lend a hand to carry the stretchers to their vehicles. The men were heavy and screams rent the air when their stretchers were unintentionally jostled. By the time her ambulance was full Alex was bathed in sweat. The men she carried were most apologetic as she helped to carry them, for they were filthy and weak and it demoralised them to put themselves in the hands of ladies, a class not one of them had ever met before. They were from all parts of Great Britain, cursing in their diverse accents, Lancashire, Yorkshire, Cornwall, Scotland and the thin reedy voices of the Cockney, but all brothers in this horror into which they had so blithely rushed.

She saw terrible things that night which were to be repeated over and over again during her service in France. Ends of bone glinting whitely through rent flesh, bodies bulging in a peculiar shape which were, she learned, dressings on opened wounds, scarlet blood that dripped to her ambulance floor, and over all the men the scurrying of orange lice which went methodically about their business across skins smeared with runnels of mud and dried blood.

An orderly shouted to her to be quick and to be back as soon as she could and she nearly snapped at him that he must be joking if he thought she could go through this again but she did, backwards and forwards, night after night, becoming proficient in letting the clutch out gently so that the ambulance would not jump forward and jostle the inmates, to take cigarettes with her which she lit, for more than one dirty face had asked for a smoke, to do her job smoothly with no mishaps, to look at each face and not see it and if nobody spoke to her she was fine. It was when one of the wounded asked her for a drink, a fag, a hand to cling to for a blessed moment that she cried all the way back to the hospital.

She learned to sleep through the barrage which seemed to go on for ever, to drive all night and, barely without a nap, spring clean and maintain her ambulance during the day. She was a skilled mechanic by now and she noticed that she was being singled out to carry badly wounded men, because if an ambulance suffered even a minor breakdown the ability to put things right could mean the difference between life and death.

Now and again as summer became autumn and still she had been unable to get leave to search for Patrick at Bailleul, which was to the south of Ypres, she and Rose sometimes managed to get an hour off together, walking out of the camp and down towards a little river that bubbled through meadows still thick with wild flowers. They lay on their backs and stared up into the sky, listening to birdsong and reminisced about days at Edge Bottom when they had wandered through fields like this at the back of the house. They exchanged news about Archie and Tom who was hopeful that he might have a little sight soon, about Dick who was still eager to get married if only Rose would agree, about Noah who was in the front line and Will who at twenty-five was the oldest man in his squadron. One subject they never touched on was the violence they had shared in the WSPU. It was as though the battles of the past had been those of children squabbling when compared to what they saw and heard and smelled in France. They could hear the constant roll of thunder that was the barrage that one side or the other seemed to keep up day and night, the bugles that echoed across the meadow as funerals, of which there were many each day, sounded on the air. When it was time they reluctantly returned to their duties, Rose to her young Jock who had a small gunshot wound in his arm which was healing nicely, to his great sorrow, for it meant that he would be going back to the line soon. He was only seventeen and cried like a baby, because he said he simply could not face going over the top again. She had comforted him and told him she would be there to kiss him goodbye and he seemed to accept.

Alex sighed sadly as she rose to her feet and brushed down the long, unbecoming skirt she was forced to wear. She still had some minor job she must attend to before going out tonight, she said, smiling down into Rose's face, for Rose was smaller than she was. Impulsively she pulled her friend into her arms and hugged her.

'I don't know what I would have done without you as my friend,' she whispered, 'now and in the past,' then turned away and began to march steadfastly towards the camp hospital. Rose followed a little way behind her and as Alex turned to wave at the gate she watched as a man in uniform approached her. Rose thought he was an orderly with bad news, for as he spoke Alex reeled back with her hand to her mouth, then reached to clutch his arm as though shaking out of him what he had to say. Rose began to run and when she reached Alex was appalled to see tears running down her face.

'What? Holy God, what is it? Not . . . not Noah?' Which surely pointed to the way her own heart was leading her.

'No, oh no, Rosie . . . that man . . . the orderly . . .'

'Yes . . . oh, for Christ's dear sake, tell me.'

'Patrick has been here,' she babbled, her eyes enormous in her ashen face. 'Patrick has been . . . he was asking for me. Oh, why wasn't I here? Why didn't I stay close to . . . Now he's gone and God alone knows when I can get down to . . . Oh, Rose, Patrick . . . Patrick was here asking for me and surely that means he still thinks of me. Rose, I must get leave . . .' looking imploringly at her friend as though it were in Rose's power to grant it.

'Of course you must, but first we shall go to the section leader and . . .'

'Oh, Rose, he was asking for me . . .' Alex's face was radiant now, colour flooding it and Rose hoped to God that Patrick O'Leary still loved Alex Goodwin.

# 16

'Absolutely not. I'm afraid we are far too busy to allow a day off, never mind the thirty-six hours you're asking for. Is he a relative?' Sister Andrews was sitting at her desk in the end hut, simply shuffling papers, or so it seemed to Alex, nothing important like nursing, or driving an ambulance or even carrying a stretcher, then she felt remorse, for someone had to do the administrative work that piled on to the shoulders of the section leader. It fell to Andrews to see where an ambulance, a nurse, a VAD, an orderly was needed and to get them there. It was like a pyramid tottering towards disaster and should one small piece be taken away the whole thing would come tumbling down. It was the end of September and the Battle of Loos was a terrible tragedy, for there had been such a loss of men.

'No, a . . . a friend.'

Sister Andrews looked up suspiciously, for none of her section were allowed to fraternise with the men, especially in the hospital grounds, so who was this man, this soldier, she presumed, whom Goodwin wanted leave to meet?

'A friend! Dear God, Goodwin, with all the wounded pouring in here, needing you to carry them to hospital, you are calmly asking for time off to see a friend. Where is this friend of yours, may I ask?'

'Bailleul, Sister.'

'Well, I'm sorry, Goodwin, it is absolutely out of the question. Besides which you are to be transferred to Number 22

General Camp Hospital between Dannes and Camiers. There are half a dozen hospitals there behind the sand-dunes of the coast, near the railway line that serves them. Casualties can be taken directly there, the worst of the cases who are to be shipped back home or who are too bad to move any further.' Sister sat back in her chair and studied Goodwin. She was a reliable, conscientious and valuable driver who could not only drive and maintain her vehicle, she was proficient in first-aid and had the right attitude to the men. She was steady and did her best to ease their suffering in the way she drove, seeming to have cat's eyes that see in the dark, avoiding the potholes that might have the men in the back of her ambulance tipped off the stretchers from the shelves on which they were packed. She had a sort of no-nonsense approach to her work which was exactly what was needed, but at the same time her steadiness appeared to be just what the wounded needed. And she could not be spared for anything as frivolous as meeting a friend. She looked desperately tired, as they all were, quite gaunt, in fact, the incredible colour of her eyes sunk deep in mushroom-coloured circles, her skin pallid, and she had lost weight.

'Sister, I have been here since April and have had no time off at all . . .'

'That will be all, Goodwin. Get ready to leave tomorrow.' Sister Andrews was sorry to be so brusque but she really could not spare anyone in this mad, mad world which it was her job to supervise. There were not only the nurses and ambulance drivers, the stretcher-bearers and attendants, she also had the task of organising the feeding of the patients and the staff, and the laundry alone was a monumental task. She herself would have liked to creep into her bed, turn off the light and sleep for a week.

Alex wanted to leap over the woman's desk and shake her. Could she not see that she must, absolutely must get to Bailleul before she went to wherever it was they were sending her?

Patrick was looking for her, believing she was here and if he should come again and she was gone, neither of them would have the faintest idea where the other was in the whirling maelstrom that was the Western Front. Wherever she went in her ambulance, whether it was day or night, she was met with straggling columns of men, glistening with sweat, loaded with so much gear it was a wonder they could walk at all, some going up the line, others coming away from the trenches, toiling along behind exhausted officers, their boots slipping painfully in the rutted mud; wounded men in blood-caked bandages who seemed to have no idea where they were going or where they had come from, with only the haziest idea of what was going on. The day she drove her ambulance to the Number 22 General Camp Hospital near Camiers it was just as bad, as many of the wounded, if they could walk, simply set off with their mates, helping one another towards the nearest hospital or casualty clearing station. As they came off the battlefield, stumbling over the dead and wounded who cried out to them for water, they first dragged themselves to the first-aid post where a bandage would be slapped on their wound and from there they were told to go to the casualty clearing station where their wounds would be assessed and from there, if it was a Blighty which, despite the agony they suffered, they prayed it was, they would be shipped home. But those too badly wounded to be moved, or not wounded badly enough and most likely to be sent back up the line were seen to and put into beds at the general hospital until they recovered.

To Alex they had become just so many parcels that she must deliver from here to there with the utmost speed. Of course she was filled with compassion for them, lighting cigarettes between her own lips and then placing them carefully between those of the wounded man. She spoke kindly words which she repeated a hundred times. 'Don't worry, lad, we'll take care of you. Just rest . . . rest, you're out of it now,' the words automatic but received with a grateful smile from the filthy face in its wrappings of even filthier bandages. Some of the men she carried had been wounded twenty-four hours previously, shunted from place to place on their way to where the real medical care could begin and she became used to the terrible smell of gangrene. Careful French farmers had scattered their ploughed fields with manure and composts to make them rich and this matter was more often than not carried into the wounds of the soldiers as they fell. Those she carried were the most badly injured come from the Battle of Loos where the casualties had been so heavy that the remnants of different regiments, which had lost one another in the confusion, were amalgamated, but Alex knew nothing of this as she went backwards and forwards in a daze of hopelessness at her missed chance of meeting Patrick.

She shared a tent with a very pretty VAD from Wales who spoke with that lovely lilt to her tongue which was almost like singing. Her conversation was punctuated with 'there now', 'well, I never did,' every soldier she spoke to was 'boyo' and every sentence ended with 'see'. Her hair was as red as a fox and her eyes a flashing blue-green and she was a great favourite with the men in the wards. Though Alex missed Rose she took a great liking to Megan and when, as sometimes happened, they were sharing the dark of the night she listened to her prattle on about the medical staff she worked with.

'Now that Sister Watson is a right beggar, so she is and there's me been a VAD for nigh on two years and she still treats me like I was no more than a cleaner, see. Do this yer, she'll say and run to there and I bet I could do an irrigation as good as her. Now that doctor that comes round, I could fall for him, so I could. Lovely he is with those brown eyes so soft and gentle when he looks at a patient and yet as cool as a cucumber when he looks at a nurse, or even the bloody sister. Five weeks, he's been yer and though there's many tried, including me, he's not interested, see. Handsome though, even if he does wear specs.'

Alex would drift off to sleep on the lilting rhythm of Megan's voice and when she woke, more often than not to the whistle and shriek of Sister Martin, the section leader, telling them that a convoy was coming in off one of the dozens of trains that came from the front, Megan would still be bubbling on about something or other. She was like a child who has been made to play with children older than herself and though the game was mature and sometimes frightening her innocence protected her and kept her unworldly.

She had just unloaded the last batch of wounded at the entrance to the operating tent from which came the reek of ether and idioform. The usual sound of the guns thundered on the still, frosty air and Alex shivered, brooding on the state the men must be in crouched in the trenches. Men like Noah whom she had not seen or heard from since her arrival in France. And Will in his flying machine who, her father had told her in his last letter, was up every day when it was not misty, performing the aerial reconnaissance that was invaluable to the allies, for it told them where new trenches were being dug and the number of German troops, which might show the extent of a large-scale infantry attack in the offing.

Alex waited for a moment at the opening to the operating tent, she didn't know why, standing to one side as pasty-faced, tired attendants unloaded mud, cloth, bandages and blood that turned out to be human beings and where an overstretched doctor-in-chief shouted orders. Ambulance after ambulance came from the lines and the doctor, whose voice softened as he bent over each stretcher, turned a little, the light shining on the spectacles he wore and for a moment she was ready to smile, for this must be the paragon of whom Megan rhapsodised. He was pointing at a man on a stretcher and as he turned further he saw her and the world about them became still and quiet. The noise of men crying out, the sharp commands of doctors and nurses, the curse of a stretcher-bearer as he slipped in the blood, the guns in the distance, the splutter of an engine as the last ambulance drove up, all disappeared and for what seemed an eternity they stood and looked at each other. They both took a step forward and had not the sister nudged him and an attendant shouted at her to get out of the bloody way they might have flown into one another's arms.

At once they were returned to this world, this real world in which both had a part to play. The noises clamoured in their ears and she saw rather than heard his lips form the word 'later', then he was gone, swept away on the tide of suffering he was doing his best to ease.

It was many hours later, the next day in fact, when she had been sitting, then walking, since it was so cold, along the peak of the sand-dunes at the back of the hospital when he came. They stood for several seconds telling each other with their eyes that the love Alex Goodwin and Patrick O'Leary had shared, still shared, could not be flung aside. That it must be recognised for what it was in this mad world of war, that it must be treasured, prized, that it was precious to them both and that it must be allowed to grow and be voiced on this day which might be their last, for both of them walked in the path of danger.

Her skin glistened like marble and her lips, just as pale, parted on a sigh. The only colour in her face was her eyes, those incredible, lavender-blue eyes which blazed their message of love.

He was the first to speak, his voice hardly more than a sigh but filled with a thankfulness that came from his heart.

'I looked for you . . . I prayed that I would find you, then I was moved. And now . . .'

'I am here, my darling.'

'Am I still that? Your darling.'

'Always.' Her voice was thick with tears and at last he put his hands on her, gently, wonderingly, just touching her shoulders, nothing more.

'I'm sorry, my dearest heart.'

'Sorry?'

'For the last time . . . Jesus Christ, it seems aeons ago . . .'

'It doesn't matter now.' Their eyes clung, sending messages of some urgency, the silent, invisible cord that bound them and which somehow had never broken despite what had happened to them since last they had met. April before the war, nearly two years and yet it still flourished. She had been to prison, been seriously ill, had recovered and though she had not consciously admitted it to herself, had begun her journey from that moment to this with the sole intention of finding him. And here he was.

'Oh God, Alex . . .' he groaned, his face drawn into harsh lines of pain. He put up a hand and removed his spectacles, shoving them in the pocket of his British warm and his smoky brown eyes were revealed in more detail. She could feel the need in him, as it was in her, to have their arms about one another, but the expression that was stamped on his face distracted her. He was a mature man, older than the boys, the gallant young warriors who were streaming over the Channel to do their bit, but there was something else there as well. He had seen suffering in his hospital in London but nothing, nothing on the scale he was experiencing now. He had grown older and there was a fine-drawn vulnerability in his body which made her want to draw him into her arms, not with passion but to provide the comfort and reassurance that a woman's body can give to a man. There was a thinning of his mouth and a fast-beating pulse in his temple and he looked as though laughter, even a smile was not something he knew a lot about these days.

At last he lifted his arms and held them out to her and she moved into them, blindly, thankfully, for it had been a long time she had searched, unknowing, for him. His lips sought hers and she gave them to him. Her arms crossed at his back, holding his body to hers, as his did and their tears mingled and fell sadly.

She was allowed a thirty-six-hour pass in May and since there was a lull in the stream of wounded passing through the casualty clearing stations and the field hospitals, a 'breathing space' as it was called, Patrick was able to manage the same thirty-six-hour leave pass. They had met as often as they could manage, having devised a system of leaving messages with a time and a place to meet, usually on the dunes, clinging feverishly to one another, as though they were afraid even as they pressed their bodies together that something, someone would tear them apart. But they could only kiss and murmur words of love, for neither of them could afford to be absent from the place where they were supposed to be for more than half an hour.

Though there was a respite in the first months of 1916 there were still casualties, 83,000 of them killed and wounded, or the 'normal wastage', as it was callously called, of trench warfare and small-scale local attacks. The British Tommy had taken over a part of the line from the French in order to relieve their badly stretched forces but on the British front there were no major battles. Still the casualties flowed in and not all of them flowed out again, and there was a backlog of men wounded in the first eighteen months of the war, the blind, the paralysed, the limbless, such patients requiring long-term care. Patrick, being the chief surgeon who had in his charge many doctors and who had been in France from the beginning, over eighteen months, had not been on leave since he arrived and he had no trouble obtaining it, indeed if she herself could have managed it was entitled to fourteen days.

Both of them were what Patrick described later when they talked as seasoned pawns in the murderous war games of

ageing generals. He was particularly devastated by the sacrifices that were being made by men who only two years ago had
been shoe salesmen, clerks, gardeners, bus conductors and the
way they had offered themselves up as sacrifices to the horror
of it. He had been initially a medical officer in the lines and his
eyes had seen crucifixions on barbed wire, the swelling corpses
that could not be recovered from no-man's-land and the stench
when they burst open. Alex had seen gassed men, burned,
blinded men and whenever she closed her own clear eyes she
could see them against the lids, and they both knew that their
spirits had been crippled by what they had seen and experienced. They were damaged, mentally drained so they had
passed beyond disillusion to a blank acceptance of evil. But
their bodies were still joyously young and in the bedroom of a
hotel in Etaples they expunged their bitter minds, their bitter
memories of the last year with an outpouring of love which
healed, for the moment, those appalling memories they shared
on the battlefields of France.

There was no end to the love they had for one another in that
seedy but enchanted hotel room which had probably witnessed
a hundred such encounters. It was clean, spartan, with a door
that locked, a bed, a chair, a window that looked out on a busy
street but none of that mattered. He undid the buttons of her
shirt, his fingers trembling, pushing it off her shoulders, then
her undergarment, concentrating sharply, she was well aware,
on the wholesomeness, the sweet-smelling, the smoothness of
flesh that was not mutilated, his hands hovering as though not
sure which part of her to caress first. He knelt to draw down her
skirt, which she was aware was stained with mud and what was
probably blood, and then her underskirt and drawers, leaning
back to study every line of her, turning her round, pressing his
lips to her belly, her buttocks and the dark, mysterious bush
between her thighs and the smooth satin skin that surrounded
it. He picked her up in his arms and cradled her as though she

were a child then laid her on the bed before slipping his uniform to the floor, his body thinner than she remembered, as was hers. He lay down beside her and they remained still, looking into one another's eyes, not touching, no more than an inch between them, then he began to talk, softly, his voice hardly more than a whisper.

'Do you know how I've dreamed of this . . .' at last reaching out a hand to cup her breasts, slowly, carefully, not wishing to neglect any of the sweet sensations his hands and heart created, for himself, for her. 'I've cursed myself a million times for the way I was the last time, the time we've wasted. My love, my heart, how beautiful you are . . . This is like the dream I've dreamed whenever I closed my eyes. You were there. Dear sweet Christ, have you the slightest notion how much I love you . . . have loved you from that first moment . . . I love you . . . I love you . . . want you . . .'

Her hand reached for his cheek, sweeping across his winging eyebrows, smoothing his hair, which she saw was no longer the dark unruly crop it had once been but was grey in swathes at the temple. She pulled it down to her breast and his mouth found her nipple and she felt it harden as his lips closed on it, while his hands smoothed the wonder of her, her flat stomach, the dimples above her buttocks until he found the hot, sweet moisture at the centre of her, the very depths of her woman's body. They were both overwhelmed by the exquisitely sensual and yet profound truth of their love. It was sharp and almost unbearable in its intensity and yet the goodness of the man, the loyal heart of the woman, the warmth, the strength, which had come from hard years of turmoil and loss, bore them up, making it unbreakable.

At last he reared up and with a great groan he entered her, arching his back and driving deeper and deeper as though he must lose himself in her, hide from the world that was slowly destroying them all, shouting her name, not waiting for her, since he was no longer himself but a man who had lost himself and was found. It did not matter to her as she cradled him against her. The lovely clean, ivory lines of her, the fresh lemon-scented smell of her, the soft whole feel of her woman's body against his was beginning the healing process which would last until the next time, for there would be a next time, she knew it. Nothing had prepared either of them for this war they fought in but they would live through it, for this was their destiny, started in the yard at Westminster.

He put on his clothes once and went downstairs, coming back bearing a tray with a bottle of wine, hot coffee, fresh bread, cheese. They ate and then slept for a little, neither of them moving as they clung together and when they awoke he made another assault upon her which she gloried in, for she knew it was mending his mind which had been damaged by what he had seen, what he had been forced to do to men like himself. He was not a self-contained, dispassionate doctor, had never been that and so he had suffered as the men he treated had suffered. He had cut off their shattered limbs, probed their poor wounded bodies, made life-and-death decisions for them, since he was forced to send back to the line men who would surely never return and it was tormenting him towards madness.

But she had given him peace, soothed his shifting nerves, renewed him with her love, with her body as she came, with him, to a climax that left her trembling and unable to speak, their mingling sighing breath no longer jagged and spiky with tension.

'Do you have any idea how much I love you?' he asked her for the second time.

'Yes, my darling, I do.'

'I can manage it if I have you nearby.'

'I'm here, Patrick. I always will be.'

'It will be a long war, my heart, we who are in it know that. They're slaughtering them – us – in their thousands.'

'I know, my love. I have seen it too.'

'Of course you have.' He sighed deeply. 'It's a bloody cock-up, hell on earth.'

'Hold on to me, Patrick. This may have to last us for a while . . .'

'I know, but at least we are near one another. Leave me a message.'

They had discovered this pile of rocks at the back of the tent she shared with Megan and hiding a tin beneath it they had found it possible to speak to one another with no one knowing. They could arrange the time and place to meet and for the moment it was enough.

'No wonder there are deserters,' he brooded, his head on her breast. 'They're not cowards as the authorities try to make us believe. They are just men who are going insane with the constant bombardment. I am getting chaps on the ward who are deaf, half mad with it and that's before they even go over the top.'

'Darling, hold me.'

'I love you. When it's over . . .'

'Yes, I know . . .'

They dressed slowly, putting on the uniforms that transformed them into other people. No longer Alex and Patrick who loved one another and always would, Alex and Patrick who were waiting for their life together to begin, but Captain Patrick O'Leary, RAMC and Ambulance Driver Alexandra Goodwin who would not even speak to each other if they met in the hospital tent lest they be noticed and this magic be taken from them.

She left first, cadging a lift from a cheerful van driver who was delivering a load of medical supplies to the hospital. She had no sooner got back and was entering her tent when the familiar whistle sounded and Sister Martin was shouting to them to get a move on. It was almost dark as Alex cranked the engine of her ambulance, which she had gone over before she left for Etaples, joining the long line of other ambulances as they headed for the station. The train steamed in as she parked her vehicle, its rear to the platform and climbed down ready to help with the stretchers. The doors opened and the usual stench to which she had long grown accustomed streamed from the carriages and with the stench came the dreadful sounds of suffering humanity.

She had learned to recognise the different types of wounds: those inflicted by the terrible serrated entrenching tools used by the Germans, shrapnel wounds which tended to tear off parts of the body and the clean, one could almost say wholesome wound from a bullet.

There was an older soldier on a stretcher, one of those who had come over with the first wave and knew the ropes. He had a cheerful grin on his face round the cigarette she had lit for him, since he had at last a wound that would probably get him a Blighty. 'Yer wanner watch that 'un, Sister' he said, nodding at the still, waxen face of a young soldier who was put in behind him. 'I reckon 'e's a bleeder.' And sure enough, when they were no more than halfway to the hospital he called out to her that the young soldier, no more than a boy, was bleeding all over him.

She sighed and, signalling to the ambulance behind her, pulled off the rutted road, leaving the engine running since she didn't want to have to crank the damn thing again. She jumped out and ran to the back of the ambulance, lifting the tarpaulin and was just about to climb up when something hit her, not hurting her at all but turning the black of night to an even darker shade which was rather pleasant. So this was . . .

# 17

The men of the East Yorkshire Regiment, who were moving up to the line and who had stepped to one side of the road as the convoy of ambulances went past, flung themselves into the mud as the shell roared over their heads, sighing with phlegmatic relief as it exploded fifty yards behind them. They got to their feet, not an easy task when carrying half their own weight in equipment, telling one another that had been bloody close, then, as someone shouted hoarsely, turned to stare in horror at the remains of the ambulance that had pulled off the road for some reason. They had passed it, noticing the figure, barely identifiable as a woman, who was fiddling about with the back flap but where the ambulance had been was now a small crater in which parts of the vehicle lay. And not only parts of the vehicle, for the shell had disintegrated the passengers in the ambulance to arms, legs and torsos, blood and pieces of the human body that none of them wanted to examine more closely. They were veterans, these men, who had seen every aspect of war in all its horror, hardened, most of them, to speaking to a comrade standing next to them in the trench and then being showered with his blood and brains, but this made even the most inured want to cry out. The woman, the nurse, the ambulance driver, they supposed she must be, had been flung into the muddy field, a small, crumpled heap of clothing and for a moment the soldiers stood, appalled, none of them wanting to approach until their officer shouted and began to run towards her, some of them following. They had stood so much, seen so much but could they face the devastation of seeing a wounded, perhaps dead woman, one of the courageous women who drove their wounded to the hospitals and the answer was that they couldn't, but, as always, they must.

Their officer was kneeling at her side. She had lost her hat in the blast and her dark hair, short, curly and soft, lay in the mud under which were thousands of decomposing bodies, and one or two of the men wanted to moan deep in their throats for her face was so lovely, unmarked, her eyes closed and it wasn't right that so delicate a creature should be flung down in the muck and muddle that was the battlefield. A battlefield over which so many had died and were still here.

They didn't know what to do for a moment. If she was dead, or if she wasn't, she must be taken somewhere decent and clean and they themselves were on their way to a place that was neither.

'She's still alive,' their officer told them, looking about him as though searching for a convenient transport but there was nothing, only miles of shattered fields and trees and the road that led through it. He was only young himself, straight from the public school that had taught him to take control of every emergency that might occur in his privileged life but had omitted this one. He was in command and it was up to him to see this poor lady back to the hospital but at the same time he had his orders to get to the line and take his men with him.

The sergeant spoke up, for if the truth were known it was he, and many other sergeants like him who guided their young officers through the maze of trench warfare they were expected to understand.

'Shall I get some of the men to make a stretcher, sir? They could carry the young lady back to the hospital and then catch us up. I'm not sure whether she should be moved, not knowing the extent of her injuries but there is blood in her hair, sir, and we can't just leave her here. There are no vehicles in sight . . .'

The men all looked round hopefully but there was nothing, just marching men who stared curiously at the little group in the field. The shattered ambulance told its own story.

'Righto, S'arnt, we'll do that.' Much relieved, the officer removed his own British warm and ordered two of the others to do the same and for a moment it looked as though there might be an argument over who should have the honour of dedicating his overcoat to make a stretcher for the poor young lady.

A makeshift stretcher was constructed and again they almost fought each other to be the ones to lift her tenderly on to it, to wrap her up and carry her to the hospital. The rest watched her go and then turned, sighing, to their march towards what was sure to be death or maiming. It was coming to something when this bloody war of which they were all heartily sick was killing women!

Patrick, or Mad Paddy as they called him at Camiers, had just returned to the hospital after his thirty-six-hour pass and he was actually smiling, which made the rest of the staff stare and exchange glances. His face was calm and so relaxed the others, doctors and orderlies, were ready to put a bet on it that he had been to meet some woman, for what else could change the irritable Irish Scouser from his usual taciturn self into this, one could almost say genial Johnny who even winked at VAD Megan Price causing her to drop a thermometer which smashed at her feet?

He had scarcely shrugged into his white coat before becoming involved in the new and exciting medical arrival that the American doctors had brought with them, which was the technique of successful blood transfusion. It was a priceless asset to the thousands of casualties who, before and during surgery, lost more blood than their bodies could stand. It would be a life-saver. Until its advent the method had been primitive and there had been a large number of failures when the donor's blood formed clots in the patient's veins so that he died of thrombosis. The Americans had developed a method that prevented the donor's blood from coagulating. The first thing to do was to get the blood group of the donor and the patient matching and a serum had been found that could do just that. Patrick was so absorbed with this and the two soldiers, one dying and one recovering, who had been wheeled into the operating room and laid side by side, head to tail, so to speak, that he was unaware of everything around him apart from the two soldiers. Everybody, even the donor, was fascinated as the blood ran from the cut on his arm up into a bottle and from there into the dying man's arm. The patient had lost a leg, amputated only the day before yesterday by Mr O'Leary, a lovely job, as neat and clean as his mother's kitchen, but the gangrene that had been present when the soldier was brought in had done its worst and he was not expected to live. He looked like death itself but the marvel of watching the colour come back into his face as the new blood ran into him had the whole bloody lot of them smiling like lunatics, the donor was to say afterwards, proud as punch, to his mates.

The commotion at the entrance to the hospital tent caught the attention of Mr O'Leary and Sister Martin who both stopped in their congratulations and turned enquiringly, for there were casualties brought in every hour of the day or night, sometimes in waves and sometimes singly as this one was and it was nothing to get hysterical about. A group of anxious soldiers seemed reluctant to part with whoever it was they carried, hanging about at the entrance, and the orderlies were shooing them away as they laid down their burden which was wrapped, they could see now, in khaki overcoats.

Megan Price was the first to recognise her, for she was nearest the entrance. She lifted her hand to her mouth and began to cry, not muffled but out loud and frightened and Sister Martin bustled forward, ready to give her a good talking to, since no matter what came through that entrance, and there had been things that would make anybody cry, you did not let the men see it, but as she approached and glanced down at the casualty, she cried out herself.

'Oh, dear God . . . I wondered what . . . her ambulance has not come back. Nurse, quickly, get a doctor . . . oh, my God . . . Oh, sweet Jesus . . .' And the staff and patients in the vicinity peered round one another to see what the devil was upsetting Sister Martin.

Megan couldn't speak, she merely took Patrick's hand and led him to the makeshift stretcher where the woman he loved lay in a pathetic, shattered bundle. For a moment he stared in bewilderment and they were not to know that the last time he had seen that face he had been kissing it, smoothing the soft curve of her cheek, tracing her lips with a tender finger.

They were all amazed when, forgetting himself in his terror, Mr O'Leary, Mad Paddy, fell to his knees and gathered the casualty to his chest.

'Macushla, macushla,' he moaned, rocking her in torment. *Macushla!* What the hell kind of jargon was that? those about the doctor were thinking. The Irish among the casualties might have been able to tell them, for it was Gaelic for 'darling'. Sister was thinking he should have known better than to sway about as he was doing, for it did no good to jostle a wounded person, man or woman, then he got a hold of himself and became a doctor again, ready to begin the task of restoring Goodwin to full health as was his purpose in life.

'Get away from her,' he snarled, making the group of appalled doctors and nurses, orderlies and stretcher-bearers who all knew her jump a foot high. 'You, fetch a stretcher and clear that small tent . . .' for he could not possibly examine her here among the soldiers, many of whom were in a poor way themselves. He needed peace, calm, cleanliness, privacy, but, pulling himself together, his face the colour of his clean white coat, he beckoned to Sister Martin and Nurse Price, for his love must be undressed and it was not seemly that he should do it. He would need help to ascertain her injuries, to treat them in the proper way, a good nurse and even, looking at the deep stain of blood on the officer's British warm, a transfusion.

The small tent was cleared of the medical supplies that were kept there and a bed hastily erected, and with infinite tenderness Patrick lifted Alex on to the bed, longing to pull her into his arms, hold her limp body close to him, cradle her, kiss her, even weep as he had seen the relatives of dead soldiers do. But he knew he must do what he did for the boys, the hundreds of boys, the thousands of boys who had passed through his hands in the last eighteen months. He must be clear-headed, detached . . . Dear sweet Mother of God . . . *detached* . . . when the woman he had loved for almost three years was lying as though dead, the blood still flowing from beneath her hair on to the snow-white sheet Nurse Price had placed on the bed.

The nurses removed her clothing, for God knew what nasty thing she had picked up, not just from the farmer's careful husbandry of his fields but from the putrefaction that heaved beneath the topsoil, and when she was naked but decently covered he stepped inside and began a careful examination of the body he had so recently worshipped, from the feet, the poor little toeless foot, every inch of her to make sure there was nothing abominable clinging to her lovely white flesh, and then her head.

'We shall have to shave her head, Sister,' he murmured calmly. 'I believe she has something . . . a splinter, a bit of shrapnel embedded and I can't . . . I must see her skull.' Without a tremble he watched as sister and nurse gently shaved his love's head of her shockingly soiled hair, wanting to weep as the VAD was doing, but holding himself steady since he must be prepared for . . . for anything. She still breathed and her blood pressure was good but her face was like chalk as the blood from her head continued to leak her life away.

His clever, gentle fingers probed the wound, the great dent in her skull, finding bits of material that would need to come out and he was aware that he would need help. This was a two-doctor operation, for the slightest slip would mean the end of Alex Goodwin, if not to death then to brain damage which was just as bad. And there was only one man he would trust to help him. He must take X-rays, get one of the other doctors to find a suitable blood donor and in the meantime Dick Morris must be found and fetched at top speed.

'But we can't just appropriate a doctor from another hospital, Mr O'Leary,' sister said, shocked and displeased. 'There will be casualties who are . . .'

But he had turned away and was shouting through the tent flap to a soldier who was just about to take off on his motorcycle with, presumably, some important message to some important personage.

'Hey, you, get over here, will you.'

The messenger looked about him as though wondering who the doctor was calling to, then mouthing the words and pointing to his own chest, 'Who . . . me?'

'Yes, you.'

'Sir, I really must protest,' Sister Martin was moaning and Megan Price leaned over the patient and gently touched her face. Since sister could hardly berate a doctor she turned in her distress to the one person she could.

'Get away from the patient, Price. I'm sure there are other patients who need your help. I don't know what the world is coming to . . .' But at the same time she moved to stand beside Goodwin, looking compassionately into the gaunt face of the wounded woman. Mr O'Leary was talking to or rather arguing with the motorcyclist who seemed reluctant to take an order from him, especially one that was not part of his duties, and

Price had slipped out to take the news of Goodwin and her injuries to the VADs, the orderlies and the wounded men, many of whom Goodwin had herself brought in. Sister leaned over the thin figure beneath the sheet and then gently touched her cheek.

'He'll look after you, lass,' she whispered, 'for any fool can see which way the wind's blowing and how long has that been, I wonder.'

It was a good job there was a bit of a lull on, Dick was to say several times during that long day and night that he and Mad Paddy worked on Alex Goodwin. They were both absorbed with the delicate surgery Patrick performed but he could not have done it without Dick, he said later. They had worked as a team at St Thomas's in London and their brains seemed to work on the same wavelength so that hardly had Patrick held out his hand before Dick was there with the correct instrument. Sister Martin assisted in the sterile unit Patrick had improvised. X-rays were done and a blood donor who was the same group as Alex was ready standing by. It turned out to be Megan Price! The whole hospital seemed to be holding its breath, for this was the first casualty among the ambulance drivers and even the most badly wounded of the Tommies asked about her anxiously. It was well known by now throughout the whole area between Dannes and Camiers where the tented hospitals lay that Mr O'Leary was in love with an ambulance driver and the questions flew back and forth: 'which one?' . . . 'that pretty one with the' . . . 'no, no not her . . . she's a bit older than the others' . . . 'I fancied him myself' . . . 'you know, the dark one with the short hair' . . . 'd'you mean the one with the limp?' . . . 'do they say she'll pull through?' . . . 'If he's anything to do with it she will' . . . 'fancy, and with that Sister Martin watching . . .'

At last they were done and with a murmur of regret Dick shook hands with Patrick. He must get back, he said or he would be shot for desertion but he knew Patrick hardly heard him. He was bending over the slight, frighteningly still figure on the bed, longing to do something for her but what else could he do? He had removed every bit of splinter he could see from Alex's skull and sewn it up with stitches so neat Dick knew his own mother, whose passion was embroidery, would have approved. Her obscenely shaved head was bandaged, again by Patrick who would allow no one, not even the competent sister, to help. Nurse Megan Price, with five neat stitches in her arm, had given of her blood and the colour was slowly returning to Alex's face beneath the snow-white bandage that reached her eyebrows. Everything that could or should be done had been done and she lay in her tent with Megan beside her, for after a furious row with sister who said she could not spare a nurse to attend *one* patient and after Mr O'Leary had snarled then he would sit himself, sister had been forced to give in. They could manage without Price but they could not manage without the doctor. They were getting ready for a big push, no one knew exactly when but there were bound to be many casualties and every doctor in the vicinity would be needed.

The men who fought the battles and who were convinced they were to spend the fag-end of their lives performing the awful cycle of five days in the line, five in support and five 'resting' in areas that came in for almost as much shelling as those in the line, surprised the nursing staff by hovering at the entrance to the hospital. They had come, they said, to enquire about the lass some of them had brought back in their great-coats. It was a damn good job it was mild, for those who had gladly donated them would have been in a state of frozen stupor had it been the depths of winter. They were delighted when they heard she was still alive though as yet had not regained her senses. She had opened her eyes and was taking nourishment but, though they did not like to say it, was still unknowing, recognising no one. They were sorry about that and the next day one of them handed in a bunch of wild flowers they had picked in a field still untouched by the shelling. Poppies, buttercups and some delicate white plant the name of which they were not sure.

Several days later Rose turned up. Dick had been in touch with her, telling her about Alex and she had managed to obtain a few hours' leave, begging a ride on the back of a willing motorcyclist. When she arrived, asking for Mr O'Leary, she was appalled at the state of him who, as she was to tell Noah whom she had been secretly meeting, looked worse than Alex.

Noah, being an American, seemed to be able to get more time off, or was it his impish grin, his charm, his cheek, his willingness to give a hand to any Tommy who needed one, his unique way of speaking which none of them had heard before, and his 'luck' in the trenches where his mates quarrelled over who was to stand next to him on the fire-step? Whatever it was, he seemed able to sneak away and wait for her when she was off shift and Rose's growing attraction towards him and his for her was a constant prickling worry to her. She was engaged to Dick who worked as hard and with as much dedication as Patrick and his letters ground her down with guilt. They were full of his love for her and his longing for the day when they would be married. Could she get a few days off, he begged her, and they could perhaps get as far as Paris, and what he had in mind was very clear. She loved him, she knew she did, but it was the love of a friend for a friend. When she had promised to marry him, had in fact become engaged to him she had not known anything else existed but the pleasure she found in his company, the way he made her laugh, his devotion which was very loveable, but what she felt for Noah, the yearning, the *secret* yearning she found herself dwelling on, to be close to him, to have him kiss her and more, much more, which had never happened with Dick, was alarming. Of course, Dick had kissed her with the reverence one shows to a . . . well, she couldn't quite explain, even to herself, but Dick did not drive her crazy with a longing for something she had never known but which just the touch of Noah's hand on her arm awoke in her.

'Dearest,' she whispered, bending over the silently staring figure on the bed. The bandage about Alex's head frightened her as did the total lack of recognition in Alex's beautiful eyes, the colour of them incredible in the pale, sunken face on the pillow. When she spoke Alex turned her head to look at her but there was nothing, only blankness, a lack of expression that frightened Rose more than the swathed bandage. Alex was alone now in the neat tent, for her health had improved in the last few days. She ate what was put in her mouth, and soldiers, total strangers, turned up at all sorts of odd times with something for the 'poorly' nurse. It had got about that one of the ambulance drivers, one of those intrepid band of women who faced death and mutilation on the battlefields of France, had herself been badly injured on one of her missions of mercy and she had become something of a symbol of hope to the men who daily passed the hospital.

Rose backed out of the tent in terror, turning wildly, looking for Patrick, for though Alex was conscious it was apparent she did not recognise the friend with whom she had shared so much.

'Where is Patrick . . . Mr O'Leary?' She grasped the arm of a passing orderly and on being told he was in the main hospital tent she hurried across to look for him, finding him bending over the bed of a young officer who was obviously dying. The boy was murmuring the word they all murmured in their extremity.

'Mother . . . Mother . . .'

'Your mother won't be long, son,' Patrick was whispering, holding the boy's hand and it seemed to ease the lad, for he smiled and closed his eyes.

Patrick turned and saw her and it was then she thought that if this man didn't get away from this hell-hole soon, taking his love with him, he would go under. For nearly two years he had taken on not only the healing of the bodies of the soldiers but, from what she had just seen, their terrible troubles in dying. They were so young. They didn't want to die. They were maimed, blinded, gassed, emasculated, burned, some of them passing the extreme limit of their endurance, for as yet there was no recognition of the condition which was to be known as shell-shock. There were heroes and there were cowards and in between a majority who could endure a spell in the line and slough off their fear the moment they were out of it.

She watched compassionately as Patrick straightened up, then, on seeing her, hurried down the ward towards her. He took her hands while those who were well enough to be curious watched with interest. Not another pretty nurse, surely, to catch the eye of Mad Paddy?

'Have you seen her?' were his first words.

'Yes. Oh God, Patrick, she didn't know me.'

'No, me neither. I did what I could . . . with Dick to help but we know so little about head injuries and the . . . the brain. Blessed Mother, have I damaged her, is it my fault that she's . . .?'

At once she became the nurse, putting on the face she showed to her patients. 'Of course not. Would she have lived if you had not done what you did, you and Dick?'

'No, she had splinters.'

'There you are then, but is she to remain here for long? And who is to look after her when she returns home? There is only yourself, Patrick, you know that. You are the best surgeon in . . . well, anywhere. How many lives have you saved, tell me that, with your skill? Now then, lad, you mustn't go under, for she needs you.'

'So do these men . . .' And he stared about him at the many, many men he was healing.

'But you are no good to them if you are constantly looking back over your shoulder to find Alex. She must go back to London, to Nan and those who can care for her and you must go with her.'

'But I cannot leave.'

'Have you been home on leave since you got here?' She tugged at his hands to get his attention.

'No. I had thirty-six hours with her before . . .' His gaunt face became soft with memories.

'There you are then. You must take her home. You are the only one who can and then, later, when she is on the road to recovery you can come back.'

'There is to be a big push. Holy Mother, what a way to describe the massacre of hundreds of thousands of men.'

'Patrick, you must go home, you must, and though I have absolutely no influence with the high-ups I'm going to find someone who has. Now, tell me about Alex . . .' leading him by the hand out of the ward and across to the small tent where his love lay.

# 18

Patrick and Alex travelled back to England together. It was obvious that Goodwin must return to her home, the Chief Medical Officer said, or to some hospital in England where she would get the necessary care, but when Mr O'Leary told him that he intended returning with his *fiancée*, taking the leave that was due him, Sister Martin, who had supported him in his decision since what he said was true, thought murder was to be done. The Chief Medical Officer, Major Alan Lang-Clausen, who was accustomed to giving orders and having them obeyed at once, took exception to Captain O'Leary's quiet statement, and not only that but in an accent that told the major he was not a gentleman. It was evident from his thunderous expression that he would have liked to have had him arrested, tried and shot at dawn for desertion. It was, unfortunately, true that the captain was due some leave and that the woman who was wounded would need an escort, a medical escort across the Channel, but it was up to him to suggest it, not *Captain* O'Leary and he was not best pleased. The woman had been wounded on duty and like every soldier had the right to decent medical attention but still the doctor's high-handed manner offended him. Reluctantly he issued the necessary papers.

She was strapped to a stretcher and, with Patrick circling the small procession like a mother hen with one chick, was carried as gently as was humanly possible by the two careful orderlies and placed in the back of the ambulance that was to take her to the hospital train. Patrick winced at every pothole and lurch of the vehicle, not certain whether it was wise to move a patient with a head injury, especially one who was so precious to him, but it was certain she could not stay where she was. She needed round the clock nursing, someone to watch her night and day, careful feeding and the presence of a doctor until she was showing signs of recovery, by which he meant when she recognised him and looked with full awareness into his eyes.

The Channel steamer was full of the badly wounded, the very decks crammed from bow to stern and from port to starboard with men who lay still and frighteningly silent, those who moaned or called for their mothers, those were known as 'boat sitting', and 'boat lying', men with different coloured tags tied to them to denote their condition and urgency of their case to those at the other end, and the nurses were kept busy. A line of blinded men had followed him up the gangplank in single file, each sightless man with his hand on the shoulder of the sightless man in front, a young doctor leading the way, a young nurse bringing up the rear.

They had reached Dover and been moved, with the rest of the casualties, on to the hospital train which would take them into Charing Cross and for the whole of the journey he hung over her, feeding her what was obtainable, mainly bread soaked in warm milk, checking her dressing, holding her hand, gazing into her strangely luminous lavender-blue eyes which gazed into his without recognition and talking to her, for though others of the medical profession laughed at him, behind his back, naturally, he believed that to talk of things, places, events they had both shared, people they both knew might reach the part of her brain that was shut off from him at the moment.

'Do you remember that first time I drove a motor car, my darling, when we went up to Grasmere? Dick's Darracq with Nan and Nelly sitting in the back holding on to each other for dear life as though the devil himself was taking them both to hell. As it happened they were right to be afraid since I had never driven a motor before. Oh, a few lessons from dear old Dick . . . and then when I did my best to teach you . . . you were always bold, my heart, wild and bold and the most courageous woman I'd ever met. I can see you now that first time, screaming into the faces of those coppers who had you by the arms. Sweet Mother, I was appalled and enraptured at the same time. I think I loved you then. I *know* I loved you then and have never stopped. Every day you were in my thoughts . . . I used to think about you when I should have had my mind on other things but this time I shan't let you go, macushla. As soon as you're well enough you and I shall be married. I'm what you might call a lapsed Catholic, I suppose, but I don't care if we get married in a Jewish synagogue or a Muslim temple as long as I can tie you safely by my side and keep you safe for the rest of our lives. Poor Dick, with that mother of his, I hate to think of Rose facing up to that. D'you think she will ever let them live their lives in peace or will she be forever interfering? That party, d'you remember, at the Ritz. She couldn't bear to see the poor chap dance with her.' He smiled and bent to kiss her parted lips which she didn't object to, which was a foolish thing to think, he told himself, when she would have allowed any man on the train to kiss her because she was not the Alex Goodwin who would have slapped his face had she the mind. 'D'you recall that walk up Rydal Fell and you just out of prison? Christ, you were stubborn . . .' and on and on throughout the journey until at last they pulled into Charing Cross where the ambulances, the stretcher-bearers, the drivers waited in silence for the boys who had come home, perhaps to live, to be put together again and be returned once more to the slaughter-house of France, perhaps to resume some sort of life with their loved ones.

And at the gate was Archie Goodwin, his face as old and drawn as a man twice his age, with Nan beside him, weeping as she watched the shattered young men being carried past her.

There was a private ambulance waiting, Archie mumbled, looking down at the slight and pitiful figure of his daughter, his face paling even more at the sight of the bandage that swathed her head, at her wan, lifeless face, and yet her lovely eyes seemed unchanged.

'Oh, my pet, my pet,' moaned Nan, reaching out a trembling hand to the girl who had been her daughter. She had not given birth to her but she was Nan's daughter just the same. The hand she put out halted then rose to her mouth as she stifled a sound but, being Nan, she pulled herself together, straightened up and led the way, not only for Alex on her stretcher, but for the dazed old man who was her father.

She and Patrick put her to bed, helped by Nelly who cried silently all the time, for Patrick told them Miss Alex must be moved as little as possible. They took her clothing from her, finding no embarrassment in her nakedness as they ever so carefully put her nightdress on her, trying not to joggle her as Doctor Patrick instructed, for they all loved her. They placed her in the soft, clean bed, smoothing the bedclothes which they pulled up to her chin, not knowing what they could do to help her.

'I'll sit with her for—' he began but Nan bristled fiercely.

'Tha'll not, the sight of yer. 'Ave tha' looked in the mirror recently? Tha' look worse than Miss Alex. Now Nelly's got tha' bed ready and when tha've 'ad a bath' – studying the stains on his uniform, of what sort she didn't know but she could imagine – 'tha' can get in it. I'll watch Miss Alex. I'll not leave 'er, you know that an' if she so much as stirs I'll send Nelly fer thi'. First tell her pa ter come an' . . . an' kiss 'er, poor old man. Go on, yer daft 'apporth. D'yer think I'd let owt happen ter Miss Alex?'

He was appalled when he woke to find he had slept for twenty-four hours, but when he ran along the corridor to Alex's bedroom in one of Archie Goodwin's dressing-gowns, naked beneath, he found the two women hanging over the bed watching Alex sleep. Or had she lost consciousness again?

'Why the devil didn't you wake me, you stupid woman?' His anger was knife-edged but Nan Meredith took no offence since she knew what drove him. He leaned over the bed and put his hand on Alex's face, laying the back of it to her forehead, then bending to kiss her lips with such love Nan had to turn away, for she felt herself to be prying on something rare. She thought for a minute he was going to lie down beside the still figure on the bed then he straightened up and as though suddenly conscious of his appearance, smiled boyishly at Nan. He put a hand to his own face and she heard the rasp of the stubble under his fingers.

'I'd best make myself decent: another bath and a shave, I think, but my uniform . . .'

'Nay, don't worry, sir. Tha's about same size as Mr Goodwin an' I've got thi' a pair of 'is trousers an' a shirt. Nelly's 'ad a go at tha' uniform an' made a grand job but the master . . .'

He had forgotten Archie Goodwin in his rapt attention to Alex and he turned abruptly towards Nan.

'Mr Goodwin, how is he? Has he been up to see Alex? I had quite . . . Dear God, for me to sleep so long when there are those who are as . . . as devastated as me. Where is he?'

'He's been up, Doctor, and sat with Miss Alex for over an hour this morning. He talks to 'er about nowt really, holding her hand and . . .'

'But that is what is needed, Nan. Or so I maintain. I don't believe that she cannot hear and, perhaps, respond in time to what is said to her. We know nothing of head wounds, Nan, but I firmly believe that those who are . . . as Alex is . . . must benefit . . .' He whirled back to the bed, the incongruity of his billowing dressing-gown appearing not to bother him, dropping to his knees and taking her limp hand, under the nails of which black crescents of oil still lay. She was washed carefully, so carefully that she was hardly moved and the oil of her engine was ingrained in her skin. He kissed her hand, gazing down with such sadness into the face he loved it was hard for Nan to quell her tears.

'Oh, Nan, I have healed so many men and yet for this one woman I cannot find a cure. What irony.'

Nan didn't know what irony was but she did know this man suffered and she, with her big heart and her own need to put things right for those she loved and admired, would do all she could to get them all well again. Miss Alex, the master and the doctor. She watched him for a moment then put a hand on his shoulder, for he seemed to have forgotten her existence as he contemplated Miss Alex's serene face.

'Doctor, will tha' not go an' get thissen washed an' dressed. Nelly'll cook yer a bit o' breakfast then Mr Goodwin would be glad of a word. He knows nowt of what 'appened. None of us do and then there's Master Tom 'angin' about at Edge Bottom waitin' on a word from 'is pa. 'E wanted ter come an' . . . well, sir, I'll stay wi' Miss Alex while—'

'Has she had anything to eat, Nan?'

'Why, bless yer, sir, she's 'ad porridge what I made wi' plenty o' milk an' toast wi' plenty o' best butter an' eats it up as good as gold. Open tha' mouth, I say, and blow me, she does, so 'appen tha're right, Doctor, about talkin' to 'er. I've medd an egg custard wi' a dozen eggs so I reckon she'll not starve, not if I've owt ter do wi' it. Now, off tha' go like a good lad' – as if he were about ten years old – 'an' come back when tha're ready.'

He bathed and shaved and shrugged into the trousers and shirt Nelly had put out for him then went down to the room where Archie Goodwin sat staring blindly out of the window. There was a newspaper in his lap but he was not reading it and as Patrick entered the room he leaped to his feet, the newspaper dangling from his hand, his face eager, not hopeful exactly, but longing to hear what Patrick had to say about his girl.

'Mr Goodwin . . .'

'Archie, please. How is she? Is she making progress? Christ, how can I stand it if . . . first my Beth, then Tom and now Alex. It's more than I can bear . . .'

'Archie, please . . . please, I am . . . she is eating the good stuff Nan produces, nourishing food, easy to digest and she seems . . . well, I am to change the dressing today and look at the wound. The stitches will be ready to come out in a week or so.'

Archie winced and put out a hand to the back of a chair to steady himself.

'Dick and I . . . you remember Dick, my colleague at St Thomas's? I believe you met.'

'Yes, nice chap.'

'He helped me with the surgery and I couldn't have had a better man. We broke every rule there is to break, neither of us caring if we were arrested for desertion or whatever the army flings at those who do not obey the rules but I think, because Alex was a woman casualty, they agreed to look the other way and . . . well the surgery went well. She was . . . her ambulance was shelled and had she not been at the back of it, we don't know why, instead of inside . . . She was thrown some distance. There were . . . I'm sorry, Mr . . . Archie, perhaps this is too much for you, she is your daughter.'

'No, no, please go on.'

'There were splinters in her skull but Dick and I removed them . . .' Making it sound so easy, those gruelling hours of careful probing, wanting to get every last scrap out and yet terrified of doing more damage.

'She has had a terrible trauma, Archie, and I believe is in deep shock but we must wait and see – pray – that she comes out of it. She is . . .' He hesitated. 'Well, sir, she is not in a . . . how can I say this? For years she has abused her own health, sir, with the suffragettes and then in the exhausting and shocking conditions she worked under in France and the men . . . the casualties she handled. There is not a stronger, more resolute woman, a braver woman in the world and I love her. When she is well . . . *when she is well*, Archie, I shall marry her and give her lots of babies so that she cannot . . . I'm sorry, Archie, I'm sorry . . .' It was evident that Patrick O'Leary was not exactly in tip-top condition himself. He had worked round the clock putting men back together again, almost as shocked as those who came wandering in a daze from the trenches, some of them on the run, throwing away their arms and as many as four a month were being shot for desertion. Poor sods, he often thought, for he could not disassociate himself from the men he tended. Detachment was what was needed and he could not seem to acquire it.

'Don't apologise, old man,' said Alex's father, putting a compassionate hand on Patrick's arm. 'Now why don't you go to the kitchen, in fact I'll come with you' – wanting to make sure this man ate a decent meal before he fell apart himself – 'since I've had nothing but a bit of toast myself. We must keep strong, the pair of us or we'll be no good to Alex. Nelly will do us some bacon and eggs . . . no, don't argue, lad.'

They took it in turns to watch over her. Patrick carefully removed the dressing on that first day, allowing no one in the room with him but Nan, who could be trusted not to weep or gasp with horror at the sight of the shaven head and neatly stitched wound. It was clean and already healing, he could see that at once, with no sign of the suppuration the medical profession, especially in the battlefield hospitals, dreaded. Nan swayed a little but she held the basin, passed the clean bandages, the scissors, the bowl of warm, disinfected water, removed the slightly bloodstained dressing, then helped Doctor Patrick, again with no embarrassment, to wash her lamb all over, a complete bed bath, Doctor Patrick said, and though Nelly was willing, nay eager to help, she would weep and that would undo them all.

They were surprised but delighted when Tom turned up a few days later, with Harry Preston to guide him. They had come by train from St Helens, a train packed with wildly cheering volunteers longing to get to the front. There was still fighting in small areas, though the rumour of the big push, which was to be a combined British and French attack, was on everyone's lips. The fighting at Verdun where the French were said to be losing thousands of men each day was in all the newspapers, but these lads who couldn't wait to be in it, were not put off, for was not one British soldier worth ten of a foreign army! Tom carried a white stick and wore his smart officer's uniform and wherever he went, he told them, ready to smile, crowds parted respectfully for him because he must be one of their war heroes, and so he was, his father said fondly, throwing an arm across his shoulders.

He had come to see his sister and to have his sight checked by the eminent eye consultant who was slowly but surely, and with the latest surgery in which Patrick was vastly interested, returning partial sight to him and hoped for even better.

After ten days, again with only Nan to help him, Patrick unwound the bandages, dropping them in the basin Nan held out to him. They were perfectly clean. Taking an instrument which had been bubbling in a steriliser for ten minutes, he cut and delicately removed the neat stitches which were almost hidden in the wisps of her growing hair. Though he knew it would shock those who loved her he decided to leave the bandages off. The scar was clean and fine, barely noticeable on her white scalp which would not really matter, for her hair was growing and though at the moment it was just a short layer of fluff, like that of a newborn baby, it would soon be the thick curling tumble again that had bounced about her delicate skull.

'Should we perhaps put a cap on her, Nan?' he asked doubtfully. 'Her father and brother might be upset when they see her as she is now. I realise she is much improved.' Even in ten days she looked better, as she was eating well and, naturally, resting which was what her exhausted body needed. He was pleased with her general health but she was still not the Alex her family was accustomed to. She was fine-drawn but with a look of serenity that was unfamiliar and brought back to him memories of the Madonna he had seen almost every day of his childhood. Not his Alex who was hot-headed and warm-hearted, who had argued and fought and frowned fiercely when she disagreed over something, which was most of the time. Please, Holy Mother, look down on this woman I love and give her back her spirit, her strength, her generous, fighting strength, her love that I cannot live without. There is a hole in the fabric of my life that will never be mended unless she returns to me. A great emptiness that only she can fill and I find I am terrified, lost in a cold world where she, the flame that is Alex has been extinguished. But all she needed now, he told himself desperately, was to sit in the warm sunshine, get some colour in her cheeks and she would at least *look* like Alex Goodwin.

'Nay,' Nelly said, her head on one side as she stood by the bed, her strong hands holding one of Alex's. 'I think she should let the air get ter that scar. Me mam always used ter say ter let the air get to it when we bairns scraped our knees. Besides, they'll have ter get used to it some time, won't they?'

'Yes, but we must not allow ourselves to . . . to . . .'

'Give up 'ope?'

He sighed deeply. 'You see, Nan, I must go back at the end of the week.'

'Go back, lad?' Nan turned astonished eyes on him.

'Yes. I'm on leave, Nan, and if I don't return they will come and get me. I'll be arrested, so I will, tried as a deserter and perhaps shot.'

'Eeh, never!' Nan was aghast. 'They'd never shoot thi'. Not a decent chap like thee. Miss Alex needs thi'.'

'And so do the casualties from the trenches, Nan. I have a duty.'

'Gerron, tha' can't just leave 'er.'

'I can if I know you're here to look after her, Nan.' His expression was haunted and the shine of what looked like tears in his golden-brown eyes was almost more than Nan could stand. She knew what Miss Alex meant to him but it seemed he was not to be allowed to care for her as she needed to be cared for and yet she felt a glow of pride that he was prepared to leave her in hers, Nan Meredith's, loving hands.

'She'll be all right with me, Doctor, but just in case . . . well, I'm sure it'll not be needed but 'appen tha'll know a doctor at that hospital where tha' worked, one tha' trusts fer me ter call on, not that it'll be needed,' she repeated hastily.

'Nan, do you not think it would be wiser to take her back to her home? To Edge Bottom House where she can recover in the peace of the country? Where Doctor Bennett can keep an eye on her? We can trust Doctor Bennett, can't we? Oh, I know he is an old man but he is a true doctor and the only one I would leave her with. Harry could fetch him in the motor to Edge Bottom. What d'you think?'

Nan's face lit up and she nodded her head in agreement. 'O' course, Doctor Patrick, where else would she get such devoted care?'

'Then let her father come to her and we will discuss it with him, so. He is a man of wealth, I believe, and a private ambulance could take her back home. There is just one thing, Nan.'

'Yes, Doctor?' Nan's voice was eager.

'Can you read?'

'Read, Doctor?'

'Yes, can you?'

'I can that, sir.'

'And write?'

'Aye, not well, but I can mekk messen understood.'

'Good, then I place her in your care. You can report to me each day in a letter and I will reply. You are a good, sensible woman and we shall make her well between us.'

Patrick O'Leary kissed his love goodbye, holding her in his arms, stroking her face, running his hands over the fluffy softness of her growing hair, no more than half an inch long but soft and sweet-smelling, for Nan and Nelly bathed her, washed her hair, brushed it and even placed a ribbon in it as though she were a baby. When the time came, not for a few weeks yet, Patrick O'Leary told them, she must be taken to her country home, accompanied by her father and brother, by Nan and Nelly, and spend the summer in the garden at Edge Bottom House, in the meadows and lanes edged with wild roses and each day he would write to her and Nan would read his letters to his love. She was to be talked to, Nan was to tell the servants, reminded of her life as a child and a young woman, the memories repeated to her again and again and she was not to sit in silence as if she were senseless. Her father could read her favourite books to her. Music, conversation, fresh air, good food and even a gentle ride round the paddock with Harry. Everything that she had done as a child, and with Doctor Bennett to oversee her welfare, she would recover. *She would recover*, did Nan understand?

Nan said she did.

Nan and Nelly cried quietly in the kitchen when he had gone, for they had come to think the world of the man who was mending their Miss Alex. Her father sat with her, watching her and dozing a little because he had grown old since his wife died and so he didn't notice that every now and again her eyes turned towards the door then back to the window where the blue sky was studded with fleecy clouds.

At the back doorstep a sound was heard and when Nelly

went to investigate a pretty little ginger cat, a young cat, sat there and eyed her sorrowfully.

'Where't dickens 'ave you come from?' she asked, still tearful, but before she could put out a hand to stop it, the cat darted between her legs, across the kitchen, along the hall and up the stairs. It mewed plaintively at the door to Alex's bedroom which was ajar and as Nelly pounded up the stairs after it, fled into the room, jumped up on the bed and pawed delicately at the still figure who lay there. Alex turned her head and the cat stared down into her face. Archie had dozed off and did not see what was happening and by the time Nelly arrived the cat was curled in the crook of Alex's arm.

'See, we can't 'ave this, tha' little devil. God knows where tha've bin.' She leaned over to take the cat from Alex's arms but as she did so two fat tears rolled down Alex's cheeks, one falling on the cat's nose. It sneezed indignantly and Alex smiled. For the first time she smiled!

# 19

They could not part her from the young ginger cat and Dr Bennett who was brought over almost every day to check on Alex's progress was of the opinion that the pretty little animal must be from part of her past life though none of them could remember her. She had certainly not been at Bedford Square when Nan and Nelly had lived there but the dratted thing seemed to know her way about the house which was a bit of a mystery. Not that she left Miss Alex's side much except when she darted down to the kitchen to eat the scraps Nelly put down for her and to roam about the long, narrow garden at the back of the house until she found a suitable place to relieve herself. A clean little thing, she was, Nan decided, but God knew where she had come from. She made up her mind that the cat must have a bath before she'd let the thing get in bed with Miss Alex, which it seemed she and Miss Alex were determined she should. And what a commotion that had caused, with both Nan and Nelly getting scratched for their trouble but she really was attractive when she was wrapped in a towel and dried, spitting her displeasure, with lovely golden and tawny stripes that rippled when she moved. In a way it was a wonderful step forward, they all decided, for it was the first sign of positive life Miss Alex had shown and hope rested in Nan's breast when she saw the devotion she and the animal showed one another.

And apart from the *cat's* cleanliness there was one other thing that brought a strange glow to Nan and that was the fact that Miss Alex never . . . well, messed herself, at least not after she regained consciousness. Not that Nan would have objected to clearing up after her, far from it. Somehow, Nan never could work out how she achieved it but she always let Nan know that she needed the pewter bedpan Doctor Patrick had left for her. She wished she'd mentioned it to Doctor Patrick before he left, for surely a woman who knows and can make them aware that the utensil was needed must surely have *something* working in her brain.

And she had taken to getting out of her bed too, so she must be getting stronger, the damned cat clutched in her arms and the animal didn't seem to mind being dangled like an old rag doll as a careless child might hold it. The cat *knew* her and Alex knew and remembered *her*!

It was three weeks later that they travelled back to St Helens. Harry had returned to Edge Bottom House and brought back the motor to London, for with Alex sitting up and even taking a few hesitant steps about the room it was decided that an ambulance wasn't necessary. It was June and the weather was perfect, not too hot but sunny and they took the journey in stages, Harry driving, the master next to him and the three women in the back. Tom remained in London in the private hospital under the care of the eye surgeon of whom Patrick had fully approved, having more surgery, and when it was time Harry would go back to London to fetch him home. In the meanwhile the five of them meandered up north, staying a night or two here and there in smart hotels where guests stared in amazement at the incredibly lovely young woman who wandered about the place with a ginger cat in her arms! When one or two approached her, wanting to stroke the lovely animal, as people do, they were even more amazed when the young woman stared at them as though they spoke a foreign language, standing still, frozen as a statue, waiting until they went away or her companion came hurrying across to get her. She was quite lovely with short curling hair and a perfectly flawless complexion but absolutely no expression, not even in her eyes, the colour of which reminded them of the lavender in the hotel garden.

Nan and Patrick exchanged letters, though Nan's were mostly a list of what Alex had eaten, with now and again a report of where they had walked each day. Patrick's were full of instructions but he also included a letter for Alex, a love letter really but with very little of how he felt in it, for he could hardly embarrass poor Nan! He wrote about the flowers, mostly scarlet poppies, he had seen growing – a rare sight – in the field by the hospital, the skylark singing above his head as he wrote his letter, a stray dog he had befriended, a soldier in the ward with a fine tenor voice who kept the wounded entertained. There were letters from Rose who wrote almost the same thing, for neither of them could tell Alex what was really going on about them! Will, who had been instructed by his father, scribbled notes, describing the colours of the sky at dusk and dawn and the narrow escape he had had when he had been forced to land his bi-plane in a field and he had been spirited away by a French farmer. Even Noah made an effort to get a letter to her though they mostly contained nothing but Rose, Rose, Rose and the few meetings they had managed. Nan stumbled through them all and Alex appeared to be attentive, her hand caressing the cat's lovely shining coat, her head cocked, whether it was to listen to the letters, the cat's ecstatic purring or Nan's voice Nan never knew.

A routine was established with almost daily visits from Doctor Bennett who held Alex's hand and spoke gently to her, of her mother, of his wife Laura who was not well, of their suffragist days. She seemed to listen, looking into his kindly old face, saying nothing, responding to nothing, a lovely, blank-faced doll who did not even turn her head when anyone entered the room, which alarmed the servants but they took their cue from Nan. They had been shocked when she had been brought home, bewildered, compassionate, treating her with hushed silence, but Nan put a stop to all that. Though they had at first felt like mourners laughing at a funeral they became used to the silent shadow who went everywhere with Nan and began to resume the jokes, the teasing and the laughter that had always been a part of their happy household. She was taken for walks in the fields and lanes, the cat either in her arms or flirting at her heels, often her hand in Nan's like a child going on a 'ta-ta' as Nan described it. The sunshine tinted her cheeks with a wash of gold and touched her cheekbones with carnation. Her figure became rounded and supple, losing that gauntness she had acquired in London. They took picnics, she and Nan and Nelly, sometimes in the motor with Mr Archie and Harry, driving to the woodland to the north of the town, sitting in the warming sunshine, shoulder-deep in bracken and fern.

And then it was July. The first day of July and the expected Somme offensive began, though those at Edge Bottom House were unaware of it for several days and when they were the newspapers described it as a great victory. In the early months of 1916, British troops in France, both the few remaining regulars from the old BEF and the eager recruits to Kitchener's New Army, were preparing for the big push. There had been a spirit of optimism and excitement among the men, for they felt, indeed had been led to believe, that this was the offensive, carefully planned and prepared for, that was going to smash the German army and bring an early end to the war.

The new offensive was preceded by five days of intensive artillery bombardment intended to obliterate the German trenches and eliminate resistance, but not only did the bombardment forewarn the Germans of the area of the attack, it heralded a total massacre. Against the German defences which had not been destroyed as the allies had hoped, eager young soldiers of Great Britain and France were thrown. They carried sixty-six pounds of equipment, rifle and ammunition, field telephones, shovels and picks. They had to struggle out of their trenches, the wounded, having once fallen, not able to regain their feet. Those who survived were to advance across no-man's-land at a steady pace in close formation and were at once mown down by the enemy's gunfire.

The first day of the offensive had broken in an ironic summer loveliness on a scene that was shortly to be one of unmitigated horror as the allies were simply annihilated, for within an hour of the attack the ground was smothered with British dead and dying, estimated at 30,000, and by midday, as the generals continued to throw troops into the battle, some 100,000 men had been engulfed in the carnage. Among them was Private Noah Goodwin, Corporal Alfie Hutchinson and his brother, Robbie, who had worked in Mr Goodwin's stables at Edge Bottom House, Sergeant Sidney Holden, one-time butler to the Goodwins, Corporal Ben Holcroft, brother of Nelly, Private George Murphy whose grandfather was brother to Abby Goodwin and dozens of others from the village and the Goodwin Glass and Brick Works, those who had all rushed to do their bit in August 1914.

Advanced dressing stations had been set up along the line with well-sandbagged collecting centres a little distance behind them. Almost from the first whistle they were swamped with a queue of walking wounded waiting four-deep for attention and although there were more medical personnel concentrated than there had ever been before it was obvious that the men would have a long time to wait, to bleed, to die. Other hospitals had been combed for all the medical staff and transport that could be spared. Specialist surgical teams of doctors, nurses and anaesthetists stood by, ready to move quickly to where they were most needed. Operating theatres were sent forward near the line to deal speedily with the seriously injured who would otherwise not have survived the ambulance journey to the casualty clearing stations. There were three empty hospital trains waiting in the area but it had soon become obvious that the provisions were far from adequate. In the first twenty-four hours 24,000 wounded had passed through the field ambulances in a steady flow and Dick Morris, who had been transferred there in preparation for the battle, worked with almost robot-like precision, sorting out those who had a chance of surviving their wounds and those for whom there was no hope, playing God, he howled into the eternal blue bowl of the cloudless sky. He slapped temporary dressings on those he could get to, while the rest lay without shelter, the first of them on camp beds, stretchers, then when they ran out, on the blood-soaked naked earth surrounding the dressing station. The guns thudded and flashed through the night, lighting the starlit sky with flashes of yellow glare while doctors, nurses, surgeons and orderlies worked flat out, but they could only attend to a fraction of the wounded who had reached the dressing stations.

Dick moved from one operating table to the next, his mind blank, dazed with the multitude of shattered men he was expected to deal with and who crowded the temporary hospital tent, even the gangways between the stretchers so that the team were forced to step over them. They clogged up the entrance and carpeted the very ground about the tent, anywhere the frantic stretcher-bearers could find a space. There were flies, for it was hot and they gorged on the blood of the men too weak to brush them off.

He stood for a moment among the agony, the filth the men brought in with them, the sickening stench of soiled clothing, the moans and the retching, the hoarse, laboured breathing, the rustles and sighs of dying humanity, the writhing sea of suffering men, and wondered if he was going mad, or was it the world, for surely a God, the God his mother purported to believe in every Sunday in church would not allow this agony and remain unmoved. The young private on the table had a leg injury on which a dressing had been haphazardly slapped, probably by one of his mates up the line, and when Dick removed it there was white bone glinting obscenely through his young flesh, a gaping slash of blood, scarlet and seeping with other matter and he knew he should take the leg off. It would be quicker, allowing him to move on to other desperate men, but something in him rebelled, something he did not recognise as part of his doctor's oath and it drove him to swear that this young soldier would walk like a man again.

'Aren't you to amputate, Sir?' sister asked him as he hesitated, watching as the anaesthetist applied the anaesthetic. 'It'll be a bad case of gas gangrene if—'

'Bugger it, Sister, I'll be damned if—'

'Sir, there's no time,' she interrupted him.

'I said bugger it. What's the poor sod's name and rank?'

'Private Goodwin. Noah Goodwin,' wondering what the man's name and rank had to do with anything.

'Really!' Dick was so surprised he dropped the sterilised scalpel which fell into the pool of blood in which they stood. He stared into the man's flushed face on the table. Sister bent down and retrieved the instrument, wiping it on a scrap of gauze, then shrugged and handed it to the doctor, for what difference would it make what had adhered to the blade. The poor boy would die anyway, especially if the doctor had, for some reason, decided not to amputate. He slaved on for another hour, finishing Private Goodwin's surgery and attending to two more and when he sank to his knees in the lake of blood about the operating table in a sort of faint a VAD put an arm about him and guided him to the entrance.

'Take five minutes, Sir,' she told him gently, for they all liked Dick Morris who had a grin or a wicked joke for everyone. 'Have a fag an' I'll have one with you.' They sat down on the ground, their backs to the tent among the carpet of sighing, crying shadows who were dying around them.

The VAD drew on her cigarette, looking up into the doctor's

eyes. His face was gaunt with none of his usual optimism. The strain and exhaustion had them all at breaking point and she happened to know that Dick Morris had a fiancée who was also a VAD. He must be worried sick about her, for whatever was happening here would certainly be happening to her as well, wherever she was.

When the first shell dropped no more than a foot from them, landing on the silent figure of a wounded man, they both turned instinctively away from it but the shell did not burst. There was a small popping sound, like a cork coming out of a bottle, then nothing. There were more, all small and landing in a neat line across the field and on to the tented hospital. Dick Morris stood up, rubbing at his ankle where a sensation of burning had suddenly begun and the VAD began to cough and retch.

'Surely to God they wouldn't shell a bloody hospital,' he managed to say incredulously before he grabbed at his throat and fell down on top of the nearest casualty.

It was several weeks before Nelly's mam got the dreaded envelope containing the brief message that her son, Corporal Ben Holcroft, had been killed in action. Nelly had screamed when her younger brother, Willy, came to fetch her, shouting that as soon as he was sixteen he was going to go over there and kill the bugger who had put a bullet in their Ben. Their Ben had not actually had the mercy of a clean bullet in him but had been blown into so many small pieces none of his mates could find him, not even his belt buckle.

'Now then, Willy Holcroft, don't let me hear you talk like that,' Nan had told him sharply. 'Tha' mam don't want ter hear it right now. I'm real sad about your Ben but tha' job now is ter comfort tha' mam. See, get your Nelly home an' I'll be over as soon as I can.' She looked about her for Mary Smith since someone must stay with Alex while Nan went to comfort the bereaved family. Dottie was a grand lass, a parlour-maid, but she was inclined to panic if there was no one to give orders and Ruth in the kitchen was a hard worker but less than useless at anything beyond scrubbing and scouring and polishing. The old man, by whom she meant her master, was not strong enough, nor well enough since the mistress had died to deal with the delicate task of watching Miss Alex.

'I'll see to her, Nan,' a quiet male voice from the kitchen door said and there was Harry, who had known Miss Alex since her birth and could be trusted to watch her with as much care as Nan herself. After all, it was he who accompanied them on their walks, dawdling behind her and Miss Alex, picking a flower to put in her hand, helping her over stiles and taking her round the paddock on the old mare.

'But what about when she goes to 'er bed, Harry? I might not be back . . .'

'Dottie'll help. She's a good lass and as long as there's someone ter tell 'er what ter do she's handy enough. Anyway, Mam'll see to it all.'

'True, true.' Nan bit her lip, one arm round the weeping form of Nelly, the other studying the quiet figure of Miss Alex who sat placidly in the rocking-chair by the kitchen fire, Cat, as Nan had named her, on her lap. 'Well, it's not far to the Holcroft cottage so promise me tha'll send Ruth for me if I'm needed. 'Appen there'll be relatives of Mrs Holcroft there an' I can get 'ome.'

The telegram boy had barely got back to the post office from his fifteenth trip out that day, for there were a lot of St Helens lads over there, when there was one for Edge Bottom House.

'Oh, sod it,' he murmured, not because he resented another trip but the Goodwin family seemed to have had more than their fair share of bad luck recently. First Mrs Goodwin dying like that, then her son, young Tom, being blinded, and Miss

Alex who had been driving the wounded in France getting a shell on her head and sending her out of her mind.

'Is it . . . is it Master Will, sir?' he asked the postmaster fearfully.

'No, but it's a Goodwin just the same.'

'A Goodwin? Who else have they got over there?'

'Nay, don't ask me, lad, but it's addressed to Mr Archie Goodwin.'

Archie reluctantly took the telegram from Dottie's hand. Dottie snatched her hand back and wiped it down her apron as though it had contaminated her, wishing she could run back to the security of the kitchen where Ruth and Harry sat with Miss Alex. But she could hardly leave the poor old man to deal with it himself, could she? What if it was Master Will, him that flew in the 'airyplane'?

Archie held the dreaded telegram in his trembling hand, staring at it with teary eyes. He knew Tom was safe in the hospital at Fulham but what of Will in that flimsy thing he took to the skies in? Who else could it be? And when, at last, to Dottie's great relief he opened it and the name Noah Goodwin jumped out at him he gave a great sigh of relief.

He was immediately ashamed but then Milly's son meant not a great deal to him. 'Wounded in action' it read and he wondered why it had come to him. Probably because Noah had given this address, being an American, as his next of kin. Now he had the dreadful task of telegraphing Milly and Todd and telling them the bald facts of their son's injury, for that was all he knew. The one person who could have told him why Noah Goodwin had given his Goodwin cousins as his next of kin was at that moment sitting placidly in the chair that Harry had placed there for her in the stable yard where he could watch her while he groomed the old mare. The cat was curled on her lap and when, from somewhere across the fields where a farmer was aiming at a fox which was decimating his hen coop, the sound of a shot lifted a flock of crows from the trees, Alex turned her head. In her eyes was a tiny prick of light and her hands clenched in the cat's fur making her squirm but Harry did not notice.

In the Quai d'Escale Hospital in Le Havre where she had been sent when the Battle of the Somme was being planned, Rosie Kellett hardly had time to look at what was going on around her but she could hear the trains, for they ran right under the wards. Day and night from 1 July onwards there was a constant rumble as they arrived to unload and immediately start off back again, empty, to the railhead to fetch the next train-load of wounded. The weather was fine and they all gave thanks for it, since there were so many to go that the stretchers were lying all over the quay waiting for a ship to come in. It was never-ending, the ships going back and forth, the stretcher cases pouring in, the most dangerously wounded kept at the hospital, the others, and really how were they to distinguish between them, going straight to England. In most cases there was not even enough time to clean them up or to change the rough dressings that had been clapped on them in the heat of the battle, hours, or in some cases, days earlier. It seemed to the frantic doctors and nurses, drivers and stretcher-bearers working round the clock in the wards, the ambulance columns, transports and trains that there must be hardly a whole soldier left at the front.

She was on night duty and had been in constant attendance on a patient who was one of those lying out on the veranda. She had put a chair next to his bed, meaning to rest for a moment but must have dozed off, for she was roughly shaken by an orderly who, with another, was placing a stretcher next to the bed of the man she was watching.

'Gas case, Sister,' they said, for they called all the nurses 'Sister'. 'His chest's bad.'

She knelt down by the side of the officer, a captain by the insignia on his bloody uniform, noting with compassion that his face was ravaged and was a livid blue and he was struggling to breathe. He was suffering from the secondary effect of gas which was acute bronchitis. She was appalled, for nothing in her experience had equipped her to deal with this terrible rasping struggle to breathe. She knew it was happening but she had not herself had to deal with it before.

'Why is he so bloodstained?' she asked the orderly as he turned away. The officer's eyes were on her face, alive and terrified, and something in them made her frown.

'He's a doctor,' the orderly said. 'His hospital was shelled by the bastards.'

'Dear God . . . oh, dear God,' she moaned, for she was looking down into the livid face of Dick Morris. He even tried to smile as the liquid in his lungs began to drown him but the dear God she had called upon had placed him in the one set of hands that could save him, not because she was more experienced than the doctors but because she loved him. Had loved him for years and was promised to him in marriage and if Dick Morris had the slightest, faintest hope of life in him, Rose Kellett would find it and restore it to him.

They travelled home on the same ship, Dick Morris and Noah Goodwin, unaware of each other and that they had left behind to fight on the girl they both loved. Dick was met at the station by his mother and father, his mother with a scented handkerchief to her nose, for really, as she said to her husband, she had no idea it would be like this. She was a lady of breeding, or at least she liked to think she was, and to be forced to look for her boy among all these . . . these men who all looked to be in exactly the same condition was too much for her to bear. Edward must look while she waited in the motor in which she expected to take her son home to Sevenoaks, to the care of the nurse they had hired, which his mother was sure would bring him back to health.

But Dick had been horribly burned by the mustard gas on his face and his body, and his lungs were badly damaged. He had nearly drowned in the infected fluid and for several weeks he had been blinded, his eyelids inflamed and gummed together and it had not been certain whether he would ever see again. The gas, lethal and invisible, had eaten through his uniform and he had suffered agonising water blisters, all of which had turned putrid, and had it not been for the personal and loving care he had been given by the VAD who had taken him over, nursing him when she was off duty and should have been asleep, he would not have lived.

Mrs Edward Morris knew nothing of this, of course, and was overruled not only by her husband and the doctor in charge but also her son himself, though he could barely speak, who insisted he was taken to the General Hospital at Wandsworth where Rosie, when she got leave, had promised to visit him. They both knew it would be a long job but at least he was out of the war and when he was recovered would resume his medical practice with her by his side. She had promised him. His mother was outraged and argued forcibly with the over-stretched doctor in charge but he simply walked away, for as he told her politely he had better things to do than argue with her over one casualty!

Further down the train a young private did his best not to cry out as the orderlies lifted him from the hospital train and carried him to the ambulance that was to take him to the same hospital as Dick Morris. His name was Noah Goodwin. Five others who had gone over the top with him, Alfie Hutchinson, Robbie Hutchinson, Sidney Holden, Ben Holcroft and George Murphy, remained in France in unmarked graves with the other thousands upon thousands who died and vanished that day.

# 20

'Imagine she is resting,' Doctor Bennett had told them, 'after a serious accident. As the body needs peace and quiet when it has been afflicted, so does the mind and that is what nature is doing with Alex. Protecting her, resting her, giving her body *and mind* time to heal. When she is totally healed she will come back to us.'

They were gathering blackberries in the field at the back of the house when Rose came upon them. The blackberries grew in profusion. Big, black, lustrous, their heady scent brought out by the warmth of the sun. The grass beneath the hedgerows was as springy as a mattress and the chestnut trees, which lined the lane from the house to the fields and which in the summer made an umbrella of pink blossom, spread a roof of green above their heads. The sun filtered through the trees playing on the quiet face of the young woman, and the servants with her, Nan, Nelly and Harry, used to her silence, scarcely glanced in her direction. She did not pick any blackberries but stood behind them, moving when they did, stroking her cat as they gossiped and laughed. They were so absorbed with the fruit, which Mrs Adams was going to mix with the apples from the orchard, promising Harry the best blackberry and apple pie he had ever tasted, they did not notice the turn of her head nor the twitch of her hand as though it would lift and pick a blackberry, as they were doing, if only it knew how.

It was almost the end of September and only yesterday the Battle of the Somme, never dormant, had erupted again, for it was said that Sir Douglas Haig was desperate to achieve a significant breakthrough before the end of the year. Again casualties were mounting by the minute and up and down the country more and more homes were receiving the brief and dreaded telegram beginning, 'It is my painful duty to inform you . . .'

It was in this month that Haig decided to play his trump card, a new British invention, the 'tank', fifty of which had been transported to France, but so many broke down or got bogged in the churned-up field of battle that the offensive dragged on, for the lumbering monsters had little effect.

Rose was so thin she looked like one of the delicate saplings Harry had planted – in lieu of a gardener – along the hedge that surrounded the paddock. She was dressed in what she must have worn over two years ago, a pretty but out-of-date muslin dress in a lovely soft shade of pink, the neck and the hemline decorated with pink ruffles. It had short sleeves revealing the stick-like fragility of her arms, the outfit hanging on her as though she had borrowed it from a woman several sizes bigger than she was. She wore no hat and her black hair, no longer as glossy as it once had been, since the opportunity to wash it in a field hospital was scarce, was still in a fat chignon at the back of her head. Her shoes were dusty, for there had been no rain for weeks and the lanes were dry and rutted.

She stopped when she saw them and began to smile. They had not seen her and for a minute or so she just watched them, then tears of joy filled her eyes. It was at that moment that Alex, as though her senses, closed to other sensations, detected the presence of another, turned her head. The three who were at the hedges all turned, open-mouthed, as she made some small sound in her throat and were amazed when she lifted her hand and pointed as though in welcome to the figure who stood in the lane. Again they turned to look where she pointed and at once all three of them began to smile and jabber.

'Alex . . . dearest Alex,' Rose cried and began to run towards her, convinced that her friend had recovered since she had received the last letter from Nan, but Alex took a step backwards, not in fear but in surprise, putting out her hand as though in defence. She clung to the cat with her other arm but strangely the animal also made a thin sound and before she could stop her, leaped from her arms and began to make her delicate, cat-like way towards Rose.

Rose stopped at once, knowing something was not as she had thought but she knelt in the dust and the cat arched her back and rubbed herself sinuously against her knee.

'Ginger . . . it's Ginger! Oh, Alex, where did she come from? I didn't know . . . in fact I never gave her another thought after the lady next door, you know, at Bedford Square, said she would look after her until we came back.' The cat purred rapturously but Alex took another step backwards and as though turning to strangers who just happened to be there, spoke to the three servants who stood as though turned to stone in the ditch beside the blackberry bushes.

'Oh please,' she said politely, 'will you not ask the lady to bring my cat back to me? She is used to me and I to her and I think she may be upset. Sir,' she appealed to the slack-jawed Harry, 'might I beg you to ask . . . I . . . well . . . I . . . you see . . . I'm not . . . and will you tell her that it's not Ginger . . . it's . . . it's . . .' She stopped speaking, looking bewildered as if for the moment she had forgotten her cat's name and at once Nan came out of her trance. Smiling with great joy and begging her with her eyes to understand, she walked towards Rose, picked up the cat and returned her to Alex's eager arms. She had not noticed how fat the cat had become and she made a vague note to tell Nelly not to feed the thing so much. Mind you, it had no exercise, lolling on Alex's knee all the livelong day.

'Oh, thank you, thank you so much. You are most kind.' Alex smiled and nodded her head, turning about as if she were to go somewhere then whirled back again for in truth she did not know where that might be.

'I'm looking for—' She stopped speaking abruptly and the three servants stared at her in consternation but Rose, with all her experience of confused, frightened, shell-shocked men, walked slowly towards her and putting out a hand placed it gently on Alex's arm. Alex flinched and her eyes were wary but she allowed it.

'Perhaps you would like to walk a little way with me,' Rose murmured. 'You and your cat. We have a house a little way along here and I'm sure someone would put the kettle on and make a cup of tea. This gentleman' – turning to smile at the delighted but bewildered Harry – 'might run ahead and warn them in the kitchen. And a saucer of milk for your cat, of course.' They were soon to learn that as long as the cat was included in any activity Alex could be coaxed to almost anything. She drew Alex's arm through hers, as a friend might, sensing that to take her hand might seem childish to a grown woman and they wandered off down the lane, Harry running ahead to warn not only the servants in the kitchen to put the kettle on but to let Archie Goodwin know that his daughter was returned, if not in *her* head, then in theirs. Nan and Nelly followed transfixed. The blackberries they had picked were left forgotten in the ditch where they had been dropped.

She was hesitant about crossing the threshold of her own home, the place in which she had lived for most of her life, or at least to where she had returned from her journeyings. She smiled politely at the man who stood stock-still, his face the colour of cement and as stiff, in the centre of the hallway and at the two maids who stood at his back. Her right arm was still through Rose's and the cat still dangled from her left.

'Is the kettle on, Ruth?' Rose said gaily to the gape-jawed kitchen-maid. 'We have a friend who would like a cup of tea and I must admit I could do with one myself. Mr Goodwin,

shall we go into the drawing-room and Dottie can bring it in.'
Her eyes were brilliant, not only with the tears she dared not
shed but with a warning to Archie not to drag his daughter into
his arms as he so obviously wanted to do. It was clear Alex knew
none of them, not even her own father. She had come back
from whatever desert she had wandered in but had not brought
her memory with her and until she did they must not rush at her
with the love, the kindness, the joy they so obviously felt, but
treat her like a guest, a welcome guest while she, Rose, led her
through the rest of the day and convinced her that it was all
right to stay with 'these people'!

They drank tea watched by Nan who sat down with them,
for Alex was her 'baby' and had been ever since Patrick had
brought her back from France five months ago. She had nursed
her, fed her, dressed her, taken her for walks, stayed with her
night and day with Nelly's help and when Nelly would have
hung back with the other servants, Nan took her arm and
coaxed her into the drawing-room with her as neither of them
wanted to miss this miraculous cure.

But it was not a cure. Certainly Alex could speak and smile,
take her tea in her hand and drink it, nodding politely at Nan
who passed it to her, but she was wary, ill at ease, holding Cat
on her lap though the animal tried several times to get down
and pad over to Rose. She had no memory of them, of the
house or the gardens and when they had drunk their tea she
stood up, as a guest would who had outstayed her welcome and
must be off home.

Rose stood up with her, smiling, then took her hands.

'Can Harry take you to wherever you're going in the motor
car? It would be no trouble.'

Alex looked about her nervously, biting her lip, clinging to
Rose's hands, letting, for the first time, the cat drop to the floor.

'I'm not sure where . . .'

'Perhaps until you remember you might like to stay with us?'

Rose asked her casually. 'We have plenty of room. I am in a room with two beds so you could share with me . . .' shooting a glance at Nan who nodded in understanding and hurried from the room. Rose was vastly relieved when Alex nodded her own head then bent to pick up the cat.

'That would be nice but . . .'

'Now don't you worry,' Rose said cheerfully. 'If anyone comes asking for you we have you here safe. Now my name is Rose and this is Nan and Nelly and . . . and Mr Goodwin' – shooting a look of apology at Alex's father – 'and you are . . .'

'Alex.' And that's how it was. Alex responded to her name as though, from the depths of her memory that was the one thing that remained and as long as Rose was with her in those first few days she seemed to be content to drift about after her. Cat was included wherever they went.

It was when Rose was telling Nan about Noah and Dick that Alex began to show signs of interest in what was happening, not just in this house and with these people who were so kind to her, but in what was happening beyond its four walls.

'There . . . there is a war?' she asked tentatively. 'I ask because you are telling Nan' – she turned to smile brightly at the woman who longed to hold her in her arms and rock her as she would her own child but must pretend to have no more than friendly feelings towards her – 'about a soldier who was wounded. What was his name?'

'His name is Dick Morris. He is a doctor but he . . .' How could she tell this child, this innocent child, for that was how Alex was, of the horror of Dick's wounds from the gas that had caught him at the front, of the VAD who had died beside him, of Noah, Alex's own half-brother whom Rose loved and who was recovering at the same hospital as Dick, of Patrick whom Alex loved and who loved her and who was still involved with the wounded from this second offensive on the Somme. He didn't know yet that Alex was . . . well, not exactly recovered, since her memory seemed to be totally buried but that she was physically Alex Goodwin again. He must be told and as soon as possible so that he could get home and perhaps the sight of him would restore the whole of Alex to them.

'And he has been wounded?' Alex looked distressed.

'Yes, but he will recover. I am to go and visit him in a London hospital where the wounded soldiers are brought.'

'You're . . . you're not to leave here, Rosie?' This was the first time Alex had used the name by which they had once called Rose. None of them had told her of it so was this another hopeful sign? She and Alex had shared the room Alex had slept in since her return to Edge Bottom, Alex sleeping in her own bed and Rose, who said she could sleep on a clothes line after her experiences in France, in the truckle bed either Nan or Nelly had used.

This was surely the time to tell Alex that Edge Bottom House was not really Rose's home. But before she could find the words, to arrange them in her mind and transfer them to Alex's troubled memory Alex burst out.

'Can I come with you, Rose?'

Rose knew that it was not that Alex wanted to go to London but that she did not want to part with Rose. It was now that she must be . . . well, she could hardly call it brutal, but she must be firm. 'No, darling, not this time. I won't be gone long and Nan will look after you.'

Alex turned a look on Nan which struck her to the heart for it told her that Nan was a poor substitute for Rose, Nan who would have given her life to save her young mistress a moment's distress. Nan who had brought her back from the brink to good health and who was now to be discarded, then Alex, with a lovely gesture that was a part of her from the old days, took Nan's hand in hers and smiled.

'I don't need looking after, Rosie. I put my own shoes on this morning and even tied the laces but I would be glad of Nan's company . . . her friendship until you return. Will that be long, Rosie?'

Nan could feel the tears welling up in her throat but knew she must not spill them, for nothing must be said or done that might upset the delicate balance of this woman's mental state. She patted Alex's hand then stood up and moved towards the door of the drawing-room where the three of them had been drinking hot chocolate, Alex's made with creamy milk, for Nan could not get out of the habit of feeding up anyone who might need it. At the moment it was the master because it was breaking his heart that his own daughter didn't know she *was* his daughter. He wanted to pet her, to put his arms about her, to kiss her, to show his love but he had been told by Rose who was, after all, a nurse, and even by John Bennett who had come over to look at Alex, that he must treat her like a guest in the house. If she had come this far she could go further and one day he would have his child back again.

Rose cleared her throat nervously as she felt it was time to test further Alex's ability to cope with the world beyond the security of Edge Bottom House.

'You see, Alex, I was a nurse in France where Dick was hurt. A VAD I was called. A member of the Voluntary Aid Detachment. I worked in several hospitals and nursed a lot of young soldiers who had been wounded. I came home to see . . . to see Dick to whom I am engaged.'

'Engaged?'

'To be married.'

Something evidently stirred in the blackness of Alex's mind, for she nodded as though she understood.

'But there was another young soldier who is . . . a relative of the people who live in this house. A cousin. An American.' Dear God, was she going too far but again Alex seemed to know what America was and she listened with interest. 'He came to fight in the war for he believed that it was only right

since he had been born not far from here. His name is . . .
Noah.'

Nan's eyes narrowed and she leaned forward, for the way
Miss Rose had spoken the name of Alex's half-brother was the
way one spoke of someone very special. Very important. Very
much loved and her heart sank: she knew that if Rose had
feelings for Noah Goodwin, where did that leave poor Doctor
Dick whom they had all taken to? And where did that leave
poor Miss Rose who was incapable of inflicting hurt on any
human being? She knew, of course, that Noah Goodwin was in
a hospital in London, for had not the master had the telegram
and the task of letting his parents know. They had been puzzled
as to why the telegram had come to Edge Bottom House but
then it had come to light that Noah had joined up in the name of
Goodwin in order not to lose his American citizenship. Nan
didn't understand it but Mr Archie had tried to explain it. The
Americans would be sure to join the allies soon, Mr Archie had
told her, but until then Mr Noah was to be Noah Goodwin.

'So you see I have to keep an eye on both these lads,' Rose
went on. 'In fact Dick is a doctor and saved Noah's life so I have
a duty to them both. I suspect Noah will come here to
convalesce though I believe his mother has come from America
to see him. So I hope you understand why I must leave you with
Mr Goodwin and Nan and Nelly and all the others who will be
there should you need them. I promise to come back as soon as
possible and I might even bring Dick, or perhaps Noah and his
mother since they are related to the Goodwins. Do you understand, dearest?'

Alex smiled. Rosie always called her dearest, which she liked.
She didn't know why but these people she was staying with . . .
her mind slipping for a moment as it considered *why*, then the
comfy mists of forgetfulness shrouded it and she looked about
her. The old gentleman who treated her with such kindness was
there, and Nan and in the kitchen were Nelly and Ruth and

Dottie and Cook and in the paddock would be Harry who put her up on the old mare and trotted her about on a lead. She had learned all their names and was happy with them, and with Cat. And Rose would return and fill in the mysterious times she could not remember and that was all she needed.

There was a bit of a crisis the next day when Cat was found to be missing at breakfast time. In fact she had not been seen since the evening before when she had wandered off into the garden to find a suitable place for her nightly relief. Alex was already asleep and did not miss her and to tell the truth neither did Rose, for she was taking the opportunity while Alex slept to pack the small bag she had brought with her.

Noah's mother was staying at Bedford Square to where she had rushed when she had heard about her son's injury, booking passage on the first available liner. Rose had not been surprised but she had been glad to get away from the cloying anxiety of Milly Woodruff, making the excuse that she must go to Edge Bottom House to visit Alex. The question of where Rose would stay until Noah was recovered was one she must address and also the answers to the other terrifying problem Dick and Noah's injuries had caused! The trouble was she had no one to talk to now that she had lost Alex and the dilemma was crucifying her!

Alex became as still and silent as the pretty statuette on the mantelshelf when Cat could not be found, sitting with her hand in Rose's, which was awkward, for Rose was just about to call a cab to take her to the station and the train to London.

'Now, don't worry, dearest,' she said soothingly, as Alex had retreated, it seemed, into that quiet world from which Rose's sudden appearance had prised her. 'Harry will find her and when I come back you will . . .' but Alex merely clung to Rose like a woman drowning.

'Oh, dear sweet Jesus,' Nan began but was hissed at from the door by a smiling Dottie.

'Tha're wanted in't kitchen,' Dottie said.

'I can't come now.'

'She's bin found but 'Arry wants a word.'

Harry was standing by the back door with a squirming Cat in his arms but he was smiling and Nan relaxed.

'What?'

'She's 'ad kittens,' he whispered.

Nan moaned, for really she didn't think she could stand much more. She could just about manage a young cat, a clean cat in Miss Alex's bedroom but knowing her mistress she would insist on the whole boiling lot of them sharing her bed!

'I've drowned 'em,' Harry murmured, looking somewhat guilty, for he was a lover of animals.

'Thank God. Tha're good lad, Harry. I don't know what we'd do wi'out yer. 'Ere, give 'er ter me,' and with no more ado she dragged the bloody cat into her arms and carried her through to the drawing-room where Alex let out a squeal of pleasure, letting go of Rose's hand and burying her face in the cat's stable-smelling fur.

'She'll need a bath,' Nan said tartly, as though the animal had been missing for weeks and had been found in the cow byre. Rose stood up and moved towards the door. 'I'll telephone for a cab,' she murmured, nodding her head in the direction of Alex who was acting like a child who has lost and found a beloved toy. 'I'll be back as soon as . . .' Her voice tapered off and when she left, climbing into the motor cab that had taken the place of the old horse cab, there was no one to see her off but Nan.

'Take care, lamb,' she told her, 'an' when tha' come 'ome I'm 'ere ter listen ter tha' trouble.'

And trouble it was that was dragging Rose Kellett down into the abyss of despair, for how was she to tell Noah Woodruff, or Goodwin as he was known, that she could not marry him since she was to marry Dick Morris as soon as he was out of hospital?

Dick was up and about now, still in hospital because his lungs were a worry and always would be. The doctors would not hear of him leaving until they were satisfied that he could breathe properly, though he himself gasped that they were a lot of old women and that now his fiancée was back from France for good, and her being a nurse into the bargain, there was absolutely no need for him to lie in bed and gaze out of the window, bored out of his mind with nothing to think about but her next visit. The burn marks on his face and body were beginning to fade and he was on the mend, but any change in the weather or if it was very cold could affect him. He still had to have oxygen to help him to breathe when he was very bad. His temperature was all over the place, as the sister in charge of the officers' ward told her and when he was better he would be sent to a convalescent hospital. The powerful phosgene in the shells needed to be inhaled for only one minute to reduce a man to helplessness and caused pulmonary lesions and to the end of his days Dick Morris would be a partial invalid. An American doctor had done lengthy experiments into the diabolical refinement of the gas, as he had called it, and his report had been given wide coverage in the newspapers and had aroused horror and indignation in the populace, and all over the country there were men who would struggle for breath for the rest of their lives, which would probably be short.

Rose pinched her cheeks as she entered the hospital, for it would not do for Dick to see her looking pale and wan. And then there was Noah!

# 21

Love, or a physical attraction sufficiently intense to pass for love had flared between them that night in the kitchen at Bedford Square and had burned long enough to overcome all Rose's misgivings, even though she was promised in marriage to Dick. Dick was prepared to wait until the war ended, he had told her. He had trusted her and she had broken that trust but it did not lessen her love for Noah.

It was not until they were both in France, he in the line, she in one or other of the hospitals behind them, that she realised that she could not refuse him, nor did she want to. They had met by arrangement, neither of them able to withstand the fierce passion that had flared up so quickly and so intensely in the fever of war and imminent death that they were both taken by surprise. He was a few years older than her and had had several encounters with young women, at university and then in New York where he worked with his father, but Rose was a virgin the first time she shared a narrow bed with him in a French inn. He was a soldier and they both knew the many ways he could die, or be viciously mutilated – shellfire, fire itself from the flame-throwers the Germans used against their enemy, mustard gas, the terrible knives they wielded – and one day she might wake up and find him a crippled, castrated wreck and so she gave herself willingly, rapturously, for she loved him as he loved her. They made no plans, for what plans can a man and woman make when either, or both, might be blown to pieces in the mud-soaked margins of battle? They were both too knowledgeable, too cautious, too superstitious to look forward to the golden future he at least dreamed about.

And there was Dick, about whom Noah knew nothing. Rose was aware that anything could happen in this vicious world they lived in and was of the opinion that to cross one's bridges before they were upon you was a mistake! When the war ended then would be the reckoning, but what was that against the threats that loomed over them now and which, in one another's arms, she and Noah could escape for an hour.

It was his constant closeness to his family in New York and his mother's possessiveness that persuaded him to stay on in England after his aunt's funeral and join the British army. He had loved Rose Kellett from the moment he first set eyes on her and though she would not admit it, even to herself, she had felt the same. While Alex was with them Rose had managed to avoid anything that might lead to a dangerous situation but now they were lovers, had been for over a year and the irony of Dick, who expected her to marry him as soon as he was out of hospital, being the one who had saved Noah's life, and not only that but the two men being in the same hospital was surely a chance in a thousand. But then what difference did that make, she thought, as she hurried up the steps of the hospital. A voice whispered in her head that the difference would have been that Noah would probably have died on the operating table. Dick had told her of the strangeness of hearing the Goodwin name just as he had been about to amputate the young soldier's leg and that had probably stayed his knife and, much against sister's will, had persuaded him to take more time and perform the operation that had saved the leg. Gas gangrene had been avoided, probably because Noah had come straight from the line to the hospital thereby avoiding the filth that soldiers picked up from the churned-over battlefield.

Dick was on the covered veranda, its door open to let in the pleasant scents of autumn: the grass that had just been cut, the massed chrysanthemums that bordered the lawn, the fragrance of woodsmoke from the fires the groundsman had lit to burn the leaves that were beginning to drift from the trees. In France the ghastly slaughter continued and men crouched in trenches with nothing but shell-holes as far as the eye could see. The wounded from the last attack lay helplessly groaning or howling but there was nothing anyone could do about them because the fire from the enemy guns trapped them. There were men there who had been buried in the exploding earth, some more than once, in the smoke, the fire, the spurting mud and when the barrage ceased they were dazed by the silence.

Dick knew, as all those who had been at the front knew, even though they were, at the moment, out of it, what their comrades still suffered. He sat in a wicker chair and the newspaper he had been reading fell from his hand, for he had been reading the list of the casualties, long and sombre and getting longer with every day. Some of the names were familiar to him. He supposed he was one of the lucky ones: at least he was still alive and he had his sweet Rosie to cling to. There was poor old Patrick still out there in the thick of it with the added misery of knowing the girl he loved was in a sort of a coma. She walked about and sat when told to, ate when told to and depended on her family for her very life but would she ever again be the woman Patrick had loved and hoped to spend the rest of his life with? She was almost in full health again except for her brain which still slept and God only knew how Patrick would ever survive it. He was off his head with worry, he said in his letters, and as soon as he could get leave he would come home to her and hoped to see Dick. Perhaps there would be a wedding, he wrote, in an effort to be cheerful and if there was Dick was not to start without him, for he was determined to be best man!

A commanding voice from inside the ward distracted him from his musings and he groaned as he recognised it as his mother's. She came up from Sevenoaks several times a week and was doing her best to get him transferred to her care or, failing that, to a hospital closer to their home where she could keep an eye on him which meant have him not only under her eye, but her thumb!

She moved in her stately way along the veranda, seating herself in the empty chair next to his. As an afterthought she leaned over and kissed his cheek sketchily, then turned to look about her at the other wounded men, some of whom, she was sure, should not have been in a ward for officers. Officers were gentlemen but this war had made it possible for the lower classes to be promoted, like that friend of his with his Irish-Liverpool accent, and she thought it a disgrace, she told her husband. It did not occur to her, nor did her husband tell her, that the casualties were so high, among officers as well as men, that there was no other way but to promote suitable rankers to officer status.

'I have just been telling that fool of a doctor out there that it was high time you were brought home, Dickon. I have a perfectly good nurse, a professional woman with excellent qualifications, ready to care for you and you would be in your own home with your own family about you. I am in a group of ladies who are all doing their bit for the troops and though I go most afternoons, Nurse Allitt would be there to look after you. And Doctor Edwards, though he is somewhat older than these . . . these boys, yes, that is what they are, these doctors, just boys, so don't argue with me, and he will be on hand. Yes, I know you need oxygen at times, the doctor out there has just told me but Nurse Allitt can administer it. She is willing to sleep in and—'

'Mother, please . . .' He could feel himself beginning to wheeze, for the life she described for him filled him with horror. Whenever he was distressed, which was seldom if left alone quietly with his fellow patients who also needed peace and who had shared with him the terrors of war, or with his Rose, he would begin one of his attacks and it was his mother who was the worst offender. Sometimes his father or his sisters came with her and they managed, as he put it, to keep a lid on her but, as now, when she attacked him singly, he could feel the trauma begin.

It was at that moment that Rose walked in through the open double door and at once he could breathe more easily. They might argue, for his mother would, as she put it, stand no nonsense from anyone, but then Rose, who had grown into a strong, confident woman since the war began, was more than a match for her and would not allow him to be whisked off to bloody Sevenoaks and be smothered.

'Rose, darling,' he managed, holding out his hand to her, the sleeve of his dressing-gown falling back to reveal the fading scars on his arm. She smiled and walked towards him, ignoring Mrs Morris, who also ignored her which was a bad sign. She took his hand and brought it to her lips, kissing the back of it and Mrs Morris tutted, for such displays were in poor taste in her opinion. She sat like stone, totally blocking any attempt on Rose's part to get to Dick but Dick winked at Rose and his eyes told her of his love, his vast relief, and his pleasure in seeing her. She had been up north to visit Alex and it was almost a week since she had been to the hospital.

'Darling, how are you feeling? Have you been up?'

'Yes, he has, and I think it's a great mistake on the part of the medical staff to have him out of his bed so soon.' Mrs Morris sniffed, in a ladylike way, of course and turned an outraged look on Rose who was forced to stand to one side since there were no more chairs and Mrs Morris blocked her off from Dick.

'Really, Mrs Morris, but I can't believe the doctors would allow Dick to be out of bed if he wasn't capable of it. The more he moves about the easier his chest will become and I believe—'

'I hardly think you are qualified to state an opinion on my son's condition, Miss . . .'

'I am a nurse, Mrs Morris.'

'Hardly! You are a VAD.'

'With more experience than you and I really think we should do exactly what Dick's doctors prescribe for him.'

'Do you indeed. Well, let me tell you I intend to have Dickon home with me by the end of the month.'

'Mother, please.' Dick did his best to gather enough breath to tell his mother to be quiet but all he could do was gasp and choke and it was then, although she had known it subconsciously ever since Dick and Noah came home, Rose admitted finally that she must give up Noah for this man needed her more than he did. Noah was almost recovered. His leg had healed and he was ready in a week or two to leave hospital. To be independent, even to be sent back to the trenches, the thought of which crucified her. Never to see him again, never to share his love in the rapture they had found, never to know if he was alive or dead, but Noah would be strong enough to survive and Dick would not and never would be. How was he to fight this ogre of a woman if left alone struggling for breath? She would manipulate him, drag him back to Sevenoaks with her, smother him, dominate him and his life would be ended. Besides if she, Rose, did not marry him he would die anyway, for she was fully aware that he lived only for her. He had loved her for three years, ever since he had patched her up in St Thomas's Hospital. With her beside him he could probably, in time, get back to medicine, live a useful life, a fulfilling life. He could give her children, she could give him peace. They would find a house in the country where the air was clean . . .

But dear sweet God . . . Noah . . . how was she to give up Noah who had become part of her and she of him and who was ready to take her back to the States with him? She felt physical pain in every part of her body. There was a great emptiness inside her, an aching, a dragging down and her eyes were heavy with a longing to weep which she could not, of course, give in to. There was a disbelief in her, a refusal to believe that she would, after she had told him, never see him again and in her mind was a yearning to have the weeks, the months, the years pass so that the pain would lessen. Agony overwhelmed her but she was forced to smile, to smile and listen to Mrs Morris who, thank God, could fill in any gap in a conversation with her opinions on everything from the doubtful cleanliness of the wards to the incompetence of the doctors, and particularly the nurses who should be at home with their families, not flaunting themselves in front of gentlemen, and those who were not gentlemen!

The sun floated behind a ribbon of grey velvet cloud as the autumn day began to fade and Mrs Morris waited for Rose to go. But Rose simply stood and stood, for she was determined to have a few minutes alone with Dick. She loved Dick and she wanted to reinforce her love, and his for her, in his arms, with his kisses before she went to the ward where Noah would be waiting for her, probably wondering why she was late.

At last, knowing that Mrs Morris would sit beside her son until the cows came home, as Nan often said, she pretended to admit defeat, though Dick's face fell and he began to gasp to her to stay, obviously longing to have her to himself. While Mrs Morris looked at him triumphantly, Rose indicated with a movement of her head that told Dick that she would be back, she moved along the veranda, through the ward where men confined to bed watched her, into the corridor and round a corner where she waited until she saw Mrs Morris come out of the ward and move towards the stairs that led to the exit.

Within two minutes she was back beside Dick where, under the gaze of the other wounded men who smiled behind their newspapers she put her arms about him and kissed him on the lips. All these men were victims of gas attacks with burns on their faces, some blinded, but even these sensed that something was happening at the end of the veranda. These men would not recover their full health, or their sight, and would never return to France, and those who could see watched as Captain Morris's pretty fiancée held him with loving arms and whispered something to him that relaxed him, which he needed after that dreadful battleaxe of a mother had visited him.

'Dick, darling, I've had time to think while I've been at Edge Bottom and—'

'How is Alex? Is she improved?' His breathing was back to normal but he clung to her just the same and she realised how imperative it was that she get him away from his mother as quickly as possible.

'Yes, physically she is quite recovered, eating well, putting on weight which pleases Nan no end and when I return I'm going to suggest to Doctor Bennett, perhaps you might agree, that she be told who she is and who the people about her are. And about Patrick.'

'You are to go back?' he asked fearfully, his grip on her hand strengthening, her reference to Alex and Patrick of no particular interest to him at that moment of crisis in his own life.

'Yes, and you're coming with me.'

His mouth dropped open and she laughed out loud, surprising herself who, half an hour ago, thought she would never laugh again. 'But I'm not sure they . . .'

'Oh yes, they will, especially if they are to release you into the custody of your wife who is also a nurse.'

For a moment he wasn't sure exactly what she meant. His mind had become a blank then it came alive again and his shout of joy as he absorbed her meaning brought the nurse running and every head in the ward and on the veranda turning in their direction.

'Captain Morris, what on earth . . .' the nurse began but Dick was so enchanted he could not speak and it was left to Rose to announce that she and Captain Morris were to be married as soon as a special licence could be obtained.

'Would it be possible for us to marry here, on this veranda, or perhaps in the garden if it's fine and then I must see Doctor Springer about taking my husband home. I have friends who live in the country and . . .'

The applause started then, every wounded man who could manage it, cheering and even whistling and the nurse was so flustered she actually hugged Miss Kellett who was soon to be Mrs Morris. Dick was beyond speech and there were tears in his eyes as he held her hand in a grip that told her he was overwhelmed and overjoyed. Everyone was happy for them and yet where her heart lay was a huge stone of lead, for happy as she was to make this dear man, she was to devastate another.

'There is just one more thing, darling,' she said, managing an expression of happiness which she hoped matched his. 'Mrs Woodruff, you know the mother of the young soldier whose leg you saved – he had joined up in the name of Goodwin since he's a cousin or something – well, she's at the house at Bedford Square so could I stay at your place?' Dick had kept on his flat at the top of the house in Queen Anne's Gate, probably in the hope that he and Rose might get leave together and spend some time there. 'And we must have somewhere to stay until I can get you to Edge Bottom.'

'Darling, darling love . . . oh, dear God, sweet Rosie, have you any idea how happy you've made me? Have you? I shall improve in leaps and bounds now that—'

'You are to escape your mama's clutches!'

'Not just that, sweetheart, but I thought it would be months, even years but now . . . and what was that about Edge Bottom? Surely we're not to spend our honeymoon there? Oh, God . . . Oh, God.' He threw back his head in a paroxysm of ecstasy and at once began to cough and it was several moments before he could be calmed. The nurse gave her a look that seemed to ask did she really think she could mend this poor broken man but Rose only smiled into his face, kissed him lovingly, stroked back his thick hair while his eyes clung to hers. They finally got him into his bed in the ward and with a last tender kiss she left him.

She began to weep then, great heaving sobs as she prepared to go downstairs to the ward where Noah lay with the 'men', the rank and file who were segregated from their officers, and tell him that she could no longer see him. From this day she would not see him and she became so distraught she opened the door against which she leaned and, finding it was a cupboard, stepped inside and sank down on to a pile of blankets. She had no idea how long she was there as she emptied the last dregs of her love for Noah Woodruff from her grieving heart. A thin anguished sound keened from her and her stomach clenched so tightly she thought she might be sick here on the pile of clean blankets. Her agony was clawing her heart to rags and she knew she must get out, retrieve her bag, which she had left at the reception desk, and clutching the key that Dick had given her find her way to Queen Anne's Gate. She couldn't possibly face Noah in this state of paralysing stupor, indeed she didn't know whether she could ever face him again.

The porter at the desk looked at her with interest and a certain degree of compassion as he handed her her small suitcase. He saw so many distraught women leave this hospital and this was one of them for she had been weeping. And yet at the same time he thought that though her unusual violet eyes were clouded with tears she still looked pretty. Not red-nosed or red-eyed with swollen lids like other women when they had been crying.

'Good luck, miss,' he said gently and she managed a smile then slipped away down the steps, striding off towards the cab rank that lay just beyond the hospital gates.

They were married a week later by special licence. The day was fine so the doctors gave their permission for them to marry on the lawn. They grouped about them, with the nurses who were thrilled at the romance of Captain Morris and the lovely girl who had been a VAD in France for almost two years. As many as could walk or be taken in a wheelchair clustered about the lawn as the simple ceremony took place and when the new bride produced several bottles of the best champagne, those who were given permission by their doctor toasted the bride who was as pale as the white rosebuds she carried in her posy. She wore a dress of palest duck-egg blue in a drifting chiffon with white rosebuds tucked into the heavy chignon at the back of her head. Her groom managed to stand during the ceremony, his eyes never leaving her face, his own scarred face smiling, and when he came to kiss her he did it so reverently it was as though he kissed a Madonna.

She left an hour later, leaving her new husband behind, for the doctor had advised another few weeks before she could take him to her friends' home in the country. He must write to this Doctor Bennett whose name the bride had given him and when he was satisfied that he was to be placed in good hands then he would allow it.

The new Mrs Morris had left instructions that her husband's mother was not to be allowed to visit her son unless his wife was with him and as she was his next of kin now and was in charge of him, so to speak, and with her telephone number to hand, they could do no more than agree.

Rose Morris dropped a letter into the postbox at the end of Queen Anne's Gate as she climbed from the cab and walked towards the flat where she and Dick would make their home until one was found in the country. She wept broken-heartedly as she pushed it into the postbox, then stumbled along the pavement to the steps that led up to the block of flats.

*My darling,*
*This is the hardest thing I have ever done in my life and how can I ever hope to make you understand. Still, I will try.*

*I cannot see you again, my love . . . yes, you are still my*
*love and always will be but I promised years ago to marry a*
*man, before the war even, and though I was going to break*
*the engagement when I met you I cannot now do it. He was*
*badly gassed some months ago and he needs me. I cannot*
*abandon him or he will die. That sounds too dramatic but it*
*is true for reasons I cannot explain to you. You are young.*
*Your leg is healed and you will be dependent on no one.*
*When you read this I will be married to him. Forgive me.*
*Forgive me, my dearest love.*
    *Rose*

She had deliberately written the letter so that he would receive it while he was still in the ward with the men, the soldiers, those who had suffered as he had. So that he would be among his own, those who would show him compassion, understand, for many of them had received letters like this as sweethearts left behind had taken up with other men. He would be devastated, perhaps unable to bear the company of the pitying men, the nurses, even the doctors who would probably be anxious that this might put him back but he would not be alone. His mother might be allowed to take him back to America, for he was, after all, a citizen of that country and though she was not certain she thought that, unlike a British soldier who could be arrested for desertion, he might be beyond the law.

She lay on the bed she would share with Dick, still wearing her pretty wedding dress, dry-eyed now, her eyelids raw, her heart dragging at her like a marble tombstone. Remorse poisoned every breath she took and the landscape of her future life without Noah in it had been turned into a blasted heath of desolation and she wondered dazedly how she was to get through it. She wanted to leap up and jump into a cab. Get to the hospital where today she had been married and before Noah could read her letter, get to him and tear it from his hands. This was his last night of peace, of believing that they were to be together for the rest of their lives and she had murdered that peace. Dear God, to save one man she had had to sacrifice another and it was tearing her apart. She felt the desolation of loneliness press down on her and with all her heart wished she could turn to Alex, the only one who would understand and give her absolution but Alex was beyond her now.

The dawn broke as she stared at the square of window.

# 22

In the commotion that was taking place at the entrance to Number 3 General Hospital, Wandsworth Common, the disappearance of one of its patients was not at first noticed.

It was a rule of the hospital that all visitors had to give their name and the name of the patient they were to visit to the porter on duty, for unknown people wandering about might upset not only some of the patients who were in a very fragile state but the staff who had, after all, a job to do.

'I have never heard such nonsense in my life,' an outraged female voice was thundering, a voice heard by not only every soldier in the wards on the ground floor but by those who were taking their first hesitant steps on the first floor, some of them in a state of nervous shock where any loud noise sent them into dithers of anxiety. Those who were recovering were allowed to wander into the extensive gardens of the hospital, the weather being fine, and they wore the hospital blue uniforms and red ties of the wounded. Several of them were making their way to the door that led on to the terraces and the soldier on crutches was not noticed among others in the same condition.

'Madam, I have been informed that Captain Morris is to have no visitors until further notice. I have the document here in front of me, signed by the doctor in charge so if you would be good enough to—'

'If *you* will be good enough to stand aside I shall go upstairs and see my son and have a word with this . . . this doctor who you say has given this order. I shall want to know why and, believe me, when I have found out you will be sorry. I shall make it my business to ensure you are severely reprimanded. I cannot believe that *any* medical man can keep a mother from her son, whatever his condition and . . .'

The porter was becoming extremely annoyed. It was his job to, if you like, protect the men who were doing their best to recover from their wounds in a place of peace and quiet, a place as unlike where they had come from in the Somme offensive as it was possible to find. If a doctor said a patient was not to be disturbed then it was his task to see to it and this woman, who he had noticed before making her autocratic way up the stairs to the officers' ward, was no different from the rest. Except she would not be ordered about by so subordinate a person, her manner said, subordinate to her that is, and told when she could or could not see her own flesh and blood and she informed him of this with great force. Men stopped to watch and from the wards on the ground floor nurses peeped out to see who was disturbing their patients.

The porter and the visitor continued their growing argument until, tutting angrily, the visitor turned away and began to make her way through the walking wounded towards the stairs with the intention, presumably, of ignoring the doctor's orders and making her way to her son's ward.

'See,' the porter hissed to an orderly who was just passing, 'get the doc, will yer, while I nip up after this bloody woman. The officer was badly gassed and any commotion can set him off and believe me, when she hears what he's bin and gone and done, there'll be fireworks. Be quick, Stan, or the old battleaxe will be at his bedside, poor sod, before anyone can stop her.'

She had got as far as the door to her son's ward when the doctor hurried along the corridor to forestall her. He actually went so far as to put his hand on her arm as though to drag her away, but with one withering glance she shook him off and was halfway along the ward when the senior doctor who was in charge of the hospital waylaid her. Captain Morris could be seen from the doorway to the terrace, wandering peacefully across the wide stretch of lawn, and Doctor Springer breathed a sigh of relief. The men who were still confined to bed watched with great interest. They looked up from their newspapers or put down the books they were reading and wondered how the doctor was going to manage this drama, for they all knew, of course, about Dick's marriage to the beautiful girl who came every day to see him and was making arrangements for Dick to accompany her up north to some country retreat in the Lake District to finish his convalescence.

'Mrs Morris, might I have a word with you in private,' they heard Doctor Springer say most courteously. 'If you would come with me to my office we can discuss—'

'Where is my son?' his mother asked menacingly and it was evident that even this prominent doctor, who had great knowledge of gas cases and was helping Dick to recover, was of no concern to Dick's mother.

'I believe he is . . . he is sitting in the—' the doctor began.

'Then why is there this fuss about my visiting him? First the porter who, I might add, was extremely rude, then the other doctor and now you and if he is fit enough to sit in the garden then I can see no reason, no medical reason, why I should not see him. Which is exactly what I intend doing so if you would point him out to me . . .'

'Mrs Morris, I insist you come to my office.' Doctor Springer was a tall, well-built man in his early fifties and had been dealing with recalcitrant patients and their relatives for many years and was not easily ignored. 'I have something I wish to discuss with you. Your son has asked me to do this for him and for the sake of his wellbeing I have agreed. He is not fit enough to . . . to face an argument. It affects his breathing and if he can't—'

'Has my son's health worsened since I was here last week?'

she said imperiously, lifting her head on which a hat of regal proportion sat. She wore a full-length fly-fronted coat in a shade of rich, ruby red and a feather ruffle with silk tassles about her neck. The brim of her hat was turned up at one side and was crowned with a great many matching feathers. She was well corseted in the fashion of the day and her bust jutted out from beneath her chin in a most aggressive manner.

'No, Mrs Morris, in fact he is improving to my satisfaction but I must insist that he remains so.'

'And you are saying I shall upset Dickon, is that it?'

'Please, Mrs Morris, come into my office. We don't want the men on this ward to be—'

'I don't care at all for the men on this ward, and as most of them are not gentlemen, as my son is, I can hardly be expected—'

'Mrs Morris, if you don't come into my office and at once, I shall call a couple of orderlies who will escort you from the premises. Your son's health is my main concern and I will not have it put at risk. Now . . .'

With a sigh of deep frustration and a look on her face that promised trouble for everyone who had thwarted her this day, she followed Doctor Springer along the corridor and into his office.

It was about two minutes later that she began to shout, not even a shout really, but a screech of pure outrage and Doctor Springer wished sincerely that Captain Morris's wife had seen fit to inform his family that she and the captain were married. He supposed this damn woman would still have come here and caused this rumpus but it might have been easier on all concerned. The captain was to be off tomorrow in the private motor belonging to friends of Mrs Morris, the younger Mrs Morris, and if this dreadful woman had been one day later . . . well, would it have made any difference to him, to the man in charge, for she would have poured the vitriol over him just the same.

It was at that moment that sister put a tentative head around the door and indicated with a tilt of her head that he was needed elsewhere. He breathed a sigh of relief.

'Stay with Mrs Morris, will you, Sister, until she has calmed down and then perhaps if you could arrange a cab for her . . .'

'Her chauffeur is waiting outside,' sister said, putting a calming hand on the shoulder of the hysterical woman only to have it flung off.

'All the better,' Doctor Springer ventured, rising from his chair and making for the door.

'His wife's here,' sister managed to hiss as he passed her then he closed the door behind him and hurried away in the direction of the slender, pale-faced but lovely woman who hesitated in the doorway to the ward.

'Doctor . . .?'

'His mother is here. I would be glad if you would go into the garden and keep him there until she has gone.'

'Is she . . .?'

'Yes, God help us. Is there any way you can get him away tonight? I won't answer for his condition if he should fall foul of the termagant who is at this moment in my office threatening me with Members of Parliament and even Asquith himself who, it appears, is a personal friend of her husband's.'

'Get rid of her, if you can, and thank you, Doctor. If I may use your telephone I'll get Harry, my chauffeur, to bring the car round as soon as possible. Mrs Morris knows where Dick's apartment is so I will take him to a hotel.'

'Dear God, some mothers . . .' And the doctor hurried away.

Mrs Morris chose to walk in a majestic fashion to the front entrance of the hospital where a harried porter had beckoned to her chauffeur to fetch the Rolls-Royce. A young doctor accompanied her and listened politely as she told him that before the end of the day she would have not only her husband, her solicitor but her local MP at the hospital to demand admission to her son and he was to tell Doctor Springer, who had not even had the courtesy to accompany her to her motor car, that his career was in serious jeopardy. Not that the young doctor gave any credence to that threat since doctors were in short supply at this crucial moment in the war. He bowed her to her magnificent motor car where her chauffeur took over, handing her into the back seat, marching to his own seat behind the wheel, started the engine and rolled down the drive to the wide gates.

Milly Woodruff, who had entered the hospital and signed her name in the visitors' book, watched the proceedings with an amused smile, wondering who on earth the woman could be to receive such servile attention. The porter pulled a face and then, remembering himself, nodded pleasantly at the handsome woman who came almost every day to visit her son in the general ward. His surname was not the same as hers but perhaps she had married again, he mused to himself before turning to the next visitor.

Milly walked along the corridor which was empty but for a nurse or two and an orderly. It was cool and smelled of disinfectant and beneath a window on a polished table someone had placed a bowl of bright chrysanthemums from the garden. She turned into the ward where her son had been slowly recovering from his leg wound but which now, thankfully, was almost on the mend. Her only worry, and it was a constant one, was that as soon as he was passed fit, he would be sent back to France. But as he was still unable to walk without crutches that would not be for a while yet. He was so cheerful, even when he had been in such agony and she supposed it was all due to the girl he loved and whom he was to marry as soon as he could get her to name the date, he had told her, the girl being, of course, Rose Kellett, who had been lodging at Archie's house at Bedford Square. A lovely girl, Milly was forced to admit, and had it not been for her constant support Noah would not have done as well as he had. She was not an American, one of the young women from the wealthy families with whom she and Todd socialised, but she was a lady, well brought up, and Milly was sure she could make something of her.

Noah's bed was empty but that was not unusual, for now that he could get about clumsily on his crutches when the weather was fine he often clumped his way along the corridor that led out into the garden.

The dressing trolley was being wheeled from bed to bed, the nurse attending to those who were still bed-ridden. Sunlight streamed across Noah's bed which was made up neatly and the man in the next bed, who was asleep, moaned slightly, startling her. She turned to look about her and caught the eye of a young soldier in the opposite bed who hastily looked away as though in confusion and for some reason Milly felt a frisson of alarm run through her. The clink of something on the dressing trolley drew her attention back to it and swiftly she approached the nurse who was bent over a bed doing something painful to the soldier's chest. The wound was weeping and the man arched his back and Milly quickly averted her eyes. The soldier saw her and with a movement of his hand indicated her presence to the nurse who turned irritably.

'Yes,' she snapped. 'Can't you see I'm busy?'

'Where is my son?' Milly demanded autocratically, just as Mrs Morris had done a half-hour ago.

'Your son?'

'Yes, Noah Wood— Goodwin. This is his bed and he is not in it.'

'I should try the garden,' a cheerful voice from another bed said. 'I saw him put on his "blues" a couple of hours since so he must have gone out.'

'Thank you,' giving the nurse a cool look.

It was an hour and a half later, after the whole of the hospital and the grounds had been thoroughly and frantically searched, that it was finally accepted that Private Noah Goodwin had deserted, for a soldier, whether he be in the trenches or in a hospital bed, was still a soldier, part of the British army and had to be in the place where they told him to be.

Milly became hysterical and Doctor Springer was heard to say he had never known such a day with mothers of the wounded disrupting the smooth running of the hospital. Milly wept copiously in his office and he was just about to ring the authorities, for he could not have one of his patients, especially on crutches, wandering about London when word came that Private Goodwin had just stumbled in through the front door. He was in a bad way, the message said, and would the doctor come and see to him at once.

They put him to bed. His mother hung over him, getting in everyone's way, begging to know where he had been, and why, but he simply turned his ashen face away and would not answer. Doctor Springer shook his head sadly, for the lad had been doing so well.

The crumpled letter was found later, clutched in his hand and though the doctor did not care to read another's private correspondence he felt it was necessary to find out, perhaps through the letter, what had turned Private Noah Goodwin from a wounded but cheerfully recovering soldier into the silent, white-faced figure in the bed. He refused to eat and even drink, but the letter, which the good doctor had read, at least revealed to him why the lad had fallen, as so many did, off the edge of the world. God damn all women, he muttered to himself, and especially those who knocked the life, which was barely surviving, out of these battered men. When they were at their lowest, their most vulnerable, to receive a letter such as this was beyond mercy.

Sighing, he left the lad with his mother and went up the wide stairway to superintend the transfer of Captain Dick Morris, who was, he kept forgetting, also a doctor, into the care of his wife and the luxurious motor car that stood at the entrance awaiting him. He was one of the lucky ones, he thought, and it was written in his face that with the lovely and solicitous woman he had married only days ago, he at least had a chance of recovery. He was off up north where the good, clear air in his damaged lungs would work wonders. He watched the chauffeur help Captain Morris into the motor car, tenderly wrapping him in rugs, then tucking the sweet-faced woman in beside him. He called her Miss Rose and for a strange moment he brooded on the coincidence of the name which was the same as the one in Private Goodwin's letter.

They all came out on to the steps to welcome Miss Rose's new husband who they had been longing to meet again ever since Miss Rose had written to the master asking for the loan of the motor car, Harry and the house in Grasmere. Nan especially, who kept telling them Dr Morris was a grand chap, could not wait to put her arms about his thin shoulders and drag him into her tight and loving embrace.

'Eeh, lad, what 'ave tha' bin doin' ter thissen? Yer like a long piece o' thread.'

'Nan,' he managed to gasp, 'have I not come all this way so that you could feed me up and get me better. I couldn't fail to improve with you at my elbow but if you don't put me down . . . I swear . . . I shall . . .' He began to gasp and at once they were all aware of the extreme delicacy of this man their Miss Rose had married.

'Nay, will tha' look at me, standin' 'ere gabbin' when tha' should be in tha' bed. Now this lot 'ere' – indicating the fascinated group of servants – 'will look after thi' so get thi' ter tha' bed and when tha're settled I'll fetch thi' summat good to eat. See . . .' clapping her hands at them all, even Mr Archie, who wanted to wish Dick Morris well and they all scattered, smiling and bobbing curtseys, greeting Miss Rose, or should they call her Mrs Morris now, who was organising Harry and the two housemaids to carry up the luggage to . . . to . . .? She turned enquiringly to Nan.

'Front bedroom, Miss Rose. It's got its own bathroom and the bed's bin aired an' the pair o' yer'll be as comfy as . . .' Suddenly aware of the picture of Miss Rose and this stranger in the same bed together, she stopped speaking and turned abruptly, only to bump into Miss Alex who was hovering timidly at the edge of the group.

'Eeh, my lass, see 'oo's ere then. Look, it's Miss Rose.' And before the sentence was finished Rose had gathered Alex into her arms and held her fiercely, for of all the people whom Rose loved this woman was surely the first. Not like Noah, of course, who had awakened feelings in her she couldn't describe, but dear as life itself.

'Alex . . . Alex, dearest . . .'

'Rose . . . oh Rosie, I've missed you. Why were you gone so long? Rosie . . . Rosie . . .'

Dick stood quietly to one side, studying Alex with a doctor's eye and saw at once what the others had missed, probably because the last time he had seen her she had been first a struggling, fighting, screaming suffragette and then the suffering, half-starved prisoner who had been released from Holloway at the beginning of the war.

At last he spoke. 'I see you love my sweet Rosie as much as I do,' he said gently. Alex whirled away from the shelter of Rose's arms though she held on to her hand.

'Sweet Rosie,' she whispered. 'Someone called her . . . called her that . . .'

'Yes, darling, it was Dick here. He and I are married now. He has been ill and I am to take him to the house at Grasmere and get him better.'

'Grasmere . . .?'

'Yes, and you and Nan are to come too. Will you like that?'

'You and . . .'

'Dick and Nan and perhaps Nelly. All your friends.'

'Will Mr Goodwin come too?'

Archie turned away and put his hand against the frame of the door to steady himself and it was then that Rose knew that it was time for the truth to be told. She had two invalids on her hands, two sick people to bring back to health and she would do it, she knew she would, for they were both so dear to her and how was she to bear it if she failed. How would Patrick bear it if his Alex was not restored to her old self? That was to be her, Rose's, future. Her life. Noah . . . Noah, my love, my precious love. How am I to manage without you in my life?

It was difficult, for Alex was reluctant to part with Rose and could see no reason why she and Rose could not share a room as they had once done, which further strengthened Rose's determination to tell Alex the truth about herself. That these kind people were her family and that Rose and Dick would one day leave her and make a life of their own. They were all to travel up to Grasmere in a week or so, when Dick had recovered from the long journey from London to St Helens and in that week she must find the strength and the words with which to make Alex, if not understand, at least accept the truth of her past life. The weather was fine at the moment, clear and cool autumn weather with the glorious changing shades of the trees, the harvesting of crops and the gathering of produce from the hedgerows for jam and jelly making. They would take walks through the orchards and woods and the gardens where the hydrangeas were changing colour, the blue smoke drifting from the fires lit by old Solly, the only gardener left. It was a peaceful time as October moved on but first she must take her new husband to bed and let him sleep against her body, for it was doubtful he could do more than that.

Alex wept as Rose and Dick disappeared into the rooms that were to be theirs and for the first time she flung Nan off and

would not be comforted or even speak. She was like a sullen
child who has been denied a treat and Nan spent a restless night
with her, sleeping, or trying to, in the truckle bed set beside her
charge. Nan wanted to say, as she would to a child, 'Now you
behave yourself or I'll box your ears,' as her own mother had
said to her but Miss Alex was not a child, she was a woman who
was sick and must be treated gently, patiently until she had
recovered.

In the bedroom they were to share Dick and Rose sat before
the fire, a table between them as Rose tried to tempt Dick to eat
a morsel of the delicious and nourishing food Nan, Mrs Adams
and Mary Smith, once maid to the dead Mrs Goodwin, Mr
Archie's wife, and who had taken on the job of housekeeper,
had put together. Mary Smith and Mrs Beth had shared some
terrible ordeals together in the early days of the suffragist
movement and Mary loved Miss Alex and indeed Master
Tom and Master Will like her own. Master Tom was to be
home soon after treatment to his eyes which had been successful and it was feared that he might be sent back to the trenches.
But they must not be pessimistic, for after all they had Miss
Alex safe and Master Will had so far survived the dangers of
the skies over France.

'Eat some of the egg custard, darling,' his wife begged Dick
but his eyes went to the bed and she knew he was afraid. Afraid
that he might fail her this night, and how was she to get him
through it without a withering blow to his male pride in his
virility?

'I don't want egg custard, my sweet Rosie, I want you, in that
bed.'

'I'm here, my love, and I'm yours. Let me help you into bed
and then . . .'

'Will you let me watch you undress? I might not be able . . .'

'Hush, darling, let's see, shall we. We are both tired and if
. . . well, let's see. We might just want to sleep and then, when

we are recovered, tomorrow night or even in the morning we shall be as' – she smiled wickedly – 'lusty as . . .'

'Oh, Jesus God, I love you. I don't want to let you down.'

'I promise you won't. Now let me . . .'

'And why didn't you tell me about Alex, my love? Not that I should be concerned at this precise moment. This is my wedding night and—'

'Alex . . . what?'

'That she is . . . Dear God, don't tell me you hadn't . . . that Nan hadn't . . .'

'What! Dick, you are frightening me.'

'That you had not realised Alex is pregnant?'

# 23

Nan cried. She lowered her chin to her chest and cried broken-heartedly. She was like a child who has tried and tried at a difficult task and, having failed, is unfairly beaten. The tears dripped on to the freshly ironed cotton of her plain gown, spotting it with large circles which spread and joined together and she would not be pacified.

'Oh, dear God, Miss Rose . . . Dear sweet God, what're we ter do? She's no more'n a babby 'erself so 'ow are we ter tell 'er she's . . . it's not possible, Miss Rose, she can't 'ave a babby, not in 'er state an' why, dear sweet Jesus, tell me why none of us saw it? She were puttin' on weight, we could all see that but we thought it were because she were getting better. Doctor Bennett's not bin over fer weeks, thinking she were on't road ter recovery, well, not in 'er 'ead like, but otherwise. I can't understand why we never noticed . . . well, her "clouts". Each month I mean. We allus wash 'em, me or Nelly, or did, an' yet none of us thought . . . or 'appen if we did we must've thought it were 'er illness, like. God forgive us . . .'

Nan sank on to the bench beside the kitchen table, put her head in her hands and moaned her pain and when Mary entered, Dick Morris's breakfast tray balanced on her hands, she came to an abrupt halt in the doorway. Her face went as white as her crisp apron and she walked very carefully across the kitchen and placed the tray with equal care on the table.

'Nan,' she quavered. They could hear Nelly singing the soldiers' song 'It's a Long Way to Tipperary' in the scullery where she was giving Ruth a hand with the breakfast pans, and when Ruth joined in Nan cried the harder.

'What'll we tell 'er pa, Miss Rose? This'll kill 'im an' . . .'

'Nan, Nan . . .' Rose sat down beside the distraught woman and put her arm about her shoulder while Mary flopped down on the other side of the table and stared at the two of them, her face anguished, for what had happened now to send Nan into such an appalling state? Nan was calm. Nan was soothing. Nan never let her composure slip, at least not in front of others and now, here she was in a state of such despair Mary was quite terrified.

''Oo . . . 'oo done this to 'er an' 'er in such a frail state an' . . .' She was just about to say feeble-minded state but she thought better of it, shaking her head sadly, beginning to pull herself together, sniffing, pulling out her spotless handkerchief and blowing her nose vigorously. ''E needs to 'ave 'em cut off, the bugger.'

'Will someone tell me what has happened, please, or I shall go mad? Is it Miss Alex? Has something . . .'

'Aye, summat so 'orrible . . .'

'Nan, no one has taken advantage of Alex's condition. Dick says he thinks she must be about five months pregnant which means this . . . this happened when she was in France before . . . before . . .'

Nan's head shot up and so did Mary's hand to her mouth as the words Rose spoke became clear to her.

'Pregnant?' Mary whispered.

'Yes, but that is not the worst of it, Mary. It's how we are to explain to Alex what is happening to her. We all know who the father is.'

'Do we?' Nan spat out.

'Of course. Alex and Patrick have loved one another for years and Patrick would have married her but her devotion to the cause of suffragism got in the way.'

'Aye,' Nan said, sick at heart.

'They were in France together and . . . well, I'm sorry to say this to two unmarried ladies but when you are living in constant danger of death or mutilation, giving and receiving vows in the wedding ceremony count for little. You might be wiped off the face of the earth the next day, or even in the next hour and so you snatch at whatever happiness, love, a feeling of still being alive comes your way.'

Rose began to weep, the tears rolling slowly and prettily down her pale cheeks and Nan knew at once that this is what had taken place in Miss Rose's war and look what had happened to Dick Morris. There must be thousands upon thousands of young men and women caught up in the maelstrom of battles who grabbed at whatever bit of joy they could find and could you blame them and that is what had happened to Miss Alex and look where that had led.

Nan stood up briskly, the other two watching her. 'Well, first thing ter do is ter get that lad 'ome an' a weddin' arranged. If she's ter 'ave a babby it's ter be born in wedlock.'

Rose looked relieved for a moment then the look of relief changed to one of despair. She rose and put her arms round Nan, pressing her tear-stained cheek to the older woman's. 'Nan, Nan, how can we marry Alex to Patrick? It is what he would want, I know, especially with the . . . the baby, but Alex is not in her right mind. She wouldn't understand the ceremony. Dear Lord . . . oh, dear Lord, what are we to do? The baby is worry enough.'

'What baby's this?' Nelly cheerfully asked as she walked into the kitchen carrying a tray piled with the pans she had just scoured.

There was a long and painful silence as the three women contemplated the appalling circumstances with which they were faced. How were they to tell not only Nelly but all the other occupants of the household? Nan sank once more to the bench and, putting her crossed arms on the table and her head on her arms, began to cry again.

They didn't know how they got through that day and had it not been for Dick Morris it is doubtful they would have managed as well as they did. Though he was himself far from well the responsibility put upon him seemed to have a restorative effect and Rose felt a moment of joy, for it boded well for their future. Archie collapsed, as they knew he would, and the servants were big-eyed with shock, but Dick sailed through it, soothing and comforting those who needed it, talking quietly to Archie and explaining what he hoped to do, which was to enquire about compassionate leave for Patrick at once.

'There must be some way that Rose and Nan can explain to Alex what has happened and what is to happen and we cannot do that until Patrick shows up. Doctor . . . Bennett, is it? Doctor Bennett will come as soon as Harry can get over there to fetch him and in the meanwhile we must, for Alex's sake, carry on as normal. It seems as long as she has either Rose or Nan in sight she is content, but after I have consulted with Doctor Bennett I believe we must try to . . . well. Mr Goodwin . . .'

'Archie, please.'

'Well, Archie, I think we must just move slowly and . . . you see, I am no expert in cases such as this but Patrick or Doctor Bennett will surely know the right man to show us the way.'

Dick was amazed at his own almost miraculous strides towards better health which had occurred in the last few days. The burn marks on his face were beginning to fade and he smiled comfortingly at the old man and was once again the engaging young man he had been three years ago. He was just twenty-nine years old but the horrors he had seen and the mustard gas attack he had only just survived had taken their toll, but last night in his marriage bed he had made love to his wife. Gently, gradually, carefully, afraid that his own weakened strength might not carry him through, his beloved wife had guided him towards a rapturous orgasm and if hers had not matched his he was not aware of it.

He did not know of the tears that she wept silently after he slept. She loved him as she had always done as a beloved friend. She had chosen to spend her life with him but he had never captured and held her heart as Noah had done. She loved him. He was one of the best men she had ever known, steadfast, kind, funny, brave and loving, but the man to whom she belonged, heart, soul, mind, muscle and fibre and always would, lay devastated in a hospital down south and would, when he recovered, if he recovered from the blow she had felled him with, go back to fight, and probably die, in France.

Doctor Bennett came just after breakfast, brought by Harry in Archie's motor car. Holding Rose by the hand Alex was led in to the drawing-room as it had been thought best not to try to examine her in her bedroom as though she were ill. Doctor Bennett questioned her gently. Had she felt sick at all, especially in the mornings? No, that was good and would she mind if he just listened to her heart. No, no, there was nothing to worry about but if he might just put his hand here, on her stomach. She was not to be frightened and when he had finished he would examine Rose who he had heard had just got married. Had Alex been told?

'Yes, her husband is . . . here he is. His name is Dick.' She smiled up at Dick and they all breathed a sigh of relief that the first hurdle was over but there was, of course, worse to come and, as Dick said, they might as well get it over and done with. He had sent a telegram to Patrick with just the bare details, telling him to come home at once, home being Edge Bottom House at the moment and was certain that he would be here within the next few days.

They agonised on who was to be present when Rose told

Alex who she was and why she was here, or at least tried to, for who knew how she would react. She was more and more herself these days, calm, quite cheerful, enjoying the company of the servants, walking down to the paddock or across the fields to the bit of woodland at the back of the house, but she still believed that these people who had taken her in were just kind strangers and if she was improving why was it that she did not question this?

Rose sat on the sofa and Alex sat next to her and in the armchair on the other side of the cheerfully blazing log fire Nan held a bit of sewing in her hand. It was the beginning of a small nightshirt, a baby's nightshirt.

'Alex, have you ever wondered who your family is and where they might be?' Rose began, her grip on Alex's hand tightening as she felt her friend tense.

'My family?' Alex quavered and Nan looked up ready to spring to the defence of her lamb but Rose held up her hand, knowing that if they baulked at this they would never get going again.

'Yes. Do you not wonder where your father and mother, perhaps sisters and brothers might be? Where they live and how you came to be here at Edge Bottom House?'

She was conscious that just outside the closed drawing-room door Dick, Doctor Bennett and Mr Goodwin sat in breathless silence waiting for any sound that might indicate that there was trouble in the room.

'Edge Bottom House?'

'Yes, that is the name of this house.'

'Yes, I know.' Both Rose and Nan straightened up and Nan began to smile. 'The man outside told me. I think he said his name was Harry. He takes me to see the horses and . . .'

'Yes, darling, but what about the others?'

'D'you mean Mr Goodwin?'

'Yes, have you not wondered who he is? Have you not

wondered why your family have not come for you? That they might be looking for you.'

Alex was beginning to get agitated and once more Nan made as though she was about to rise but Rose persisted. Some instinct told her they *must* go on. That the truth must be *forced* on Alex if she was to be restored to herself. If she could talk to and listen to these members of her family and the servants who cared for her she might be guided back to what she once had been. Memories, images of her childhood, of her young womanhood might prick some shell that was covering her past and once that prick occurred and the shell was torn, surely it would all come flooding back. It was a physical trauma that had caused this amnesia, some damage perhaps to her brain, but if they didn't try to get through it she might remain in this state for ever and with a baby she didn't know was hers! If only Patrick could get here soon . . . Dear God, please, dear Lord let her not be doing harm to this lovely woman when all she wanted was for her to be returned to them.

'Alex, I'm going to tell you something that might surprise you.' Rose pulled Alex into her arms, kissed her, then placed her carefully a foot away, holding her gaze, smiling, stroking her cheek, ready to weep at the obvious anxiety Alex was displaying.

'Do you trust me, dearest? Do you believe I would never, ever lie to you, hurt you in any way? That I love you dearly?'

Alex relaxed and smiled back at her. 'I love you too, Rose.'

'I know. Now then . . .' She turned to smile at Nan. 'Nan has known you since the day you were born. When was that, Nan?'

'Twenty-eight years ago last March.'

'And I have known you for over three years. You were born close by here, Alex, but this is your home. Mr Goodwin is your father and you have two brothers, Tom and Will. Tom is to be home soon and I believe Will, who is a flier, is to get some leave from the war. You know there is a war on, don't you, Alex? We have spoken of it. You were involved in that war, sweetheart. You were very brave. You drove an ambulance taking the wounded to hospital and you yourself were hurt. Wounded. Your head was hurt and it has . . . has taken your memory. One day it will come back and you will remember all these people who love you but until that happens we are here to help you, to take care of you and to try to make you happy. You must not worry. Bits of the past will come back to you a little at a time. Like your cat who we used to call Ginger. And you remembered when Dick called me his sweet Rosie, didn't you? Let us help you. Let us talk to you about the Alex before the accident, tell you, remind you of your life and then, gradually, you will remember yourself. Are you happy about that? Nothing will change. You will stay here with your family until you are better. Do you understand, dearest?'

There was no answer and Nan rose to her feet, for her lamb was wobbling and her face was screwed up in a tight grimace then Alex began to cry desolately. Rose pulled her into her arms and made the sounds mothers make to comfort a hurt child, but Alex pulled away and they were amazed to see her smiling through her tears.

'Oh, how lovely. I have always liked Mr Goodwin and now I can love him since he is my father. Where is he? Please, I must see him and then I'll tell the others that they have known me since I was a baby. To think all this time Harry and . . . oh, Nan, will you tell me what I did? And there is so much I must know. Why is my foot as it is. I have wondered . . .'

Nan pulled her to her feet and clasped her fiercely in loving arms. 'Oh lamb . . . my lamb, welcome 'ome. Eeh, we've a lot ter talk about, thi' an' me but first, come an' say summat ter tha' pa.'

For a moment Alex hung back and Rose hoped fervently that Nan, in her excitement and relief, as though she were convinced that now Miss Alex knew who she was, she would be the same as she had been, mightn't say too much. Restored to the family and able to chat of old times, or at least listen to tales of old times. She must speak to them all, the servants, to Nan and Nelly, even to Mr Goodwin, and tell them not to be too . . . well, she wasn't sure what the word was: perhaps enthusiastic. They must let Alex ask the questions, not force reminiscences on her. They must not use the word *remember* all the time, for Alex would not remember and must be led gently along the path of her past.

She rose to her feet and moved slowly across the rich carpet which never failed to amaze her, for she herself had been brought up in genteel poverty and the carpets in her father's house had been threadbare, the chairs and sofa and beds old and sagging, the curtains mended and patched by herself, and the luxury of the Goodwins' home was a wonder to her.

Nan was drawing a very shy Alex into the hallway where Mr Goodwin, Doctor Bennett and Dick rose slowly to their feet, their faces filled with apprehension. She knew both Dick and Doctor Bennett had had reservations on the best way to go about bringing Alex from her forgotten past in the way Rose had, but then the mind was an unknown quantity to the medical profession and whatever way they approached it was a chancy thing.

'Alex,' her father murmured, his face very gaunt, thin, his eyes set in deep pouches, for Archie Goodwin had gone through hell in the past year. He wanted to hold out his arms, Rose could see that, and have Alex run into them as she once had done but he restrained himself, for Alex did not yet think of him as her father but a kind stranger. Rose had told her who he was, and who Alex was, but they must move slowly.

'Yes,' Alex whispered, then moved hesitantly towards the elderly man. They were both trembling but Alex put out a hand and he took it, bringing it to his cheek where a tear fell on it.

'Oh, Alex . . . my lovely girl . . .' He tried to smile reassuringly. She seemed to be acting on some instinct and with a lovely gesture she stretched up and placed a kiss on his cheek.

'Did I call you . . . Father . . . or . . .'

'You called me Father, my darling, and I would be so glad if you could bring yourself to do so again.'

'Yes . . . oh yes, I will try. I know you . . . have known you for . . . how long is it?' turning to Nan.

'Four months, lass.'

'Four months as a . . . very kind . . . gentleman but now . . . you are my father. Father!'

Very gently he put his arms about her and drew her to him and she went willingly, and Rose drew a sigh of relief as it seemed another step had been taken. Dick and Doctor Bennett exchanged glances for it seemed Rose's instincts had been correct. Alex understood who she was and what her place in life was. She would take time to get used to it but it seemed she had left behind the tragic small girl she had been all these months and become a woman. True, a woman without a memory but surely, with the help of them all, it would be restored to her.

They could not go now to Grasmere, that seemed to be understood because they must wait for Patrick to return from France, which surely he would soon. There was still the matter of Alex's pregnancy which must shortly be explained to her, for even she would soon realise that she was putting on weight. She had been so slender and was one of those fortunate women who do not immediately show their state when they are with child but that would not last. Doctor Bennett was brought over almost every day, to Alex's surprise, but as she did not know, or at least remember the ways of medicine, she accepted his constant examinations though, of course, these were all super-ficial and did not require that she remove her clothing. He told Rose and Nan privately that she was in splendid health and should have no trouble bearing the child, but the dilemma of when and what to tell her loomed over them all. Patrick would know, they kept telling one another. Wait until Patrick arrived, for they were all convinced that Alex would know Patrick at once since they had been lovers, that much was obvious.

In the meanwhile they wrapped up warm against the October winds, and went for walks on the moors to the east of St Helens, not Nan, of course, for she was far too old for that sort of thing, she said, wrapping a warm scarf about her lamb's neck, but Rose and Alex, and if it was not to be far Dick accompanied them. The cold affected his chest badly and Nan transferred her devoted cosseting to Miss Rose's husband, watching wistfully as Miss Alex tramped off with Miss Rose, not exactly wishing that Alex was still the little girl who had clung to Nan for months, but at least dependent on her a little bit. Alex thrived and it was not unusual to find her sitting in the stable with Harry talking about the days before the war when she and Tom and Will rode their wild little ponies over the moorland. Well, Harry did all the talking while she listened in total absorption, both of them sitting on upturned buckets, with the cat purring round their legs. Harry asked her, after discussing it with Miss Rose, if she would care for a puppy as he had heard of a litter over at Wildwood Farm and was delighted with her response.

'I would love it, but what about Cat, Harry? D'you think she will mind? I don't want to upset her for she's been a good friend to me.'

'Has she, Miss Alex? What makes you say that?'

'I don't know really. I seem to . . . to remember her, as if we had been together. Oh, I don't know, she is special to me but I would love a puppy. Can we go and see them, Harry? I could ride and you could lead the way.'

She was quite put out when Harry, who had had strict instructions from Doctor Bennett, would not allow her to get up on the old mare's back.

'But you always allowed me to ride Molly,' she said, to

Harry's amazement as it was the first time she had called the animal by her name. He told Nan you could have knocked him down with a bloody feather but, as instructed by Miss Rose, he made no comment.

All these events took place over a few days, which surprised them all at its speed, but she seemed to have recovered something she had lost – not unfortunately her memory – which Rose decided was her identity. It gave her strength and confidence and in such a short time they were amazed. Perhaps it was time to tell her that she was to have a child, probably about December, Doctor Bennett thought, revising his opinion of how far along she was. It was difficult to tell when faced with a woman who did not know when her last courses had taken place, or was even aware that there were such things. One could only put one's hand on the woman's belly and guess.

They waited, Rose and Dick, Archie Goodwin, Nan, Nelly and the rest of the servants for the arrival of Patrick O'Leary who, it was whispered, was the father of Miss Alex's child, for surely when he came some magical thing would happen and their Miss Alex would be as once she had been. There would be a quick wedding, a quiet wedding and then they would await, with a great degree of pleasure, the birth of the child. Naturally the child's father would have to return to France, for he was a surgeon and much needed in that terrible place where men were dying or being returned to their loved ones changed beyond measure by their wounds. In St Helens alone were lads who had joined up in their Pals Battalions, lads who had grown up together, gone to school together, lived in the same street and died together. It was said on the first day of the Battle of the Somme that 5,000 men from London alone had fallen and in Manchester 3,500 and that villages all over the country had proportionally been hit even worse. But Patrick was surely on his way home by now and they waited patiently, the two girls in the kitchen earnestly discussing what they would wear for the wedding, not in Nan's hearing, of course, nor in Nelly's nor Miss Smith's, for they had been told that if Miss Alex spoke to them they were only to speak of the past, not the future. Still, it was exciting, wasn't it, they whispered to one another as they waited for the bridegroom to come home!

# 24

The armies pushed on through the months of September and October, but now – particularly among the Australians of the Anzac Corps which was bearing the brunt of the fierce fighting in the middle of the sector – there were murmurs of 'murder' and 'slaughter'. Some battalions had lost so many men, had been reinforced by so many drafts that they now contained very few of the original members of their ranks. When the 13th Battalion of the Australian Imperial Force was relieved after forty hours' desperate fighting they sent in a casualty list of ten officers and 231 men and in those forty hours they had also won between them thirty-two military medals and had triumphantly reinforced the reputation implied by their nickname of 'the fighting thirteenth'.

By 26 October they were again up to their full strength and were sent north to the Ypres salient but those who had been wounded were left behind at Number 55 Casualty Clearing Station where Patrick O'Leary was standing beside the bed of a young private from Toowoomba in Queensland, pondering on the rather bleak prospect of saving the lad's leg. He had been a sheep shearer in civilian life and it was difficult to shear a sheep on one leg, he told the doc, his eyes filled with terror and Patrick was – in his head – performing the operation that might save the young Australian's leg when the telegram was handed to him. From further down the tent the Aussies, those whose wounds were lighter and were recovering, were quietly singing a song to the melody of 'Moonlight Bay'.

*I was strolling along*
*In Gillymong*
*With the Minnywerfers singing*
*Their old sweet song . . .*

'. . . so you see, Doc, I don't care what it takes but I must get off that bloody boat wi' both me legs,' he was saying, but the doc was reading his telegram and as he read it his face drained of all colour and with an oath he turned from the poor lad and began to run between the beds as though the bloody Minnywerfers them-selves were after him, leaving the young Aussie with his mouth hanging open and his chances of saving his leg dropping to nil!

The Chief Medical Officer for the area was in the wooden hut where the administration for the hospital took place. He was just about to move on to Dernancourt, behind Albert where he had further administrative duties to perform, when Patrick O'Leary, the best surgeon in the unit, burst in waving a telegram, startling not only him but his staff, and was not best pleased by the frantic stuttering of the man who most of them called a 'cold bastard' or, more kindly, Mad Paddy. Not to his face, of course, and it had been noticed that he was compas-sionate with his patients. Confident, transferring it to the wounded. He was patient and willing to give his free time, which wasn't much, to the men in his care. Now he was babbling like a lunatic and it was some time before they understood what it was he wanted.

'. . . compassionate leave. I must have it, sir. I must get home at once . . . oh, I know we are in the middle of a battle but then when aren't we? I have not had leave for months, of any sort, perhaps a day here and there . . .' His face twisted as though at some memory, then he blundered on, waving what looked like a telegram in the officer's face.

'Calm down, Captain, calm down, man. You know you can't be spared.'

'I must, sir. With respect, I must insist. A week, no more.'

'What is it? Who is it that has you in such a—'

'My . . . my fiancée, sir. She is—'

'*Your fiancée!* Not even a relative.'

'Soon to be, sir. But she was wounded; perhaps you don't remember. A head wound which has left her without memory. She was an ambulance driver, wounded on duty, like any soldier. I operated with Dick Morris and took her home but she is . . .'

'Yes?'

'Read it, sir, I beg you.' The officer took the telegram from Patrick O'Leary's shaking hand, wondering who this woman was who had the cold bastard in such a ferment. It read: 'Come home at once. Alex needs you,' and was signed 'Dick'.

'But this does not even indicate what is wrong with her. You apparently healed her head wound and—'

'She has amnesia, sir. Sir' – his voice became strangled – 'sir, I must go.'

'I can't just allow—'

'I am due leave, sir.'

'But the wounded are . . . High Wood, Delville Wood, Mamtetz Wood . . . well, need I go on? Every doctor is needed.'

Patrick O'Leary was seen to grit his teeth as though he longed to smash his fist into his officer's teeth but he controlled his explosive anger at this waste of time and waited while the man dithered about with bits of paper and muttered discussions with his aides and at last got the precious scrap of document that gave him ten days' leave beginning the next day.

He left at a run and if his absence from that moment on was noticed by his fellow doctors they kept it to themselves; within ten minutes of leaving the Chief Medical Officer's hut he was on the back of a messenger's motorbike, speeding towards the railway station at Etaples and the boat to England. The boat was full of the suffering humanity, the victims of the brutalising war in the trenches, but Patrick stood aside from it, his whole being concentrated on the woman towards whom he was moving, at a snail's pace it seemed to him.

He drove up to Edge Bottom House in a motor cab thirty-six hours after he had received the telegram, haggard, un-shaven, his uniform crumpled and stained with the mud of France.

They were at dinner, the startled maid told him, eyeing his dishevelled state with some trepidation, not recognising him and was even more alarmed when he summarily pushed past her and strode across the wide hallway and flung open the door to the dining-room.

There were four of them round the oval, highly polished dining table, candlelight reflecting in its surface, the two women, not in evening dress as had been the rule before the war, but wearing pretty afternoon gowns of floating chiffon and satin ribbons in the style of 1914 when they were pur-chased. The two gentlemen were in lounge suits, smart but casual. They all stared for a moment then Rose jumped to her feet, and with a muffled cry flung her arms about him and held him fiercely to her. She smelled lovely, he had time to think, the stench of gangrene and disinfectant still in his nostrils, then his eyes went to Alex, who had recoiled against the back of her chair, her lovely eyes wide and startled, but looking so radiantly beautiful he could hardly believe it. If ever a woman could be said to be blooming it was Alex and he was ready to lash out at Dick for terrifying him so. Nan was there, standing beside the serving table and her eyes were filled with tears and at the same time she smiled as though in relief.

But he had no time for any of them. Not Dick or Rose or Mr Goodwin, but walked slowly towards Alex who crouched even further back in her chair.

'Careful, old man,' Dick murmured, putting out a warning

hand as though to stop him but Patrick was beyond stopping, beyond any reasoning or caution. There she was, his beloved girl, his macushla and seemingly in the best of health.

'Patrick . . .' Dick warned again and as he spoke Rose came forward and took Patrick's arm. He tried to shake it off, for there was nothing more he longed to do but to hold out his hand to Alex, help her to her feet and take her in his arms. In his right mind he would have known this was not the proper thing to do, for if she did not remember him it would frighten her but at that moment his mind was *not* right. It was bemused by the loveliness of her and by his love for her, by his own sense of homecoming, of being here where she was, with love and peace and relief that she was so obviously recovered. For a second he wondered why Dick's telegram had been so urgent, then he felt Rose's hand grip his arm in a vice and though he tried to brush it off impatiently she would not let him, was, in fact, doing her best to pull him away.

'Patrick, come away,' she said, her voice artificially bright. 'It's lovely to see you, isn't it, Archie, but you must be famished after such a long journey.'

'No, Rose.'

'Yes, Patrick. Nan, set another place for Patrick. We are just about to start our main course but I'm sure there is some soup left.'

'I don't want any bloody soup, Rose, just let me—'

'*No*, Patrick.' And all the time Alex stared at the stranger who seemed to be having a struggle with Rose. He was a soldier, she could see that, and, it seemed, a friend of Dick and Rose. Her hand trembled a little where it rested on the table and her father took it in his and she turned to him with relief, for this strange man was causing her some anxiety.

'Perhaps Patrick would like to clean up a bit,' Dick said in a loud voice, anything to get him out of the room and explain, but he began to cough quite violently and it was perhaps this that finally dragged Patrick from the trance of love he had fallen into at the sight of his lovely Alex.

'Dick . . .' he faltered, turning to him in alarm and it gave Dick time to take him by the arm and lead him, unprotesting now, towards the dining-room door.

'Dick,' he said again, turning back to look at Alex who watched him with uncomprehending eyes, but Dick drew him out of the room, across the hall and into the fire-glowed drawing-room.

'Dick, please, why have you sent for me? It's not that I'm not glad to see her. God, I love her, but there seems to be—'

'She's pregnant, Patrick,' Dick said baldly, catching Patrick as he swayed and steering him to the sofa beside the fire. Patrick sat as though felled, which he was and Dick hurried to the drinks table and with a shaking hand poured a liberal brandy into a glass and passed it to Patrick. Patrick stared at it but when Dick told him to drink up, he did, draining the glass. Dick sat down opposite him and waited.

For perhaps five minutes, as the drink steadied him, Patrick stared at nothing, then, leaning forward, put his elbows on his knees and lowered his head.

'No wonder she looks so bloody marvellous. Pregnant women often do. Sweet Christ, what are we to do?' He had at last grasped the implications of the situation. He knew the child was his, of course, and in some sweet corner of his soul he was elated, but with Alex not having the faintest idea of who he was, that had been obvious, nor that her body contained the growing symbol of their love or even of how it had got there, what the hell were they to do? They must be married, naturally, before he went back and she must be told of her condition, but how, dear God, how?

At last Dick broke the silence. He knew that Rose would be fidgeting about, longing to come and see what was happening, what was being said, but they must not upset Alex who was settling quite nicely into the knowledge that she was in her own home with her own family about her. Now they were to spring this on her and how the devil were they to do that?

'Patrick, come and have a wash and a word with Nan as to where you are to sleep. Have something to eat, a night's rest, for I can see it's a while since you had any and then in the morning Nan can take Alex out, we'll send for Doctor Bennett and five of us will talk it out. Perhaps Doctor Bennett will have some ideas. But you're too tired to think straight and the shock . . . come on, old son, let me give you a hand. Oh, and another bit of news . . .'

'I can't stand any more shocks, Dick.'

'No, lad, you'll like this. Rose and I are married.'

'You always were a lucky swine. Oh, Dick, I'm sorry and you with . . . well, it can't be any fun being gassed but with Rose to nurse you . . .'

'Bugger that, she's my wife,' leaving Patrick in no doubt that Dick was fulfilling his husbandly duties despite his incapacity.

'Now isn't this pleasant?' Archie said as he sat down on the sofa after dinner, his daughter beside him. Introductions had been made between Alex and Patrick, which was somewhat of a farce in view of their relationship but it had to be done. Patrick was an old friend of Dick's, Alex was told, and of them all really, since before the war he had stayed at Edge Bottom House and even been on holiday with them at Fellgate House by the lake in Grasmere.

'Was I there?' Alex asked, wide-eyed with wonder that this stranger was so well known by her new family.

'Of course you were, dearest, though I wasn't,' Rose said. 'You and I hadn't met then. It was not until we were together in the . . .'

'What, Rose?' Alex asked eagerly.

Rose hesitated. 'Have you heard of, or read about' – for she had introduced Alex to some books as despite her loss of memory she could still read and she had encouraged Alex to go through the newspapers so that she would know what was going on in the world Alex had forgotten – 'the suffragettes?'

'No, I don't think so. No.'

'I'll tell you about them some time but that was when you and I met, and Dick . . . and . . .'

'And Patrick,' smiling shyly at the man who sat opposite her. He was beginning to nod in total exhaustion and Dick was ready to get him to bed but at the mention of his name on his love's lips Patrick glanced up and his face softened and glowed and Alex felt something strange happen inside her. A sort of warmth and yet a tingle, almost a recognition of something which slipped away as soon as she tried to grasp it. They had met before, she had been told that. She liked the look of him. He wore spectacles but as they looked at one another he took them off and she noticed the colour of his eyes for the first time. They were a smoky brown with stripes of gold coming from the dark pupil to the whites, very unusual but, despite the exhaustion in them they seemed to be saying something to her, though again she could not grasp it. He smiled, his lips curling over straight white teeth and she thought, How . . . how . . . what . . .'

She turned uncertainly to Rose, Rose who was the true cornerstone of her life. Nan was kind and loving and so was the man they told her was her father but there was some bond between her and Rose and it was to Rose she always turned when she was doubtful about something.

Rose smiled at her reassuringly. 'I really think we have all had enough for one day, don't you, dearest?' She stood up, drawing Alex with her and taking her husband's hand. 'Shall we all get to our beds and then in the morning, when Patrick has had a good night's sleep we will talk again.'

'I think I might . . . sleep by myself tonight,' Alex told them hesitantly, smiling at Nan then looking about her as though expecting one of them to disagree. Nan, who was included in all discussions regarding Alex and had been ever since she had taken up residence at Bedford Square in the days of the militant suffragette activities, returned her smile. She sat by the window, saying nothing much but listening, for it was in her mind that though there was nothing she wanted more than to see her lamb married to Patrick O'Leary before he went back to France in ten days she was a practical woman and could not see how this was to be achieved. Miss Alex must be made aware, gradually and gently, that she was carrying a child and that the father of the child was the man who was doing his best not to fall into exhausted sleep on the sofa, which in Nan's mind was strange since he was so deeply involved. She was not to know that he had been on duty without sleep for fourteen hours even before he received the telegram that had brought him here and it had taken him thirty-six hours to travel the distance from the casualty clearing station to St Helens. And was it likely, now that he *was* here that Miss Alex was going to agree to marry him? Not in ten days, she was not!

She felt her heart drop, since it seemed Miss Alex's child was to be a bastard. Illegitimate. Dear sweet Lord, what was to be done? They must put Miss Alex's health and peace of mind first. She and Miss Rose must find some way to tell her what was to happen to her and if she could not be persuaded to marry Patrick, who was a lovely man and would make her an ideal husband, where would it all end? The pair of them must have been in love and . . . and in France . . . well, there was no other way to put it, had an affair and this was the result.

'Right tha' are, Miss Rose. You an' tha' 'usband get off. I'll see ter Miss Alex an' then get ter me own bed. Tha' knows which room tha's in, Doctor?' she said, addressing Patrick O'Leary.

'Yes, thanks, Nan.' He could barely put one foot in front of the other but Patrick felt he could not merely go to bed without speaking to Alex. She was looking at him with a lovely shyness that took his breath away and for a moment he had the most desperate need to put his arms about her and crush her to him. Shake her! Tell her who he was and what they meant to one another. Speak of their child that was growing inside her, the child he had put there. The frustration was so great he actually began to tremble with his need but Dick stepped forward and took his arm, leading him towards the door.

'Goodnight then,' Patrick said quietly, turning back to the others but with his eyes on Alex. 'Perhaps in the morning you can show me round, Alex. The gardens and . . . and . . . well, but I'll say goodnight and apologise for being such a . . .'

'Patrick, old lad, we realise what you have been doing these last months and how difficult the journey from the trenches to here has been.'

'The trenches?' Alex questioned.

'Now my lass, Doctor'll tell thi' all about it in't morning, won't thi', Doctor, so off tha' go an' sleep well.'

He did sleep well, in fact for so long Alex wanted to go and knock at his door and wake him because she was eager to take him round Edge Bottom and show him the horses, the cat, and even to show him the farm, Wildwood Farm, where Harry had taken her to see her puppy.

'Leave 'im be, Miss Alex. He'll wake when he's ready. Tha've plenty o' time an' the lad's exhausted.'

He came running down the stairs at noon, apologising profusely for the lateness of the hour, washed, shaved, dressed in a pair of corduroy trousers, a shirt and jumper that Archie had lent him since Nan swore he couldn't get back into his uniform until she had cleaned and pressed it. He looked as though he'd fallen off a flittin', she told him, which he understood being Liverpool Irish! They sat round the breakfast table with him, Archie, Rose, Dick and Alex, watching him eat the enormous plate of bacon, eggs, fried mushrooms, tomatoes and toast that Nan urged him to 'get inside tha'. He drank a potful of tea and laughed as they watched him, saying he felt like a small boy being urged by Nanny in the nursery to eat every mouthful. Not that he had had a nanny or seen the inside of a nursery and when pressed by Alex, who hung on his every word, told them of his childhood in Liverpool, of his Catholic upbringing, of his days at school and university and his first job as a junior doctor.

'Won't your mother and father want to see you, Patrick?' Alex asked, shooting an affectionate glance at her own father whom she had learned to love in the last few months.

'Indeed, and when I can I'll get over there, to be sure, but at the moment I have more important matters to see to . . .' then came to a full stop for how could he tell her what those important matters were, but she was becoming more the Alex of the old days and though she did not remember them, her stubborn will was returning day by day and she was not satisfied with the answer.

'Perhaps you could telephone them and . . . I know . . . invite them to come here. That would be lovely, wouldn't it, Rose?' She turned eagerly to Rose who put out a tentative hand as though to stop a runaway child.

'Darling, Patrick has only a few days with us and there is so much. . . .' She stopped, as Patrick had done, turning frantically to the others for inspiration but Patrick had the answer and he said smoothly. 'My parents don't have a telephone, Alex, so they don't, and beside my father has the shop, so.'

His Irish accent was becoming more pronounced as he did his best to head off the charming child Alex had become. Alex was a mixture of woman and child and he wanted her badly but the bloody thing was so impossible. Like Nan he was well aware that he could not marry Alex before his leave was over. He must leave her to bear their child without him and if he should be killed in the destruction that was taking place across the

Channel she would be the mother of an illegitimate baby. Sweet Mary, Mother of God, what was he to do? As he looked about him at the others he could see the same despair on all their faces.

Suddenly he stood up, so suddenly they all jumped, but as naturally as once he would have done he held out his hand to Alex. 'Come along, macushla, let's start on that voyage of exploration you promised me. It's a lovely day, just right for a walk. Are you ready?'

She stood up, her movement the exact opposite to his. Slowly, so slowly and on her face was an expression of gladness, which lit it up and put stars in her lavender-blue eyes.

'Someone used to call me that. Was it . . . was it you, Patrick?'

'Yes.' He could say no more, for his throat was thick with tears.

'I like it. I don't know what it means but I like it. Now then, let's go and look at the stable. Oh, and you haven't met Cat yet, have you?' She took his hand and led him from the room, still talking of the wonderful things about the place she was to show him and those left let out their breaths on a concerted sigh.

'Well!' said Nan. 'I've come mazy all over.' She shook her head in bewilderment. 'That's fair flummoxed me.' And it seemed it had fair flummoxed them all!

# 25

She seemed to consider Patrick her own private property and the household held its collective breath, for though they were all aware that in the time limit of ten days Patrick and Alex could not build up that relationship they had once known it was a good beginning. She called him her friend and, moving carefully, patiently and at the same time with extreme tenderness, he built up her confidence. They roamed the meadows and woodland about the house, just the two of them, and Patrick even rode the old mare with much hilarity, as he had never been on the back of a horse in his life, he told her, as he slithered off for the umpteenth time. Where he had grown up there had been no such things as riding stables and the only animal he had been familiar with was the old horse that pulled the rag and bone man's cart.

The rag and bone man's cart? she questioned him which led to further discussions about the streets of Liverpool, the dockland where he had watched the sailing ships come flying like birds up the river, the river itself on which the sailing ships were nearly extinct as steam took over and at each conversation the route of it led on to another. She was quite fascinated with him, it seemed, and the others realised that they had not *extended* her mind, that they had cosseted her, loved her, protected her as they would a child while her mind, which had lost the first almost thirty years of her life, was still curious, intelligent, quick to learn. And so it was when they were on one of their rambles that Patrick told her she was to have a baby of her own. He loved her and with his love had come an intuitive knowledge of her capacity to absorb, as she had done in the week they had been together. The others left them alone though Nan lamented that she was not sure about this, this neglect, as she saw it, of Miss Alex by Nan herself who had cared for her for so long, by Rose, by Alex's own father and by Doctor Dick. Was it proper? she questioned, for Nan came of the era where a well-brought-up young lady was never left alone with an unmarried gentleman who was not a relative. Really, Rose said to her and what of the days when she and Alex had walked the streets of London, alone and together and had been in the company of men who were a far greater risk than Patrick!

But Dick was none too well at the moment, his lungs at risk as the mildness of the autumn became colder, the cold entering his lungs, reacting to it, making him cough and wheeze. He kept to the bedroom he shared with his wife, a blazing fire in the hearth, wrapped about in a shawl and her loving care, with Nan's potions and egg custards so that Alex's wanderings with Patrick were really a godsend.

They had walked that day to Wildwood Farm, Alex in the warm, ankle-length coat she had worn before the war, scarf wrapped about her by Nan, warm woollen gloves and a pair of stout boots. Patrick was still in the cords and sweater lent to him by Archie but over it he was swathed in an old Chesterfield overcoat and similarly scarved by Nan so that even his ears were covered.

The puppies were enchanting and Patrick watched as Alex knelt in the straw of the barn, a leaping tumble of growling, yipping puppies about her, mother crouching warily nearby to make sure her offspring were safe. She was a sheep dog, used by the farmer to herd his small flock of sheep, with black and white markings and pale blue eyes but some 'bloody mongrel must've got to 'er and these 'uns is the result'. They had their mother's colouring but they were finer boned, with a short plumy tail and eyes the colour of peat. 'Gawd knows what sort,' the farmer continued, 'but these're no bloody good ter me . . . pardon, miss,' suddenly realising he was using language that was not suitable in front of a young lady, but Alex was squealing as loudly as the puppies, doing her best to avoid sharp teeth and licking tongues. 'Yer can 'ave which yer like o' them two. T'others is spoken for.'

'Oh, I can't leave one behind. I'll have them both, if I may,' she told the resigned farmer. 'When can I have them? Can we take them now?'

'Not yet, miss. They're not weaned but 'appen in a week or two if you was ter walk over.'

Later they sat with their backs to a tall grey-pitted rock in a semicircle of others, looking out over the smoky yellow pall which lay over St Helens, having walked up the low moorland that surrounded the town. It was open country up here, unspoiled, wild and uninhabited, too poor to be cultivated. There were small, heathery shrubs at the back of the circle of rocks: bilberry, heather, gorse, sedge, cotton grass. There was bog moss divided by tracks and rocky outcrops and grazing peacefully were small, sturdy sheep who sheared away as Alex and Patrick approached. Patrick had brought a groundsheet at Nan's insistence, for she didn't want her lamb sitting on no damp grass, she told him sternly. He spread it out and they sat down and gazed over the low countryside at their feet in the bowl of which the town of St Helens lay.

They were companionably silent for a while and Patrick wondered at it, for he was coming to believe that their shared past still lived in some small place in Alex's mind which was not yet fully revealed. He believed her body recognised his even if, as yet, her mind did not. They were *easy* with one another, with no need to talk and yet when she did begin there was no end to her questions. Was she like this with her? he asked Rose. Or Nan? The answer was no. Of course she asked questions but not with the same intensity nor interest that she employed with him. She sat beside him, her knees drawn up, her arms clasped about her knees and, sighing with growing content, he lay back on the groundsheet and closed his eyes.

Alex was still excited about the puppies. *Two* puppies and she delved into her knowledge of the things she had recently read and tried to decide on names for them. None came readily to her but she had a week or two, the farmer had told them, to decide. She did hope Cat, who had tried to come with them this morning, would not mind. Poor Cat, she had been shut in the scullery, protesting loudly, for, as Patrick said, they could hardly take her to the farm where the dogs, and there were more than one, might set on her. Her mind was still busy with names when a picture flashed across her astonished mind. It was of a lady walking along a street and going into a shop called . . . called Derry and Tom's, a lady whom she thought was her mother . . . so pretty, so elegant, smiling, and in another flash she saw a girl with a hammer lift it and smash it against the glass window of the same shop. Lord, what on earth . . . who on earth . . . what were they doing this lady and this woman, this destructive woman who . . . who she thought might be herself?

Alarmed, she turned to Patrick, for it was somehow right that it should be to him that she should speak about it but he had his eyes closed and the bewildering questions she had to ask drifted away as she looked at him. She had never seen him asleep before, had she? How did she know . . . but leaning closer she studied the relaxed lines of his lean face. He had removed his spectacles and held them loosely in one hand which rested on his flat stomach. His breathing was deep and even and she leaned even closer, watching the sweep of his long lashes which you didn't notice much when he had on his spectacles. They were a deep brown but the tips were gold. His skin was smooth and because they had been out each day in the autumn sunshine it had changed from the pallor he had brought with him from France to a pleasing amber. His mouth, which curled up intriguingly at each corner, seemed to have a smile on it and she put out a tentative finger as though to touch his lips then drew back quickly. He was so nice to look at, so kind, so funny at times he made her laugh and yet he was serious, treating her and her questions seriously. She had one for him now but didn't like to wake him.

Suddenly his eyes opened and since their faces were no more than six inches apart, though he seemed undisturbed she became flustered.

'May I kiss you?' he asked her just as though what he was asking were of no more importance than 'may I help you to your feet?' His breath was warm and sweet on her face and she thought it might be rather nice so she nodded breathlessly.

It was she who leaned forward and placed her mouth on his and it fitted there, was at home there, in its rightful place. He moved his lips slightly, opening them, parting hers, his breath again warm and sweet in her mouth and when she lifted her head and looked into his face she sighed contentedly.

'We knew each other, didn't we?' she said.

'We knew each other, macushla, and it's time we talked about it.' He sat up and put an arm about her shoulder, cradling her to him and she sighed again as she nestled close.

'I don't remember, Patrick,' she warned him.

'I know you don't but there is an intuitive sense in you that recognises me and we must just trust it. I can tell you all you want to know. You have only to ask but first . . .'

Patrick paused, bending his head, for this moment was to be the most important in his life and he must not make a mistake. She must first be made aware of the child and then, from there, not on this leave as he was to go back tomorrow, they must be married. He must apply for further leave. Thirty-six hours perhaps. Rose could bring her to London where they would get a special licence, but there was this to be got through first.

'Those puppies,' he began quietly. 'Do you know where they came from?'

'Where they came from? Well . . . no, not really, Patrick but their mother was there so she must have something to do with it. All creatures have a mother, horses, dogs . . .'

'And human beings, macushla. Your mother died last year but your father still lives.' He pondered for a moment or two on whether to introduce the complexities of her natural mother and father then decided it would not do to involve her further in what was not really needed at this time.

'Yes, I see, but . . .' She looked up at him and giving in to that instinct that so far had not deserted him, he placed his lips on hers again, soft, they were, like satin, warm and willing. Jesus, Joseph and Mary, things were going so well he could hardly believe it. She liked him. She was happy and safe with him and she was also, though she wasn't aware of it, physically attracted to him!

'One day Rose and Dick, who love each other and are married . . . you understand?' She nodded, her eyes on his. 'Well, one day Rose will have children, like the dog at the farm had puppies. Because they love each other Rose and Dick will . . .' Holy Mother, give me the right words to make her understand but not to frighten her. Jesus, he was a doctor, he should be able to . . .

'They sleep together and love one another and the result will be a baby. It will grow in Rose's belly and after nine months when it is able to survive outside her it will be born.'

'Really!' She was quite fascinated and not a bit alarmed. 'Will this be soon?'

'It might or it might not but since Dick and Rose love one another it will be a happy event. That is what some people call it. A happy event.' He drew her closer and laid his lips on her short hair, which had grown into a dark cap of curls since it had been shaved off in May. 'That is what happened to you and me,

Alex. You know you were in France, driving an ambulance, Rose told you that.'

'Yes.'

'And were in an accident. Your head was hurt which is why you can't remember anything before that, but you and me . . . we loved one another. I still love you, so much and one day I hope . . .'

She drew away from him in confusion and he felt his spirits sink, for it seemed he had gone too fast but though her face was serious her eyes were clear and it was evident that she knew what he meant. Not the exact details of how this sort of thing happened, what was done when a man and a woman loved one another but that the thought of sharing it with Patrick was not one that dismayed her.

'You . . . you loved me?'

'I still do and when we were in France because of how we felt about one another, we shared a bed, as Rose and Dick do.'

'Even though we weren't married.'

'Yes. The war has changed so many things. You have read the newspapers and seen the casualty figures. Young men and women who don't know whether they will still be alive tomorrow, they . . . they . . .'

He turned away from her and gazed out over the moorland, his eyes unfocused, his face sad, so sad she took his hand in hers and held it to her cheek. He bent his head to smile down at her.

'Do you think you could become . . . fond of me, macushla?' he asked her delicately.

'I must have been more than . . . than fond, Patrick,' she told him earnestly.

'Yes, and there is something more that you must know.'

'Yes?'

'Remember I told you about the puppies and that one day Rose might have babies.'

'Yes.'

'You and I made a baby, macushla, when we loved one another. It is growing inside you. Your child. My child and in a few months it will be born. A happy event, you see. Will . . . will that . . . will you . . . would you like to have a child of your own, my lovely girl?'

She was so still he felt his breath stop in his throat, for if she panicked, said she didn't want a baby, that he was to go away and she never wanted him to come back he thought he might simply walk into no-man's-land and let them shell him out of existence.

He cleared his throat and leaned back against the rock, his eyes staring out over her shoulder, for should she be looking at him with horror he knew he could not bear it. Oh, Holy Mother, he prayed, though he was not awfully certain such a being existed, let her accept. Should she want me to leave I will go but don't let her be hurt, give her peace and contentment and . . .

'Will Nan and Rose stay with me . . . be with me?' she asked doubtfully.

His heart began to lift, to sing because it seemed the first step had been taken and accepted. She looked down at her stomach which had the slightest curve to it and put her hand on it, seeming to stroke it. 'A baby in there?' she murmured. 'My baby . . . and yours?'

'Yes, macushla, and I think it would be a good idea for you to see Doctor Bennett so that he can explain to you what . . . how it got in there.'

She took his hand. 'Why can't you do it, Patrick? I'd rather you did it. Tell me what we did to put it there.'

She had gone to bed and when he had peeped in she was fast asleep, her face serene. Cat was with her, curled up by her side and he wondered what she would do when the puppies came. Derry and Tom, she was going to call them, she had told the astonished company at dinner. Why? Because she had seen a lady going into the shop and another lady, she thought it might be herself, breaking the window. She said it so calmly none of them liked to question her further, for as yet she and Rose had not discussed their activities in the suffrage movement. Yes, the name of the shop had been Derry and Tom's and since it was the first thing she had remembered she thought it was . . . was . . . what was the word? turning eagerly to Patrick . . . yes, appropriate to call her puppies that.

He and Rose sat in the drawing-room, gazing into the crackling log fire, absorbed with their own thoughts, and when Nan popped her head round the door to see if there was anything further they might need, Patrick turned and asked her to sit with them. It was about Alex and so it was right that Nan should take part. Archie had gone up to his room soon after Alex and Dick was still confined to his.

'I told her this afternoon,' he said calmly. 'I had the perfect opening with the puppies, you see and then, forgive me, Rose, but I said that you and Dick, being married, would have babies one day. That men and women who loved one another usually had a family, a child, and . . . well, she's very astute, you know, and she realised that she and I . . . I told her about France, you see, and that we . . . we had loved one another and that I still loved her. I told her she had my child growing inside her because of our love and she seemed to accept it. I don't think it's as real to her as are the puppies which was why she was full of them at dinner, but she knows and when she's ready she'll speak to you about it. I even told her' – he smiled wryly – 'though how I managed it I don't know, how the baby got inside her.'

'Doctor O'Leary . . .' Nan gasped, her face as red as a tomato.

'I had no choice, Nan. I wanted to leave it to Doctor Bennett but she wouldn't have it. She begged me to tell her so I did, as matter-of-factly as I could and she did not seem shocked or frightened. I think she knows inside the feelings I have for her and the child to come and now you can talk about it, buy things for the child, get her interested, explain to her what is to happen to her. She asked if you and Nan would be with her and I said you would, so as far as that went she was calm. The thing now is for you to persuade her that she must marry me. I could do it myself, given time, for I believe she has feelings for me, buried deep but still there, and they will come back. I mean to get a thirty-six-hour pass on compassionate grounds, travel from the front to London where you will meet me and we will marry by special licence. I will return to France and you to Edge Bottom House to await the birth of the child. I know I can rely on both of you to take care of her for me. I wish to God I could stay with her but I can't, so . . .'

Rose dropped her face into her hands and began to weep. Nan went across to her and took her in her arms, rocking her and patting her and planting small kisses on her brow. It was plain that her love for Rose was almost overwhelming her. If it hadn't been for this woman she would never have got through the last months and now, with this wonderful man, everything would be as it should be.

'There, there, chuck . . . there, there, our lass'll be all right now. Eeh, Doctor Patrick, if there's owt I can ever do fer thi', tha've only ter ask. My lamb'll be wed and the babby born in wedlock and then, when this bloody war's over an' done with . . . Pray God, it's soon.'

She cried broken-heartedly when he left the next day and tears wet his own face as Harry ran him in the motor to the railway station. She had clung to him, her face a pale mask, her eyes enormous and drowning in it.

'I don't want you to go, Patrick. There are so many things I wanted to ask you and now . . .'

'Write to me, macushla, and I promise I will write to you

every day. Tell me anything, ask me anything and perhaps in a few weeks – soon – I will come to London and we will meet there.'

'Oh, Patrick, you won't forget, you know . . . about the baby?'

'My little love, how could I? It is our baby, part of you and me and . . . I must go, macushla. There are wounded soldiers who need me. They have no one to look after them, not like you with Nan and Rose.'

'Yes, of course.'

'Goodbye.'

'Goodbye, macushla,' she said to him.

In the wet, cold days of early November troops at last managed to take the village of Beaumont Hamel, battling across a field carpeted with their own unburied dead. The cost of the Somme offensive begun on 1 July had been enormous, the gains minimal. Now, as it came to an end a great silence fell over the shattered and leafless valleys of the Somme as winter began to descend and the fighting was halted. So many men were reported 'missing, presumed killed' that the Red Cross set up a special bureau for tracing them. In most cases there was not much that could be added to the bald information sent to frantic families.

Day in and day out, all through the Somme campaign and long after it ended, in the wards of hospitals at the bases in France and in hospitals the length and breadth of Britain, Red Cross workers and volunteers, armed with long lists of names, gently interrogated the wounded who might know something of the fate of their comrades.

Long after the battle had died down the work of tracing the missing, burying the dead and tending the wounded went on. Another year was dragging to a close and it was already the third Christmas of the war that everyone had said would be 'over by Christmas' more than two weary years before.

On Christmas Day every sick or wounded soldier in every hospital, casualty clearing station, hospital ship or train, in every theatre of war, received a message from the King telling them that he and the Queen were thinking of them. But in London where a thick black fog rolled over the city on Christmas night, seeped into every crevice and clung thick in the air for the next two days, the gassed patients coughed and choked and died for want of breath.

Doctor Bennett judged that Alex was about six or seven months pregnant and Nan was becoming quite frantic that unless they got a move on the child would be born out of wedlock. Patrick had written to Dick that he hoped to be in London two days after Christmas and so on that special day on which the birth of Christ was celebrated, they all gathered round in the drawing-room and began to prepare Alex for the trip to London. They had, of course, spoken of it often. Her wedding day, making it sound special and exciting, for they were still inclined to treat her like a child who has been promised a treat. A new gown had been made for her since she could no longer fit into any of her clothes. A lovely dress with which she was enchanted, the local dressmaker who had for years made gowns for the Goodwin women coming in to measure her blooming girth, her face straight and expressionless, for it was nothing to do with her, was it. She was aware that Miss Alex was not *right* but if she was to be married, and it needed to be soon by the look of her, then she supposed it was for the best.

Alex was quiet on the train, travelling first class from St Helens to London, looking forward to seeing Patrick, she said, just as though the significance of the journey was unclear to her.

Dick, who had hoped to be best man at his friend's wedding

was strictly forbidden to accompany Rose and Alex, since the killing fog still hung about in London, and so was Nan, for who would look after Dick if both of them travelled up there? The train was filled with hundreds of soldiers travelling to the front, not many of them cheering and eager to get there as once they had done. Two years had taught them the cost of this journey which many of them had done more than once. Alex clung to Rose. It was as though some chink had opened in her damaged mind, allowing some tendril of memory to escape, some reminder of the days when she herself had travelled with men like these, but suddenly Patrick was there, somewhat uncertain, wanting to open up his arms to her, to clasp her to him. She saw him and her face split in a wide and welcoming smile and despite her cumbersome state she flew along the platform until they were face to face.

'Patrick . . .' she ventured shyly.

'Macushla, my little macushla . . . oh, my love . . .' And with a groan of relief, for who knew what might have happened in her mind since last they met, he held her to him, their child squirming between them.

# 26

If the registrar was confounded at the size of the pregnant bride he did not show it, for there were many such weddings in this day of 'live for today for tomorrow might never come', and frequently it didn't. The bride looked quite lovely, glowing with something that seemed to shine from inside her, clinging to the arm of the gaunt-faced major who was in the Medical Corps. Patrick had been promoted, he had told Rose, God knows why, but it meant he could manage two days with Alex before he went back, but they must not tell Alex this, not yet. They were so afraid of upsetting the delicate equilibrium of her mind, but when they did she was calm, saying, to their amazement, 'Then we must make the best of what we have.' She had seemed so genuinely pleased to see him, holding his hand and gazing up into his face with a heart-stopping smile and it occurred to Rose that Alex was falling in love all over again with this man who was to be her husband.

She wore a small pearl-covered Juliet cap which nestled among her riot of glossy curls. Her dress was of white silk net over a chiffon foundation, very simple but with clever draping that did its best to hide her vast stomach and she carried a single white rosebud which Patrick had given to her. Her low-heeled shoes were of white glacé kid with a white rose decorating the centre front.

Patrick had gone to a great deal of trouble to look good for her. He had sponged and pressed his uniform, removing the detritus of the casualty clearing station, the hospitals, the wounded men he dealt with and the war itself. His knee-length boots were polished until you could see your face in them, his breeches, rather like the ones gentlemen wear on a horse, though somewhat faded, were clean and his jacket well brushed. The badges on his collar and his cap were bright and gleaming and the belts about his waist and across his shoulder were as well polished as his boots. He wore leather gloves and carried a swagger-stick. He was tall, straight-bodied and by no means ill-favoured. His thick straight hair had been brushed to a smooth gleam and his eyes were lit to a brilliant whisky-coloured brown as he looked with tender love and pride at his beautiful bride. She carried within her his child which was visibly stirring as they made their vows to one another.

She smiled up at Patrick as she repeated the words the registrar spoke and which Rose had coached her in and at the end she lifted her rosy mouth for his kiss.

'I love you, macushla,' he murmured to her and the rather dour registrar smiled despite himself.

She astonished both Patrick and Rose as they left the registry office, standing in the cold winter air on the steps by saying breathlessly, 'Can we go to the Ritz? We always liked the Ritz, didn't we, Rose, with you and Dick.'

Rose was busy wrapping her in a long, white velvet cape and her hands stilled on the clasp. 'How did you know that, sweetheart?' she asked incredulously. 'Did someone tell you? Was it Dick?'

'No, I just seemed to . . . remember.' She smiled up at Patrick, then put her hand in his arm. 'Sometimes little things jump into my mind and I recall . . . did we dance, Patrick?'

'We did, macushla, and if you want to dance again, we shall.' The image of the heavily pregnant woman waltzing round the ballroom at the Ritz under the astonished gaze of the officers and their elegant women did not seem to concern him.

★      ★      ★

It had taken a great deal of patient dialogue, not exactly to persuade Alex to marry Patrick since it was obvious she had taken a great liking to him, but to explain that because they had made this baby together, they must make a safe place for it to grow up in, and that meant with a mother and a father in the home to protect it. A home such as Rose and Dick were to have as a married couple and where they too would have children, dogs and cats and make a loving family. There was the question of Cat, Derry and Tom to consider, for the puppies had been introduced to Edge Bottom House soon after Patrick left for France and Miss Alex was determined to take the three animals with her to London as she could hardly leave them, could she?

'I'll see to 'em, lamb,' Nan had assured her. 'Now tha' trust me, don't tha'? Would I let owt 'appen to 'em, would I? Nay, they'll be 'ere safe as 'ouses an' when tha' comes back, they'll be waitin' on tha',' wondering if the rest of them would survive 'safe as houses'. Bedlam, it had been, Nan complained, with the dratted things that excited and Miss Alex not helping by joining in their mad gallop and poor old Cat condemned to the top of the wardrobe in Miss Alex's bedroom. She had put her foot down, backed by the master, when Miss Alex had wanted the puppies in the bedroom with her, but an old laundry basket had been found and the pair of them had settled down well enough in front of the kitchen fire.

Christmas had come and gone with a lovely tree brought in by Harry and decorated by Rose and Dick and Alex, which was promptly brought down by the wild antics of Derry and Tom and Nan said privately to Nelly she honestly didn't think she could cope another day, which Nelly knew to be untrue, for as long as Miss Alex needed her and was happy, that was all Nan asked for. And she was happy. She begged anybody who was passing to feel the movement of her baby which was doing cartwheels in her belly, she told them, much to the embarrassment of Harry and old Solly.

And the day after Boxing Day she and Rose left, Alex ready to weep, for she had never been parted from Nan since the day she came home and her animals . . . how would they manage without her? But at last they had her in the motor car and on the way to the railway station.

They had pondered at great length on whether Alex should go back with her new husband to his rooms or whether it would be better if she returned to Bedford Square with Rose. Willing as she had been to become his wife was she ready to spend the night with him? Rose knew with great certainty that Patrick would do nothing to alarm her. Was he to share a bed with his new wife? She had not liked to ask him but Alex was his responsibility now and she was pretty sure that if Alex showed reluctance to get into bed with him he would do nothing to persuade her. But now, here she was, wanting to go to the Ritz and *dance* with her new husband.

'Patrick must return to France tomorrow, Alex,' Rose said dubiously, 'and you and I will be catching the train to Edge Bottom. Don't you think it would be better if you had an early night? It's been an exciting day and you must be tired.' At the last minute Rose was having doubts as to whether Alex understood what had happened to her and what, normally, would happen to a woman just married. Always at the back of their minds was Alex's vulnerability but she had improved enormously recently, her health blooming, and she realised it was since Patrick had re-entered her life.

'Sweet Rosie, this is my wedding day' – startling them both – 'and I want to dance on my wedding day.'

'And so you shall, macushla.' Patrick put a comforting hand on Rose's arm, a hand that said, 'don't worry, I'll look after her' and Rose knew he would.

She caused a sensation at the Ritz. She was so obviously a bride in her lovely white dress and Juliet cap, and so obviously happy, uncaring, it seemed to those who watched speechlessly, of her condition. Her husband, a major in the Medical Corps, soon had them a table and a waiter hung round ready to serve them, for he had been given an enormous tip. They drank the best champagne and Alex was radiant, telling her new husband she hadn't had such a good time for ages. She frowned slightly as she said it, as she could not remember when that was but Patrick knew, telling her of Dick's birthday and how they had danced and she listened raptly to his every word, for this man knew her and her past so well she need never fear her loss of memory.

They danced, a slow, dreamy waltz, forced with much laughter to lean away from one another slightly since their child kicked between them. He kissed her, watched by the other guests but somehow it did not seem improper because the bride was so lovely, so happy, and besides, things had changed in the last two years, for who cared about such things in today's uncertain climate?

They took a cab back to Smith Square, where he told her on the doorstep that it was customary for the bridegroom to carry his bride over the threshold. What fun, she replied, giggling like a child, but surely she was too heavy, whereupon he asked her, frowning, if she thought he was a weakling who could not lift his own wife and child, sweeping her up into his arms and so, with much laughter, their marriage began.

Her suitcase stood in the hall and holding her hand he carried it to their bedroom, serious now, for whatever was to happen next was up to her and was she ready to make so momentous a decision? He had made up a small bed in the spare room and would, if she showed apprehension, sleep there. She was heavily pregnant and was he a brute who would have his way with her despite her condition? But her trust in him was implicit and when he offered to help her undress she complied. She seemed to find nothing embarrassing about her nudity and when he sank to his knees before her and kissed with great reverence the swelling of their child she put out a hand and laid it on his head. Something in her, a tiny compartment of memory, still lived and he thought that made her accept this as natural, for so he had worshipped at her feet when they were together in France. Her breasts were swollen, ready for the child, the areola a dark brown and he longed to cup them, kiss them, suck them as the child would do, but though his manhood strained against the crotch of his breeches he stood up, reached for her pretty, lace-decorated nightgown and slipped it over her head.

'Into bed, macushla,' he said briskly, 'and sleep well. Sleep well, Mrs O'Leary.' She smiled and reached for his hand.

'Be quick, Patrick,' she murmured, her eyelids already drooping, and it was clear she was expecting him to share the bed.

She was asleep when he slid in beside her, wearing the respectable pyjamas he had brought with him, for though they had slept naked in their past life he did not want to alarm her. She turned as she felt him close to her, then, with a sigh of content she put her arm across his chest and her head in the curve of his shoulder.

He was bloody uncomfortable, for his masculine blood was up and it had been a long while but at the same time he was elated as it seemed she had accepted the situation. She *trusted* him, that was the first and most important factor of their relationship. They were married and even, God forbid, should anything happen to him in that holocaust over there, she was safe and their baby had a name.

It took him a long while to go to sleep but he did, then when he woke the next morning he found that they were curled up together snugly and trustingly, like two spoons, her back to his chest, his hands cupping her breast. At once he moved them then was confounded when, still asleep, she put them back.

★    ★    ★

He took her back to Bedford Square later that morning. He had helped her to dress in the full dress and coat she had travelled in, groaning inwardly for she was so lovely, flushed with sleep, her hair curling about her head, her ripe body inviting him to move forward but he knew it was not the time, not yet. They breakfasted with Rose who kept looking anxiously at Alex but Alex was all smiles until the time came for him to leave.

'Don't go, Patrick,' she wept then, resorting to a child again in her anguish, clinging to him with fierce hands. 'I need you. Who will tell me about the past?'

'Rose will, macushla. Rose has known you as long as I have and she'll tell you all you want to know.'

'Patrick . . . Oh please, Patrick.' She was desolate and Patrick felt her desolation and wondered at it. It seemed she had become dependent on him in a remarkably short time and though he was exultant about that, as it boded well for their future, how was she to cope without him until he came home? But he must go. Although he had been given two days' leave, travelling from France and then back again took up a great deal of those two days. His face was stiff with pain as he turned to Rose appealingly and Rose, understanding, took Alex from him and held her as he walked without a backward glance down the steps of the house and into the waiting cab.

'I do so like Patrick,' Alex sniffed disconsolately as they turned indoors.

'I know dearest, and he likes you. Indeed he loves you and I believe that you love him.'

'I do, Rose.'

'And he is your husband now and soon, when the baby is born, he will get leave and come and see you both. You can look forward to that. Perhaps while we are in London we could buy some clothes for the baby. Would you like that? We can go home tomorrow. I'll telephone your father and tell him not to expect us until then.'

It was the hardest winter anyone in France had ever experienced. The hills were drifted in snow and the ponds and water-filled shell-holes were frozen to a depth of ten inches. Along the vast frozen length of the line there was a lull in the winter's fighting but despite this it was not possible to withdraw large numbers of men to the rear. Many of them succumbed to exposure, pneumonia and trench feet. Special orders were given that every man must carry a spare pair of dry socks at all times and at least once a day the soldiers must remove their boots and stockings and rub their feet with whale-oil.

Patrick and the other doctors found it was not easy to persuade a shivering soldier to divest his icy feet of what protection he had and when the ice thawed the men were knee-deep in layers of icy slush. The infantrymen's feet turned into one excruciating chilblain and with frostbite added walking was impossible. Men limped into the hospital and in severe cases had toes amputated and were sent home. As the winter of 1917 continued, although Patrick was a surgeon he found himself dealing more with bronchitis and rheumatism rather than wounds. Young men absolutely crippled, sometimes doubled up as if they were men of eighty instead of boys in their twenties. The surgical service was light now while the medical service became heavier and as January moved into February Patrick waited for news of Alex. She wrote to him every day in a round childish hand, telling him of the activities of Derry and Tom and Cat and he wrote back, telling her of the cheerfulness of his patients who, despite their pain, continued as the young do to joke and tease the nurses. The sick outnumbered the wounded now with fewer serious cases, fewer operations and fewer deaths, and consequently at the end of February he was able to contrive five days' leave.

He arrived at Edge Bottom House at the same time as his daughter!

Alex was woken by the whimpering of Cat who was roaming about the bed in a great to-do. Cat always slept on her bed once the dogs had been fastened in the kitchen, curling herself in the curve of Alex's back, a warm patch of comfort which tonight was very restless.

'What is it, Cat?' Alex murmured, wondering why Cat was sort of moaning, then she realised that it was not Cat who was making the noise but herself, the noise disturbing Cat. As though to confirm that there was something not quite right someone slashed at her in the small of her back where Cat usually slept and she cried out in pain and fear. Cat jumped down from the bed and scurried towards the door which was slightly ajar, almost tripping Nan who cursed her silently. The animal streaked down the stairs making for the dining-room where there was a high shelf that the dogs couldn't reach, settling down indignantly after having her sleep disturbed.

Nan moved swiftly to the bed, switched on the electric light, then knelt down, taking the restless hand that crept about the quilt.

'What is it, my lass? Is it . . .'

'A pain in my back, Nan, and I'm afraid I've wet the bed,' Alex told her apologetically. They had done their best to explain to Alex what would happen when her baby was born but the breaking of the waters must have been overlooked and Nan cursed herself.

'Nay, lass, 'tis nowt ter worry about. Tha've not wet bed, not . . . well, like a baby does but yer waters've broke.'

'My waters?' Alex quavered.

'Aye, it's what babby floats in inside o' thi'. It wants ter come out now so waters've gone and soon, yer babby'll be with yer. But tha' mun be brave fer it'll be . . . it'll hurt a bit. Now let me go an' fetch Miss Rose an' send Harry fer't doctor. Now rest, lamb . . . nay, I'll not leave thi',' as Alex showed signs of distress. 'I'll shout fer Miss Rose,' which she did, moving only as far as the bedroom door and bellowing her head off so that the whole house was raised. Nelly, so excited she ran out in her nightgown, hammered at Harry's cottage door just beyond the stables and within five minutes he had the motor car out of the stable which had been converted into a garage and was off in the direction of St Helen's and Doctor Bennett's house. In no more than an hour the doctor was at Alex's bedside, kneeling on his old and painful knees, for he was getting no younger he complained regularly to his wife. It was time he gave up, he often added, but the trouble was none of his patients would let him and besides, she answered him, what on earth would he do if he had no one but her to boss about?

It was almost like a party at first with everyone coming and going, Mary and Ruth and Dottie, who couldn't sleep anyway, popping in to see her, to ask if she wanted anything, even going so far as to sit down with her and drink a companionable cup of tea. Miss Alex had changed so much since she had come home wounded from the war it was almost as if she and they were of the same class. She sat with them in the kitchen, showed interest in their families, even helped them in their duties and was eager to learn how to cook and make bread, would you believe. It was as though she were a *new* person, a person made up from the one who had been their master's daughter. She did not stand on ceremony. They knew that times had changed since the days of the old mistress, the master's wife and the mother of the woman about to give birth to the first baby in the house for over twenty years. They longed to be a part of it, to help her, to add their knowledge to that of Nan and Miss Rose.

Archie Goodwin wobbled about between the drawing-room and the landing, not sure it was proper for a man to be included in the birth of his grandchild, but things were so different since his Beth had given birth to Will twenty-six years ago he supposed it was all right. No one seemed to mind. Rose was there, and Nan and Doctor Bennett, but though Alex had begged them to let her have Derry, Tom and Cat with her, Doctor Bennett refused, telling her they might be afraid which was enough for Alex.

It was almost morning when she had been in the first stages of labour for five hours that Doctor Bennett shut the door on them all except Nan and Rose. The others drifted about, boiling water, fetching clean towels and sheets, talking in subdued murmurs. The faint contractions Miss Alex had felt for the past few hours were becoming stronger and nearer together, which was a good sign as it meant that the time was nearly here and when some faint sound – was it Miss Alex? – came through the closed door and floated down the stairs to where Dottie and Ruth sat on the bottom step, they turned their heads in dismay, then smiled nervously at one another for all women had a bit of a shout when in labour. They themselves came from big families and hadn't their own mams skriked a bit.

It was full light when Doctor Bennett put his head round the door. The master, who had been leaning against the wall, straightened up in fear, for Doctor Bennett looked strange, pale and a bit funny round the eyes.

'Fetch Dick, would you, old chap,' he said to the frightened father. 'I might need a bit of help here.' Miss Alex was moaning and even as the doctor closed the door and Archie stumbled along the hallway to the room where Dick was sleeping – how could the man sleep with all this going on, he thought, then was ashamed, for the winter was hard on poor Dick's chest – they heard the shrill sound of Miss Alex, her voice rising to a peak on the name 'Patrick'. She was calling for her husband and him many miles away in the thick of it at the front, poor sod.

It was clear Doctor Dick was not really fit to be out of his bed as he blundered along the hallway behind Archie. It was not going well, they whispered to one another, and why had Doctor Dick been summoned when Doctor Bennett was a perfectly competent doctor who had delivered babies by the score?

Their anxious questions were answered when Doctor Bennett emerged from the bedroom, his face like suet and his hands clutching his chest, falling like a log into the chair at the top of the stairs. 'My bag,' he managed to gasp to the master and when it was put in his lap, his trembling hands, helped by Mary Smith who was a rock in situations like this, were guided to a bottle from which he took a pill. Again helped by Mary he got the pill in his mouth and sat back, floundering like a fish on a line. Mary knelt at his feet, smoothing his hands and they were relieved when a bit of colour returned to his cheeks and he smiled, shaking his head.

'This damned old ticker of mine,' he said and though they were not sure what he meant they smiled with him. 'I'll go back in now.' But Mary clung to his hands, patting them, appalled really, for they had never seen the old doctor anything but spry. But after all, he must be in his eighties because hadn't he attended the Goodwins since the grandmother of the woman giving birth had been a young woman?

They heard it then, the thin wail of the newborn and all of them, Ruth and Dottie huddled on the stairs, the old doctor and the woman at his feet, let out their breath on a long sigh of relief. The women began to cry, as women do, floods of tears running unchecked down their faces in sheer thankfulness. The old doctor rested his head on the chair back. It was over. She could rest now with her baby beside her in its spotted net cradle. She could be pampered and spoiled, surrounded by fresh fruit and chocolates and flowers. The excitement was intense as they waited for Nan or Rose or Doctor Dick to come out and tell them that Miss Alex was well, that the baby was well and of course, was it a girl or a boy? They longed to go in and tell her how clever she was, what a beauty the child was and could they have a hold, but when the door was at last opened, revealing the plump figure of Nan with the shawl-wrapped bundle in her arms they knew sadly that none of them would ever get a look in, for Nan stood proudly, protectively with what she considered her baby in her arms. Her face was wet with tears but her eyes were smiling as she allowed them a peep at the bundle in her arms.

'It's a girl,' she crowed. 'Miss Claire O'Leary, an' in all me born days I've never seen one bonnier. Miss Alex is sleepin' so tha' can't see 'er,' warning them that unless she said so none of them would get over the threshold.

They were all astounded when the front door crashed open and footsteps thumped on the stairs and coming up them was Major Patrick O'Leary, still with the mud and muddle of the trenches on his greatcoat. Nan's triumph didn't last long, for with a great shout the major took his daughter from her arms and bundling Dick and Rose before him shut himself in with his wife and child.

# 27

'Well,' said Nan, 'tha'd think tha'd give someone else a look in, is all I can say. Not even allowed ter bath little lamb an' every time I go up they shut door in me face. I've 'ad the lookin' after of all Goodwin babbies ever since Mr Will were born an' even before when Miss Alex come from Thornley Green but no, "we can manage, thank yer, Nan", 'e ses, an' now, only three days after child's born they're off fer a walk down ter't paddock ter show Miss Claire th'orses. Three days, I ask yer. It's not right, Nelly, an' I'm going ter tell 'em so.'

'Nay, Nan, major's ter go back day after termorrer an' yer can't blame 'im fer wantin' ter spend all 'is time wi' 'is wife an't babby. Even Mr Archie an' Miss Rose 'ave 'ad their noses pushed out but when he's gone tha'll . . .'

'It's Miss Meredith ter you, Nelly Holcroft an' I'll thank you ter remember tha' place,' said Nan in high dudgeon. 'Doctor Bennett said she could get outer bed but not go prancin' off ter't paddock.'

'But major's a doctor, *Miss Meredith*,' emphasising Nan's name, 'an' 'e should know.'

'That don't mean owt, my girl. 'E's a surgeon an's 'ad nowt ter do wi' babies an' such. Any road, I'll be glad ter see't back of 'im an' then lass can get proper looked after an' the bairn an' all.'

'Eeh, Miss Meredith.' Nelly was shocked. 'Don't say that, poor lad.'

Nan had the grace to look suitably chastened and Nelly put a hand comfortingly on her arm, for she knew Nan didn't mean it. Devoted she was to both Miss Alex and Doctor Patrick but she had been smugly under the impression that when Miss Alex's baby was born she, Nan, would have sole control of it, especially with Miss Alex being the way she was. She had not expected to be totally excluded by Miss Alex and her husband who, it seemed, were determined to enclose themselves in a warm and loving circle round their baby to the exclusion of everyone else.

She and Nelly were sitting at the kitchen table having their elevenses, sipping the hot, strong tea to which they were both partial, Nelly buttering one of the scones that Nan had just made and brought out of the oven. Mary was up in Dick Morris's room helping Miss Rose to 'do' for him since he was still in a wheezing, gasping state due to the cold, damp weather and had been ordered by Doctor Bennett to stay in his bed. Poor Doctor Dick, a young man but condemned to the life of an invalid by the gas he had inhaled in France. It was pitiful to see him struggling for breath and his face took on a blue shade caused by the acute bronchitis; until the warmer weather came he would be as he was. Doctor Bennett was of the opinion that the milder air of the southern counties might be better for him than the sharp winds and damp climate of the north and Rose, who had been studying medical journals advertising practices, was to travel, perhaps to Cornwall or Devon to see if she could find a small country practice where they could settle. If he had some work to do, and in a milder climate, he might regain some of his health, she and Doctor Bennett had decided and Patrick agreed.

In the scullery Ruth and Dottie were preparing vegetables for the family's evening meal, both of them singing, 'If You Were the Only Girl in the World' in what they thought was harmony and with great enthusiasm, the song a particular favourite with the soldiers, it was said.

Nan 'tchhd-tchhd' impatiently and then shouted to the pair of them to keep the noise down since it was giving her a headache. They all knew it was no such thing but just the sight of Miss Alex and Doctor Patrick with *Nan's* baby in Doctor Patrick's arms, boldly walking through 'her' kitchen that was causing her irritation. She had done her best to protest but after all it was their child and the child's father was a doctor so she hadn't a leg to stand on, had she, she moaned to Nelly, and if that bairn took cold or Miss Alex had a relapse she'd never forgive him, blaming him for what she saw as interfering.

She suddenly shook her head and returned the pressure of Nelly's reassuring hand. 'Nay,' she said. 'God forgive me. I shouldn't talk like this, Nelly. Wicked I am, wicked, but I were lookin' forward ter seein' ter't child meself an' now . . . Well, he loves that babby an' so does she, an' she's that 'appy.'

And Alex was happy. The birth of her child had been hard and she understood now why they called it 'labour', for that was what she had done. Laboured to bring forth a child. But when, still with the detritus of birth about her they had put the baby in her arms and she had looked down warily into its face – not a *her* at that moment – it all faded away into the haze of forgotten memories like the ones she must have known before she was wounded. Then, as though to add to the magic, Patrick was there, kneeling at her bedside, gathering her and the baby into his arms, his wet cheek pressed against hers, his spectacles knocked sideways, holding them both to his chest so that she began to laugh, for he was smothering her in his rapture.

'Macushla . . . my macushla and my wee macushla . . . a girl, they say and I love you and her and the Holy Mother answered my prayers and allowed me to be here as she was born. Oh my love . . . my love.' He removed his spectacles and flung them on to the table. Behind him Nan and Rose and Doctor Bennett were ready to go mad with the excitement and the little dear hadn't even been washed yet. She was, as yet, nothing more than a screwed-up face as though annoyed at the world for dragging her into it, red and somewhat fretful, a wide-open mouth in which a tiny tongue quivered, eyes tightly closed and long, fine eyelashes, but Nan was obviously longing to get her hands on her. Her hair was still wet with smeared blood but it was dark and had a wave to it as though it might be inclined to curl. She was beautiful and she was Nan's to care for or so Nan believed, but she had soon learned different.

Now Alex leaned against her husband as they strolled towards the paddock, her husband who had, despite Nan's disapproval, shared her bed since he came home though he had done no more than curl up against her and sleep and sleep and then, when he was wakened by the child's cry, had helped her to put the rosy quivering mouth to her breast. The baby had sucked and sucked ecstatically and Alex had felt the milk spurt and then Patrick had held her and the feeding baby in his arms and slept again. He had allowed Nan and Rose to get Alex into a bath and back to bed, then watched anxiously as Nan bathed and changed the baby, had a bath himself and from then had gently ushered them all from the room, allowing in only Doctor Bennett to examine Alex.

They were well wrapped up, she and Claire, and Patrick wore the clothes her father had lent him on his previous leave. Patrick had apologised to Archie for monopolising his daughter and granddaughter but the old man seemed to understand and told him to carry on, for they would have their share when Patrick returned to France, and so husband and wife, with their precious child, were left alone for the space of three full days.

He cradled the child to his chest with one arm and with the other held Alex close to him, supporting her as they walked the short distance to the paddock. It was a fine day with winter sunshine falling weakly over the pathway from the house. All along the path daffodils bobbed cheerfully. A blue tit pulled at a worm that had been foolish enough to poke its head out of the cold earth and under the trees in the woodland, violet roots were sending up little trumpets of green leaves. There was gorse blossom in the hedges and as they approached the paddock the old mare and the donkey heard them come, pricking their ears and wandering across the paddock to greet them. The old mare whinnied a welcome as she recognised them and high above them a lark sang, the first of the year.

'I don't know how I'm to part from you, macushla, from you and Claire. I won't even be here to see her christened. Who will you have for godparents?' Seeing she did not fully understand he explained the significance of it all.

'Oh, Nan and Rose, of course, Patrick, but can't we wait until you're home again before we have her christened?' she said, looking down into the peacefully sleeping face of her child. *Her child!* She could hardly believe that this tiny beautiful human being belonged to her, to her and Patrick and the only sadness was that Patrick must leave soon and, like him, she couldn't bear to contemplate it. She recognised that this man whom she had only met a few months ago, at least in her present life, though she understood she had known him before, was the man she loved. Had always loved and would always love and having talked at great length to him about what he did in France and having read the newspapers and the casualty lists they contained, she realised there was a danger that he would never come back to her. It seemed so unfair that they should have known one another for such a short time even though they had met in 1913, almost four years ago. Such a lot was hidden from her. Patrick and Rose told her of her days as a suffragette but she didn't really understand it, or the mind of the woman she must have been. She could hardly believe that she, Alex Goodwin, or O'Leary now, had actually smashed windows, set fire to postboxes, climbed railings to get to the King, gone on protest marches, shouted rudely in court and even gone to prison for her beliefs that women should have a vote as men did. So strong, so true to her cause, so brave, so foolhardy, another woman to the one she was now, for all she wanted, all she could ever imagine wanting was a home with her husband and baby in it. Perhaps more babies, for Patrick had said that the next time he was on leave they would try and make another! Perhaps this was why she felt so close to the scrap of humanity she held in her arms because it was as though they had been born at practically the same time. Claire, like herself, knew nothing of the past, existing for this moment, as Alex did, waiting, as Alex did, for her father to come home when they would begin the future!

The dogs swirled about their feet but did not attempt to go into the paddock, for Harry had trained them not to go near the horse or the donkey, and idling behind, keeping a distance from the dogs who ignored her now, was Cat, her tail in the air, a look of uncaring dignity in the way she walked.

'When I come home we will take her to church and have another ceremony, macushla,' Patrick said in answer to her question. 'Just you and me and Claire but we must go back now or we'll have Nan out here with a broom handle to teach me my place. She's longing to get her hands on our daughter.' Suddenly he was anxious. 'Will you manage, macushla? With the feeding and the bathing and the changing as you and I have done together. Perhaps you had better—'

'I mean to take care of my own baby when you've gone, Patrick,' but on the last two words her voice wobbled and he hugged her to him as he read her mind.

'I know, love, but get your strength back first. Let them help you for a while.'

'Patrick, I just wanted to say . . .'

'Yes, macushla?' He turned his head blindly towards her, for his own eyes were filling with unmanly tears.

'I love you, Patrick. I know I loved you before but now I love you again. Come back to us . . . please.'

'I promise you. You are my one bright star in the dark of the sky. You will guide me home.'

They stood quietly for another minute or two, their child held close, then turned and walked slowly back towards the house.

It was a week later when Rose announced she was to go to London and then on to Cornwall. She and Dick had been discussing it for weeks, she told them, for they could not impose on Mr Goodwin's hospitality for ever. They must start a new life together, somewhere that suited Dick, and they had seen a practice advertised for sale just outside Falmouth. Rose was to go to see it and report back to Dick. They all knew Doctor Bennett's views on the northern climate and Dick's chest would benefit from the soft Cornish air. The practice for sale: so sad, the doctor's two boys had both died of wounds on the Somme and the doctor, one of whose sons was to have taken it over, had not the heart to carry on and was selling up. She thought she might travel up to London in April.

They had all been amazed and pleased when, two weeks after Patrick had departed for France there was a telephone call from St Helens railway station to say that Lieutenant Will Goodwin had managed to get a week's leave and was there any chance of Harry coming over in the motor car to pick him up? Tom, whose sight had never been the same, had not been returned to the front and was being trained by his father to take over the running of the Edge Bottom Glass and Brick Works. He was doing well and had revealed to Rose, though she had been for the moment sworn to secrecy, that he had met a young lady, a VAD from the Fulham Eye Hospital, and was, in fact, stumbling somewhat in his confusion, in love, and so was she! With him!

Will had that rather dishevelled look about him that all the men from France brought back with them, even though he was a flier and rarely went near the trenches, as though they had done their best to be smart for the folks back home but the mud and other substances that adhered to them were hard to dispose of. He wore the new 1917 Pattern jacket with his rank on the shoulder straps. His breeches were khaki like his jacket, with stockings to his knee and shoes that he had done his best to polish. He had on what was known as a 'Gor Blimey' cap with stiffening in the crown which had a neck flap with a supplementary fabric chin strap which could be let down in foul weather to create a sort of balaclava. He was in his best suit and wore his observer's wings over his left breast pocket. Over the lot he wore the comfortable and convenient fur-lined British warm with leather buttons, breast pocket and a fur collar.

'Well, tha'll not catch cold in that lot,' Nan screeched as she dragged him into her arms for he was her 'first baby'. His duty as pilot observer was to ascertain the position of the allied troops. He made landings in odd fields up and down the line and took a few bullets in his fuselage which he made light of, though Nan held her hand dramatically to her heart. He made friends with French farmers who fed him fresh baked bread and home-made butter so that they began to imagine he led the life of Riley! He did not tell them that at twenty-six he was the oldest pilot in his squadron and the only one left of his original group. He did not tell them of the flimsy bi-planes he had seen go down in flames nor of the terrible burns of the men who survived. His eyes were the eyes of an old man who has seen war, bullets, flames and every other way a man can die and has survived it, wondering when his turn would come. He was flippant, amusing, teasing, charming and only when his eyes met Dick's did they look away hastily. He was amazed and delighted to find his sister recovered from her wound and married to that grand doctor chappie and the baby was a popsy and he only wished he could stay a few more days but he had promised a fellow from his squadron he would meet him in

London. He must see *The Bing Boys are Here* and that new show *Zig-Zag* from which a new song, 'Over There' was emerging. It was rumoured that the Yanks were about to enter the war and the song was bound to be a big hit, though the troops, the British troops that is, were sceptical about the Americans arriving in much time to do any good and they developed their own ironic parody of the song.

> *. . . over there . . .*
> *and they won't get there 'til it's over, Over there.*

Rose left for London in April after the christening of Claire Elizabeth. She and Nan were godmothers and Nan was so proud and so fiercely possessive of her godchild one might have been forgiven for thinking the baby was hers and hers alone. She was six weeks old and the house revolved round her and her needs though Alex turned out to be a good mother who, though she was indulgent of the woman who had cared for her for so long, did not allow Nan to take over completely as she would have liked. She bathed and changed the child, fed her, kept her cradle in her own bedroom and when Nan shrieked that that blessed cat, who still slept on her bed, might smother the little lamb, had Harry make a strong netting cover to put over the cradle and protect Claire as she slept. She was a good, contented child, thriving on her mother's milk and the loving care she was given. Her cheeks were rosy and rounded, her eyes the exact shade of her mother's, a rich, lavender blue and her pouting lips as pink as coral. Her hair was thick and curling, a dark shade of brown and her fat little hands lay like starfish on her mother's full white breast as she nursed her. She wore white, simple little dresses embroidered with pale sprigs of lavender and even, because of its thickness, had a lavender-blue ribbon tied about one fat curl. Her feet kicked in little white satin slippers and she smiled at her mother when she was six weeks old though Nan swore it was wind. Alex worshipped her and longed for the day when Patrick would come home to see their beautiful child, but Patrick O'Leary was up to his elbows in blood, allied blood due to the misguided optimism and arrogance of General Robert Nivelle who was confident he could break through the German lines with little loss of life. He could not have been more wrong. An attack at Arras and the storming of Vimy Ridge ended in disaster and some 120,000 men fell before the German machine-guns for an advance of 600 yards. And all fought on Easter Monday in a blizzard which struck as the troops went over the top to fight the Battle of Arras in the first move of the long-planned spring offensive.

The big push was to start soon and it was on Easter Monday that Rose saw Noah again. She was on her way back to Bedford Square after returning from Falmouth where she had known at once that this was the place where Dick would recover his health. Though it was only April the air was balmy with spring sunshine and she had unbuttoned her coat as she walked through narrow twisting streets that led to the Market Strand. There were small sailing boats dancing on the bluest of sparkling seas and a larger windjammer coming in under the white towering pride of her sail making for her anchorage in the Carrick Roads. The harbour was the loveliest she had ever seen and the air like wine as she drew it deep into her lungs and she knew that with this before him and inside him Dick would recover. There were little steamers and yachts with brilliantly coloured sails, the water so smooth they were reflected in its gleaming surface.

The old doctor, old in his grief if not in years, asked a ridiculously small price for the practice he had hoped to pass on to his son and she promised to bring Dick to meet him.

'Gassed, you said?' the doctor asked gently. 'My boys . . . just disappeared. Missing believed killed, both of them.'

As she walked away from the lovely little house which looked out over the wide waters of the English Channel her eyes were wet with tears. She marvelled at the amount of tears shed in this dreadful war!

She decided to walk from Paddington Station, along Marylebone Road, turning into Tottenham Court Road to Bedford Square as she carried only a small overnight bag and a cab seemed unnecessary. She was just about to turn into the square when she saw him. He was standing on the corner, gazing into the oval gardens around which the houses were situated, his back against a wall. He was cluttered with the paraphernalia of war which soldiers were forced to carry about with them: his rifle and tin hat, his haversack and water bottle and the iron rations he must always have with him in case of emergency. His greatcoat was stained still with the last battle he had fought in but it hung about him in empty folds as though he had shrunk and had two holes in the sleeve, neat and round. A door banged somewhere in the square and he recoiled violently, looking about him in a haunted sort of way, ready to jump over the wall against which he had been leaning. He was whole, unscathed but that light-hearted, carelessly good-natured, untroubled look of the man she had known and loved since the day they met had gone for ever.

He saw her come round the corner and though he was already pale, gaunt, every vestige of colour left his face, and she felt the same happen to her. He straightened up and tried to smile, to act the part of a man who just happened to be passing, but he failed pitifully. It was two years since they had first met and while they had been in France they had been lovers. She had loved him then and she loved him now and her heart constricted with the pain she had caused him when she had married Dick last September. She had had no word from him or of him except in casual references made by his mother in her letters to Archie from America. She had known he had recovered from his leg wound and had returned to the battlefield and now here he was looking just like the hundreds of thousands of other war-weary soldiers come from the front.

He hitched his rifle up on his shoulder and did his best to smile but when she began to weep, the tears raining down her cheeks and dripping on to the front of her coat he seemed to dissolve, dropping everything he carried with a clatter and hurrying towards her. His arms came round her and she sank thankfully into his embrace, home at last, in that place that had grown so familiar to her and which had got her through the horror of her days in France.

'Sweetheart, oh sweetheart,' he whispered repeatedly, his grip tightening. Passers-by smiled in sympathy, for they were well used to such scenes by now. Men come home to their women, men shattered and in despair, women the same, longing to comfort, to speak of their love and understanding but then, unlike this woman, not sharing their experiences and unable to do so.

'I never hoped to see you. I thought you were up at Edge Bottom with your . . . with . . . I heard he had been gassed . . . oh, my love . . . my love,' he groaned, bending his head so that his face was buried in her shoulder. His cap had fallen to the ground along with his other accoutrements and her bag went with them and still they stood as though fixed to the pavement.

She stepped away from him at last and looked into the depth of his deep brown eyes which had come from his mother, from the Goodwin side of the family. She cupped his face with her gloved hands, then impatiently, pulled off her gloves and held his stubbled cheeks between bare hands before leaning forward to kiss him, soft as thistledown, all pretence gone, for this man was her man and always had been. She had married Dick for pity, compassion, with the knowledge that he would not survive without her. She had travelled to Cornwall to set up their future life together and had every intention of doing so but here was Noah needing her just as much as Dick, his eyes filled with the nightmares that had tormented him and millions of others during the past three years. The United States had declared war on Germany at last and though it would be a while before the war machine rolled into action it had raised morale at home and surely, surely it would be over soon. There was to be a big push very soon and Noah Woodruff, alias Goodwin would without doubt be in it, but in the meantime he was here and Rose was here and men and women like them had learned to live for the moment.

She took his hand and led him to the Goodwin house.

# 28

She took him straight to bed in the room that had been hers since she had first come to live with Alex Goodwin before the war. She undressed him, anguishing over his thin frame, his ribs which protruded over the concavity of his stomach, the loss of muscle in his broad shoulders, the still raw-looking wound in his leg.

She remembered the first time they had been here in this house with Alex when Noah had been intent on joining up. What a cheerful lad he had been, making them laugh with his quaint way of talking, the 'swell' omelette he had made them, his engaging good looks, his tall, rangy figure. He had worn a casual knitted jersey and a cap with a button on the crown, a tweed jacket, and they had fallen in love scarcely without realising it, easily and naturally. She knew she loved her husband but this man was her soul mate, the other half of her, and she would love him all the days of her life. She had left him cruelly when he was at his weakest but he had been returned to her and she would never desert him again.

When he was naked in her bed she removed her own clothing slowly because she knew he wanted to look at her. At a body that was whole and clean, a woman's body that smelled of the French perfume she favoured. His male body had been beautifully made when last she saw him naked, with long graceful bones and flat muscles that flowed smoothly from chest and shoulders to belly and thigh, but all that was gone in the deprivations of war. Still she loved him and when she climbed in with him his arms went round her at once, pushing her on her back, parting her thighs with one knee and sinking into her and into the oblivion that had not been his for a long time. He was harsh with her, hurting her, groaning with each thrust but she knew he needed it and when he collapsed on to her and fell immediately into a deep sleep she held him to her. They had barely spoken but they were as they had been in France: one entity, one love, one body still joined together and her heart broke, as it had done before, since she knew she could not leave him again.

When he woke after ten hours of death-like sleep she could hardly move she was so stiff. Again without speaking he lifted her tenderly and carried her to the bathroom where he filled the big bathtub with hot water, still holding her in his arms, then put her in the water and climbed in himself. He soaped her and himself with the lemon-scented soap the Goodwins always used, even washing her hair and his own. They lay, her back against his chest, his arms about her, one hand cupping her breasts, his penis thrusting against the cleft of her buttocks and when she turned and sat across his thighs he entered her again, hard but sweet with tenderness and the softness of the soapy water. This time he brought her to arching orgasm, knowing her, taking her to that special place as he had done when they had been lovers.

'You're mine, Rosie, mine and no one shall take you from me, not even that man you married,' he told her hoarsely, his mouth hot on hers. She did not tell him that as yet she and Dick had barely consummated their marriage, for Dick was still not strong. It had not concerned her unduly and she supposed in a way she had been pleased, for when she married him she had wondered how she would manage to make love to one man when she loved another.

They dried one another, laughing softly, exchanging kisses, warm, moist, gentle, tongues touching and he brought her once more to rapture, lifting them both on a high wave of love, murmuring her name as his back arched above her on the bathroom floor.

He had three days' leave and they spent it in the house at Bedford Square. He wore a dressing-gown that belonged to Archie Goodwin and she a light and pretty negligce, an almost transparent coffee colour edged with lace, one she had bought and at the time wondered why. Now she knew. She telephoned Edge Bottom House and explained to Archie that she had been held up, glad it was he who answered the telephone, for he was the last one of the household who would ask why. His nature was sweet and trusting and he would tell Dick and Alex that she would be home soon, he promised.

She woke on the last night to sounds of his distress. He was tossing restlessly, calling out names, the names of men along-side whom he had fought.

'Freddy . . . bloody hell, Jack . . . watch it . . . watch it . . . *keep down, damn you, keep down* . . . aah . . . Sammy . . . someone shoot him, for Christ's sake . . . he's being crucified . . .' Then he sat up and in the light from the streetlamp she could see the horror on his face. She put her arms about him and drew him down to her breast as he wept for comrades long gone and when he slept she wept too for this man, these men who were on the edge of madness in the madness in which they lived.

He would not let her come to Victoria from where the leave trains departed, saying goodbye in the hallway of the house, holding her in arms that were inclined to tremble.

'Promise me you'll be here when I come back.'

'I promise. I promise.'

'No matter what.'

'No matter what.'

'You'll write to me. I can manage it if you'll write to me.'

'I'll write to you.'

'Will . . . will you let me write to you? Will it be possible?'

'Yes, I'll say it's from a VAD friend,' not caring about deceit or lies or indeed anything but this man who had come back to her. She didn't know how she was to manage it. There was Dick. There was the practice they were to buy in Falmouth. There was Alex and a thousand obstacles in the way but she would overcome them.

When he had gone she closed the door and leaned her back to it then slowly slid down to her haunches where she squatted for an hour in the deepest most desperate moment of her life.

Dick was enthusiastic, gloriously so, about the medical practice in Falmouth and couldn't stop talking about it, but Alex, of them all, noticed that Rose was quiet on the subject and seemed curiously disinclined to go into details.

'When can we go and look it over, my love?' Dick asked her as April moved into May and June approached but she gently put him off, telling him they must wait for the warmer weather. He was getting better, his chest beginning to clear of the matter that clogged it and she took him for walks in the grounds of Edge Bottom House, moving towards the trees, his hand in hers, their faces dreaming but of different things. She had had two letters from Noah, filled with his love and his hopes and his rememberance of the three days they had spent together at Bedford Square. He did not speak of his days in the trenches nor the words that said they would soon be in the thick of a big battle but of them, Rose and Noah, and what they would do when the war ended. Dick Morris did not seem to exist in his mind, nor in her life and when she was alone she wept, for how was she to be with this man and not destroy Dick who loved her just as much. He was getting better but would he ever be as he once had been? Was he recovering? He was damaged and frail still, subject to setbacks but he was cheerfully certain that one day soon they would travel down to Falmouth and he would take up the life she was designing for him.

The telegram arrived on 11 June. It was addressed to Mrs Patrick O'Leary and for several fumbling, heart-stopping moments they stood, even Dottie and Ruth who had heard of its arrival, with faces like frozen stretches of snow, expressionless and without colour.

'Dearest . . .' Rose whispered, ready to take the telegram from Alex's hand but Alex was a mother now and the role had given her a strength she had never before known. She read it and as she did so the colour flooded back into her face and she threw back her head with a shout of joyous laughter.

'Patrick's got forty-eight hours' leave. Not enough time to get to Edge Bottom but he wants me to meet him in London. To bring Claire and—'

'Eeh, never, Miss Alex. Tha' can't tekk the bairn all that way. Trains'll be packed wi' soldiers an' . . .' Nan was horrified and, putting her hands on her hips, moved towards the front door as though she would physically stop the first person who tried to get past her.

'Nan, dearest Nan, you would come with me and Harry would take us in the motor. Patrick will probably only be able to stay one night.' She studied the telegram carefully. 'He doesn't say but he must be allowed to see his daughter. She'll be walking before he might get another chance. Oh, do say yes, Nan.'

Nan, somewhat mollified, shook her head at Miss Alex who was inclined towards exaggeration. After all, little lamb was only three months old. 'Well, it'll tekk a fair bit o' plannin' but I expect . . .'

'Today, Nan, we must go today. He's to be at Victoria on the leave train tomorrow and I must be there to meet him.'

'Terday!' Nan shrieked. 'Nay, we can never be ready ter go

terday. Miss Claire's not 'ad 'er mornin' nap yet and can tha' imagine what us'll 'ave ter tekk fer a baby not yet four months old. Nay, Miss Alex, it's outer't question. We shall need a charabanc to carry all 'er stuff an' then there's . . .'

But Miss Alex, with Rose hot on her heels, was halfway up the stairs and Mary and Ruth, galvanised by the excitement of it all, were sent off to search the attic for Miss Alex's small suitcase as she wouldn't need much for one day. She would travel in her new tailor-made tweed costume with the 'military' jacket which had a belt and four practical pockets. It had a flared skirt which reached the top of the gaiters she wore over her high-heeled shoes. Under it went a crêpe-de-chine blouse that matched the camel and cream of the costume with a plain turn-down collar. A hat, no she wouldn't bother with a hat since she would be in the motor and would someone run and tell Harry to be ready to drive to London in half an hour? She wanted to be there before dark and if Nan and Ruth would pack all the necessary things for Claire . . . no, not her bath, she could be bathed for once in the kitchen sink.

*The kitchen sink*, Nan echoed as she began to run here and there in search of all the paraphernalia a young baby would need for two nights away.

Rose was a rock, directing operations, for Alex was too excited to be of much use. She kept picking objects up and putting them down again, a pink teddy bear, a silver feeding spoon which had been a christening present, a white woollen blanket edged with satin, until Rose pushed her into her bedroom and told her to decide what *she* needed and the rest of them would see to Claire.

Harry was at the front door as ordered, his face a picture of excitement, for he did love to get the motor out for a good long run. It did the engine good, he told old Solly who didn't know one end of a motor car from the other but went off to cut some flowers for Miss Alex to take to London, for there'd be none at

Bedford Square. Harry had filled up the petrol tank which would see them a good way on their journey and they were off within the hour, all the household standing on the step to wave them off. The dogs raced about, doing their best to climb into the motor car, and Cat sat on the wall to the side of the house, conveying her disdainful indifference to the whole affair. Even the servants crowded into the garden, Ruth inclined to shed a tear as if they were off to the North Pole, her pinny to her eyes.

Claire, tucked into her small basketwork cradle, slept as good as gold for the first two hours, the cradle crammed at the feet of the two women in the back seat. When she woke Alex fed her beneath the folds of a sheltering shawl while Harry kept his eyes strictly to the front. In the boot of the motor were suitcases of baby clothes for every conceivable change in the weather, for as Nan said firmly, daring anyone to argue, it was as well to be ready for anything.

'I don't think it's going to snow in June, Nan,' Rose said wryly, holding up a garment that would have been suitable for the Arctic, but Nan had her way. She herself took only her long flannel nightgown, her woollen dressing-gown and her old slippers in case she should need to get up to Miss Claire in the night, since it was her opinion, which she kept to herself, that Miss Alex would be too busy elsewhere to bother about her child!

They arrived as dusk fell, tired and irritable, especially the baby who was not used to having her routine altered. There was no food in the house but Rose – how would they ever manage without her when she went to Falmouth? – had packed a picnic basket to see them through until tomorrow.

Harry wanted to drive her to Victoria Station. After all it was not long since Miss Alex had been a woman without a memory so would she remember how to get from Bedford Square to the railway station and Nan was giving him merry hell for even listening to her, let alone allowing her to persuade him to let her walk it.

'Nan, I can't remember anything of my previous life in Edge Bottom but you and my family are giving it back to me. I know about my mother and my grandmother, my relatives in America' – she still couldn't bring herself to call Milly Woodruff 'Mother' – 'and one day I'm sure it will all come back to me, but somehow the journey from here to Victoria is fresh in my mind. I suppose I made the trip so often when I was an ambulance driver that it remains there indelibly. Now it's a lovely day and I want to walk and when I've . . . I've picked up my husband we will walk back.'

She stepped out along the length of Charing Cross Road, Nan's chiding voice in her ears, for she had no hat and a lady did not go outside, even in her own garden, without a hat. Her hair which she had kept cut short was a heavy, glossy tangle of curls about her head, lifting a little in the warm breeze. She felt so happy, so alive with anticipation she could not help smiling at passers-by who, surprised, smiled back. The war was entering an even more desperate area and there was little to smile about but Alex O'Leary was on the way to meet her husband, the husband with whom she had fallen in love twice in a lifetime and her step was light as she moved through Admiralty Arch, across St James's Park, round Buckingham Palace where once she had hung on the railings and screamed her defiance at the King, and down Buckingham Palace Road to the railway station.

The hordes of soldiers and their wives and sweethearts were everywhere. There were leave trains coming in disgorging mud-spattered, exhausted young men into the arms of those who waited for them, and leave trains returning to the front with equally strained but cleaner warriors who had women clinging to them, trying to smile, determined to hold back their tears until their men had gone. It was total chaos and for a fleeting moment Alex faltered, huddling against a pillar, for she had not been out alone before, then he was there, pulling her into the shelter of his arms, holding her against him with the fierceness of desperation, his pack and the rest of his equipment draped about him so that it stood between them. With an oath he tore it off, dropping it to the ground and drew her once more against him.

'Macushla . . . macushla . . . oh, Alex . . . my love . . . you're here . . . by yourself . . .'

'Yes, Patrick . . . I'm better now and I seem to remember London, I don't know why. I wanted to come and meet you without . . . I walked down. I left Claire with Nan. Oh, my darling, darling, hold me tight.' For the surging crowds of soldiers, some coming, some leaving, were threatening to tear them apart. He buried his face in her springing hair, wondering how she knew that this was what he wanted, his face in her sweet-smelling hair with no hat to come between his lips and the softness of it. They strained against one another, a pair among so many other pairs, desperate young men and women, the men knowing what the odds of this happening again were. Desperate sons, no more than schoolboys who had been thrown straight from school into the trenches and wanting nothing more than to be in their mothers' safe arms.

At last they parted, though he kept an arm about her, leading her back the way she had come towards Buckingham Palace Road. They walked the length of it until they came to St James's Park. As Rose and Noah had done, they barely spoke. Lovers in this war seemed to have no need of speech, or perhaps there was nothing to speak of in this horror which might separate them for good. Those at home had no inkling of what it was like in Flanders where the next battle would be fought and those who had witnessed such things, survived such things, could not speak of it. So the soldiers merely drank in the goodness, the innocence, the cleanliness, the sweetness of the women, the children they left behind, storing it within themselves against what they were to return to.

They sat on a bench, his arm about her while she spoke of Claire, his head against hers, her sweet breath in his nostrils, his eyes filled with the brilliance of the herbaceous borders that lined each path. The colours hurt his eyes. Lupins of yellow, blue, purple, pink, red and white, delphinium of vivid blue, phlox of violet and the white of lilies. Just this day and then tomorrow he must come back this way, not bringing her with him, for he could not stand to see the agony and terror in her eyes when they parted. He must get Nan to help him but now all he wanted was to get to Bedford Square, have a hot bath, meet his child of three months and then take his lovely wife to bed. That would be the pinnacle of these days, and perhaps the hardest to reach, for was she ready to be his wife in the truest sense of the word?

He held his child in his arms, rocking by the kitchen fire, the child looking up into the strange face above hers, a bit unsure but ready to smile if he did. He was watched for a moment by Nan who then quietly slipped away and left them to it. 'Call me if tha' . . .' she murmured, meaning when the two of you are ready to be alone and when that time came he kissed his daughter's round, pink cheek, handed her to Nan and led his wife upstairs. They had dined on what Nan had found for them at the market, where they remembered her, and drunk a bottle of wine he had brought with him and now it was dark and they were together in the softness and loveliness of the bed-room where once she had slept alone.

He was exhausted, war-weary, bone-weary, his mind fogged with memories of broken and mutilated men, but he wanted to love her, to take back with him the image of her curving, womanly body, the wrenching loveliness of her as she stood before him, her body white and mysterious in the light of the candles. He moved slowly, carefully, afraid he might alarm her but it seemed her body remembered his and responded to it though her mind was still hazy. He lifted her on to the bed beside him then leaned to kiss her. She curled her legs up, feeling the warmth of him. They were intensely aware of one another but a shade awkward, then she pressed herself against him and he whispered something against her hair.

'I want you so much.' And again she felt what she would probably call shy but their bodies had shared a language before she was wounded and now her body recalled it. She pressed her hips sharply against him, grasping his, the curve of his buttocks and then their senses took over. They came together, softly at first, then ferociously, loved, sighed, kissed, murmured, caressed and then slept, their arms tight about one another until dawn pricked through the curtains and it began again. Her breasts were filling with milk and she was aware that she would have to see to Claire soon but for one last time she gave herself to him, and him to her.

She argued fiercely when he told her he was to go alone to Victoria, but over her head Nan nodded at him, taking her forearms in her strong hands, holding her back until he had slipped through the door and into the waiting motor car with Harry at the wheel. He had gone before she could get to the door and when she rounded on Nan, Nan held her firmly in her arms and shushed her as she did Claire when she was upset.

'See, lamb, why don't tha' go to that shop, what were it called, the one what sells baby carriages, that's it and buy our Claire a perambulator. Tha' can tekk 'er a walk in't park this afternoon and then tomorrow we'll go 'ome. Nay, don't skrike, lass, 'e'll be 'ome soon . . . eeh, this bloody war, what'll it do next?'

She spent a lovely hour in the shop which Queen Victoria had made famous in the 1840s when she bought three ready-made carriages for her children. They had become known as Victorias and were pushed from behind like a bath chair, but designs had changed since then and now the one who pushed faced the baby who could lie or sit in a large boat-shaped body with solid wooden coachwork. The body of the 'pram' as it was now called hung on leather straps attached to two large C springs. It was a lovely shining silvery grey with a navy blue hood and Alex wanted to push it back to Bedford Square at once, wishing Patrick could have seen it. As the thought entered her she felt as though a fist had struck her in her ribs, a heavy blow that took her breath away, for by now Patrick would be speeding away from her through the English countryside towards the coast and the steamer which would take him to France. She felt quite faint and the shop assistant, a well-dressed young man with pomaded hair, urged her to sit down for a moment.

She paid for the pram which the young man told her politely would certainly be delivered this very afternoon, then led her to the door of the shop where a doorman hailed her a motor cab. She had bought several little garments for Claire which she knew would not meet with Nan's approval, for Nan believed that any child in her care *in their class* should only wear what had been hand-made for her. The doorman handed her and her purchases into the cab and after telling the driver where she wanted to go, bowed his head respectfully as he closed the cab door.

The traffic was heavy. A train carrying wounded had just entered Charing Cross Station and the wounded, transferred to ambulances, were moving slowly towards the hospitals of their destination so that all vehicles were held up until they had passed. Regent's Park where she and Patrick had kissed beneath the canopy of the trees was a glory of summer colour and though she could not remember the event Patrick had told her all about the wonder of it and how they had returned to his rooms and made love to one another. So many memories, all stored in Patrick's mind and transferred to hers. The wretchedness of being parted from him overcame her for a moment and the world misted with her tears.

'You all right, miss?' the cab driver asked her sympathetically. He had many such passengers in his cab, women who were parted from their men or grieving for those who had gone never to return.

She heard the strange thuds as the cab turned into Tottenham Court Road and though she could not identify them her heart began to thud in unison. She leaned forward and peered out through the windscreen. Both she and the cab driver stared with amazement then with horror as a great plume of smoke rose before them and Alex began to whimper, returning momentarily to the mindless child she had been last year.

'Bloody 'ell,' the cabbie whispered, gently putting his foot on the brake and coming to a stop, for all of a sudden chaos reigned. The woman in the back opened the door and leaving her parcels began to run towards the corner of Bedford Square. She was screaming as she ran. He felt like screaming himself!

The seventeen Gotha bi-planes, heavy bombers, had taken off from Belgium and flown across the English coastline, heading for London. Their flight took them over East Ham, Liverpool Street Station, Aldgate, Whitechurch and Poplar. They dropped their bombs injuring 437 civilians, and killing ninety-seven, eighteen of them five-year-old children at Upper North Street School.

One bomb fell at the edge of Bedford Square, demolishing two houses at the end of the row.

# 29

The new offensive was launched north of Messines on a twenty-mile front between Warneton and Dixmude on 31 July but by the time the men went over the top they didn't care what part of the country or even the world they were in, for the preliminary bombardment, the heaviest so far mounted and lasting two weeks, had driven them almost senseless. And it did no good, merely churning up the sodden land whose drainage system had been destroyed by years of artillery fire into a vast morass of craters filled with water through which the debilitated British soldiers were expected to advance.

They died in their thousands for slices of ruined land that were indistinguishable from the ruined land around them and it was said that the explosion of nineteen underground mines had been heard on the south coast of England and even felt in Number Ten Downing Street.

The newspapers described it as 'a slight advance on the Messines front'. In a deep shell-hole that he shared with eight others Noah clung on to his sanity, to the walls of the shell-hole which was half filled with filthy water and to life itself by the simple expedient of filling his eyes, which could see nothing, his mind, which could sense nothing, with images of Rose as he had last seen her. The man next to him was calling for his mother, a young soldier called Billy who had been brought up with others to replace the multitude who were vanishing in the mud. He was missing a leg and was beginning to ramble and Noah knew he would not last long. He kept slipping down towards the water and though each man with a bit of strength did their best to haul him up again they all knew it was to no avail. There was no sign of rescue. The sky was full of flashes and the second night was coming on fast. They were all stupid with fear and fatigue and would, unless someone came for them, undoubtedly slip down into oblivion in the morass at the bottom of the crater.

As dark fell, apart from the occasional flashes, those who could walk said 'bugger it' and decided to leave the shell-hole despite the intermittent firing, carrying those who were wounded, for no matter what happened, or how bad a state they were in, none of them would leave a mate. The comrade-ship in the trenches never faltered and many of them admitted that when they were on leave they could not wait to get back to their mates who were the only ones to understand. The relationship between the men was extraordinary and one that would never break. The world of home was precious but it was not real. This was the real world, this horror they shared and they felt no compunction about getting away from their fa-milies when the leave was over.

Noah had young Billy on his back, the weight of him nearly bringing him to his knees and he knew if he should slip on the duckboard both he and Billy wouldn't have a chance. They would be drowned in the slime that surrounded them. As hard as he clung to Billy he clung to his vision of Rose, his sweet Rose whose name was so appropriate and which was like a prayer that repeated often enough would be heard and would get him through this and back to her.

He delivered Billy to the field hospital where a doctor who seemed vaguely familiar to his tired brain gave the lad the once-over, directing him to another part of the tent where it seemed there was a queue waiting their turn for the operating theatre. Overhead there was a great deal of activity and he and his pals watched for half an hour the air-battles that raged in the skies as the British and French air forces sought to make the task of the German gunners impossible by destroying their air balloons and shooting down their reconnaissance aircraft. In one of the airplanes was Noah's cousin Will Goodwin, though Noah was not aware of it. It was raining as it had been since 31 July, a constant drizzle that had filled the craters, including the one from which Noah had just climbed, with muddy slime.

'Come on, lads,' one said at last. 'We're for the rest billets behind the lines,' which proved to be something of a luxury for it was a quiet country place with a river flowing serenely beside it. They slept and smoked and bathed in the river and Noah dreamed of Rose and wondered where he had seen the haggard face of the doctor who had taken in young Billy. In this, the third Battle of Ypres, or Passchendaele as it was to be called, he supposed it was easy enough to cross the paths of men, most never to be seen again but others slipping into your life for a second time. He had himself been in a field hospital when he was wounded in the leg and he had been told that a surgeon had saved the limb when others had wanted to cut it off. He had a feeling that this was the same man and on the tip of his tongue, teasing the edge of his memory the man's name lingered. An Irish name and now he came to think of it they had called him Mad Paddy. But try as he might he could not bring his identity to mind. But the poor chap had looked to be on his last legs. Well, let's hope he did as well for Billy, Private Billy Hartley as he had done for himself. Mind, he couldn't put the poor young bugger's leg back could he?

The boy in the end bed with only one leg left to him, probably no more than seventeen years of age, cried softly and monotonously for his mother. She had to clench her jaw the better to withstand it, trembling though she did her best not to, for it would not do to let the boy see her own exhaustion or grief.

Besides, sister would not allow it. There were a lot of things sister would not allow, but the most important was not to let the men see you as anything but strong, willing, competent and able to deal with anything. Even openly to show compassion, or any sort of soft emotion was frowned upon by Sister Hammond. Not that it made any difference, for the girls she worked with, most from genteel homes, once they had overcome their fear and dread were filled with pity for the poor shattered young men they nursed. When she was on night duty, which seemed to be the time most of the men were at their lowest ebb, she often sat with a soldier in the deep shock of his terrible wounds and held his hand, murmuring his name, speaking softly of his home, his wife, his mother, for she made it her business to find out these things about every man in her care. She soothed them, quietened them, helped them through their agony, which eased her own as though taking on another's pain into the space where her own lived diminished it fractionally.

She walked softly to the bed where the boy lay, aware of the rustling sighs, the muttering, moaning, restless movements of the badly wounded men in the beds down each side of the room, leaving the table in the centre of the ward in a pool of shaded red light, moving into the shadows and sitting down in the chair. She took his hand which twitched and fluttered and held it in one of her own while the other moved to his forehead, brushing back his fair, feathery hair then, knowing no one saw her, bent to place a light kiss on his eyebrow. At once he sighed and quietened, turning his head towards her.

'Mam . . . ?' he quavered.

'No, Billy, it's not your mam. Your mam will be here to see you soon. She's to travel a long way, you know, from Carlisle, but she'll be here soon. Why don't you go to sleep . . . no, don't cry . . . I know it hurts but in the morning the doctor will be here to give you something . . .'

'Nurse, can yer not give us summat now? It 'urts terrible bad, like.'

'No, Billy, I'm not allowed to give injections but I'll sit here until you go to sleep. You're a brave lad, Billy, your mates at the field hospital said so, those who brought you in.'

'Aye,' the boy sighed, 'me mates, they brought me in . . .' He began to shudder at the memories those few words brought back but she squeezed his hand gently.

'None of that, lad. That's all over. You're here safe with me. See, we're holding hands, you and me, and I'll stay until you sleep and then when you wake it will be the day your mother arrives. Sleep now, Billy, rest your head and sleep.'

She had been at the hospital, Number 3 London General Hospital, Wandsworth, for three months now, living in the nurses' home, her room, one of a dozen or more no bigger, no more comfortable than a cell. She wore the VAD uniform of mauve check in a hardwearing cotton, a great trial to many of her colleagues who were accustomed to silks and satins but to her it meant no more than something to cover her nakedness and certainly was a vast improvement to the prison garb with which she had once been acquainted.

Her life was narrow and she had become totally absorbed in the ward and her patients, giving herself willingly to the institutionalised world of the hospital, not wanting to think of the outside world, spending all her time and energy on her patients. She had passed the first month in a confusion of sounds and smells which had failed to sicken her, to terrify her as they did the other girls, for had she not seen it all in France and become hardened to it. The horror of wounds that turned *their* stomachs had no effect on her and besides, what did that matter when inside her the worst suffering dwelled? Pain was no stranger to her, physical pain that is, but the mental pain she was gripped by was something she could barely contain. But she did. What she saw in the wards steadied her and she gave herself to it whole-heartedly. It became her world. The night duties with the red shaded lamp, the endless echoing corridors where at first she had lost herself; sister's sharp voice, impatient with the nurses, gentle with the men, the sounds of men in agony, the deathless silence of the dying, sterilisers, sink rooms, appalling stenches, vomit, blood and the patient smiles of the men who had lost legs, arms, sometimes both, and who had no understanding of where they had gone.

The handbell clanging in the corridor woke her each morning, the frantic fumbling into her uniform, the days filled with exhausting, mindless work until the moment she was allowed to tumble into her cot at night. She learned to use a thermometer, to make beds, to wash helpless men who gazed at her with an apologetic smile, ashamed of their own weakness, to give enemas. Though their pain crucified her she taught herself to look away from vacant, staring eyes and turn deaf ears to senseless, incoherent mutterings, to hold stinking stumps for bandaging, to shave men and feed them and clear away the mess they made of their sheets.

But worst of all was the laying out and preparing for the grief-stricken families the broken bodies of those who did not survive. She never wept. She had no tears in her which confounded the VADs with whom she worked, for they believed she was heartless. She was good with the living but the dead were dead and apart from her sympathy for the sorrowing families who came to take them away, she was like stone. She had passed her First-Aid Certificate and though the other VADs at first invited her to a night out, or a day out on their days off, they had become used to her refusal.

'Come with us,' Evvie Winters begged her. 'Maude's got her brother's motor and we're taking a picnic while the weather's fine. We thought we'd drive out to the country. Maude tells us there's a wonderful old inn out there where we can drink cider and be human beings for a while without sister. Wear our own clothes instead of these shapeless monstrosities. Oh, do come. You've been here three months and not once have you had a moment off and really, it's not good enough.'

The nurse smiled and shook her head. These young girls, no more than twenty-one, which was the age they were allowed to become VADs, were so much younger than she was. They were away from their families for the first time in their lives and if they could escape from the hospital and have a bit of 'fun' that's all they asked. They worked hard and saw sights that their parents would be horrified at but most of them were prepared to get on with it, not shirking, nor moaning at the state of their hands or their aching backs or swollen feet. She admired them for it and would have liked to become one of them, for she had never had a true, free girlhood, being occupied with other things, but it was not possible. She dared not leave this deep hole she had dug for herself, pulling it in over her head, and go out into the world these girls moved in lest she lose herself in the whirlpool of menace, of danger, of terror, of grief that waited for her out there. She was safe here, or as safe as any woman could be who had lost everything in one mad moment, lost everything that was her life.

'Nurse, may I ask what are you doing sitting by that soldier's bed when there are others wanting your attention? He is asleep and does not need you.'

Though Sister Hammond spoke in a quiet voice it seemed loud and the nurse jumped. She turned, not guiltily as other nurses would do when found going against sister's orders but with that impassive face that they had all become used to as though there were nothing going on in the head of this excellent VAD who had come to them from the Red Cross in London. She was older than the others and looked as though a feather would have her over but she worked like a Trojan, refusing no task no matter how arduous nor how repulsive. Her hands were badly scarred, the nails broken almost to the quick, half-healed scars running down the backs and though she had been questioned as to how they had got into such a state they could never get a sensible answer from her. Many of them picked up infections from the wounds of the men they nursed and they supposed that was how she had come by hers. Only she knew!

Rose Morris put her arm about her husband's shoulders and eased him back on to his pillows, wiping his sweated face with a clean white cloth. As his head settled into the pillow she leaned over him and kissed him lovingly. His eyes smiled up at her and she marvelled that this man who had once been a virile, strong and vigorous doctor who had given all his energy to healing the sick, who had once played rugby and all manner of sport, whose life had been filled with laughter and his heart with love for mankind, was reduced to this pitiful wreck and yet could still smile at her. He couldn't speak and if he could she knew he would have made some joke and told her not to worry. He raised his eyebrows wryly and she could see he was trying to say something. She leaned closer until her ear was to his lips and heard him whisper, 'Falmouth . . . soon,' then he closed his eyes as though the effort of those two words had felled him.

She kneeled down and put her arm about his head. 'Yes, my darling, as soon as this bout is over and you are feeling stronger we will go and look at the practice. Doctor Woods wrote to me the other day saying he was in no hurry to sell and will wait for us. Come spring and at the first sign of warmer weather we'll get Harry to take us in stages by motor car. Have us a holiday. You'll love Falmouth. Mary can manage here for a week or two, can't you, Mary?' turning to the woman who stood by the window folding the sheets they had just taken from Dick's bed ready for the laundry.

Mary smiled and nodded, turning away from Dick and Rose so that they would not see the expression on her face. She had been with the Goodwin family ever since her early twenties when she had been friend and companion to Beth Goodwin, the master's dead wife. Nearly thirty years she had lived at Edge Bottom House and had become part of the family, struggling with them through the tempests that had beset them and there had been many of those. She was neither house-keeper, housemaid, nor any of the roles servants have in a household but was something of them all. She had stood in for Nan when Nan had nursed Miss Alex and had always been there for anyone who needed her, a rock in a maelstrom to which they had all, in their turn, clung, and now she helped Miss Rose with the terribly sick man who was her husband and who, in Mary's sad opinion, would not last the winter. He was still breathing noisily, every breath rasping like a saw through wood, his ragged lungs dragging at every wisp of air and with a sigh Mary watched as Miss Rose put the oxygen mask to his face and held it there since he was too weak to hold it himself. Almost immediately she saw the relief on his face and that special look he kept for his wife.

'Sit with him, will you, Mary, and hold the mask until he's easier?' Mary sat in the chair Miss Rose had just vacated and took the mask. Rose put a hand on Mary's shoulder and squeezed it. Dick needed night and day nursing when he was as bad as this, for the gas he had breathed caused acute bronchitis and oedema of the lungs which in its turn could bring on death by asphyxiation. The winter cold, the damp of the northern air that lingered over this part of the world had affected him very badly and sometimes he simply couldn't get his breath. He coughed and coughed and had been confined to their room ever since November. The hope that they might have got to Falmouth and the softer warmer air there had, of course, been out of the question since last June, for if they left Edge Bottom House who would hold this sorrowing household together? Without Nan to 'see to it' as she would have put it, Rose was the mistress here, the one who directed them all, who did her best to hold the master together and at the same time nursed her husband. She could not have managed without Mary!

She picked up the basket of bedding and, putting it on her hip, left the room, conscious that Dick's eyes followed her. She knew she was keeping him alive, not with her nursing but with the love they bore one another, for Dick was like a climbing plant that, its host removed, will fail and die. They had suffered another blow, as if what had happened in London wasn't enough and that had been the sudden death of old Doctor Bennett. He had seen this family through sickness, death, tragedy, so many hardships and they had relied on him, three generations of Goodwins, and now he was gone. A young doctor who had been invalided out of the army when he had been burned by a flame-thrower as he was leaving a field station just behind the lines had bought his practice and with a young wife and two children had proved to be popular with his patients, those he had taken over from Doctor Bennett. The lower classes, those with men at the front, took to him, for after all he had suffered what their men were suffering and those who had depended on Doctor Bennett, of what might be called the 'upper class' knew him for one of their own. He was clever, kind, intuitive and was up to date with all the latest medical developments learned during his time in France. He spent time with Dick, sitting by his bedside, talking about anything Dick fancied, sharing his experiences with the men in the trenches and Dick liked and trusted him. There was little he could do for Dick since his damaged lungs could never be repaired but Doctor Newcombe's very presence seemed to give courage and even invigorate the sick man.

Rose took the bedding down to the kitchen where Ruth and Dottie were preparing the simple meal which was all the two maids could manage. Nan and Mrs Adams had been the cooks in this kitchen, planning, supervising the preparation and cooking of the splendid and nutritious meals that had been part of 'her' family's diet. Dottie was a kitchen and scullery-maid and Ruth parlour-maid and there was a laundry-maid who came in twice a week. Everything had once worked like clock-work but things were different now.

'Everything all right, girls?' Rose asked brightly. 'What have you in store for lunch today?'

They exchanged glances. Miss Rose was lovely but surely she knew that neither of them could do no more than knock up something plain, the sort of meal they had eaten when they were children living in a labourer's cottage: a decent stew made with shin of beef, for there were always plenty of vegetables provided by old Solly, perhaps a steak pie, for at least Ruth's mam had taught her how to make pastry, a chicken, a rabbit pie, since Harry had taken to setting traps in the bit of wood-land at the back of the house, jugged hare, herring from the coast and liver and bacon when they could get it. Food was scarce now what with them blasted Hun submarines sinking ships and becoming scarcer as the war continued. Where once everything had been delivered to the back door now one of them had to go to town and queue for food and there was even a form of rationing to get tea and butter. They ate tripe and onion which none of the family cared for and once would never have eaten as it was considered to be a dish for the very poor! Still, they had no choice but to eat what was put in front of them. Actually Doctor Newcombe had told them that tripe and onion was very good for them and they were to give it to Mr Morris!

Ruth was chopping carrots and turnips which they were to have with what was left of a chicken they had eaten for their evening meal the night before and Dottie was making celery soup. Old Solly had just brought a head of celery in with a couple of onions so with that to start with it would do very well.

Rose nodded as they explained to her what they were doing but they could see she wasn't really listening but was just being polite. Poor Miss Rose had gone to skin and bone since last June and could you wonder, for it took all her time to see to that poor man who was wasting away before their very eyes. Not that Ruth or Dottie saw much of Dick Morris now he was confined to his bedroom. Earlier in the year before the cold wet of winter set in he used to come through the kitchen on his way out to the gardens, the meadow, the paddock and the woods but that had not happened for a while. He'd been such a good laugh, poor soul, teasing them, untying Dottie's apron strings as he went past, pinching Nan's biscuits, then running away into the yard before she could catch him.

Rose carried the laundry basket into the scullery and set it down on the bench ready for the laundry-maid who would come first thing in the morning. There was always a great deal of laundry these days for Dick sweated so much his bed was constantly in need of changing and then there was the rest of the household.

'Has Mr Archie had a drink yet, Ruth?' she asked the maid, who at once began to rush about ready to make the chocolate the master liked mid-morning but Rose put a hand on her arm.

'No, Ruth, I'll see to it. You have enough to do. I don't know how we would manage without the pair of you. So many maidservants have left to go into munitions and yet you two have remained loyal when I know you could earn so much more.'

She bustled about, putting the milk on to boil, setting out two tall mugs on a tray, mixing the chocolate while the two maids continued with their chopping, their faces wreathed in smiles as it really was lovely to be so valued and for Miss Rose, who was kindness itself, to say so. They were well aware they could earn twice as much in the munition factory in St Helens. Why, Annie Furness, who had been kitchen-maid to a family in town, had bought herself a *fur coat*, would you believe.

Rose carried the tray with the chocolate in to the drawing-room where Archie Goodwin sat hunched over the fire, pretending to read the newspaper. He turned as Rose entered and stood up, taking the tray from her and she wondered if they all looked as bad as he did. Sometimes, as the days and weeks passed, it was easy not to look too closely at those with whom one lived. You became used to them and their appearance and did not notice the terrible deterioration wrought by the tragedies of the war, but now and again your eye saw clearly for a minute and their image swam into focus. Archie was an old man. Bent of back where once he had been straight and tall and vigorous. He had lost so much in this war and yet they could thank God that young Tom had been spared and his sight restored. He kept the works going and when he could he persuaded Archie to go with him, which he hoped would give the old man something to cling to.

'Come and sit down, Rose,' he said, 'and tell me how Dick is this morning. I have been reading the casualty list and—'

'Oh, Archie, you shouldn't. It does no good. You know if . . . if anything were to happen to Will they would send a—'

'It's not just Will, Rose.'

No, she thought despairingly, it was not just Will. She had received no letter from Noah in the last three weeks and her heart lurched sickeningly in her chest at the thought that in this disintegrating world he could be dead in one of the dozens of horrifying deaths that came to claim those in its sights.

They sat silently sipping their chocolate, both busy with their own sad thoughts, then a sound from above made them both lift their heads and smile.

It was the sound of a child crying.

# 30

Every soldier in the trenches knew there was an attack coming. They had been driven back as far as the old battlefields of the Somme as they retreated, in what was to be called the Battle of Picardy, before the enemy, leaving behind vast amounts of artillery which they could ill afford. The German army numbered 750,000 men, the British 300,000. They had been told of Field Marshal Haig's famous message, 'Backs to the wall. Every man will stand and fight and fall. No more retreating,' which was all well and good, the soldiers muttered, but it wasn't him who had to do the standing and fighting and bloody falling! Had he ever tried to advance over battlefields that were no more than churned-up fields, shell-holes filled with slime and mud and the remains of their comrades who decomposed there, up to their knees in mud and muck, forced to pull their feet out of it and in great danger of losing their boots in the process? The great thaw had begun on 15 January and was so complete the ground just collapsed about them. Dugouts fell in and men were buried and would have suffocated if their comrades had not frantically clawed them out, most of them gibbering in terror, for to be buried alive was second only in horror to being crucified on the wire.

Early on the morning of 21 March the expected blow fell. Between Arras in the north to the south of the River Somme the enemy had mustered every gun, every shell of every variety ever devised: shrapnel, shells, high explosive, gas shells and the lethal 'blue cross' containing two-thirds high explosive and one-third gas which not only mutilated but left their lungs cracking like sheet ice on a lake, their ribcages bucking and heaving in an effort to draw breath.

The field ambulances, the casualty clearing stations, the field hospitals well behind the lines awoke to the thunder of a thousand guns and the shattering blast of shells. The men in Noah Goodwin's regiment were completely pinned down by the German bombardment. They had little shelter from the explosions, swearing and cursing and blundering about in the chaos. They were blinded and dazed by the fumes and the gas that thickened the morning mist into a suffocating fog. They were unable to escape and there were not many units left with enough strength to stand fast and put up more than a token resistance when the enemy infantry followed on the heels of the preceding inferno. Noah and the remainder of his company were quickly overrun and as the Germans moved across the shattered trenches, deep with dead, the demoralised survivors were rounded up and sent stumbling eastward to captivity.

Noah was not among them. As a shell came over, landing about a yard from him, a splinter caught him across the temple, blinding him with blood and then another entered his leg. The same bloody leg that he had nearly lost last time and he remembered thinking that the buggers were determined to have it off him. He lost consciousness then and slipped away beneath a pile of his dead comrades, fortunately with his face uncovered so that he was able to breathe and as the enemy ferreted about looking for prisoners, seeing his bloody features and his closed eyes, they took him for dead and moved on.

Stretcher-bearers found him hours later but might have missed him had not his hollow voice – since he had now regained consciousness – spoken to them from beneath their feet.

'Hey, guys, you took your time,' he said faintly, grinning at them from his blood-caked face, giving them quite a turn, they said, his American accent catching their attention as much as the sound of his voice.

They took him to an advanced dressing station where the usual argument took place across the stretcher as to the advisability of taking the leg off and again he seriously startled the doctor by swearing obscenely and threatening to break the bloody nose of any man who cut off his leg. There was no way he was going to kiss his girl tottering about on one bloody leg, he told them. The doctor shrugged, put him to sleep, stitched his wound and put a dressing on it. The next he knew he was on a Red Cross hospital train that took him to a hospital just outside Calais. His leg was hurting like hell but it was he himself who had shouted at the doctor not to cut it off so he supposed it was his own fault he was in such agony. Would it have hurt as much if they had taken it off? he wondered. He had heard men say that an amputated arm or leg could still hurt even when it had gone but what did it matter? He was going home, not to America, his birthplace, but to Rose who was his real home. He supposed he was lucky when he looked about him on the dockside where men were writhing and groaning, men with hastily applied and often filthy bandages caked with the mud of France clapped to their faces, to their chest and stomachs and one who seemed to be clutching at his genitals, his mind gone along with his manhood. This bloody war which he had been so eager to be involved in had shattered and mutilated a whole generation of men, not to mention their families who had lost them. But he was going home to his Rose!

'All right, mate?' he asked the chap next to him who appeared to be dying silently in his own blood, speaking in the vernacular he had learned from the Tommies in the trenches. Stretcher-bearers were lifting the wounded, khaki-clad bundles unidentifiable as living, dying men, staggering with them up the gangplanks and placing them on any spare bit of space on deck. Noah was lucky enough to be sailing on a cross-Channel ferry but hundreds and hundreds of casualties were to be taken to Blighty on any sort of vessel that was available. Pleasure steamers, cattle boats, anything that could be pressed into service was used. They were packed on to hospital ships not only into the wards and saloons below but into the sisters' and doctors' own quarters and when even they were full they laid the stretchers on the deck alongside the 'walking wounded', that is those who had wounds above their waists. The agony, the filth, the sickening stench of soiled clothing, the moans, the retching, the rustle of breathing, the gurgling, the writhing sea of men, the mad mêlée that went on around Noah was mercifully concealed from him by his own fevered state, for when you are in a madhouse you become slightly mad yourself. He was well aware that the allies had taken a massive setback in the last encounter. Not only were troops retreating but also the hospitals, the personnel, the wounded were making for the base camps and the English Channel beyond and the sense of defeat hung like a pall across the Western Front in the bright spring days of Easter week, made all the worse because no one knew quite what was happening, only that they were too busy to brood. As the troops and the clearing stations fell back they were swamped with convoy after convoy of casualties and many of those who should have been stretcher cases were staggering in the same direction, ragged, dirty, tin hats still on, wounds patched together any way, some not even covered.

Noah had been placed near the rails of the ship and, as they cast off, turning his head he looked at the heaving dockside where whole convoys of wounded soldiers waited patiently to be shipped directly to England. He was aware of a filth-encrusted, mud-encrusted, blood-encrusted chap bending over him, his rank hidden beneath the detritus he had brought with him from the regimental aid post, the field dressing station, the casualty clearing station or base hospital from which he had retreated. He wore no cap but about him were the accoutrements that every soldier carted with him. The soldier put his hand on Noah's forehead, his eyes soft, haunted almost as though the agony around him was more than he could stand.

'All right, Laddie?' he asked with what seemed to be an Irish accent but Noah drifted off into unconsciousness with the thought that though they might still cut off his bloody leg he was one of the lucky ones. Soon he would be with Rose. Rose's husband was not even considered.

She had just come off duty and was about to fall into her hard, narrow bed, aching in every bone and muscle, when the call came that she and as many VADs as could be spared were to go with the ambulances to Charing Cross to meet the Red Cross trains that were bringing in the wounded. She had had a heavy day, for the hospital was already packed with the badly wounded. Though sister was on the lookout she had managed to spend as much time as she could with a very young lad who had had all his genitals blown off. He was cheerful about it, which made her want to cry, for even while she dressed his wound he managed a grimace of a smile. The wound was no more than a hole but it had to be packed with gauze with just a silver tube coming out of it that was connected to his bladder. Despite his brave spirit, during the night, when the men were at their lowest, he had drifted into unconsciousness and the doctor had been called to him. The doctor had shaken his head, and just as it was getting light, as she sat and held his hand, he opened his eyes, smiled at her and quietly died.

She had offered to lay him out, but strangely sister had told her she would help as though she knew this lad had been special and behind the screen, just for that moment, sister was seen as a human being and not the martinet they had all thought her as she bent and kissed the boy's beardless cheek.

'The things we have to do,' she said sadly, then was herself again.

The rumour was that the Germans had broken through and a big retreat was in progress. The casualties were heavy and every hospital in London and the districts about it were to be called into action. There was talk that the wounded were to go as far as Yorkshire since there were so many of them, most in a poor state, for in the retreat they could not be attended to in France.

'Come along, Nurse,' Sister Hammond was calling down the corridor, herself dressed in a uniform so immaculate the others often wondered if she ever went to bed. At all times of the day or night she was starched and pristine, her three-cornered handkerchief headdress pleated and stiff about her calm face.

'Nurse', as she was anonymously called, hastily fastened her own headdress, her belt in her hand, her shapeless coat flung about her shoulders, colliding with Evvie and Maude and the others who were in much the same state as they moved hastily along the corridors. She had tugged on her shoes and stockings and was dreadfully afraid her stockings were about to fall down but in the panic to get to the ambulances waiting in convoy at the entrance she had no time to stop and adjust them.

Scores of ambulances were already lined up at Charing Cross Station as they arrived, one VAD plus the driver to each vehicle. It was very quiet as the nurses, the VADs, the stretcher-bearers, the drivers stood waiting for the long grey trains with the red crosses on the outside.

Waiting for the name of their hospital to be called she stood beside Evvie and Maude and the drivers of the three ambulances that were to be in their care. The train chugged slowly into the station, pulling up gently beside the platform, so gently she decided that even the engine drivers were conscious of the need to be careful with their suffering burden. Even before the doors of the compartments were opened they heard and smelled that suffering burden. These men were the most serious *cases*, if such a casual word could be used. Those less badly wounded and able to stand the journey were to go on to hospitals in the Midlands and the north.

Very soon the platform was covered, every inch of it, with stretchers bearing what remained of men come from the mud of the trenches in which they had fought and from which they had been forced to retreat. These were the lucky ones, many having been left to die alone as the enemy tramped over them. Evvie began to whimper – and Evvie prided herself on her stoicism – as a stretcher was placed at her feet, the man on it with his face covered by a black cloth as she thought but then she could see that the whole lower half of his face had been blown off and what had appeared to be a black cloth was actually a hole. She turned away ready to retch, ready to faint but the words of sister pierced her mind: 'Always look a wounded man in the face, Nurse,' and she steadied herself, even putting out a hand to touch that of the wounded man. He clasped it gratefully.

'Come on, Ev,' Maude said, ready to faint herself. 'Pull yourself together, old girl,' for that was how 'gals' from her class spoke to one another.

They moved backwards out of the way as the stretchers were carried as gently as possible along the platform to their designated ambulances but inevitably there were hold-ups and several of the wounded men screamed as they were laid once more on the platform.

It was then that she saw Noah. He had his eyes closed. There was a mask of dried blood on his face and a filthy dressing was slapped on his leg. He looked peaceful and for a moment she thought he was dead then he opened his eyes and they looked directly into hers. His brown eyes, once a lovely glowing brown like a polished conker, those her brothers had played with as boys, were dull, barely focused, but as he looked at her they lit up and he lifted his hand to her.

'Alex, so there you are,' he murmured, as though she had been missing for a few moments but was now returned. 'It's swell to see you. Where . . . where . . . ?' then his voice tapered off to a whisper then to nothing as he fell into a mercifully deep hole. She held his hand, her heart beating frantically, looking about her as though she had to run, had to find some place to hide as she had been hidden for the past nine months but there was nowhere to go. Noah was picked up and carried away, put in an ambulance with four others with a VAD to attend to them and she heard the man in charge give the order 'Lewisham' and knew that her half-brother was not to be taken to the hospital where she nursed. Her heart slowed to a more or less normal beat and she leaned for a moment on a pillar, catching her swirling thoughts and doing her best to direct them to what she must do here.

Her turn came as four stretchers were designated hers, all of them bearing soldiers with their legs missing. They were in the greatest pain, for the amputations had been newly done. They were placed into one of the three ambulances.

'Take it easy, Ted,' she said quietly to the driver, for if the ambulance lurched the men were nearly knocked off their stretchers. They would scream and she would be forced to do her best to hold on to them, talk to them, calm them and in any way she could ease their agony. They always wanted a cigarette and though she knew it was dangerous to put a lighted cigarette between the lips of a badly wounded man she did it if it gave them something to help their suffering. Anything to comfort them, talk to them, tell them they were safe now. She had been given a kitbag containing a water bottle, a tourniquet, scissors and an emergency bandage just in case she had to rip anything off to try to stop a haemorrhage. Evvie and Maude would be doing the same.

The walking wounded and the doctors and nurses sent with the casualties to look after them on their journey were moving tiredly along the platform, their job done for the moment. They looked as though they could barely put one foot in front of the other and she sympathised with them, for she herself had had no sleep, nor even rest, for a day or a night. She had climbed inside the ambulance and was about to close the door when she saw him. He was limping and her instinct and the love she bore him, which had lain dormant all these months, nearly had her out of the vehicle and running towards him. Damn the rest of them, let someone else look after them, for she could see this man needed her, not just her nursing experience, but the comfort, the ease, the release from the suffering he must have known at the loss of his wife and child. But she was not prepared. She couldn't face it. She had only just survived in this small cubby-hole of blackness that had covered her for all this time. All of us have a fortress in which we can take refuge when the enemy attacks and though hers had been severely damaged, even totally destroyed, she had managed to build a little hut, flimsy and insecure, where she had hidden all these months.

She remembered that day on which her world had ended and her own fortress had been destroyed and though she had flinched away from it a hundred times, it was still there and always would be. She could clearly see the rescue team as they stared with horror at what was left of the house at Bedford Square, but clearly at the same time her eye had been caught by the multicoloured mass of the flowers planted in the garden in the centre of the square. She could see and smell the smoke and the pall of dust, the dazed figures wandering from undamaged houses and yet, in the silence that followed the blast she heard a blackbird singing its heart out in blithe ignorance of the tragedy that was taking place. She had begun to scream even as she and the cab driver flung themselves from the cab and began to tear up the pavement towards the devastation and she saw again the way he had flinched from the sound she made directly into his ear. She remembered flying like a mad woman up the smoking heap of rubble and beginning to dig frantically with her bare hands which within seconds were torn and bloody. She remembered shattered window frames, shreds of material, shards of crockery, tatters of carpet, plaster, clocks, books, fractured pipes from which steam erupted and exposed electrical wiring. But worst of all was the stuffed rabbit whose name was Tabitha, though of course Claire couldn't as yet say it. She clutched it to her breast. She still had it.

She had continued to scream and seriously damage her hands until some burly policeman pulled her away, making the sort of noises that are supposed to comfort but they didn't comfort her. She had simply run away from it all, from Nan and Claire who were dead beneath the obscene pile of rubble, from the tortured remains of her world, from her own mind which had mercifully closed down.

How had she known where to go? she had often wondered. How had she remembered the den she crept into which was Patrick's empty flat, an animal injured beyond bearing, needing to lick its wounds in privacy, to die in privacy, for there was nothing else to do, nowhere else to go but into the eternity she craved. She remembered the blood on her hands and on her face where she had scrabbled at it. She had a dim recollection of people stopping to stare at her, some even trying to stop her, to help her, for surely she must have been in an accident, but she had evaded them all until she found what she was looking for, more from instinct than any conscious thought. These were the memories of the past which had hidden her.

Later she had gone to the Red Cross headquarters in Pall Mall where they were asking for volunteers for the VAD and having been accepted without much questioning since nurses were so desperately needed, she had been directed to the Number 3 London General Hospital where she had been ever since.

She had been glad of the bank account her father had opened for her when she came to London to become a member of the militant suffragist movement almost nine years ago and from which she had scarcely withdrawn a penny, as she had not needed it while she had lived beneath her father's roof at Bedford Square. She had never been a woman especially concerned with clothes or fashion and so when she became a VAD she could support herself since, being a voluntary service, the VADs were not paid.

She had spent her first weeks taking trolleys round the wards at the command of sister, scrubbing floors, sterilising instruments, helped with the mountains of washing-up to be done, taken round trays, working harder than the lowest paid skivvy in the home of the upper classes. With the others whose hands before the war had never touched a dishcloth or a sweeping brush she scrubbed and polished until her arms ached, running at the beck and call of harassed nurses and sisters until her feet swelled through the laces of her sensible shoes, emptying bedpans, holding kidney trays of instruments in operating theatres, looking on with detachment while nurses and doctors probed wounds so terrible that only the most hardened of stomachs could look on. She had passed the test. She had moved on to dress cuts and grazes, which described the slighter wounds of the casualties, and to bandage broken limbs. She had smoothed pillows, made beds, but as time and the war progressed and the shortage of nursing staff became even more acute she had been allowed really to nurse these broken men, performing medical procedures that only a fully trained nurse should do. She had worked with girls who, before the war, had never lit a fire, cooked a meal or swept a floor and had watched them with admiration, for these women deserved what she and Rose and hundreds of others had fought for in the battle for female emancipation.

She had survived. She had found a life of sorts, one she could cope with and in the knowledge that her family believed her dead, perhaps buried deep beneath the remains of Bedford Square, she had found the strength to continue. The pictures in her head of Claire's baby body smashed to pieces beneath the tons of rubble which she herself had done her best to crawl into, her smiling, crowing face disintegrating into blood and pulp, the gurgling sounds she was beginning to make silenced for ever, the images carved into her brain, pictures of horror so great her mind had become distorted and the pain and grief of those she left behind did not concern her, including Patrick whom she had loved above anyone. They would have kept it alive with their own sorrow, their compassion and she would never have had a chance to live again. And Nan, dear Nan who had been a second mother to her, wiped off the face of the earth and with her went Alex O'Leary who had become Nurse Annie Smith, as the other nurses called her.

She was fully occupied with her four casualties as they drove carefully through the morning traffic towards Wandsworth. It was recognised by any vehicle on the road that they were to move aside to let the easily recognisable ambulance convoys get through to the hospitals as quickly as possible. Smoothly Ted negotiated the roads, not stopping for anything, for a few minutes might make the difference between life and death to a bleeding man. Alex allowed nothing but the plight of these, 'her men' to enter her mind. It would come soon enough, what she was to think, to do in the next few hours. First let her pass over her charges, her moaning, writhing charges to other waiting hands – though that might be later than she thought since these men and the ones in the rest of the ambulances must be washed, changed, their wounds attended to, and there was already a shortage of nurses and doctors at all the hospitals.

*Patrick!* What was Patrick doing back in England? He did not appear to be wounded and yet he had moved like an automaton along the platform. Was he wounded? Please, dear Lord, no . . . not Patrick . . . not . . .

The man on the bottom stretcher became very still and as she knelt by his side the drip of blood that ran from him on to her uniform turned into a flood, and banishing Patrick and Noah and indeed every other part of her life that she had abandoned, she tore off the bandage from the stump of his left leg and began the task she had learned from watching and helping the medical staff at the hospital. A tourniquet first, then a bandage and not until the flow of blood had stopped did she lift the flap between her and the driver.

'If you can go any faster, Ted. We've a bleeder here.'

'I'll do me best, lass.'

It was not until well on into the afternoon, her patients safely in other hands, her tired body given the heavenly bliss of a warm bath and the rough blankets of her bed beneath her cheek that she gave herself up to her sad thoughts, to her fears, for there was nothing more certain than that the black hole in which she had buried herself was about to be uncovered.

# 31

Patrick climbed wearily into a cab and directed the driver to take him to Smith Square, where he let himself into the flat he had kept on, he often wondered why, dropping his kitbag and the rest of the paraphernalia every soldier was forced to carry about with him to the floor. Not that an officer was as dragged down with accoutrements as a man in the trenches, but he was so bloody bone-weary even his kitbag felt like a ton weight. There would be no hot water, of course, but he was prepared to wait until the boiler, when lit, produced enough for a bath. He would clean himself up, sleep for a while and then he must find out where Noah Goodwin had been taken, which, being an officer and a doctor, he would find easy to do, and go and have a word with him. The poor chap had been wounded once before and returned to the front and now, in this disaster that had come upon the British army, it seemed he had 'copped another Blighty one' as they said.

He rubbed his hand over his chin, the stubble of his two-day growth of beard rasping under his fingers, and flopped down into the kitchen chair while he waited for the water to heat. It was as he sat there, gazing around him indifferently that he noticed the clean, neatly piled crockery, the folded tablecloth, the teapot and the remains of a loaf, green with mould. Some-one had been here since he had last been on leave, which was before the big push in June of last year, the time when he and . . . Sweet Jesus, don't let me be punished further . . . but the thoughts, as he had learned, could not simply be turned off and her face as he had last seen it in the hallway at Bedford Square, struggling with Nan, for she had been determined to come to Victoria to see him off, invaded his vision. He shouldn't have come here. He had meant to go straight to St Helens but the sight of Noah had changed his plans, for though poor old Dick wasn't aware of it since Rose kept it hidden, he himself knew she loved Noah and he loved her and she would be glad of news of him. He had seen them once in France, before Rose came home, first to help nurse Alex and then, when Dick was gassed, to look after him, to marry him. Noah and Rose had been clasped in one another's arms behind the hut where Rose and the other VADs slept, so still, so silent, so anguished it was obvious to anyone that their hearts were being torn apart as they themselves were being torn apart. He had not approached them. It had not seemed right to intrude on such a moment. Rose had given herself to nursing her sick husband and Patrick had admired her for it, but at the same time he had shared the torment of her loss, for had he not himself lost the only woman he had ever loved, or would ever love? True, they had never found her body but the leader of the rescue team when he had called round at the station had told him compassionately that there were people missing in a number of the houses that had been bombed that day, the buildings so flattened, so pounded into the ground that bodies had simply disintegrated. Dear God, he was sorry to be telling him this, he had said, his own face ravaged, but what other explanation could there be? His wife was missing, gone, and from that day there had been no word of her.

So who had been in his flat, made tea, eaten bread that had been left to go mouldy? His tired brain, which had been forced to assimilate so much over the past three and a half years, not just in the ocean of sickness and suffering that beggared description in France but in his own heart which had known a loss greater than he thought he could bear, faltered in the chaos. It could not seem to get to grips with the possibility that someone had broken into his flat and made themselves tea and the act seemed so paltry that he could not be bothered with it. He would have his bath, shave, drink a cup of tea without milk and then find out what had happened to Noah before he took the train to Edge Bottom House.

She must be walking now, saying her first words, and he could not wait to see her, hold Alex's daughter in his arms, that sweet baby flesh that had come from . . . Dear Mother, Blessed Virgin, help me, help me get through this . . . to obtain comfort from the child. The same member of the rescue team had told him that a woman's body must have protected the baby, then only four months old, for it seemed Nan had sensed the disaster to come and had lain across Claire who had survived with no more than a few cuts and grazes.

He found Noah Goodwin in a military hospital in Lewisham where, the doctor in charge told him irritably, the foolish lad would not let him take his leg off.

'Is there gangrene?' Patrick asked politely.

'No, not yet but it's a nasty wound and the lad says he'll fight anyone who comes near him with a saw. It's been dressed and we're irrigating it with hypochlorous acid quarter per cent solution so that might save it. Er, are you a relative?'

'In a way. He is my . . . my wife's half-brother. I thought if he was up to it I might have a word with him. With your permission, of course.'

'Well, I don't see why not. He's asking for writing paper at the moment, completely irrepressible it seems, which I've found to be a characteristic of the Americans.'

Noah was sitting up glaring at the door of the ward in direct contrast to the rest of the patients who were either staring quietly at nothing or mumbling in delirium, restlessly moving their tormented bodies to gain some respite from their suffering.

Noah was drawn, his face bruised, looking far older than his twenty-eight years, but he was alert. About his head down to his eyebrows was a snow-white bandage. The moment he saw him Noah's mouth fell open in astonishment, for he recognised him now that Patrick was cleaned up. He had met him briefly, he could barely remember when but he knew him now for Alex's husband. He also knew of the dreadful tragedy Patrick had suffered when the bombs had fallen on London and Alex had died in the air-raid. He had been about to write to Rose to tell her the strange but joyful news because on no account would they, meaning the hospital authorities, allow him to get out of bed to use the telephone which he had begged to do. A telegram would not do either, for though it would get there quicker what could he say in a few words that they would understand? But this man smiling briefly at him from the doorway must be the one who had spoken to him on the ship, murmuring his name, laying a hand on his brow and now, for some reason, he was here just as he, Noah, was dithering on how he was to tell them about Alex.

'Noah,' Patrick said, 'I thought I would just come and see how you were . . .' then was surprised when Noah grabbed his hand and began to shake it as though congratulating him on something. His eyes were shining with excitement and his face, which had looked old and gaunt, took on the boyish grinning delight that he had shown before he had been drawn into the war machine.

'Patrick . . . dear Lord, Patrick, I can't believe it's you and that you are here just when . . . I was going to write to Rose but . . . Jesus, Patrick, I hardly know how to tell you this, in fact it might be better if you'd sit down. Oh, Patrick . . . Patrick . . .' His hand gripped Patrick's with such intensity Patrick winced and the expression on his face changed to one of amazement as Noah began to speak. At first he could hardly understand what it was his wife's half-brother was telling him but Noah was aware of its monumental importance and was shaken by it. Noah knew what it was like to love a woman deeply, profoundly with every beat of his heart and could not imagine what this man had gone through with the loss of his wife but he felt honoured – was that the word? – proud, certainly joyful to be the one to tell him.

His tone was solemn. 'She's alive, Patrick, I saw her at the railway station. She was with the VADs. I was in a bit of a state and . . . well, I wasn't up to conversation, in fact I think I might have fainted but it was her, Patrick. It was Alex. I don't know where she was going, to which hospital, I mean, but . . . here, Patrick, do sit down,' for Patrick was crumbling before his very eyes, ready to fall across his bed, although in his face was the beginning of something that might be wild happiness, a happiness so great he was unable to speak. It shone from his eyes, turning them from the dull brown they had been when he walked in to such a glorious, golden tinted colour, Noah was speechless at last.

Patrick sat down heavily in the chair beside the bed. His face was the colour of the ash in a dead fire, only his eyes alive. He opened his mouth several times, then closed it as though the words he would speak, the questions he would ask were stuck in his throat. The sister who sat at the table in the centre of the ward watched curiously, wondering whether she should go across to Private Goodwin's bed and enquire if something was wrong, for both Private Goodwin and his visitor looked very strange. Not that she was unduly worried about the visitor since he was not her responsibility but Private Goodwin was and the doctor who had done rounds with her this morning had asked particularly that she should keep a special eye out for the soldier who had flatly refused to allow the surgeon to amputate his leg which was in a bit of a mess. It was not often that a patient was allowed to dictate to a doctor about his treatment but perhaps it was because the patient was an American. The

Americans were in the war now and in reality the soldier should perhaps be with his own but if he should show signs of a decline the doctor was to be called at once.

Noah put out his hand and took one of Patrick's in both of his, watched not only by the sister but by one or two patients who still had their wits about them, for it was most odd to see one man holding another man's hand. They could not hear what was being said. The man in the bed next to Noah was unconscious anyway but when the visitor folded his arms on the private's bed and put his forehead on them the sister thought it was time she went over there, for she did not want her patient disturbed.

'It's all right, Patrick,' she heard Private Goodwin say, patting the man's shoulder. 'I should feel the same if it was Rosie who had vanished and then returned. All this time and not a word and God knows why not but she was injured before so perhaps it was that . . .' His voice died away as Patrick turned up his tormented and yet at the same time enraptured face and looked into Noah's compassionate eyes.

'Noah . . . Jesus, Joseph and Mary, are you sure it was her? You were . . . not yourself . . .'

'Oh yes, I'm sure, Patrick. She held my hand and I spoke to her. God knows what I said but it was her.'

'Where was she going? Which hospital?'

'Gee, Patrick, I don't know but the medical authorities would. If you were to contact the . . . the Red Cross perhaps . . .'

'Yes, yes, and I must telephone Rose and Archie. Let them know.'

Patrick could feel the life pour into him as if his veins, the vessels through which life itself flowed, had been empty and were slowly filling up. His body was renewed and his mind surged, overloaded with thoughts, with promises for the future, with what he must do next. Where first? Sweet Mother, let this be true, for if Noah, in the fevered delirium of his wounds, should be wrong and this wonder be taken away again he really didn't think he could live with it. Not even for the sake of the child whom he scarcely knew but who was blood of Alex's blood, bone of her bone and who was being cared for by Rose. Dear Rose, he blessed the day Alex had met Rose all those years ago, for it was she who had got this family through the misery and sorrow that had plagued them ever since Alex was injured in France. She had her own troubles and grief, the adversity of Dick's illness which was slowly killing him; her love for this man from whom life had parted her and yet she was the strength, the rock, the anchor to whom they all clung. Once there had been Nan to help her, now she was alone, for even Archie Goodwin relied on her for his own sanity.

But Alex, his lovely Alex who they had lost for all these months was somewhere in London, still alive, probably still suffering the amnesia that had come on her after her accident, for what else would keep her from her daughter, from her family, from him who loved her more than life itself? He had drifted helplessly through the months since she had gone, automatically doing his job, mending broken men, his own mind concentrating on nothing but their recovery, eating, sleeping, performing the tasks set him by the army and by his own nature, which was to heal.

And now she was with him again and he must find her. He wanted nothing else, cared about nothing else but having her in his arms, in his life, in his heart where of course she had always been. He had lain on his camp bed when he was off duty and relived every moment they had known together, memories, images of her during her suffragette days, her bravery, her defiance, her determination, her desire to help her sisters to a better way of life. To those enchanted days when she had loved him, given herself to him, taken him to herself and made him what he was, and now, if Noah was to be believed, she was here in this city and he would find her, take her home, put her child in her arms and then take her into his and love her for the rest of their days.

Noah was watching him anxiously and the sister was watching them both. A nurse came into the ward pushing a trolley, the contents covered with clean white cloths, ready, Patrick thought, to begin changing dressings, for one or two of the men began to show signs of distress, the distress of realising that they were going to be hurt despite the nurse's care.

He stood up and without a word held out his hand to Noah.

'How can I ever thank you? Begorra, do you know what you have done for me . . .'

'Not me, Patrick. I simply saw her at the station but . . . well, you could do something for me.'

'What? Tell me.'

'Let Rose know where I am.'

He moved from hospital to hospital in the city and beyond, jumping in and out of taxicabs, starting at dawn and not finishing until dark fell, for there were many hospitals filled to overflowing with the wounded who still poured in from the Western Front. He had a week's leave but when he had applied for compassionate leave on the grounds that his wife, whom he had thought dead, was actually still alive but perhaps wounded, he was granted a further two weeks to search for her. No more could be allowed him, for the British army was at its lowest ebb as the Germans pushed forward and those doctors who had crossed the Channel with the first wounded were ordered back to man the hospitals that would be needed when the allied troops regrouped. The Germans had met with glittering success in their offensive yet the very speed of their advance had brought their armies to exhaustion and General Sir Hubert Gough and General Sir Julian Byng were planning a counter-attack.

Patrick was barely aware of what was going on in France or indeed anywhere except in his own small world. The joy at Edge Bottom House had been overwhelming when they had been told the news of Alex, and Rose had been determined to come to London to help him. She had been in touch with Doctor Newcombe who had taken over from Doctor Bennett and he had not only found a competent, experienced nurse, Molly Hughes, who would live in at Edge Bottom House while Rose was absent and care for Dick, who was improving slowly as spring came, but would himself visit Dick every day to keep an eye on his progress. There was Mary Smith who, though she was getting on a bit, was very capable, Dottie and Ruth who longed to help to bring Miss Alex home, and there was Archie who, after hearing the news of his daughter's resurrection, so to speak, was eager to take his turn at not only caring for Dick but for his baby granddaughter. Abby and Noah Goodwin, sending word from Lytham where they had retired, both in their seventies, had offered to help in any way they could. Sally Preston, once lady's maid to Milly Woodruff, Abby and Noah's daughter, Sally Ward now, for she had married a Lytham fisherman, had offered her young seventeen-year-old daughter, Harriet, as a nurse for Claire when Claire had been brought home last year. She was a good, decent, willing girl whom they trusted with the baby and so, with every contingency covered, Patrick, with Rose to help him, set out to look for Alex.

They stayed at Patrick's flat and the mystery of the stacked dishes, the tablecloth and the mouldy bread was cleared up at once by Rose whose brain was much sharper than Patrick's at that moment.

'It must have been Alex, Patrick, don't you see? You say there was a broken window in the pantry. I don't know why but she mustn't have been at Bedford Square when the bomb fell and we'll never know until we find her. Oh, yes, Patrick, we *will* find her but I think she must have had a relapse of some sort, brought on by shock. You had just gone back to France and then when she returned from wherever she had been she found the house . . . gone. Claire and Nan . . . Dear God, it would be enough to send the steadiest woman out of her mind. She ran to shelter and the only place of shelter she knew was here. Then, believing her baby was dead she . . . well, I can only guess.'

'But she still had me, Rose.'

'No, she didn't. You were gone to God knows what disaster . . .'

'But she could have come to you.'

'She wasn't in her right mind. Now what made her become a VAD I cannot imagine but she did, we know that now and we must find her. Take her home to her child. Dear God, Patrick, what she must have suffered . . .' Rose began to weep, putting her face in her hands then lifting her head and sniffing disconsolately, while Patrick watched compassionately, wanting to weep himself.

'Patrick, I must . . . I promised myself that I would devote all my energy to finding Alex but tomorrow, would you mind if . . . if I was to go and see Noah. I feel it would help his progress if . . .'

Patrick took a step forward and put his arms about her, holding her to him as he might any wounded soul who needed comfort. 'Rosie . . . dear sweet Rose, how would any of us have managed without you? Of course you must go, for I know that . . . well, I once saw you and Noah and . . . you love one another, don't you. No, no,' he added hastily, 'Dick doesn't know. Jesus, Joseph and Mary, what a mess this bloody war has made of so many lives.'

The hospital was calm now after the last influx of casualties. They had all been attended to and were presumably tucked up in their beds. She was told to wait since it was not visiting time and even if she was Private Goodwin's cousin come from up north where they had just heard of his injuries, she was not certain she could make an exception, the starched sister told her. She must remember that the men in the ward with Private Goodwin were seriously ill and must not be disturbed, looking at Rose who was exceptionally pretty as though she might encourage them, being men, to get out of their beds and throw themselves at her feet, to flirt and laugh and generally upset sister's strict routine.

He was in the end bed next to a window. He was sitting up, his head swathed in a bandage and a cage over his legs and though the view from the window was very pleasant in the early April sunshine, daffodils dancing, tulips nodding, he stared resolutely at the door through which she entered. When he caught sight of her she saw him relax visibly, the breath easing from him in a long sigh of relief.

'Thank you, Sister,' she said to the disapproving nurse who nodded and moved away to a bed nearest the door where, from past experience, Rose knew the most seriously wounded soldier lay. A screen was round him and she heard him moan and then give a shrill scream as the nurse began to remove his dressing. One or two of the others stared at her as she moved down the ward towards Noah, for she was reckoned to be a lady and this was a ward for the ranks.

He watched her come and when she reached him held out his hand to take hers which had already risen to him.

'Kiss me, for God's sake, kiss me,' he said hoarsely as though he were at the end of his tether. His hand was like a vice holding hers and when she bent towards him, towards his lips, she saw the tears start in his eyes though they did not fall. His lips were chapped but she put hers against them and with her other hand cupped his face.

'Oh God, Rose, I thought you'd never come. I waited and waited and tried to be patient. They wouldn't let me use the bloody telephone and I'd no idea if Patrick . . .'

'Yes, my darling, we're here now looking for Alex.'

'Jeez, you look beautiful. Your hair . . . let me touch it.' And his hand rose and brushed through her glossy black hair which was uncovered and which she had never had cut. The enormous coil at the back of her head was disturbed and tendrils drifted down about her ears. She wore a simple cream shirt and a tweed skirt in colours of camel and cream and over them a three-quarter cashmere coat of camel with a tied belt. Her perfect oval face was tinted with the apricot flush of her love and her long-lashed violet eyes gleamed into his.

'Your head . . .'

'Just a scratch,' rubbing his thumbs across the backs of her hands which he held. His eyes, such a deep and glowing brown, brilliant with the depth of his love for her, searched hers and as she sat down beside him he reached up and kissed her again, watched this time by every man who was conscious and two nurses in handkerchief caps and bibbed aprons who had just entered the ward with the tea trolleys. But all her attention was on him. He looked so thin and drawn and the fine amber tint of his skin was gone. His hair, so thick and dark but with a hint of the copper both his mother and his aunt had once had, fell uncut from beneath his bandage.

'Your leg?'

'Is still there, my love.' His voice was soft and the tenderness in it almost toppled her resolve not to fall on him and cradle him in arms of love. She loved him and always would, she knew that, and he loved her and what they were to do was something unknown to either. She saw the strain in him, for he loved another man's wife, the tired weary torrent of despair that engulfed them both. He was studying her face with careful, minutely searching scrutiny and she knew he was committing to memory every curve of her eyebrow and lips, every eyelash and in his eyes was what she knew was in hers: the passion they had known and remembered and the haunting agony of whether they would ever share it again. She had come to London just when he needed her most but she had come not to be with him but to help Patrick search for Alex. A perfectly legitimate excuse but one that might not come again. His leg was suspect now and it was doubtful he would ever go back to France so what was he to do? It was in both their minds. Could he simply go back to America and never see her again? It didn't bear thinking about but it was all he *did* think about as he lay here in this ward of suffering men.

He lifted one hand, tenderly and smilingly tucking a drifting curl behind her ear. She caught the hand and bringing it to her lips pressed a kiss into the palm. God, he loved her, wanted her even now with his bloody leg crocked up. He could feel the need at the base of his belly and he knew she knew of it. Her eyes were clear, steady and calm, the eyes of a strong woman and suddenly he felt her calm wash over him and through the pain, the sorrow, he was aware that this would not be the end for them.

'You'll come again, my love?'

'Yes, before I go back. When we have found Alex.'

'Promise me. I must have something to . . . to cling to.'

'I promise.' And under the fascinated gaze of every man and woman in the ward, those who were not asleep or unconscious, she kissed him lingeringly, yearningly and there was not a man who watched who did not envy him despite his leg on which he might never walk again. She was so exquisitely lovely.

# 32

Matron called the VADs into her office several weeks later and told them that three volunteers were needed to go to France urgently.

'As you may know the Germans have made huge advances and the allied lines have been broken. At the moment everything seems to be in Germany's favour but naturally we will overcome and fight back. Since the retreat many medical staff returned to England with the wounded, so fresh nurses and doctors are needed and each hospital has promised volunteers. Over the next few months there will be fierce fighting and the consequence will be many casualties. Are there any of you who would be willing to go?'

Matron's glance played over the group of young women who stood before her, her eyes, as usual, noting anything in their dress that might be considered careless: a stain on an apron; a belt set just not quite right; a cap worn at too jaunty an angle, for matron was a firm believer in not just the nurses' competence on the ward but in their appearance. Lack of care showed lack of competence, in her opinion, and she noted that Nurse Smith had as usual something that might be blood on her shirt cuff. Nurse Smith was a good nurse but she was inclined to ignore matron's and sister's rules, saying that she believed the men came first and that a spot on an apron, or a ladder in a stocking were surely not important where their welfare was concerned.

As she had expected Nurse Smith spoke up first. 'I'll go,

Matron.' That was all. She was a strange woman, older than the rest and in these last weeks had looked even more gaunt than usual, with deep rings beneath her eyes and an unhealthy-looking pallor to her skin. Not that she complained about feeling ill. She was always there at sister's elbow, quiet, patient, impassive, ready to do anything she was called upon to do. It was only when she was with a soldier that she became soft, matron would call it, smiling, even holding a man's hand, kneeling at his bedside in the night and she had been spoken to sharply about it on a number of occasions. But she was so willing, so conscientious, so hardworking, the best nurse matron had ever worked beside.

'Very well, Smith. You will sail tomorrow. Anyone else . . .' It was evident from Smith's smile she was glad that Winters and Chadwick volunteered. Not that they were friends exactly, for Smith made friends with no one. Matron had discussed it with sister and they had both come to the conclusion that Smith had suffered some great sorrow and was therefore inclined to keep to herself, which was no bad thing in their opinion.

Nurse Smith lay in her bed that night, her duty at Number 3 London General Hospital done with for the moment and wondered, almost idly, why she had volunteered to go to France. They would find her soon enough if she remained in London, she knew that, since Noah would have revealed that she was still alive and she supposed that Patrick would come looking for her. It didn't seem to matter and again she wondered why she felt as she did. Her baby and one of her dearest friends had died and her heart had broken, she accepted that. Inside her something had been smashed apart and no amount of trying would mend it. Nothing made sense any more. She was no use to anyone except the soldiers she nursed. That was what kept her from simply flinging herself into the murky waters of the Thames, the thought that someone had use for her, but what would become of her when the war ended she couldn't imagine so she didn't try. The truth of it washed over her like ice and she knew that something inside her would never be warm again. In a way she thought that perhaps it was guilt that made her as she was. Who knows, if she had not been so eager to get out of the house that dreadful day she might have been able to save her child, even Nan from the fate that had overtaken them. She was younger than Nan and more lively and there might have been a chance that had not been presented to Nan to . . . to . . . Lord above, what was the use in wondering? Tomorrow she would go where the danger lay and perhaps it would find her and that would be the end of her. She could fight no longer. All her adult life she had fought for something, for the suffragettes and the women who could not fight for themselves. Then for the soldiers she had carried from the trenches to the hospitals, saving lives where she could, endangering her own as she had done before the war in Holloway. Now she was to fling herself without fear into the frightful obscenity of the lives her young patients floundered in before they were wounded. She was not afraid, for if life has no value what is there to fear? She felt quite calm and as she settled herself in the coarse nightdress nurses were allocated under the even coarser blankets, she felt herself drifting into a deep and dreamless sleep. Under her cheek was a soft woolly rabbit called Tabitha.

'There's a Mr O'Leary, a surgeon, wishes to have a word with you, Matron, if you can spare the time. He is in uniform, a major, and says he won't keep you but a minute.'

Nurse Cameron, her hand still on the doorknob, popped her head round matron's door. Matron looked up from the notes she was reading and tutted irritably and Nurse Cameron got ready to run for it as each and every one of the nurses were scared to death of her. Just a glance from her reduced even the sisters to tatters.

'What does he want, Cameron?'

'I don't know, Matron. He did say it was very important.'

Matron sighed. Running this enormous hospital which was at the moment filled from cellar to attic with seriously wounded men took every moment of her time and she was not prepared to waste it on some caller, even if he was a doctor, who probably had trivial questions to put to her. She could not exactly say what trivial questions she had in mind but whatever it was she really hadn't the time to . . .

The door opened abruptly and Nurse Cameron was gently put to one side, her mouth agape, her eyes wide with fascinated surprise. 'Excuse me, my dear,' the officer said, the light from the window glinting on the spectacles he wore. He was very smart, his uniform freshly cleaned and pressed, she thought, and she wondered what he was doing here when every doctor who could be spared was being rushed to France.

'Well!' said matron, seriously affronted, standing up and puffing out her formidable bosom and Nurse Cameron, feeling she was no longer needed, was glad to escape though she was sorry she would not be privy to the major's requests.

Patrick shut the door behind him and with a smile asked matron if he might sit. She nodded, ready to give the man the length of her tongue then suddenly she changed her mind as he sank into the chair before her desk because she had never seen a man, and she had seen many, who looked so despairing, so desperately weary, so weakened by something that was tearing him to shreds.

'I'm sorry, Matron, this is monstrously rude of me, for I know how busy you are but I . . . I'm looking for my wife.'

'Well, I'm sure I do not have her, Doctor, and I can't for the life of me—'

'I'm sorry, Matron,' he said again, 'but I believe she may be working here as a VAD and—'

Matron, annoyed at being interrupted, interrupted her visitor.

'We do not employ married woman, Sir, as you must know.'

'Yes, but she would be posing as an unmarried woman, you see.'

Matron did not see. 'Mr . . . er . . .'

'O'Leary.'

'Mr O'Leary, the ladies we employ are very carefully vetted. The Red Cross would not—'

'She would lie, Matron. She suffered a severe accident, you see. Before we married she was an ambulance driver in France and then . . . last year, when she was recovering, our child was involved in the bombings that took place over London. She believed the child, our daughter, had been killed with her nursemaid but she wasn't. Alex did not know that and . . . and simply ran away from it. She was seen several weeks ago in the uniform of a VAD by a young relative of ours who had himself been wounded, so you see I am searching for her. She is . . . will not be herself and I am . . . quite simply, Matron, I am out of my mind.' Patrick bowed his head and the compassionate heart that beat beneath matron's starched exterior went out to this man, and to the woman he looked for.

'I'm sorry. I presume you have looked in the other hospitals?'

'This is the last but I must report for duty myself in the next few days. I have had compassionate leave but with the way things are in France I am to return.'

'Of course.' She grew brisk, stood up and moved towards a small cabinet at the far side of her office. She took out a decanter and poured a stiff brandy into two glasses, for matron often needed a heartener to get herself through the trials of her day. She thrust one into Patrick's hand. They raised their glasses to one another, neither knew why but it was a habit, and downed the contents.

'What is your wife's name?' She waited with her pen poised.

'Alexandra O'Leary, or perhaps Goodwin. I'm not sure . . .'

Matron lifted a large notebook and opened it. 'This would have happened on . . .'

'June of last year.'

'So I need go no further back than that?' She ran her blunt finger down the names that were written in the notebook.

When she came to the end she lifted her head sadly. 'There is no VAD of that name, Mr O'Leary. They are all here, coming and going and where, if they have left, their destination.'

There was silence for a moment then she glanced once more at her notebook. 'Three of my VADs volunteered for France. They left only a few days ago. Winters, Chadwick and . . . and Smith.'

'Smith?'

'Yes, Ann Smith. How old is your wife, Mr O'Leary? Smith was older than the others.'

'She was thirty in March.'

'Aah . . .' Matron closed the book and leaned back in her chair.

Patrick stood up and held out his hand to her. 'Thank you, Matron, I shall know where to look now.'

She rose and took the hand of this desperate man who searched for a woman who obviously did not want to be found.


The Channel crossing was stormy, the troopship packed with quiet soldiers, most going back from leave, knowing what was in store for them, wondering if they would ever see home again. Alex stood by the rail and stared unseeingly towards the coastline of France hardly aware of the troops about her. It was a dense grey day and the soldiers peered through the Channel mist until the hospital tents which lined the clifftop encampments swam into their vision. For miles and miles they stretched from Calais to Wimereux and straggled up the slopes of the hill round Boulogne and ranked behind the lines of sand-dunes along the road to Etaples, on and on, and before long they would all be filled with fresh casualties.

Number 49 General Hospital, Etaples was a vast city of matchwood and canvas, rows of wooden huts and drab khaki tents, one of which Alex shared with Evvie. Their new home had a floor of rough duckboards, two camp beds, two collapsible washstands and two small metal lockers.

They barely had time to pin on their caps and aprons before reporting for duty. Evvie was in immediate trouble for dropping a jar of thermometers and breaking the lot but she and Alex were old campaigners and not easily intimidated even though the sister in charge put both her and Alex on their knees scrubbing out a hut that had contained cases of PUO – pyrexia unknown origin, or 'trench fever'. As Evvie said cheerfully they had scrubbed more miles of corridors and wards than sister had had hot dinners but both of them were longing for 'real work' which they had been performing at Wandsworth. The next day they had their wish, for they found themselves in total charge of a hut full of twenty wounded men. They had an orderly to help with the lifting and could run to sister in an emergency.

And there were to be many of those as the Germans continued to deliver heavy blows against the British. On 27 May they launched the third major attack, smashing the allied defences and pouring forward until they reached the Marne. They had taken not only the hard-fought-for ground but 40,000 prisoners and up to 400 guns. Even more demoralising, particularly for the French, this brought the German heavy artillery within range of Paris.

Alex, Evvie and the other VADs and nurses were exhausted. The Germans were moving their airfields forward to keep pace with their advance and not only did they have the casualties to deal with but they were bombarded by the German planes which came over every night and seemed hell-bent on hitting the hospital. They had no lights, only candles in the ward and the doctors who had been operating steadily for twenty-four, thirty-six and even forty-eight hours did dressings almost in the dark. Sometimes there was such a rush of casualties the wounded had to wait a long time to be seen. They simply poured in and worst of all they were depressed, low in spirit. Once they had been cheerful, full of hope, but now one of them said to Alex, 'You know, Nurse, they'll be over the Channel by next month at this rate and we can't do anything about it.' She and Evvie and all the others never left the hospital, never went into town, and barely were allowed a half-hour in which to walk in the hospital grounds. Nurses were supposed to have leave every six months, a half-day weekly and a full day monthly but it never happened. They stayed in the base in case they were needed to load up the drums for sterilising or indeed might be called on at a moment's notice to take charge of a ward filled with dying men. There were emergency operations at all hours of the day or night but still there was a steady stream of ambulances bringing in the wounded, an unending stream that took on the proportions of an avalanche gathering momentum as it rushes onwards.

Alex was made the senior VAD nurse, probably because she was the eldest, she said to the others. She was put in sole charge of two huge emergency huts with stretcher beds on the floor and not even a proper nursing orderly. She started at seven fifteen in the morning and sometimes it was midnight or even one o'clock the following morning before she finished. She would snatch a few hours' sleep after she had made the men comfortable and then they had to be left alone for there was simply no one to replace her.

It was early June when she began to notice that the *ill* patients were outweighing the wounded and she herself did not feel well. Not just tired and drained, which they all were, but really ill and when she simply fainted dead away at the end of a bed, the wounded man on it, who was in a state of what was called shell-shock, began to babble hysterically, deprived of the crutch that Alex had been to him. Men who were not unconscious tried to sit up to see what was going on and for several minutes there was pandemonium as the nursing orderly had left the hut for a moment and there was no one to attend her.

'Nurse what is it? Get up, lass,' one seriously wounded Lancashire man begged her and even tried to get out of bed to go to her aid. They began to shout and the shell-shocked soldier screamed in terror, for any unexpected noise drove him, and many others like him, into a frenzy.

The screaming soldier brought them running from other huts and for a moment they thought the shell-shocked soldier had attacked her. She was put to bed in her hut and since there wasn't a spare nurse to sit with her she was left alone until a doctor could be found who had the time to diagnose her. She had come round from her faint and seemed confused, asking for someone called Patrick, but she was, apart from this, quiet and still. It was not until the American doctor who had come over with the American soldiers had a look at her that it was decided she had influenza.

'They say the Germans have thousands of cases in every division. Have you German wounded in the hospital?'

'Yes, a few, but I don't think Nurse Smith has been near them.'

'Well, she's caught it from someone. Keep her in bed and if a nurse can be spared to look in on her she should be on the mend in a few days.'

Evvie had just dropped off into the almost deathlike sleep which took them all over in their exhaustion when she became aware of movement in the bed next to hers. Annie had been quiet these last few days and so, thinking to let her have peace in which to recover they had left her alone. Evvie herself had crept in during the day to make sure Annie was drinking, for it seemed there was little else to be done and she seemed to be recovering though she was still dreadfully thin and weak. But she was determined to return to work, she told Evvie hoarsely. She ate every nourishing scrap of food Evvie managed to scrounge for her and after a week in bed during which she slept most of the time she was back on the ward.

And thank God for it, sister was heard to say, for she was not the only sufferer. An epidemic of enormous proportions was gathering among the tents and huts of every hospital along the coastline and as June passed into July it was decided that an influenza hospital must be opened to contain the epidemic. It was reported from their hospital alone that over 230 cases a day were coming in and they could not be left to lie with the wounded who were already weakened. A vast general hospital was taken over and with the addition of Nissen huts and marquees they were able to accommodate 2,000 seriously ill sufferers. Thirty nurses and forty medical officers were drafted in to care for them. They had to be kept in an even temperature and given plenty of fluids, but since most were out of their minds with a high fever they were all incontinent and the overworked medical staff, even the doctors, none of them in the best of health, were forced into changing beds and patients, helping with the laundry. Even after almost four years of nursing men with ghastly wounds, one nurse was heard to remark that the influenza epidemic that had hit them was the worst thing she had ever known. Soldiers, orderlies, nurses, doctors were dying like flies and those who were still on their feet began to give the sick blood transfusions in the hope that if they could keep them alive until they got over the main symptoms they might live. It was rumoured that more people were dying in this world epidemic, which was reaching every corner of the globe, than had died during the war.

Volunteers were asked for from the hospitals that were not yet affected and among those who volunteered was Patrick

O'Leary. Another was Nurse Annie Smith who, having had and recovered from a bout of the illness, was considered perhaps to be immune and therefore a great asset in the wards.

She had been on duty for thirty-six hours and sister had told her to go to bed and if she could to snatch an hour or two of sleep.

'We'll come for you if we need you, my dear,' sister told her gently, for she greatly admired this nurse who did the work of three and seemed ready to try even more.

'Sister, there are so many of them still coming in. Are you sure?'

'If you don't rest for an hour or two you'll collapse completely. Now go.'

She fancied she could hear a baby crying and though at the edge of her consciousness she knew it could not be hers she pushed back the blankets that covered her and tried to get out of bed, for when the baby cried someone must go to her. She didn't know where she was for a moment or two so deep had been her sleep, but something made her fumble for her cap and apron which she had removed before she lay on her camp bed. She had eaten nothing before she flung herself down and her head was aching badly, but again some voice within her was urging her to look lively, to get on her feet and return to the ward where she knew every pair of hands was needed. Sister would probably speak sharply to her but she would be glad of her in the terrible chaos of the epidemic. It had broken out in June and had seemed to be abating, herself one of its targets but now it was appalling and the number of sick men being taken in had risen to 500 and 600 a day.

A convoy had just come in as she arrived back at the ward and though Sister threw her an exasperated look, for she had been gone no more than an hour, she was glad to see her, she knew. Sister relied on her, for she was clear-headed, calm, confident, seeing what was needed and what to do, but then sister didn't know that Alex O'Leary was all these things because of who she was and what had happened to her. She had no worries, no problems, no troubling thoughts about family or friends who might be vanishing in the destruction of a whole generation of young men. Alex O'Leary was already in the land of the mindless, even the dead and so could cope with anything.

'Start where you can, Smith,' sister told her wearily. 'It makes no difference, for they are all semi-conscious.' Sister was not inhuman but merely a human being doing her best to cope with this horror that had crept up on them when they were at their lowest ebb. They would all be seen to when they could get to them, her grey, ravaged face said, but there were men, and women now, with bronchial pneumonia and septicaemic blood poisoning. The fluid movement of troops was carrying this killer across the world but they were concerned with this tiny corner of it and though at the end of their strength, which had kept them going for nearly four years, they were doing their best.

Alex nodded her head then moved round the screen where an orderly was starting to strip and wash a man whose face was already dark blue, which was the worst sign, especially the screen for that meant he was dying and might upset those who were aware of him.

'Poor sod,' the orderly murmured, placing a pair of spectacles on the locker beside the bed, then standing up to move round to the other side and as he did so her heart kicked her savagely, so savagely she felt the agony of it ripple through her body, for the man with the darkening face was Patrick. *Her Patrick. Her dying Patrick* as she had seen that awful colour so many times in a man's face.

She leaped forward and pushed aside the orderly, screaming at him to leave her Patrick alone. She would see to him, she shrieked furiously and if anybody, God or anybody thought she was going to lose him then they were bloody well mistaken. If that Blessed Mother Patrick had been heard to call on thought she was going to have her Patrick then she could think again.

The whole of the ward heard her and for a moment everything became still and those who were capable of it decided the nurse had gone out of her mind and could you blame her. It was enough to send the strongest to the verge of madness. The orderly was flabbergasted, for Nurse Smith had never, in all the time he had known her, shown the slightest *personal* interest in any patient. Oh, she was good and kind and would work herself to a shadow for the lowest of them, even the bloody German sick and wounded but now she was hanging over this chap's bed, this poor chap who was obviously in the last stages of the illness, covering him as though in protection with her own body.

'Leave him,' she said harshly. 'I'll see to him.'

'But Nurse—' he began to argue.

'Leave him, you fool,' she shrieked at him. 'He's my husband and he's not going to die, d'you hear?'

# 33

Sister ordered her to return to her duties at once saying she would have no more of this nonsense and Nurse Smith must surely know that there were literally hundreds of extremely sick men who needed her attention. The orderly would continue to see to the soldier but she must continue her duties as a . . .

'Get out of my way, if you please, Sister. This man is not just a soldier he is my husband and I will nurse him as a wife should.'

Sister's mouth fell open and her eyes popped out of her enraged face. This VAD had been under her command for no more than a few weeks and had been one of the best and most dedicated she had ever known and to be told that she had a husband, which was strictly against the rules, left her speechless.

'I swear to God,' Alex went on, 'that if you continue to obstruct me, I shall strike you. Yes, I am aware that I am . . . *was* a VAD which as you know means I nurse voluntarily. I am not paid a wage as qualified nurses are and therefore I am beholden to no one. I may resign when I like and that is what I am doing. I am a civilian from this moment on. I am aware that every pair of hands is needed but my husband comes before all others.'

'Nurse Smith,' sister thundered while all about them sick men, wounded men, nurses, VADs, doctors and orderlies held their breath and for several seconds the frenzied activities of the ward were paralysed, for never in the whole history of nursing in this dreadful war had any member of staff ever been allowed to interfere with the treatment of casualties, then they hurriedly resumed their duties as they could not afford to dither about when so many men sadly needed their care.

'It is not Nurse Smith, Sister,' Alex told her quietly, for she had regained her composure now. She could not nurse Patrick if she remained in the state of hysteria the sight of him had brought on and she meant to nurse him, bring him back to full health and take him home. 'My name is Alexandra O'Leary and this man is my husband, Patrick O'Leary. For almost four years he has given his life to saving others. He has healed literally thousands of men, most of whom, to his anguish, were sent back up the line. Now he is very ill and as his wife it is my duty to do for him what he has done for others. I'm sorry for the men who are . . . are dying here but I cannot leave him to nurse others. He is my one concern and until I can make arrangements to take him home I am making this *his* sickroom, his exclusive sickroom,' indicating with a wave of her hand the small area behind the screen where Patrick lay. 'There is nowhere else to take him. I myself have given my . . . my time and devotion to caring for the men who are being wounded in this war. I have lost . . . lost loved ones and I do not intend to lose him. Now, if you forbid me to nurse him here for a few days I shall have to take him . . . I don't know where but believe me if any man in this war deserves all the care that is available, he does.'

They left her alone then. They had no time to be concerned with one man and one woman; and the space they took up, the nurse, the patient and the narrow camp bed he lay on, was very little. She asked for no help, not even to lift him as she changed his bed, for he constantly soiled himself. She fetched water, lugging buckets from the tap that stood just outside the hut, politely brushing past the straggling lines of sick and wounded, hardening her heart to their piteous cries for help for, since she was still in her stained uniform, they thought her a member of the nursing profession. She was obliged time and time again to clean Patrick's wasting body of the stinking fluids that ran from him, holding him in her arms to quieten him, for he had begun to be delirious, thrashing about the small space and threatening to knock over the screen that contained them. He fretted under her hands as she bathed his body, his bones ready to break through the flesh so emaciated had he become. There was nothing she could do for him, nothing any of the nurses and doctors could do for any of them, for they had never experienced anything like it before. They had no conception of where this had come from, this deadly influenza epidemic. Some said Spain, others France. Others believed the epidemic was a biological warfare tool of the Germans but since as many Germans were dying of it as British that was hard to believe. Some gave their opinion that it was the result of trench warfare, the use of mustard gases and the generated smoke and fumes of war, but wherever it had come from it was killing men at a faster rate than bullets or shells.

He opened his eyes once as she was dripping liquid between his lips and she leaned forward eagerly, taking his hand, but he stared unseeingly at the roof of the hut.

'Patrick, macushla,' she whispered, touching his cheek. His hair was matted with sweat, standing about his head in a thick, sticky mass, but when she put a hand on it he moved irritably. 'For God's sake,' he said hoarsely, 'I'm not taking off that leg . . . no . . . no . . . leave it . . . he's young, so he is, and healthy . . . no . . . no . . .' He was quiet for a while then, 'Where is she, Rosie, where is she? Dear Mother, if I don't find her . . . what will I do? And Claire?'

*Claire!* Claire! She sat back on her heels, her legs spasming in agony, for she had been kneeling beside him for what seemed days. Why had he mentioned the name of their dead daughter? she agonised. She knew he was not of this world, that he roamed in the shadows, the vacuum into which his illness had spun him, but he talked as if . . . as if . . . what? She didn't know and she supposed at this moment it did not matter, for he was fighting for *his* life. *She* was fighting for his life but the layers of his flesh were melting away before her eyes and there seemed to be nothing she could do to keep him from that brink of death into which so many were falling. And yet some recovered, still frightfully ill, but hanging on to life but, despite her care, her individual attention, he seemed to be slipping further and further away from her. She couldn't bear it, she moaned inwardly though not a sound escaped her. It was strange really because she had deliberately kept herself apart from him and now, as he lay on the edge of the valley of death, she could not even remember why. She could not even think of losing him without every muscle in her body seizing up in agony. She loved him. *She loved him*, needed him, couldn't he sense that as she hung over his bed, breathing her own breath into his open mouth. Soldiers who had survived battles and appalling hardships were dying right here in this ward and so, it seemed, was Patrick. It was like a forest fire, destroying every scrap of energy these men had in a matter of hours but they had so little energy to start with after what they had gone through, and Patrick was one of them. His body was on fire and she longed for packs of ice, for surely that would bring his temperature down. He did manage the sips of water she constantly dripped between his cracked lips hour after hour and she took hope from that.

He must have quietened because she woke to find herself sprawled on the duckboards which did as a floor, her body so cramped, so painful, so *dirty* she thought longingly of the bath at Patrick's flat where once they had lain in sensual pleasure. Would those days ever come again? she agonised. Would they regain the enchanted nights and days they had once known, the companionship, the love, the joy of just being? It seemed with every hour that ticked by Patrick sank deeper and deeper into an appalling state of insensibility and it was then that she knew she must get him away from this place of death, of pain, of noise, cries of pain, moaning, weeping, even the shouts of the despairing doctors as they cursed whatever had sent this plague on them.

The battle going on in this ward was still being repeated on the battlefields and for once it was the allies who were gaining the upper hand. The Germans had been caught unawares as Australian and Canadian troops made a rapid advance of seven miles or so near Amiens and although there had eventually been fierce resistance some 16,000 Germans had been captured and it was whispered, though they hardly dared believe it, that the German high command no longer believed they could win the war. With the massed deployment of that much-despised weapon of war, the tank, preparation began for an attack by the allies along the whole front, from the fortress of Verdun to the North Sea.

Evvie Winters crept in on the third day of Alex's vigil by Patrick's bedside, her innocent eyes wide and wondering as she exchanged a glance with this nurse they had all known as Annie Smith.

'I can hardly believe it,' she whispered. 'All this time we thought you were . . . well, I don't know what to call you, Annie or Mrs O'Leary . . .'

'Alex will do.' Alex tried a smile but everything about her ached and she hoped to God she was not going down with this dread disease, for who would look after Patrick then? The smile was stiff, as was the rest of her body and she thought she would never walk upright again.

'And this is . . . your husband?' Evvie leaned forward to look at the unexceptional face of the man who was Annie Smith's, or should she say Alex O'Leary's, lost husband. It looked bruised, gaunt, sunken, like hundreds of others in the hospital in the depth of this hideous illness, all somehow alike in their semi-conscious state.

'Yes, and I must get him home, Evvie. I need help to nurse him and I can't get it here. Sister allows me to remain with him, to keep him isolated but I know she is fast running out of patience. Whether he will survive the journey home is . . . is questionable. He is so weak but I must try. Would you do me a favour, Evvie? I can't leave him. To tell the truth I daren't take my eyes off him but I must send a telegram to my family. My friend who lives with my family would meet me at Victoria . . . that's if I can get Patrick on to a hospital train, and she has nursing experience. She would be there for me, I know, that's if . . . Oh dear God, Evvie, life is so bloody complicated. Rose, that's my friend, also has a husband who was wounded in France and whether she can leave him . . . but I must try, Evvie. You do see that, don't you?'

'What do you want me to do, Annie . . . Alex?' Evvie put a hand on Alex's arm and smiled pityingly into her ravaged face. Evvie had never been in love and wondered at the state into which it spiralled men and women, but it appeared that Alex was at the end of her ragged tether and if Evvie could manage it, whatever it was in this mad world, she would.

The telegram arrived at Edge Bottom House the next day and as Dottie put it into Miss Rose's reluctant hand she stepped back as though contact with the appalling item would con-taminate her. Up and down the country families were receiving these obscene messages of grief, sorrow, pain and now there was one here, so was it Mr Will, or perhaps Doctor Patrick who had been adopted so to speak by the Goodwin family?

'Thank you, Dottie.' Rose's voice trembled as did her hands as she tore the envelope open. She read the words on it and Dottie watched her. In the garden stood old Solly, for he had seen the telegram lad come wobbling up the drive on his bicycle. At the kitchen door Ruth, Nelly and Mary hovered; though they did not want to hear the bad news these dreaded things contained they could not leave Miss Rose to deal with it by herself. The master was in his study, but, concerned by the silence that followed the ringing of the doorbell he came into the wide hallway. He had a small girl by the hand.

Rose began to shriek, not with pain but with joy, laughing and crying and ready to whirl a bewildered Dottie round and round the hall and all of them began to smile, then laugh, though they didn't know why.

'Oh, sweet God,' she cried, crumpling the telegram between her clasped hand and throwing back her head so that the enormous chignon at the back fell down in a swirl to her waist.

'Rose . . . Dear Rose, what is it?' Archie quavered and the little girl, probably no more than eighteen months old, clung to his leg.

'Oh, Miss Rose . . .'

'What . . . what's happened? It's not . . . not . . .' Mary didn't know what to say because it seemed it was good news and did that mean Master Will was coming home? But that surely wouldn't have Miss Rose is such a transport of joy, dearly as she held him in her affections.

Rose composed herself and turning to face them said solemnly, tears now running across her cheeks. 'It's from Alex. Our Alex is coming home. Oh, God, I can't believe it, all this time . . . we thought she was lost to us and now this says she is coming home. We don't even know where she has been or what has happened to her. Why. Alex, our Alex is alive and coming home and . . .' She uncrumpled the telegram and studied it again. 'And she is bringing Patrick. She wants me to meet her at Charing Cross . . . he has the flu . . . and that's all. Oh, Archie . . .' She stepped forward and was just in time to catch the frail old man as he swayed into her arms.

'Archie, darling, your daughter is coming home and . . . and Claire's mother.' She bent to put a hand on the child's head and watched as she firmly plugged her thumb into her rosy mouth. It was a gesture with which they were all familiar, for though the child was dearly loved and wanted for nothing in the way of hugs and kisses and the attention they all gave her, she had no mother nor father and somehow it was as though, even at her age, she knew there was something lacking in her life. She sucked her thumb whenever she was distressed and this hullabaloo which she did not understand frightened her. They were all laughing but at the same time crying and she was not sure what her part in this was.

Aunt Rose swept her up in her arms and kissed her soundly on the cheek, then put her in Mary's willing arms. She was about to say, 'Your mama's coming home, your mama's coming home,' but she stopped herself in time, for the baby would not understand. That was all she was, a baby who had suffered an experience no child should suffer and she must be led very calmly, peaceably, lovingly back to her mother and father who were coming home. Slowly, one tiny step at a time until she could accept them . . . that is if Patrick lived, for there were hundreds of thousands dying all over the world of this terrible plague, *millions*, and if Patrick did not survive, how would that leave Alex? Dear God, what a turmoil they had in store but the first thing was to get in Molly Hughes to look after Dick while she, Rose, was absent, to get in touch with Doctor Newcombe, to see to the hundred and one things that needed seeing to before she could take the train . . . No, not the train, the motor car with Harry at the wheel as Patrick must come home in comfort. Harry had been hoarding petrol, which was hard to come by, and with what they had in the garage they should be able to manage the journey to London and back. Patrick would be nursed at home, in the bed that had once been Alex's and with Alex and herself to look after him he would recover. He *must* recover, for had not Alex suffered enough over the past years and did not she, Patrick and their child deserve some happiness?

And perhaps, *perhaps*, if she and Harry left at once and moved swiftly there might be a chance for her, for Rose, to see her love. Noah was staying in Patrick's apartment, not sure yet what he was to do, reluctant to return to America, though his family pressed him, and leave Rose behind. He had been discharged from the army on medical grounds and there was a job waiting for him in his father's business but he could not bear to put the Atlantic Ocean between himself and Rose. She knew, although he had an allowance from his indulgent father and was not short of money, he was bored and miserable without her as they waited − for what − and they were both guiltily ashamed to admit it was to be together in some way and what way was there while Dick was her husband? In his last letter he told her he was doing voluntary work at the hospital, as an orderly or wherever there was a need, unpaid work that helped those he had once fought beside. He found he got a great deal of satisfaction from helping the sick and wounded and was considering a career in medicine; what did she think? Here or in America, but he would not leave her.

The ferry from Boulogne across the Channel was choked with the sick lying stretcher to stretcher in their own waste with no more than half a dozen medical staff to look after them. They simply died where they lay, even on the short journey, with temperatures of 105 degrees. Patrick tossed on his stretcher, ready to throw himself off it and on to the deck.

'Hush, darling, hush,' Alex soothed him, doing her best to keep him still, to keep him covered, to keep him from flinging himself on to the stretcher of the still soldier beside him, until, in desperation she lay down beside him, his head in the hollow of her shoulder, his arm across her breasts, hers wrapped about his sweat-soaked body. He quietened then but still muttered of medical matters, of Dick and someone called Albert who was to bring him something or other and once he murmured her own name. She wept then, for she knew she herself had brought this on to the man she loved. Not the illness but his inability to cope with it. He had nothing to live for, with her and their child dead and so he was slowly sinking into the oblivion he craved. She kissed him and caressed his face, whispering his name and when they arrived at the dockside where the hospital train waited she knew she could not carry on for much longer. She had not slept for days except for the occasional doze from which she jerked awake, her heart beating frantically until she ascertained whether he had died while she slept.

It was chaos at the train station and the journey to Charing Cross seemed to take days. She marvelled at Patrick's strength which kept him alive while all about her men died, quietly or noisily. The stench was appalling but she barely noticed it, for not only was she accustomed to it but was aware that she smelled as badly as any man on the train. She had not washed nor combed her lank, lifeless hair since . . . well, to be honest she couldn't remember.

The train slowly puffed into the station and there were the usual nurses, orderlies, stretcher-bearers, VADs, women who had come in the hope of finding a loved one, and as the door opened and she stepped down on to the platform as though by a miracle there she was, Harry beside her and without hesitation she was pulled gently into Rose's compassionate arms. She was not aware of the shocked look on Rose's face nor the appalled expression that crossed Harry's. He was to say later that he would have walked right past her she was so changed. Their Miss Alex, so pretty with eyes the colour of the lavender in the garden at Edge Bottom House, clear and steadfast, usually with a mischievous smile on her face, and now she looked as though she had been buried and dug up again, in a worse condition than the soldiers who had come from the trenches. Like a scarecrow with huge, unseeing eyes, shambling, barely able to put one foot in front of the other and he would have bet his last couple of bob she hadn't had a square meal since God knows when, mumbling in the last stages of exhaustion.

They took over, he and Miss Rose. Miss Alex directed them to Doctor Patrick through the stinking mess in which their brave soldiers had travelled and when they had him, Harry at one end of the stretcher and Miss Rose at the other, they carried him as though he was no more than a feather along the platform, Miss Alex staggering behind until they reached the motor car. Harry had laid down the passenger seat and with a bit of manoeuvring they inserted the stretcher the length of the car. Miss Rose helped Miss Alex into the back seat, squashing in beside her and they weaved their way through the congested traffic to Doctor Patrick's apartment where Mr Noah waited.

For the next hour it was like a madhouse, he told the others later, if you could imagine a madhouse that made very little noise. Quietly Doctor Patrick was stripped of his clothing and Mr Noah washed his poor body with Harry's help then put him in his own clean bed where at once Noah began to spoon some nourishing liquid into him, slowly, patiently, with Harry standing by in case he was needed. Doctor Patrick was semiconscious but he took it, his eyes staring at the ceiling, muttering in between sips of the horrors he had seen over the past four years and Harry thought he might make a fool of himself and weep for him, for how could one man stand the suffering of the thousands he had cured, mended, soothed, eased, comforted? Harry didn't know.

Rose took Alex into the bathroom where Noah had filled the bath and with gentle, consoling movements, eased Alex into the warm water. She washed her flesh through which every bone in her body protruded, soaping her with lemon-scented fragrance, holding her by the shoulders as she had done with young Claire lest she slip beneath the water in her weakness. She washed her hair which at once stood up in the exuberant curls that had been hers since it was cut. She helped her out, dried her, dabbed perfume behind her ears, for surely every woman feels more feminine with perfume scenting her skin. They did not speak as it was apparent Alex was already half asleep. Leading her along the passage to the kitchen she fed her some of the nourishing broth Noah had spooned into Patrick's mouth, then, allowing her one peep in on Patrick who seemed to be sleeping under the watchful eye of Noah, led her to the small, spare bed where she covered her with clean sheets and watched her as she fell instantly into a deep, healing sleep.

Noah stayed with Patrick, dozing in the bedside chair and Rose slept fitfully on some cushions beside Alex. No words had passed between any of them and the present circumstances and those of the past when Alex had been missing for all those months were ignored for the moment. Harry curled up on the sofa and the night passed peacefully. It was as though Alex knew her beloved husband was in safe hands, the only hands she would trust to take him and so she could sleep, the sleep that she had denied herself ever since she had found Patrick behind the screen in the hospital. There was so much to be said, on the part of them all but the next few days must be got through before either of them, Alex or Patrick, would be strong enough to engage in any sort of discussion. Alex was not even aware that her daughter was alive.

And then there was the danger of the influenza epidemic that was sweeping the towns and cities not just of this country but of the world. Apart from the congestion around the stations where the sick and wounded were being deployed, the streets were practically deserted. Noah, when Rose had rung him and told him the joyous news that not only was Alex found and was to come home with her husband but that she, Rose, and Noah were to see one another, had promised to scour the shops for food so that when the patients arrived there would be no need for him to go out again until the epidemic had died down. He himself was strong and healthy now he had recovered from his wounds and Rose and Harry, cut off in the country as they were, had kept clear of the illness. It was said that the war was winding down and that peace was on the horizon. Since the Americans had joined the fight they had brought the allies closer to victory against the Germans. But the flu was most deadly for people between the ages of twenty and forty and that was the majority of soldiers in the trenches. But people walking the streets were struck down with the illness and died rapid deaths. In the house next to the one in which Patrick had an apartment four ladies were playing bridge on the day he was brought home and by the next night they were all dead. Men and women dropped in the streets struggling to clear their airways of a blood-tinged froth that gushed from their mouths and nostrils. It was no wonder that people kept to their homes.

But in Patrick's apartment the two sufferers slept on. One with the illness, the other with the effects of nursing that illness and in the few precious moments that Rose and Noah managed alone while Harry watched the two patients, they shared what might be the last hours they would have together.

# 34

She was crouched over Patrick's bed, her face no more than six inches from his, studying the ravages of his face left by the illness that had had him in its grip for the past ten days. The weight he had lost was appalling and his cheekbones stood out almost ready to pierce his skin. He was still now and both she and Rose thought his temperature, which had been up to 105 degrees, was beginning to drop. Every few minutes she gently parted his lips and dripped a few drops of water into his mouth and then smoothed a tiny fingertip of Vaseline along his cracked lips. He was breathing hoarsely and she shuddered as she heard the rasping in his chest. She touched his cheek, then ran her finger along his eyebrow, bending to kiss where her finger had been, moving her mouth as delicately as a butterfly's wings down his cheek to his jawline and up to his mouth.

Once he had opened his eyes and the faint glow in them told her he knew her. She was elated, bending forward from her position beside his bed from where she had not moved since she herself had woken from her deathlike sleep, except to make a necessary trip to the bathroom. Rose watched him, or Noah, or even Harry who longed to help but most of all Harry wanted to take him home. Harry had gone out in the motor car, bringing back news of deserted streets, people who were out hurrying by with masks over their mouths, of men spraying the streets with chemicals but still people were dying in their hundreds each day. He had even seen a body lying against a wall, an old man, probably a tramp who had no one to miss him but he had not dared get out of the motor lest he bring fresh contamination back to Smith Square. Even the King had the influenza so what chance did the rest of them have? he said gloomily. He shopped where he could and as soon as Patrick was strong enough they intended taking him back to Edge Bottom.

He had smiled that day when he had opened his eyes.

'Macushla?' There was wonder in his voice.

'Yes, my darling, I'm here . . . oh, thank God . . . my love . . .' beginning to weep and when he did his best to brush her tears away with his fingers and found he hadn't the strength to lift his arm she wept even more.

But it had been only a temporary recovery as they were to discover over the next few days. His face took on a dark, brownish purple and he began to cough blood. His feet turned black and they were all terrified, for none of them knew what it meant. He gasped frantically for breath and appeared to be drowning as his lungs filled with some dreadful matter, then he slept or dropped into an unconscious state and when he came to he seemed better. That was how it was, recovery then relapse, but Alex would not give up nor give in to Rose's plea to get into the spare bed and sleep. A proper sleep. Surely she knew she could trust Rose, but she would do no more than doze in the chair beside Patrick's bed, unaware that Rose and Noah slept together in the small bed in the spare bedroom, for the lovers knew that Rose must soon go back to her husband and that they must snatch at any moment to share the lovely passion that was theirs. If Harry knew he said nothing. He could sleep anywhere, he told them and had made a bed on the sofa in the drawing-room where he was as snug as a bug in a rug.

When she and Patrick were alone she talked to him.

'Patrick, don't leave me, don't go, you are everything to me, my life, my beloved husband, my friend, my lover and I cannot imagine this world without you in it. I left you for months and I will never forgive myself. Cruel and wicked I was but I didn't know how to bear my loss, you see. On my own was all I could think of, with nobody knowing who I had lost or even that I had lost anybody. To remember Claire and Nan, with no one speaking of it or looking at me with pity, with sympathy. In that way I could just about hold myself together so I ran away from it, from you all and now this is my punishment. Patrick, Patrick . . . stay with me, stay with me.'

In an agony of grief she lay on the bed beside him and lifted his wretchedly thin body into her arms. He weighed nothing, skin and bone and bits of muscles holding it all together. His head fell against her breast and she rocked him passionately, her anguish so great he stirred restlessly then sighed and in her agonised sorrow she did not feel the gradual, *peaceful* sinking of his body against hers. A sigh fluttered from between his lips and a name which might have been 'macushla' came with it, then, like a tired child, he fell into a deep and natural sleep.

She slept too, holding him against her and when Rose put her head round the door then stepped closer to peer at the couple on the bed she felt her heart give a giddy leap of joy, for Patrick, his long eyelashes resting on his high, prominent cheekbones, slept like an infant does in its mother's arms. She went to fetch Noah and Harry and together they felt the joy flow through them, because it was evident that Patrick had climbed out of that black pit into which he had fallen and though there was a long way to go to reach a state of full health, he was better than he had been. They didn't know how they knew really, for he still looked ghastly and without Nan's broths and soups and the nourishing tit-bits she had always contrived for those who were 'poorly' how was he to regain his strength? Perhaps if they telephoned Mary or even Nelly, for they had both worked side by side with Nan, something might be learned as to the best way to give Patrick back his vigour, his virility, his maleness.

'An empty sack won't stand,' Nan used to say and this sack

must be filled at once, Rose realised. Alex was still too weak herself to think of it rationally so it was up to her. She left the two men still gazing in wonder at Alex and Patrick and moving into the hall lifted the receiver and asked the operator to put her through to the number at Edge Bottom House. She telephoned the Goodwin home every day but this time asked Archie, who always answered the telephone, if she might speak to Mary.

Mary's hesitant voice warbled over the telephone line, obviously afraid, not just of the telephone but of what Miss Rose was about to say to her.

'Mary,' Miss Rose said briskly. 'Do you remember any of Nan's recipes? Or perhaps she wrote them down.'

'Beg pardon, Miss Rose?' Mary gasped, but when Rose told her what was needed of her she grew excited because she knew Nan had kept a recipe book in the drawer of the dresser and there was a part in it that referred solely to food for invalids. In fact she made Doctor Dick many of them. And Nelly had a wonderful memory and would be bound to know.

'Send them to us, Mary and ask Nelly to come to the telephone.'

'Oh, I don't know about that, Miss Rose,' Mary had said doubtfully.

'This is for Patrick, Mary. You must persuade Nelly to overcome her fear of the telephone. Say I must speak to her.'

And so a constant supply of barley gruel, beef tea, baked calf's foot, chicken broth, eel broth, egg wine, rice milk and a dozen others made their way from the kitchen, where Noah and Harry, following the instructions in Nan's book, found out they were grand cooks, to Patrick's bedside where Alex tenderly spooned food into him even though he complained that he was not hungry, she was wicked to force him, that he would get fat. They laughed together for the first time, though Patrick did it very carefully lest it make him cough.

Rose knew the time had come for her to return to Edge

Bottom. She had been absent from her sick husband for too long and she was well aware that he would not survive without her, despite the good offices of Molly Hughes. She telephoned every day and spoke to Archie and Molly but Dick was too weak to come to the telephone in the hall and so messages of love had to be transmitted by others and she was aware that he would be fretting. He would do anything to help his old friend, she knew that, but there was really no need for her to stay at Smith Square any longer. Noah would remain to help Alex, and Rose would return by train, for the minute Patrick was fit to be moved Harry would drive him and Alex to Edge Bottom. But first there was something she must say to Alex now that the crisis with Patrick was over. He could barely speak and then only in whispers, except with his eyes which followed Alex about the room, never taking them away from her face when she fed him, but he was gathering his strength for his fight towards complete recovery.

'Let's try him with pobs,' Alex had said the minute it was clear that Patrick had turned that dangerous corner.

For the space of several seconds the two women had looked sadly at each other, for the memory of Nan stood beside them. It didn't matter what was wrong with you, if you had no appetite and could barely keep anything down, 'pobs' was the answer. Bread and milk with a small teaspoon of sugar slipped down easily with no effort at all and what was best of all it rested delicately on the stomach and gave it a lining that enabled more solid food to be accepted. This was in the beginning.

'Well, he's only just conscious, darling, and might choke on it.'

'I won't let him. Do you think I would chance losing him again, Rose, do you?' Alex's face was as flushed with joy as a child who has just been given the one present she has always longed for. It might have been Christmas, or her birthday, for her eyes were a bright gleaming lavender, clear and steadfast and though she was still dreadfully thin she ate every single meal, whatever it was, that was put before her, scraping her plate clean as she knew she had a long battle ahead to get Patrick back to his former self and she must be strong herself if she was to do it.

Rose looked at her then drew her into her arms. She loved this woman who was so brave, so fragile, so strong and honest. She had supported Rose through thick and thin, protecting her in the old days of the suffragettes, her friendship the one sure thing in Rose's often rocky world and even now, knowing what she did, of course, of Rose's love for Noah, not judging her but there beside her in whatever Rose decided to do.

Noah sat with Patrick, recounting to him the news of the war, which was nearly over, his voice quiet and patient because he was aware that Patrick would fall into a healing sleep within minutes, for the war was over for Patrick and the finishing of it did not greatly concern him now.

'Dearest, I have something to tell you,' Rose began, 'and I fear it will be a shock so I think we will go into the kitchen, sit down and have a cup of hot chocolate before—'

Alex clutched at her and her face lost that lovely rosy colour that had returned with Patrick's improvement. 'Oh, please, Rose, I couldn't stand another blow, really I couldn't . . .' she began to babble but Rose put her arms more tightly about her.

'This is wonderful news, my dearest friend, but nevertheless it will be a shock to you.'

'Patrick, I must be with Patrick.'

'Patrick knows of it, Alex, and if we could have found you we would . . . But still, we must not go into that. We understand what you went through and . . .'

Alex began to cry. 'Oh please, Rose . . . don't hurt me . . . I can bear no more pain.'

Rose stood up, moving away from the kitchen table where

she had placed Alex, then turned and drew Alex to her feet, put her arms about her once more as though physical contact would make her stronger.

'Listen . . . oh, Alex, dearest, how am I to say this to you? Claire, your daughter, did not die with Nan. Nan protected her with her own body and Claire was pulled out alive. She has been living at Edge Bottom. Oh, darling, she is lovely, your daughter. Oh, see, sit down,' as Alex began to sway. Her arms fell to her side and had not Rose pushed her roughly into the chair before the fire she would have fallen. Her face was like unbaked bread and her eyes stared and stared into Rose's. Her hands wavered, looking for something to hold on to so Rose knelt at her feet and held her hands firmly in hers. She squeezed them as she thought Alex might faint, or vomit, or start to scream, for how does a woman react to the news that the child she thought was dead was, in fact, alive? She was shivering, her head wobbling dangerously on her frail neck and her mouth kept opening and closing on the questions she wanted to ask but could not form.

At last she managed to speak. 'Patrick . . .?'

'Patrick loves her, naturally, though they scarcely know one another. I have . . .'

'. . . cared for her . . .'

'Yes.'

'Of course, you would. Dear God, Rose, it was a blessed day when Helen Craggs was arrested for trying to set fire to a house.'

'Alex?'

'The day you and I met when driving the gig. When we distributed *Votes for Women*. Don't you remember? The day you met Dick.'

They fell into one another's arms and their tears which for so long had been sad and ravaged with pain were warm with anticipation of the future, the welcome tears of the happiness that was to be theirs. They clung to each other then stepped apart and smiled into one another's eyes.

Rose climbed out of the motor cab that had brought her to Edge Bottom House and as the front door opened was overwhelmed by the welcome that poured out to her even before she had turned to pay the cab driver.

'Oh, Miss Rose . . . Miss Rose, 'tis you . . .' Nelly was gabbling, while behind her Ruth and Dottie hopped from foot to foot, laughing and crying at the same time. Nelly even went as far as to throw her arms about Miss Rose's neck, forgetting their respective stations in life in her joy at seeing this dear woman again. She was not a Goodwin, but she had become one ever since Miss Alex had brought her here all those years ago. ' 'Tis good ter see yer and with such happy news. About Doctor Patrick and Miss Alex, I mean. Won't Doctor Dick be pleased ter see yer and see, here's Miss Claire and Mr Archie wantin' ter give yer a hug. Oh, Miss Rose, what a happy day, and them dishes of Nan's brought Doctor Patrick to 'imself. Eeh, Nan would have bin right medd up if she'd known. Eeh, if only she'd known, bless er . . .'

Archie put his arms about her and held her to him for a long time, his tears creeping down his gaunt face, for the war had cost Archie Goodwin dear and though he was not yet sixty-five he looked older. His daughter was returned to him though he had not yet seen her. She was well and her husband was recovering, thank the Blessed Lord. Holding on to his leg, with her thumb in her mouth, was his beloved granddaughter, for they were devoted to one another. Without her he believed he might not have survived. The war over, or as good as, his son's sight returned and his Will, who had come through against all odds without a scratch, was soon to be home.

'You'd best go up to him, Rose,' he said quietly. 'He's

waiting for you. He . . . well, off you go. Of course, a kiss for Claire, then . . .'

Dick lay in the bed from which he had not risen since the winter set in. There was a great fire in the hearth and the room was cosy, warm, fragrant with flowers and from the chair by the fireside Molly Hughes rose to her feet, smiled, put her hand on Rose's arm then quietly left the room.

'Darling . . . darling . . .' She moved across the room and as he opened his stick-thin arms to her she lay down beside him and with her head on his shoulder stroked his face.

'I missed you,' was all he said for a moment.

'I know, my love. I promise never to leave you again.'

'I couldn't bear it, my sweet Rosie.'

'I'm here now.'

'And Patrick. Tell me, how is he? Mary says he is recovering slowly.'

'Yes, darling, but it will be a few weeks before Alex can bring him home. Now, let me take my hat off.'

'Bugger your hat. Just stay with me.'


It was after Christmas before Patrick was strong enough to be put in the motor car and brought home to Edge Bottom House. He knew Alex was fretting to get home and see their daughter so he obediently 'ate up like a good boy' as she ordered him, though often his appetite failed. He had put on some weight and could walk from his bed to the blazing fire in the drawing-room where he sat in the protection of his wife's arms and soon, she told him, on a nice day, she would let him try for the corner of the square. They had sent Harry home several weeks earlier, for he himself had been chafing to get back to his duties. He knew that old Solly was to be trusted with the mare and the donkey, besides his other duties, but he had little to do at Smith Square besides tinker with the motor car and was eager to be with his family, as he called the Goodwins. His old parents,

Ruby and Olly, were still alive and his father would help Solly where he could but despite being over fifty Harry had taken a fancy to a nice little widow woman from the village, a bit younger than him but she seemed to have a taking for him and he was anxious that no other bugger would snap her up while he was gone. The influenza pandemic had vanished just as quickly as it had come and things were getting back to normal though it was said worldwide it had killed millions.

He returned to London with the widow's promise that she would wait for him and after a sad farewell to Noah who was to stay on at the flat and resume his voluntary work at the hospitals until he could get into medical school, they had set off on a day that seemed to contain the promise of not only a lovely spring but of the future to come. It was almost mild, a winter's sun doing its best to make the world believe that spring was already here though it was still January. They took two days, stopping halfway and at once putting Patrick to bed.

'I'm not stopping here by myself,' he complained, 'so you had best get a meal sent up and then you can hop into bed and do your wifely duties. By God, I'm feeling well so you'd best watch out. Send Harry to the bar and then . . .'

'Patrick O'Leary, if you don't behave I shall ask the landlord for another room.'

'Will you so? Woman, just try it and . . . oh, my Alex, I love you . . . I love you . . .'

They spent an hour telling, and *showing* one another how much each loved the other until they were both not only rumpled and flushed but breathing so heavily Patrick's chest began to wheeze.

'This bloody chest . . .'

'Give it time, sweetheart. Look how much better you are already. Before Christmas you couldn't even . . .'

'. . . you,' using a word a soldier uses, at which she gasped with shocked laughter.

'*Patrick O'Leary!*'

'Mrs O'Leary? Are you complaining?'

Their homecoming was muted, for in the bedroom he shared with his wife, Dick Morris was very ill. They all wanted to sing and dance and shout their joy for Miss Alex's return from the dead so to speak, but how could they do all these things with a sick man doing his best to draw breath into his damaged lungs, every one threatening to be his last. Doctor Newcombe was with him now, and though Rose came downstairs for a moment it was clear she was eager to get back to her husband who, it seemed, could not stand her out of his sight. Patrick could go up presently when the doctor had gone but he must be prepared for a great change in his old friend, she said, holding on to Patrick's hands. Their eyes met, telling Patrick all he needed to know.

'Can I . . . ?' Alex began but Rose shook her head.

'Not just now, dearest. When he is . . . is stronger perhaps.'

In the doorway of the kitchen Dottie lifted her apron to her face and melted back into the kitchen, followed sadly by the rest, not even stopping to watch Miss Alex bend down to her daughter nor see the smile that creased both their faces.

The apple trees were in blossom and blackbirds sang in the shrubbery on the day they buried Dick Morris in the old churchyard that lay to the east of Edge Bottom. Swallows were flying high and over the fields between the church and the house every imaginable tint of spring foliage, touched by the sunlight, glowed with loveliness as though to honour the good man who had gone. Everywhere a wealth of flowers sprang up, wild primroses and violets, the rich colours of crocus in the garden, tall soldier tulips and proud trumpeting daffodils and narcissi. Buds on the oak trees were opening and about the churchyard the ancient beech trees stood like the soaring columns of a cathedral, with their smooth, silver-grey trunks and the spring leaves breaking into leaf, a bright, shining, almost translucent green.

The men had carried the coffin across the fields, Harry, Will, Tom and Doctor Newcombe who had become a friend to the grieving family. Dick was buried beside Beth Goodwin who, said Archie tearfully, would keep an eye on Dick until he found his feet up there. It was a simple service, for Dick had not been religious, attended only by what they called the family. Rose had asked Alex if she thought she should invite Dick's parents but Alex had thought not, for his mother would only upset those whom Dick had loved. A short letter had been written to inform the Morrises that their son had died from the wounds he had received during the conflict that had ended in November. No reply had been received.

The others had drifted off across the fields towards the house. Mary, Ruth, Dottie, Nelly, Harry and his parents, Molly Hughes, all subdued in their best Sunday black which would last them a lifetime. Following slowly, their arms linked, were Archie and his two sons, their passage through the field lifting the wild flowers' fragrance, causing them to sigh at the loveliness of it all. What a beautiful day nature had provided for the man they had all come to love. It seemed right somehow and though it was sad, Dick had suffered enough.

Alex and Rose, who had stood for a few minutes at Dick's grave, both placing a red poppy on the heaped-up earth, holding hands and shedding tears for their dear lost friend, turned away and began to follow the others who could just be seen across the field. They still held hands.

'Was I right not inviting his family, Alex? It worries me; after all he was their son.'

'Would Dick have wanted his mother here?'

'No, I don't think so.'

'There you are then.'

There was silence as they sauntered towards the house, its chimneys just visible in the distance. The old house that had seen generations of Goodwins come and go, love and laugh and weep, and though Dick had not been a Goodwin by blood, he was in spirit, his loving ghost mingling with all the others who had gone before him.

'What will you do now, you and Noah?' Rose showed no surprise at the question that might have offended on the day her husband was buried.

'Wait a few months, then we will be married and go to America to see his family.' Alex made a small sound of distress and at once Rose turned to her and looked fully into her face. 'Oh, we'll be back, dearest, don't fret. I have come to believe that you and I are . . .'

'Sisters, sweet Rosie, from the very first on that gig. We cannot be parted. Patrick is to resume his duties at St Thomas's for he is, after all, a surgeon, and if Noah is to attend the London School of Medicine he could be of invaluable help to him. We are to look for a house somewhere in the suburbs. But what of Noah's mother? Will she . . .?'

'We must make our own lives now, Alex. You and me. We have given so much of ourselves, not just in France but in the fight for women. Do you realise that now you are thirty you will have the vote? And soon, all of us will be enfranchised for we damn well deserve it. Dear God, will you listen to me. I sound like some moaner continually picking over old sores. Darling, we have so much to look forward to now . . .'

'I am to have another baby, Rose.'

'I know, darling. Patrick told me.'

'The tattle-tale. I'll give him the rounds of the kitchen when we get home.'

They were silent for a moment, their hands swinging between them. 'Dear Nan . . .' Rose murmured, for that was what she had threatened them with so many times.

They sighed then turned to smile at one another.

'Claire will be waiting for me. I promised her a ride on the donkey. Race you home,' Alex cried and the two women began to run giddily towards the gate that led to Edge Bottom House.